RITA

Barbara Freethy

"TUGS ON THE HEARTSTRINGS."
Romantic Times

"MAKES BELIEVERS OF US ALL."
Debbie Macomber

And More Praise—

"COMPELLING AND WONDERFULLY WRITTEN."
Romantic Times
(on *Almost Home*)

"FANS WILL BE EAGER TO DIVE INTO THIS TALE."
Publishers Weekly
(on *Just the Way You Are*)

Love Will Find a Way

"Gary is a good man," she said desperately.

"The best," Dylan agreed. He cupped her face with his warm, strong hands. "But you have to be sure, Rachel. This is too big a step not to be sure."

"I know," she whispered. She looked into his eyes and saw the glitter of desire, the gleam of recklessness as his head drifted down toward her.

She had plenty of time to move, but she didn't. She had plenty of time to say no, but she couldn't. It seemed to take forever for his mouth to touch hers, each second strung out like a long, taut wire, until finally, finally, he kissed her.

BARBARA FREETHY

Love Will Find A Way

AVON BOOKS
An Imprint of HarperCollinsPublishers

This is a work of fiction. Names, characters, places, and incidents are products of the author's imagination or are used fictitiously and are not to be construed as real. Any resemblance to actual events, locales, organizations, or persons, living or dead, is entirely coincidental.

AVON BOOKS
An Imprint of HarperCollins*Publishers*
10 East 53rd Street
New York, New York 10022-5299

First Avon Books paperback printing: March 2002

Avon Trademark Reg. U.S. Pat. Off. and in Other Countries, Marca Registrada, Hecho en U.S.A.
HarperCollins ® is a registered trademark of HarperCollins Publishers Inc.

Printed in the U.S.A.

10 9 8 7 6 5 4 3 2 1

To my husband for always being there

Chapter 1

At twelve stories, the Caldwell Court Hotel wasn't even close to being the tallest building in San Francisco, but Dylan Prescott still felt like he was standing on top of the world. With a hard hat on his head, the roar of drills and saws in the background, the chill wind coming through the framing for the windows, the distant hum of the traffic below, and a stack of blueprints in his hand, Dylan felt completely in his element.

This was his world, a world where numbers added up, where perfect angles met and meshed, where someone's dream came true. He found himself smiling at the errant thought. He'd left little time in his life for dreaming. That had been his best friend, Gary Tanner's, department, not his.

Gary . . . Dylan took a deep breath as the smile faded from his face and the almost unbearable grief threatened to choke him. It had been six months since Gary's tragic death. This hotel was the last building his best friend had designed. Dylan still couldn't believe there wouldn't be any more buildings that were designed by Tanner and built by Prescott. They had made a hell of a team, and now one of them was gone.

It was easier to imagine that Gary was working on the other side of the country, that he would call at any second and tell some lame joke or put forth a wild idea for his next building, or ask him what the Giants were thinking when they'd traded their best pitcher to the Yankees. Dylan could almost hear Gary's energetic, laughing voice in his head, especially his familiar parting comment, "Don't do anything I wouldn't do." As if he would. Gary owned the patent on crazy. Dylan usually just went along for the ride.

Although, truthfully, there hadn't been many rides in the past few years. Gary's little spare time had gone to his family, and Dylan—well, he had no spare time at all. He kept himself busy from morning to night, ten hours a day, seven days a week. The past nine years had been like running in a marathon.

But that's the way he liked it, frantic, intense, no time for idle hands or idle thoughts. And if his latest bid went through, in three months he would tackle the biggest project of his life, the soon-to-be tallest skyscraper in downtown Los Angeles. Getting that job would put him at the top of his profession. A voice inside his head questioned what the hell he'd do then, but he ignored it.

"See you in the morning," one of his co-workers called out. Dylan suddenly realized that the buzz of work had come to a grinding halt and his crew was headed for home. Checking his watch, he saw it was past five, and the sun was drifting over the horizon.

It was late September and already the days were getting

shorter. Soon night would descend, and the lights would come on in the other buildings. It would be a magnificent cityscape, a sight that always made him catch his breath. He just needed a cold beer and a best friend to share it with, the way he and Gary had done so many times before.

Get over it already, he told himself. Just get over it. But that ruthless order didn't work any better now than it had any other day for the past six months.

His cell phone rang, and Dylan slipped it off his belt, grateful for the distraction. Work was what he needed to focus on, and nothing else. "Prescott," he said briskly.

"You've got a little problem," his secretary, Connie, informed him.

"What's up?"

"Remember all those messages I gave you from Rachel Tanner?"

Dylan had been avoiding her calls since last Friday, and it was Wednesday now. He kept telling himself he'd call her back, but he never quite got around to it. He didn't know what to say to her. And he couldn't understand the sudden flurry of phone messages from Gary's widow. He'd offered his help at the funeral, but Rachel had turned him down with a polite "No, thank you, we'll be fine."

He'd believed her. Besides that, she had her family, her friends. Now that Gary was gone, they had nothing more in common. Unless this was about the house, the dream house Gary had wanted him to build for Rachel. It was the only one of Gary's jobs that Dylan had turned down.

"Oh, boss." Connie's voice brought him back to reality. "Are you there?"

"I'll call her back. Just brush her off. If she calls again, tell her I'm out of town or something."

"But—"

"Tell Rachel whatever you have to. I can't deal with her right now."

"That's too bad," a woman said from behind him. "Because as far as I can see, you're not out of town."

Dylan's chest contracted at the sound of her voice, the voice that had haunted his dreams for so many years, the voice he'd tried to forget, just as he'd tried to forget everything else about her. He was her husband's best friend, and she was his best friend's wife. That's all they would ever be to each other. All they ever could be.

He heard Connie say something, but he simply closed the phone and forced himself to turn around, to face Rachel. She was dressed in black, the way she'd been at the funeral, her long blond hair hidden by the incongruous hard hat on her head. Her face was pale, her blue eyes dimmed, shadows of fatigue drawing lines around those eyes. Dammit, she was too young to be a widow, not even thirty yet. But then, Gary, at thirty-five, was too young to be dead.

"Why didn't you call me back?" Rachel's steady gaze wouldn't let him look away. It had been that way once before, a long, long time ago, when she had looked into his eyes and asked him a question he hadn't been able to answer. Not in the nine years since her wedding had she ever looked him straight in the eye again, the way she was looking at him now. He found it unsettling and was reminded of exactly why he'd wanted to avoid this moment.

"I've been busy. I'm sorry." And he *was* sorry. Looking at her now, he realized what an ass he'd been to avoid talking to her. She was Gary's widow. She deserved his support, his friendship, anything she needed.

Her fingers played with the strap on her purse, and he saw that her nails had been bitten down to the quick. Her arms were thin and pale. She'd lost weight in the past few months, along with everything else. He should have offered his help. At the very least, he should have returned her calls.

"You told me if there was anything I needed . . ." she said haltingly.

"Yes, of course."

"Don't answer so fast." She licked her lips and took a deep breath. "It's not that easy, but it is important. That's why I'm here—why I couldn't wait another second for you to call me back."

Dylan couldn't help wondering what she'd come to ask him. She sounded so dramatic. It had to be something minor, he told himself. She needed extra cash, advice on a plumbing problem or the construction of her house or something equally mundane. She couldn't possibly be here for any other reason.

"There's a problem with Gary's life insurance," she said in a rush.

"What?" He rocked back on his heels. He certainly hadn't been expecting her to say that. "What kind of a problem?"

"They don't want to pay."

"I don't understand."

"I don't either." Her voice shook with emotion.

He tried to make sense of her words. "Didn't Gary pay the premiums?"

"That's not it. They said they think Gary . . . Gary . . ."

"Gary what?" he asked impatiently.

"They think he drove off that mountain on purpose."

Her words hit Dylan like a solid punch to the gut. He couldn't believe what he was hearing. "Say that again."

"I can't say it again." She turned away from him and walked toward the edge of the building.

He stared after her in confusion, her words still racing around his head. No matter how many times they went around, they still didn't make sense. Gary's car had gone off the side of a mountain road in Lake Tahoe. It had been an accident, pure and simple.

"My husband would not have driven himself off of a cliff," Rachel said forcefully. "It would be like me jumping off this building right now. I couldn't. I wouldn't."

"Gary wouldn't either," he said, coming up behind her. "How can you think he would?"

"I don't think it," she said fiercely, turning back to face him. "But the report they gave me said Gary was seen driving erratically minutes before the crash. There was an eyewitness who saw him drive straight toward the edge. There were no skid marks on the road, nothing to show that he attempted to stop."

"Maybe the brakes didn't work. Maybe the eyewitness was wrong. And—and I thought insurance paid off even if, even if . . ." He couldn't continue.

"It was a new policy. Gary took it out last year. They have a two-year clause for, well, you know. The thing is, I didn't even know about the policy until I started cleaning out the desk last month. Gary paid all the bills. He took care of our finances. I thought all we had was the twenty-thousand-dollar policy Gary took out when Wesley was born. When I saw there was more, I assumed Gary had finally gotten around to realizing we needed a bigger cushion." She cleared her throat. "The insurance company thinks it's highly suspicious that he bought a half-million-dollar policy two months before his accidental death. But they're wrong."

She shook her head, as if to rid herself of any doubts. "I know it was an accident. Gary took the curve too fast, or a deer ran in front of him, or he got distracted, or something." Her gaze drilled into his once again. "You have to help me, Dylan. You're the only one who can. You have to help me prove this was an accident, that Gary had no reason whatsoever to kill himself. You have to."

"Jesus! Slow down." Dylan ran a hand through his hair, trying to think, but he didn't have a clue what to think. His mind was in utter chaos, emotions denying all logic. Only one thing was he certain about. "Gary didn't kill himself. That's nuts. He had everything to live for. He had a great life."

"Yes, he did." Rachel spoke with a tenseness in her face that seemed to belie her confidence. "He—we—we had a great life. God, this is making me crazy!"

Dylan felt another wave of guilt at her words. He told himself he'd had no way of knowing, but, dammit, he should have returned her calls. Unfortunately, his instinct for self-preservation was well honed, especially where Rachel was concerned.

"In the last few days, it occurred to me that perhaps there are answers to be found at Gary's apartment here in the city," Rachel continued. "I have his key ring, but I don't know which key it is. And I'm sorry to say I'm not even sure where the apartment is. I haven't been there in a while. I'd like you to give me the address and tell me which key, or else give me another one."

Oh, boy. Dylan hadn't seen this coming either, although he didn't know why he hadn't. When he'd bought an apartment building four years earlier, he'd offered Gary one of the units as a place to stay when he worked late or didn't want to face the sometimes-two-hour commute home. Gary had jumped at the idea.

On the weekends, Gary would drive home to be with Rachel and their son, Wesley, but when he wasn't traveling on business, he usually stayed in the city a couple of nights a week. Since Dylan owned the building, he hadn't worried about the apartment sitting empty, and he hadn't been able to bring himself to clear it out. He'd gone in right after the funeral and left just as quickly, the pain still too raw to deal with. Now Rachel wanted to go there, and Dylan felt a sudden protectiveness toward his friend. Maybe he should go through the apartment first, just in case.

"Unless you've rented it out already to someone else?" Rachel asked hesitantly. "I guess I should have been paying the rent, but Gary never said what it was."

"I didn't charge him rent."

"Oh."

She would probably want some of Gary's things, too, Dylan realized, maybe even the furniture. He should have gone through the place, boxed everything up, and shipped it to her months ago. That way he could have made sure there was nothing . . . Damn! What was he thinking? He had no reason to believe there was anything in that apartment that Rachel couldn't see. No real reason anyway. Nothing concrete. Nothing definitive.

"What's wrong, Dylan?"

"Nothing. I was just thinking maybe I should take a look and let you know."

"Let me know what?" Her voice filled with painful confusion. "Let me know Gary had some secret? Is there something you know that I don't?"

"I don't think he had a secret, but it might be hard for you to see the place."

"It was hard for me to learn my husband was dead. It was even harder for me to learn that some people think he killed himself. Frankly, I don't think there's anything in that apartment that could be any more difficult."

She had a point. And the fiery light in her eyes made him feel better. Anger was good. Anger could get a person through tough times. Rachel seemed stronger than he remembered, but then, his memories were mostly that of a beautiful, blond, nineteen-year-old girl in love with his best friend. She'd been laughing all the time back then, a smile so inviting you couldn't help smiling back. Of course, Gary had always been one to make a girl laugh, and Rachel had been no exception.

Over the years, Dylan had had only limited contact with Rachel, an occasional phone call or a brief appearance at a christening or a birthday party. He could count on one hand the number of times they'd stood this close together. And there had been a good reason for that, a very good reason.

"I need to go to the apartment," Rachel said firmly. "I'd like you to take me."

"All right."

"Thank you." She paused as she took in her surroundings for the first time. "Is this one of Gary's buildings?"

"Yes. The—" He stopped himself from saying "the last one." But he could see her finish the sentence in her head.

"He was a good architect, wasn't he?"

"One of the best."

"I've only seen a couple of his buildings. He'd show me the pictures you sent, but he rarely took me to see the real thing."

"Gary wasn't much on the final product. He liked the dream. Once it got down to nails and bolts, he moved on to the next project. I always sent him a picture just in case he wanted to know if I'd messed up anything."

"He said you always knew what he wanted, even when he didn't spell it out right."

"I don't know about that. I'm the kind of guy who follows the blueprints. Gary was the one who had to face the blank page. He had the harder job."

Rachel nodded, then shivered. Dylan suddenly realized how late the hour was getting. It would be dark soon. "I'll take you down now. It's a good thing you aren't afraid of heights. Some people don't like being up this high without closed windows around them."

"I didn't even think about it." She offered him a bewildered smile that cut through the years between them. For one second she was the young, innocent, carefree woman he remembered. "I keep doing that, ending up places and wondering how I got there," she added.

"I've done that a few times, too," he admitted.

"Maybe I was wrong to come here, but I didn't know where else to turn. I can't let some insurance company's doubts become my doubts. I have to prove they're wrong. I have to."

"I understand. And I agree."

"Do you? Because there was a look on your face a few minutes ago that made me feel like you knew something I didn't."

"I don't," he said immediately. Gary had been his best friend. That's all he wanted to think about, nothing else.

Dylan walked over to the elevator and pushed the button. Rachel came to wait beside him. They were standing so close he could smell her perfume, or maybe it was the lingering scent of apples. The first time he'd met her she'd smelled like a warm summer day, lush with the scent of flowers and apples. His chest tightened, and he forced the memory out of his head. He couldn't go back there. It had been a long time ago. And Gary had met her first. The only time in their lives the happy-go-lucky and perpetually late Gary had gotten somewhere before the ever-punctual Dylan.

The elevator doors opened, and they stepped inside, silent on the speedy descent to the ground. Rachel didn't have anything to say and Dylan didn't know what to say. He couldn't believe that Gary had killed himself. It made no sense whatsoever. The insurance company had to be wrong. There was no other explanation. But . . .

Gary had been stressed, tired during the weeks before his death. He'd been working hard, traveling a lot, but he certainly hadn't been suicidal. Still, he'd gone to Lake Tahoe alone, for reasons he hadn't shared with Dylan, and that in itself was odd.

"You're doing it, too," Rachel said as the elevator came to a halt.

"Doing what?" He held open the door for her.

"Going over those last few days in your head."

"I think it's a mistake, Rachel. I honestly do." They walked out to the street; dusk was settling over the city. "Where's your car?"

She pointed to a white minivan. "Shall I follow you, or do you want to give me directions?"

"You can follow me." He tipped his head toward the silver Mercedes parked across the street.

She raised an eyebrow in surprise. "Not bad. I always pictured you in a truck for some reason."

"Well, as long as you didn't picture me with a beer gut

hanging over my belt and the infamous butt crack when I squat down, I'll still feel good about my profession."

A smile blossomed across her face. "It was never that bad."

"Thank God." He paused. "Okay, then. I'll wait for you to turn around."

Rachel pulled the corners of her smile back as she walked to her car. There were moments in time when she forgot the sadness, when a smile broke through her tight lips. But then she'd feel guilty that she'd forgotten her pain, if only for a second. Some things, some people, should never be forgotten, and Gary was one of them. Dylan was, too, unfortunately.

The two men were as different as night and day, Gary with his golden-blond looks, Dylan with his midnight-black eyes, Gary with his sunny disposition, Dylan with his dark moods.

Dylan. Today her faded memories had been washed in bright, beautiful color, and the shadowy figure in her mind had become vibrant and real and distinctly unsettling.

As she got into her car, she told herself it was the circumstances that bothered her, not the man. There was too much at stake to allow a momentary indiscretion from a long time ago to get in the way of what she needed to do. Dylan had probably forgotten all about it. Chalked it up as no big deal. He probably didn't even realize she'd been avoiding him all these years.

It had been easy not to see each other. She lived more than an hour away. When Gary was home on the weekends, he was with her family, her friends. Dylan had rarely invaded that space.

Gary had always told her that Dylan felt more comfortable in the city, and she'd accepted that explanation.

Whether or not it was true didn't matter. And whether or not Dylan made her uncomfortable didn't matter. What did matter was that Dylan had been Gary's best friend for more than twenty years. If anyone could help her figure out what had been going on in Gary's mind the last day of his life, it was Dylan.

Rachel started the engine and pulled out behind Dylan's car. It seemed ironically fitting that their vehicles so perfectly represented their lives, Dylan in his fast, big-city, successful guy Mercedes and she in her practical-mom minivan. The minivan was exactly what she needed to drive Wesley and his friends around, but she couldn't help admiring the sleek lines of the car in front of her.

Within minutes, Dylan pulled up in front of a four-story apartment building in Pacific Heights. He waved Rachel into a driveway, for which she was incredibly grateful, since she was reluctant to park on the steep hill.

When she got out of the car, she was dazzled by the view, the shimmering blue waters of the San Francisco Bay turning silver in the moonlight, and the gleaming lights of the Golden Gate Bridge brightening the darkening sky. She was more comfortable with wide-open spaces and endless quiet, but there was a beauty here that she hadn't expected. For the first time, she wondered how Gary had felt living with one foot in each of his worlds.

"Ready?" Dylan asked her, meeting her by the front door.

She nodded and followed him into the elevator and up to the third floor, where he inserted a key into the lock and opened the door.

For a second she froze, suddenly terrified to step inside. Did she want to know—if there was something to know?

Wouldn't it be better to keep her memories, her love, her faith, intact? But they *were* intact, she reminded herself. She just wanted one last look at the other part of Gary's life—the part she hadn't really understood.

Gary had taken the apartment for practical purposes. With his long hours and long commute, it made sense for him to have a place in the city. She hadn't been able to argue with his reasoning, although she'd never gotten used to the idea of her husband having another home. Whenever she'd raised her concern about the distance between them, Gary would pull her into a big hug and tell her they had the best of everything.

She'd believed him because she wanted to believe him, and perhaps because changing the status quo might have meant having to come with him and live here in the city, she thought guiltily.

"You don't have to do this," Dylan told her. "I can check things out and let you know what I find."

"I've come this far." Squaring her shoulders, Rachel walked through the doorway and halted just inside to get her bearings. It was a man's apartment: heavy, dark furniture; a big-screen television set; a state-of-the-art stereo in one corner; a treadmill in the other. Her gaze moved from the big stuff to the little stuff: the pair of tennis shoes kicked halfway under the couch; sunglasses on the counter; a newspaper spread out on the dining room table the way Gary had always spread it out, driving her crazy by never closing one section before opening another right on top of it. Oh, God! She put a hand to her mouth, feeling suddenly sick.

"Are you all right?"

Dylan's voice sounded like he was speaking underwater. The blood pounded through her head so loudly she couldn't hear a thing. She found herself being pushed down onto the couch, her head forced between her knees.

"Breathe," Dylan ordered. "Just take a breath."

She forced some air into her lungs and began to feel better. Embarrassed, she sat up. "I'm sorry. I don't know what came over me."

"It's all right. I should have cleaned this place up a long time ago. I had the same reaction when I walked in after the funeral. I guess that's why I didn't come back. I should have sent the cleaning lady in. The dust is an inch thick." He got up from the couch and dug his hands into his pockets as he walked toward the window.

Rachel was grateful for the chance to regroup. "It wasn't your responsibility, it was mine. But the apartment was never a part of my life. After Gary's death, I forgot about it." She picked up a childish drawing from the coffee table, Wesley's birthday card to his father. The words *I love you, Daddy* were scrawled across the page. Rachel's heart broke just a bit more. "What am I doing here?" she murmured, a tiny sob escaping her throat. "A man who saves a little boy's cards doesn't kill himself."

Dylan turned around at her words. "Why don't I pack everything up and send it to you? You can go through the boxes when you're ready."

Rachel stood up, thinking that was a good plan, although she didn't quite trust the expression on Dylan's face. He seemed uneasy. Of course, after her reactions, almost fainting, then getting soppy over a silly card, he probably wasn't sure what she would do next.

"Won't it be hard on you?" she asked, instead of saying yes.

Dylan shrugged. "I can handle it." He cast a quick

glance toward the bedroom door, then looked back at her. "I'll walk you out."

"Maybe I should check the bedroom." It wasn't what she meant to say; it wasn't even what she wanted to do, but once the words were out, she couldn't take them back. So she walked into the bedroom, telling herself with each step that it would be fine. There were no monsters here. This was just a place where Gary stayed during the week. No big deal.

The bed wasn't made, no surprise there. The half-open closet door revealed a pile of dirty laundry in a hamper, suits and shirts hanging from the rack. They were Gary's work clothes, his architect clothes, not the comfortable Dockers and polo shirts he wore at home. She began to breathe more easily as she looked around the room. These were her husband's things. True, she didn't recognize many of them, but so what? That didn't mean anything.

"Are you done?" Dylan asked from the doorway.

"Yes." But as she turned, her gaze caught on the dresser, on a strangely shaped glass bottle. It drew her like a moth to a flame. She knew it was perfume before she crossed the room. She knew it wasn't her perfume before she reached the dresser. But she didn't know the bottle was only half full until she picked up. "Oh, God!" she whispered as she turned around to face Dylan. "Who does this belong to?"

His face grew so tight she wasn't sure he could answer even if he wanted to. It quickly became apparent that he didn't want to.

"Gary always said you were an honorable man, someone he could trust. Does that also mean you would keep his secrets?"

"Don't do this, Rachel."

"Was he having an affair?" She put a hand to her heart as her voice filled with the doubt she'd been trying to suppress. "Oh, my God, was he having an affair?"

Chapter 2

Dylan's breath stalled in his chest at the look in Rachel's shocked eyes. A dozen answers came to his mind, but it wouldn't matter what he said. She was too caught up in some unspeakable scenario of betrayal that her imagination had conjured up. Despite the fact that his own stomach had taken a nosedive a second ago, he couldn't let her go in that direction.

"Stop it," he ordered. "Just stop it. You jumped about a million miles in logic. There's a perfume bottle sitting on a dresser. So what?"

"So what?" she echoed in disbelief. "It's not mine. That's so what."

"Maybe it belonged to a client."

"What kind of a client? Why would Gary be holding business meetings in his apartment?"

"I don't know, but neither do you. Think for a second. We don't know who left the perfume bottle here. We don't," he repeated when she opened her mouth to argue. "It could be perfectly innocent. In fact, I'm sure it *is* innocent. And you should be sure, too."

"You're right. I should be sure. I *am* sure," she added, deliberately raising her voice. "I knew my husband. I knew him. I did."

She was trying to sound convinced and was failing abominably. Dylan didn't know what to say. He wanted to reassure her. He wanted to defend his friend. He wanted . . . Hell, he wanted everything to be the way it had been. No, that wasn't even true. The way it had been hadn't been right either, but it had been better than this. Anything was better than this.

"I can't be here right now," Rachel said. "Nothing makes sense here. I don't know this place. I don't understand it."

"Then go home, Rachel. Go back to your apple farm and your son and your family. I'll box everything up and ship it to you."

"Not the bottle. Don't send me that bottle." She wrapped her arms around her body as if she could somehow protect herself from it.

"I won't."

"No, you should. It could be a clue. No, don't. Oh, God, I don't know. Tell me what to do. Please. Just tell me what to do."

The painful plea in her eyes made him want to pull her into his arms and protect her. But he forced his hands deeper into his pockets. The very last thing he needed to do was touch her. "I think you should let it go," he said. "Gary is gone. None of the rest of it matters."

"But it does matter."

"If you need money—"

"It's not just the money, although God knows I'm not sure how I'll manage without it. But that's not it. I can't stand these doubts I have. Gary deserves my loyalty, yet there's this little voice inside my head telling me something is wrong with the way he died. I think I felt it even before I talked to the insurance company, but when their report said suicide, I couldn't run from the feeling anymore. I want to know what Gary was thinking when he drove down that mountain road six months ago. I want to know why he took cash from our bank account. I want to know why he bought the life insurance policy without telling me. I want to know if I somehow missed something. Maybe if I'd paid more attention, been a better wife, I could have stopped him—"

"Stopped him from what?" Dylan interrupted. "From dying? How could you have done that? How could you have possibly done that?"

"I don't know, but I was his wife—"

"And I was his best friend," he said harshly. "I could have stopped him, too. If you want to blame someone, blame me." Because if Gary had driven himself off that road, then Dylan should have seen it coming. He'd always been able to gauge Gary's moods, but not this last time. This last time he hadn't asked any questions, hadn't inquired why Gary was heading up to Tahoe on his own, hadn't pressed him about why he looked so tired or seemed so distant. In retrospect, Dylan knew that things hadn't been right, but he'd hesitated to ask, because . . . well, because he'd been afraid Gary was cheating on Rachel, and he hadn't wanted to hear it. Dammit, there it was. But he couldn't tell Rachel that. God, he couldn't tell her that.

"I can't blame you," Rachel said, catching his gaze and

holding on to it. "Gary loved you, Dylan. You were his best friend in the world."

Her words pierced his heart like a knife to the chest. "Yeah, I was a hell of a best friend." He drew in a much-needed breath. "Look, this isn't getting us anywhere. None of this was your fault. In fact, I don't think it was anyone's fault. I think it was an accident. Gary took a curve too fast and lost control of his car." Maybe if he said it forcefully enough, he'd believe it, too.

She stared at him for a long minute, searching his face for something, but he wasn't quite sure what. "I have to know, Dylan, and not just for me, but for Wesley. I have an eight-year-old son to protect, a little boy who loved his father and still can't accept the fact that he's gone. I can't allow any doubts, any secrets, to jump out and hurt him even more."

"That won't happen."

"I won't let it happen. I can't. But I wish this wasn't happening. I wish I'd never filed that insurance claim."

"So do I," he said heavily. But neither one of them could go back in time.

"Will you help me, Dylan? I hate to admit it, but I don't think I can do this alone."

Such a simple sentence, yet such a difficult request, for so many reasons.

"Gary would want us to do this together," she added.

Rachel was probably right. Gary had always wanted them to get along better, never understood why neither one of them had shown any interest in the other; but then, Gary had never known that once, just once, the distance between them had been covered by a kiss—a kiss they said they would never remember, but one that Dylan had never forgotten.

He owed Gary for that lapse in loyalty. And he'd been trying to pay off that debt for the past nine years. This might be his last chance to make things right. He needed to restore Rachel's faith in Gary. He needed to protect Wesley's love for his father. It was the least Dylan could do for his best friend.

"I'll help you," he said.

She looked him straight in the eye. "And you'll tell me the truth, no matter what?"

"I can't promise that. Gary was my best friend."

"Well. I guess I know where we stand."

"Where we've always stood," he agreed. *With Gary in between us.*

And just like that, they were back to the beginning.

His blond hair glowed in the afternoon sunlight, like an angel's halo, Rachel thought whimsically as a handsome young man walked up to the apple stand, where she'd been selling fruit for the better part of the day, and asked for directions. She couldn't answer right away, caught up in the blue of his eyes, the dimple in his cheek, the mischief in his smile. Then she realized he was laughing, and she was staring. She blushed with embarrassment.

"Gary Tanner," he said, extending his hand. "And you are?"

"Rachel Wood," she stuttered. She put her hand in his, expecting a brief handshake, but he curled his fingers around hers and a shiver ran down her spine. "Where—where did you want to go?" she asked, finally pulling her hand away from his and surreptitiously wiping her sweaty palm on the side of her shorts.

"I'm not sure," Gary replied with a thoughtful tip of his

head. "Maybe I don't want to go anywhere. I think I just found what I was looking for."

Rachel's heart took a tumble. All the coldness that had gripped her in the past month in the wake of her daddy's illness was suddenly wiped away by this man's warm smile.

"But my friend, Dylan, will probably kill me if I come back to the car without directions. This is about the hundredth time I've gotten us lost," he confided with a mischievous grin. "Dylan doesn't understand that sometimes the most interesting and prettiest sights are found on the side roads."

Rachel felt the heat creep back up her neck and across her cheeks. She wondered when she'd outgrow the terrible habit. She wasn't a child anymore; she was nineteen years old. She needed to stop acting like a foolish schoolgirl. But this sophisticated young man was so different from the boys she was used to seeing around the farm.

"At least you're willing to ask for directions. Some men would rather die first," she said, trying to sound casual and worldly at the same time, as if she knew all kinds of men and their subsequent habits.

"Well, we have been driving around in circles for about an hour," he admitted. "Can you tell me if I'm anywhere close to the Redwood Highway?"

"Oh, sure, you're not far at all. Just a mile farther down this road. Make a left past the railroad tracks, go two blocks, and you'll see the highway."

"Sounds easy enough. Thanks. Now how about . . ."

He paused for so long, she thought he was about to ask for a kiss. A kiss! Her heart thudded against her chest in anticipation as they both seemed to be leaning forward.

"Hey, what's the holdup?" a man asked, coming up behind Gary. "Did you get directions, or are we destined to drive past the same cow for another hour?"

A flood of disappointment swept through Rachel at the interruption. She fixed an annoyed glance on the dark-haired man who seemed as cold and impatient as his friend was warm and friendly.

"I got the directions. I'm just picking up a few apples while we're here," Gary said, giving Rachel a wink. "Which of these are the sweetest?"

Rachel made a sudden and impulsive decision. She reached behind her into a canvas bag and pulled out an apple that was a rainbow of pinks and reds. "Take this one. It's special."

"Special, huh?"

She shrugged her shoulders, feeling a bit silly. "Well, there's a legend, but it doesn't matter. It's still the tastiest apple you'll ever eat. It's on the house," she said when he reached into his pocket.

He turned the apple in his hand. "A legend? As in magic?"

"Gary, we don't have time for this," Dylan said impatiently.

"Maybe I'll have to come back, and you can tell me the story," Gary said with an appealing grin.

"I'm counting on it," she whispered as he walked away, taking the other man with him. She hoped there really was some magic in that apple. Because she had a feeling about this man, a really good feeling.

A little magic, Rachel thought with a sigh as she drove over the Golden Gate Bridge and headed north to the small town of Sebastopol; she could sure use a little magic now, too. Not even magic really, just answers, truth, light— something to take the queasiness out of her stomach and the heaviness off her shoulders. She felt lonely, scared and completely overwhelmed, so different from the time her heart had been filled with hope, excitement and anticipation when she'd met Gary. All of that was gone.

One day she was a wife, the next day she was a widow. Somewhere in between she'd lost her heart, her soul and her spirit. She had to find a way to get them back. She had a child to raise. And there wasn't just Wesley, but her sister, Carly, her grandmother Marge, her grandfather John, her aunt Dee and everyone else who depended on the orchards, on *her*, to keep things going. How would she manage that if she couldn't keep herself going?

The same way she'd managed before, she told herself firmly. When her father had died, she'd felt the same crushing grief, but she'd pulled it together. She had made good on her promise to keep the orchards alive, hold the family together, and she'd continue to do that. Because home and family were everything.

Suddenly she couldn't wait to get home and put on her old, faded blue jeans with the rip at the knee and her comfortable sweatshirt. Then she'd heat up last night's lasagne and listen to Wesley talk about his day. It would be familiar and safe. And she wanted safe. She wanted sameness, habits. She wanted comfort, love, a man's arms around her shoulders, a reassuring voice in her ear, a shared smile, a hope in the future . . . oh, how she wanted. The ache seemed to grow with each passing day instead of fading as it was supposed to.

Rachel turned on the radio, desperate for a distraction, but everyone was singing about love and heartache. She turned it off just as quickly, the gesture reminding her of another time, another trip from San Francisco to Sebastopol. She'd been ten years old, and her father, Vince,

had been driving his 1969 Mustang convertible. Her little
sister, Carly, age three, was asleep in the backseat, completely unaware that their lives were changing forever. But
Rachel had known, and she'd been grateful to have the top
down, the breeze blowing in her long blond hair, because
then she could pretend that the wind was making her eyes
water and the drops on her cheeks weren't really tears.

She wasn't supposed to be crying. She was supposed to
be happy they were going back to live on her grandparents' apple farm. And in a way she *was* happy, because
their five years in the city had been filled with nothing but
fights as her parents battled over everything. Her mother
complained that her father had no ambition, that he
wasn't a good provider. Her father complained that his
wife had no love in her, that she wasn't a good mother.

In the end, they'd broken each other down. Her mother
had taken a job in Chicago and her father was bringing
them home to the farm he loved, back to the place where
nothing ever changed except the seasons. A place where a
person could count on apple blossoms in the spring and
long, hot days in the summer, a bounty of fruit in the fall
and cold quiet in the winter. She would love it there, he
told her, and she believed him. She wouldn't have her
mother, but she would have him and the farm. It would be
enough.

Since that trip, Rachel had never wanted to live any-
place else, especially not in the city, where they had been so
unhappy. Gary had understood—not all of it, of course,
because she'd never told him all of it. And he'd never
asked—not really, not like he had to know.

Maybe that's what had been wrong between them, the
not wanting to know and the not wanting to tell. But she'd
been a young bride and a young mother, caught up in the

demands of life and family. She'd been happy enough; she thought he'd been happy, too.

As the miles drew her closer to home, Rachel gained strength and resolve. It had been a mistake to go to the city. She couldn't believe in anything she found there. She certainly couldn't let a perfume bottle shake her faith in her husband. That wouldn't be fair to Gary. And she wanted to be fair. She wanted to be loyal. She still wanted to be the best wife she could be; it was all she had *ever* wanted.

Dylan knew that.

Dylan. If Rachel hadn't been driving, she would have been tempted to close her eyes and let his image play in front of her. Even now she could see him in her mind, penetrating eyes, stubbornly proud jaw, a generous but ruthless mouth. He'd always had a presence, a dark, brooding intensity to him. At nineteen, she'd found him both attractive and frightening. At twenty-nine, she felt pretty much the same way. And they had a history, a past, a kiss. Just one kiss. One shameful kiss, exchanged the night before her wedding.

Dylan had apologized and begged for forgiveness. He'd told her they'd never speak of it, never consider doing it again, never, ever betray Gary the way they had. The words had poured from his mouth, building a wall between them that would last forever. But then, that's the way Dylan built things—so they would never fall down. Gary had said Dylan was the best builder he had ever known. Rachel could only agree.

As she turned off the highway, she veered away from the town center and headed down the country roads that led toward home. She opened her window, eager to breathe in the cool night air, which was laden with the sweet fragrance of apples. The trees were heavy with fruit and ready to be harvested. It was her favorite time of the year, and with each breath she felt calmer. This was her place in the world—where vineyards and orchards lined the hillsides and fields of wildflowers adorned the highway. This was home.

She turned under the arched sign that proclaimed AppleWood Farms and drove the half mile up to the main house, a large two-story building that had sheltered six generations of her family.

After her father's death, she and Gary had moved into the master bedroom. Wesley and Carly had taken over the other bedrooms on the second floor. Her grandparents, Marge and John, lived in a separate, small cottage a hundred yards away that had been built by her great-great-grandfather Joseph Wood at the turn of the century.

There was history in the two houses, love, joy, sorrow. So much history. And maybe a little too much sorrow. Her father had died in his upstairs bedroom, just after her twentieth birthday, just after her one-year wedding anniversary, just after Wesley's birth.

Rachel knew she should have been grateful that her father had seen her marry, that he'd held his grandson in his arms, but there was so much he had missed, so much he was still missing now.

She wondered if they were together somehow, her father and Gary, looking down at her, probably shaking their heads in amazement that she'd actually gotten into her car and driven to San Francisco, which only showed how desperate she was to know the truth. Because if she couldn't believe in the life she'd had with her husband, in the love they'd shared, then how could she believe in anything?

Faith, her father would say, as he'd said to her the last

day of his life. *Rachel, honey, have faith in yourself. You're strong. You'll be the one to keep the family together. I'd like to say you got your strength from me, but in truth, I think you got it from your mother. Only it's love that drives your strength, and in the end, that's all that will matter. Just promise me one thing, Rachel. Promise me you won't ever give up.*

"I'm not sure I can keep that promise, Daddy," she whispered. "I'm not as strong as you think I am." Rachel stopped the car at the end of the drive and turned off the engine. She leaned her head against the steering wheel and closed her eyes. Even before Gary's death, she'd had her hands full with the orchard and her family, but at least she'd had Gary on the weekends to share the burden, to make her feel like she wasn't alone. Now she didn't have anyone around whom she wasn't taking care of.

Enough, she told herself, lifting her head. Enough self-pity. She would make it all work. There was no other choice. She opened the door and got out, looking toward the house as the back door banged open and a childish voice rang across the yard.

"Mommy," Wesley cried, hurtling himself down the steps, across the lawn and into her arms. She hugged him tight as he murmured, "You're back. You're back," over and over again.

Rachel heard the uncertainty in his voice and squeezed him tighter. "I'm here, honey. I told you I'd be back before bedtime." She let him go and smiled into his face, which was so like Gary's it made her head spin. Wesley's hair was a white blond, his eyes a brilliant summer-sky blue. The freckles that ran down his nose and across his cheeks were the same freckles that had kissed his father's face. Some-times it hurt her just to look at him. But he was her child,

and in him she would always see the man she had loved
and married. That was a gift in itself.

"Where's Aunt Carly?" she asked.

"Inside."

"Did she help you with your homework?"

Wesley rolled his eyes in another gesture reminiscent of
his father. "Aunt Carly isn't good at math. I did it myself.
But you can still help me if you really want to."

She smiled at him. He was so obviously concerned
about her. It wasn't right for an eight-year-old to be worrying about his mother. "So what *is* Aunt Carly doing?"

Rachel saw a sudden gleam come into Wesley's eyes.
Whatever Carly was doing had Wesley looking guilty as
sin. She hoped there wouldn't be any consequences like an
explosion or a trip to the county jail. At twenty-two, Carly
was supposed to be an adult, but so far, Rachel had seen
little sign of any maturity. Her sister was already in her
fifth year of college, changing majors with every season.
She was supposed to work in the farm office when she
wasn't in class, but never quite got there. She seemed to be
drifting through life. Although, come to think of it, Carly
had mentioned something last week about a plan . . .

"She's just cooking," Wesley replied.

"But—" Rachel prodded.

Wesley darted another quick look at the house, then
lowered his voice to a whisper. "She's making a magic apple pie."

"Oh, dear." Rachel had a feeling that Aunt Carly's new
plan had nothing to do with finishing her education.

Chapter 3

Carly wiped her flour-covered hands on a dishtowel and glanced out the kitchen window. She could see Rachel and Wesley on the lawn. The poor kid had been worrying himself crazy for the past hour, asking every two minutes when his mommy would be home. Carly had tried to distract him as best she could, but she knew he wanted only his mother; no one else would do. There was a bond between Rachel and Wesley that was so strong it could never be broken.

That's the way it was supposed to be between a mother and a child, but certainly not the way it had been between herself and her own mother. No, her mother had decided a career was more important than her children. Carly had been raised first by her father until age thirteen, then by Rachel, who had taken over after their father died. Her grandparents had helped out, too, but Rachel had been the one in charge, acting as both mother and father. Unfortunately, what they'd never really been was sisters, which was the one relationship Carly wanted. Especially now.

They were both grown up. Rachel was reeling from Gary's death. It was time for Rachel to turn to her for comfort. But Rachel wasn't turning anywhere. She was holding it all in, the way she always did, which made Carly feel helpless and frustrated.

Of course, there were other reasons that she felt helpless and frustrated. Actually, one reason. One person. Antonio Paccelli. Just thinking about him made her smile. He was the most gorgeous, sophisticated male she had ever encountered. He wore Armani suits and Fendi shoes and smelled like heaven. His skin was a dark olive, his eyes and hair a jet black, his body as buff as any she'd ever seen. She was in total and complete lust. But Antonio either ignored her or, worse yet, followed Rachel's lead and treated her like a kid sister. He was thirty, just eight years older than she. Well, enough already!

Antonio would be in Sebastopol for only a couple more weeks. He and his father, Gianni, had recently purchased the failing Rogelio Winery, and Antonio had come here to oversee the renovations and hire new workers. He'd been in town six weeks and the work was almost finished. Soon he would return to Milan or New York or perhaps L.A., for his family had offices in all three locations. But he wouldn't be going alone if Carly had anything to say about it.

She'd been flirting with him for weeks. Now it was time to bring out the heavy-duty artillery. Thank goodness her great-great-grandmother's special apple tree had bloomed this year. It was another sign that it was time to take action. The harvesting of this tree had always turned the tides of love. It had been that way since the tiny seeds had been planted in the ground, and her great-great-grandmother Elaine had enticed the man of her heart with the perfect apple.

The tree had offered only a few apples ripe enough to pick, and those special apples were now simmering in Carly's pie. By this time tomorrow, if her favorite legend had any teeth, Antonio would be hers.

Carly opened the oven door and took a look at her pie. The crust shimmered with sugar. Inside the slits, she could see the apples bubbling. She could smell the cinnamon, and she drew the scent in, all the way in, inhaling it like it was her last breath. Well, she was getting desperate, that was for sure. She was twenty-two years old, and all of her friends were either graduating from college, finding new jobs or getting married. She was doing none of the above.

She couldn't contemplate the idea of spending the rest of her life in a small town, picking apples every fall, worrying about pests and pesticides and harvests. Her whole life would not be about fruit. Of that she was certain.

Sometimes that sense of certainty scared her the most. She'd heard the bitterly whispered stories of her mother's passion for painting, for a life that didn't include family and children. And sometimes, deep in her soul, Carly wondered if she wasn't like her mother. The fear that she was made her hide her own art. She'd pretended all through school that she couldn't draw anything but stick figures. Because if she could, what kind of person did that make her? Someone like her mother, who everyone said was a terrible person? And how could Carly argue that her mother wasn't terrible? She still felt the sting of rejection, of abandonment.

Gary had understood. He'd been the only one she'd ever told about . . .

The kitchen door opened behind her, and she quickly shut the oven.

"Carly?" Rachel questioned as her sister turned around. "You're baking?"

"Yes," she replied lightly, casually, as if it were no big deal. But Rachel's eyes narrowed suspiciously.

"It smells wonderful. When will it be ready?"

"It's not for us," Wesley interjected. "It's for—"

"Someone else," Carly finished abruptly with another bright smile in her sister's direction.

"Wesley, why don't you get your math homework, and we'll take a look at it," Rachel said. After Wesley had left the room, she turned her attention back to Carly. "Now, what's going on? Did you pick some apples you shouldn't have?"

"I might have."

"Oh, Carly. For who?"

"I don't think it's any of your business."

"Antonio is not the man for you."

"How was your trip to the city? Did you learn anything?" Carly felt guilty for bringing up the sad subject of Gary's death, but she didn't want to discuss Antonio with Rachel. Besides, Rachel's problems were more important than hers. And she did want to be a good sister. She was rather pleased that Rachel had confided in her about the insurance. Well, maybe not *confided*. She'd sort of accidentally overheard Rachel telling their grandmother . . . but that was beside the point.

Rachel set her purse down on the table, walked over to the refrigerator and took out a bottle of mineral water. "It was . . . I don't know. I just don't know." She sat down at the table and sipped at her drink.

"Did you find Dylan?"

"Yes. He took me to the apartment."

"And?" Carly didn't like the evasive look in Rachel's eyes. "What happened?"

"Nothing."

"It looks like something."

Rachel shook her head. "It was strange to see Gary's things. That's all."

"What kind of things?"

"His clothes and stuff." Her eyes softened. "Wesley's birthday card to Gary was on the coffee table."

"So you didn't find anything out of the ordinary?" Carly tried to sound as if she couldn't imagine what Rachel would find. But she *could* imagine, and she hoped her imagination was wrong.

"No, not really."

"Not really or no?"

"No," Rachel said quickly. "I didn't find anything. I didn't think I would. This is all just a terrible mistake."

"I'm sure it is." Carly was unable to read her sister's mood. Rachel had always been difficult to read. As she'd gotten older, she'd become even more private. Sometimes Carly wondered if her sister was hiding something. "What does Dylan think?" she asked.

Bingo. Rachel's entire body stiffened. Something had happened. But what?

"He doesn't know what to think. He was shocked." Rachel stood up and walked restlessly around the room. "I don't think he knows any more than I do." She paused to read the phone messages on the notepad by the phone. "Wesley's teacher called?"

"Yes. She's very concerned about how he's handling Gary's death. Apparently he keeps insisting that his dad will be home soon."

"I know. I can't seem to make him stop," Rachel said wearily.

"She asked if you could come in after school on Monday for a conference. She also said something about his test grades. I didn't quite catch what she was saying. But, heck, he's only eight. He's had a rough year."

"You can say that again. So what's with the pie?" Rachel changed the subject as Carly took it out of the oven. "Are you really planning to feed it to Antonio?"

"Don't worry about it, Rachel. You have enough on your mind."

"Too much to be worrying about you doing something crazy," Rachel replied sharply. "So please, don't go overboard."

"I know exactly what I'm doing," Carly said coolly, placing the pie on the counter.

"Which is what? Trying to seduce Antonio? He is completely wrong for you, not to mention too old. And you're not the kind of woman who—well, you're not his type."

"Thanks a lot," Carly snapped. She'd always known she wasn't as pretty as Rachel. She'd had to inherit some recessive red-hair gene when everyone else in the family was blond. And she had way too many freckles because she liked the sun far too much. And her eyes changed their color with her moods, so no one could ever write a poem about her wondrous green eyes or her golden eyes or her sky-blue eyes, because no one could ever remember what color her eyes were.

"That's not what I meant," Rachel said.

"Well, I may not have the face, but I do have the body." And she did, long legs and a big bust, her two best selling features.

"You're gorgeous, you know that. But you're a small-town girl. Antonio is a man of the world. You have nothing in common. You barely know him."

"I know Antonio better than you knew Gary when you gave him one of our special apples," Carly said pointedly.

"That was different."

"It sure was different. It was crazy. You were nineteen years old, and he was a stranger. You didn't know if you'd ever see him again. But it didn't stop you. And it worked. You found true love. Well, I'm going to find it, too."

"I want you to be happy, Carly, but—"

"But you don't think I know what I'm doing," Carly finished. "What else is new?"

"I don't think you realize how different your lives are. Antonio travels all over the world. He's a playboy, Carly. He knows lots of women."

"And he knows how to make women happy. Frankly, I don't see the problem. And I want to travel. I'd love to see the world. It's not like you married a stay-at-home guy. Gary was always on the road. You made your marriage work."

"Did I?" Rachel sighed and rolled her head around on her shoulders. "I'm not sure anymore."

Carly frowned, hearing the doubt in Rachel's voice. "It sounds like you're starting to believe the accident wasn't an accident."

"No, absolutely not. I know it was an accident. It had to be. It just had to be." She shook her head. "I thought we were talking about you and Antonio."

"There is no me and Antonio—not yet anyway." Carly plunged ahead before Rachel could respond. "So what will you do now? Did Dylan have any ideas?"

"I'm not sure I can work with Dylan on this."

"Why not? I know you never liked him, but he was Gary's best friend."

"It's not that I don't like him. It's just . . ."

"Just what?"

"I'm not sure I can trust him."

"Do you need to trust him to get answers?"

Rachel hesitated, her eyes troubled. "I have to know the truth, Carly, whatever it is. I'm not sure Dylan will tell me the truth, not if it could hurt Gary's reputation in any way."

"Hurt his reputation? I don't understand."

Rachel looked away. Her usually unreadable face was clearly lined with worry.

"Oh, my God," Carly breathed, her mind racing to the only logical conclusion, the one she hadn't wanted to believe. "Gary wasn't having—"

"Don't say it," Rachel warned, cutting her off with steel determination in her eyes. "Don't say it."

"But you're thinking it."

"No. I'm not."

"Then what *are* you thinking? I want to help you, Rachel, but I have no idea what's going through your head."

"I know you want to help, but you can't. As for what I'm thinking—right now I'm thinking I never should have gone to San Francisco. I never should have contacted Dylan."

"Because . . ." Carly prodded.

"Because he's going to make it harder. He's going to make it a lot harder."

Dylan woke up the next morning with the same thought he'd had when he'd gone to bed. He wished Rachel had never come to the city, never told him the suspicion that Gary's death wasn't an accident, never gone to the apartment, never stood so close to him. Damn it all. Why couldn't he be free of her? It was as if someone had cast a spell over him ten years ago and he couldn't break it. Keeping his distance certainly hadn't done the trick. Maybe if he'd spent time with her over the years, gotten to know her better, he wouldn't like her so much. Maybe more familiarity would have bred more contempt. Maybe he was kidding himself.

Rachel had a piece of his heart and always would. Deep down, he knew it wasn't just Rachel who had gotten to him all those years ago; it was the life she represented: the happy, meddling family in which everyone loved each other no matter what; the big old house with the long, wide porch and the swing on which she and Gary watched the sunset or, better yet, watched their little boy playing on the lawn. That was the last image Dylan had of the three of them together. After that night, he'd promised himself he'd never go back, because it hurt too damn much.

He'd always wanted a family like that. He'd had one once, when he was a child, until everything had broken apart. So how could he begrudge Gary the family he'd always wanted?

For he and Gary, two kids from broken homes, had both seen a future in Rachel's eyes, only Gary had seen that future first and grabbed it. Now that he was gone . . . well, some men might have considered trying to step into that empty space, to take what they'd always wanted. But not Dylan. He'd been second best before, tolerated, liked but not loved, not wanted, not really wanted. And he deserved that, dammit. He deserved that.

Rachel might be back in his life now, but she wanted his help—she didn't want *him*. And he couldn't forget that. He'd promised to help her, too. For Gary's sake, he told himself for the hundredth time. Not because he wanted to spend time with Rachel, but because he wanted to clear Gary's name. He wanted his friend to rest in peace, so he'd keep his promise. Then he'd say good-bye to Rachel and never look back.

With new resolve, Dylan got dressed, then went downstairs to Gary's apartment. The perfume bottle called to him like a beacon in the night. He found himself standing in front of it, staring at it as if it would suddenly speak some truth. But there was nothing except silence in the bedroom. He had no idea whom the perfume belonged to. Even if Gary had had some woman in the apartment, it didn't mean he'd had an affair. It certainly didn't mean he'd killed himself.

In fact, Dylan still couldn't wrap his mind around that possibility. Gary had come from a troubled background, but unlike Dylan, who tended to hold everything inside, every hurt, every slight, every word of anger, Gary had always been able to let things go. He'd been the one to tell Dylan not to take life too seriously, to live in the moment, to forget about the past and stop worrying about the future.

So why would a man who wanted to live only in the now kill himself?

Had Gary changed over the years? Had Dylan missed some sign that something was wrong? They hadn't seen each other much in the months before Gary's death. Work and other commitments had kept them moving in different directions. A distance had developed in their friendship, which Dylan now deeply regretted.

His gaze turned away from the perfume bottle to the dresser below. He didn't want to go through Gary's drawers, but it would be him or it would be Rachel. He had a feeling that Gary, if given the choice, would prefer him to do it.

Pushing the last bit of doubt out of his mind, Dylan opened the first drawer, then the second and the third. He was relieved to find nothing but clothes. He was about to shove the last drawer closed when he realized that the piece of clothing sticking out was lace, white lace, *female* white lace. Oh, Lord!

He pulled it out like it was a bomb about to explode in his face. And in truth it was a bomb, a ticking time bomb, for he couldn't think of one good reason why Gary would have female white lace apparel in his sock drawer.

Dylan sat down on the floor. He leaned against the bed, holding the piece of lingerie in his hand. If Rachel saw this, she'd freak. And what if there was more? What should he do? Throw it away, pretend it didn't exist? Stuff it into a box with everything else and ship it to Rachel?

Wait. Maybe it was Rachel's. She must have spent at least one night at the apartment.

Before he could come up with an answer, his cell phone rang. For a panicked moment he thought it might be Rachel, but she didn't have his number. "Yes," he said warily.

"Hi, boss. Sleeping late?"

Connie, his secretary. He blew out a breath of relief. "I had some things to do this morning. I'll be in later."

"How much later? You have a lunch meeting at twelve with the architects from Martel and Howard."

"Right. You better cancel. I have something more pressing to take care of."

"Anything I can help you with?"

"I don't think so."

"Does it have to do with Rachel Tanner?" Connie asked cautiously. "Yesterday I tried to warn you she was on her way. I didn't tell her where you were, but she got the information out of the temporary receptionist."

"It doesn't matter. I needed to talk to her anyway."

"Which is why you avoided her calls the last few days." His secretary, a forty-something mother of four, was too perceptive sometimes.

"Yeah, well, she found me, so that's that. There is one thing you can do. Find a moving company willing to box up an apartment and ship everything to Sebastopol ASAP."

"Gary's apartment?"

"Yeah."

"Is there much to pack?"

He fingered the lace teddy. "There's enough, more than enough." He paused. "You and Gary had some conversations, didn't you?"

"All the time, boss, usually about you. Why?"

"Do you think he was acting differently before he died?" Connie didn't answer right away, and Dylan's suspicious antennae went up. "Well? Don't hold out on me now. It's important."

"Why would it be important now?"

"It just is."

"Gary said someone had recently come back into his life," Connie finally replied. "He wasn't sure how he felt about it."

"A woman?"

"He didn't say. Why?"

"I can't tell you why. It probably doesn't matter anyway."

"He was a good guy, too young to die, that's for sure," Connie said. "How's Rachel holding up?"

"All right. Are you sure Gary didn't say who the person was who'd come back into his life?"

"No. He just made some joke and changed the subject and that was that. I only remember the conversation because I thought at the time how rare it was for Gary to speak seriously about anything. He was such a joker and probably the biggest flirt on the West Coast. I miss his phone calls. And I really do feel sorry for his wife and child. I wonder what happened to that house they were building."

Dylan had no idea what Gary had done with the plans for Rachel's dream house, as he'd called it. In fact, Dylan had tried not to think about it. Just hearing about the house had made him realize that he had to draw a line somewhere. He could be supportive of their marriage, but he sure as hell couldn't build their dream house.

"So when will you be in, boss?" Connie asked.

"Not for a couple of days," Dylan said, making a sudden decision.

"You're taking a vacation? Hold on, I may have to faint. I don't think you've taken a sick day in the last five years."

"Then I'm due. Tell Tom he's in charge. But tell him I will be back, so he shouldn't get any big ideas about redecorating my office."

"He is ambitious."

"A young hotshot," Dylan agreed. Tom Landers had joined his company right after college, and for the past four years he'd worked his way up to become Dylan's right-hand man. It was Tom who'd encouraged him to go after bigger and bigger jobs, including the skyscraper in L.A., and Dylan had to give the younger man credit for always wanting to shoot the moon. Like himself, Tom was single, no family or kids to think about. They had no reason not to go for everything they could get. Because what else was there, really?

"You'll have your cell phone?" Connie queried.

"Yes. If anything urgent comes up, let me know."

"And you'll be where?"

"I'll be in Sebastopol."

"Are you sure that's wise?"

He uttered a short little laugh. "No, I think it's damn stupid, but I made a promise, and I'm going to keep it."

The drive north gave Dylan a dozen chances to reconsider, but he hadn't gotten where he was in life by allowing himself to get sidetracked. Right now he had to focus on helping Rachel learn the truth about Gary's death. Then they could all get on with their lives.

In the backseat of his car, he'd placed a couple of boxes filled with Gary's personal papers and other small trinkets he'd found in the apartment. The movers would bring the rest of the furniture next week. The white lace teddy he'd stuffed into his own bag. He'd keep it there for the time being. There was no point in throwing more fuel on the fire. They needed to move slowly, think matters through, talk to Gary's other friends and associates and figure out what to do next.

As the freeway turned to highway, and the city sights gave way to rolling green hills, Dylan's resolve began to weaken. This was Rachel's turf. He didn't belong here. It was too quiet. There wasn't enough traffic. There weren't enough buildings. There were too many damn trees. Apple trees, probably, he thought with a scowl.

He hadn't been able to look at an apple without seeing Rachel at nineteen, standing in the middle of a ridiculous fruit stand wearing cutoff blue jeans and a bright yellow tank top. She'd had a golden tan, flowing blond hair and a wide-eyed, innocent smile that promised the world.

He'd tried to get that image out of his head for years, but it kept coming back. He had a feeling it was indelibly printed on his brain. He'd had other women in his life, quite a few other women, if the truth be told. Only one or two whom he could remember now, but none who stood out so vividly.

Dylan looked out the window of the car, trying to distract himself. He saw a structure up on a small hill and realized the worst was yet to come.

Off to the left side of the empty road that led to Rachel's apple farm was the beginning of a house, a framing, a skeleton of what was to come. He knew it before he knew it. It was Gary's house. It was Rachel's house. It was their dream house. Dammit. It was the last thing he wanted to see.

But he found himself slowing down, and when the driveway appeared, he took the turn. He drove up the dirt road toward the front of the structure, shut off the engine and stepped out.

Even though only the bare bones were there, he could see how the house would look when it was finished. It would be spectacular, proud and grand, the way a house should be. There would be a big porch, perfect for some comfortable chairs. He turned his head to look out at the valley that spread before him: vineyards, trees and wildflowers. It was a stunningly peaceful sight, but Gary wouldn't be here to appreciate it. Rachel would sit on the porch alone.

His stomach turned over, and he knew he had to leave, but then he heard the sound of hammering coming from the back. The knocks were short, then fast. A board clattered to the ground. He didn't see any cars, although he supposed there could be someone around the back. In fact, there should be lots of someones. The house should be going up. He wondered why construction had stopped. Had Rachel run out of money? She'd mentioned something about missing cash. He wondered now how much cash. But that would have to wait. Right now he wanted to find out who was hammering like a five-year-old.

He went up the front steps and through the various rooms, turning a corner, only to stop dead in his tracks. It wasn't a five-year-old hammering, but it was close.

Wesley!

When the boy turned his head, Dylan could have sworn he was looking at Gary, a younger Gary, the boy he'd first met at the age of eleven . . .

"Hey, there," Dylan said, clearing his throat somewhat awkwardly as he tried to think of what to say.

Wesley stared at him, blond hair, blue eyes, freckles— Gary's face. The sight almost made Dylan lose it. He struggled for control, composure.

"Who are you?" Wesley asked.

"I'm Dylan. Do you remember me? I'm a friend of your dad's. I was at one of your birthday parties, the one where the clown came and did the juggling act. I think you were turning five."

Wesley slowly nodded, looking a little less uneasy.

"I don't see your mom around. Is she here?"

Wesley didn't answer, just shrugged.

"So what are you doing?" Dylan asked.

"Building my house."

Dylan squatted down in front of the boy, giving him a

friendly smile. "It looks pretty good. I'm a builder, too, you know."

"You are?"

"Yes, I am. Is that your hammer?"

Wesley flushed somewhat guiltily. "Yeah."

"It's kind of big, don't you think?"

"It's okay. I have to go back to work now."

"Maybe you could use some help."

Wesley shook his head. "We can't afford any help, not until my daddy comes back."

Dylan's heart stopped. Did Wesley really think his father was coming back? He knew the boy had been at the funeral. But Rachel had told him Wesley was having trouble understanding that death was forever.

"He's coming home when it's done," Wesley said fiercely, as if anticipating an argument. "He said we would live in the house together all the time, just like a real family. He promised."

Dylan had no idea what to say, but thankfully, he heard the slamming of a car door and a very familiar, worried voice.

"Wesley. Wesley," Rachel yelled.

"He's back here," Dylan replied.

Rachel came around the corner with a shocked look on her face. He didn't know if she was more surprised to find him or Wesley.

"What are you doing here?" she asked as he got to his feet.

"I was on my way to your place. I saw this house, and I had a feeling . . ."

She frowned and glanced over at Wesley. "And what are *you* doing here? I told you to stay on our property."

"This is our property."

"You knew what I meant. I don't want you coming over the hill on your own. And I certainly don't want you here alone."

"I'm working on the house. Someone has to," Wesley said defiantly. "Else Daddy can't come back and live with us."

Dylan heard her sharp intake of breath, but he had to give her credit for holding it together.

"I told you that I'll hire someone to finish the house as soon as we get through the harvest season," she said.

"That's too long. Don't you want Daddy to come home?"

"Of course I do. But he's not coming back. He's in heaven. You know that, Wesley."

"No, he's not in heaven. He's on a trip and he's coming back when the house is finished. We have to finish it. We *have* to." Wesley picked up the oversized hammer and swung it down so close to his fingers that Dylan had to react. He grabbed the hammer from Wesley before he could strike again, but the boy's eyes filled with outrage and unbearable pain.

"I'll finish the house," Dylan heard himself say. "I'll finish it for you, Wesley."

"Dylan, don't," Rachel said. "Don't make a promise you can't keep."

"I never do," he replied, making a sudden decision.

"You will?" Wesley asked hopefully. "You'll finish the house?"

"Yes."

"Wait a second," Rachel interrupted. "Slow down. I can't pay you, Dylan. I don't have the money. That's why I stopped the construction."

"You don't have to pay me. I want to do it—not for you, for Wesley."

Rachel looked at her son, who was listening intently to their conversation. "Go get in the car, Wesley."

"But—"

"Now," she said in a mother's tone that allowed no argument.

"You promised," Wesley told Dylan. "Don't forget."

"I won't."

"Are you crazy?" Rachel asked as soon as Wesley was out of carshot. "You can't finish this house."

"Why can't I?"

"Because, because . . ." She waved her hand in the air, searching for words. "Gary said you didn't want to work on it. He offered you the job a long time ago. You said no."

"I've changed my mind."

"Why?"

"Because I want to do something. I need to do something," he said, realizing how true that was. "And this I can do."

"But you have other jobs—"

"And lots of employees."

"This could take weeks."

He nodded slowly as reality seeped into his brain. Maybe he was crazy, volunteering to work on a house that was just down the road from where Rachel lived. She'd no doubt be by all the time. Well, what did it matter? Whether she was down the road or an hour away, he'd probably still be thinking about her. And now that he'd seen the house, just begging to be finished, he knew he couldn't walk away. He had to finish it. He would make Wesley happy and maybe, somewhere, Gary would be happy, too. Gary had wanted Dylan to work on the house all along.

"I keep thinking things can't get any worse, and then they get worse," Rachel murmured, running a hand through her hair. "I knew you would make this harder."

"I don't want to make it harder. I want to make it easier. This is something I can do. Will you let me do it?"

"I should say no."

He saw the expression on her face and suddenly knew for sure that she hadn't forgotten the past any more than he had. "Say yes," he whispered recklessly. "Just say yes."

Chapter 4

"You'd better come up to the house," Rachel said. She tried to think logically, which was almost an impossibility considering the way her pulse was jumping. "We can talk about it, think about it."

"There's nothing to think about. Gary wanted me to build your house, and Wesley wants it finished. I owe both of them. It's what they would want."

"And what about me? What about what I want?"

"What do you want, Rachel?" He gazed intently into her eyes. She had to look away, afraid of what he would see there. She was too vulnerable right now to deal with Dylan, too mixed up, too lonely, too scared.

"I don't know," she said with a sigh. "I don't know if I even want to finish the house. Especially since Wesley has it in his head that Gary will come home at the end of it all. I've tried to make him accept the truth. But he won't."

"Maybe he needs to let go in his own time."

"But everything I read about kids and grief says you should be up-front with them from the beginning. Don't give them false hope. Don't let them wish for the impossible. Make them face reality."

Dylan snorted, feeling an old anger sweep through him. "You can't make someone forget or give up or accept, Rachel. You can't make them do that just because it makes you feel better."

"It's not about me, it's about Wesley."

"That's what my mom used to say. 'It's not about me, Dylan, it's about you.' You need to forget."

"Forget what?" Rachel asked in confusion. "What are you talking about?" She'd rarely heard him speak of his family, and Gary had been silent on the subject as well.

"Nothing. It doesn't matter."

"I thought your parents were divorced. I didn't know your father had died."

"Not my father."

"Your stepfather? One of your stepsisters?" she queried, trying to remember the makeup of his family.

"No. It was before the stepfamily. My first family, I guess you could call it. I had a little brother named Jesse. He died when I was ten years old." Dylan walked away from her without any further explanation.

Rachel caught up to him at the front door of the house. "Hang on a second. You can't just say that and leave."

"I shouldn't have said it at all."

"I don't remember you ever mentioning that you had a little brother who died."

"I don't like to talk about it."

"What happened, Dylan? Please tell me."

"It was a long time ago," he said slowly. "Jesse was eight,

the same age as Wesley. He had cerebral palsy. He spent most of his life in a wheelchair, but his spirit was as free as a bird. When he died, everything else died, too."

"Why?"

"The family didn't work without Jesse in it. We'd focused everything we had on him. My parents split up. My mother wanted me to accept Jesse's death so she could go on. I hated her for rushing me." He paused. "Give Wesley a chance to let go of his father when the time is right for him, not when it's right for you."

Rachel was touched by his story. "Of course I will. I wish you'd told me before, Dylan. All those talks we used to have and you never once mentioned Jesse." Another thought occurred to her. "Gary never said anything either. Did he know? Of course he knew," she murmured, answering her own question. "He kept your secrets, didn't he?"

"Yes, he did." Dylan met her gaze head-on, with no apology.

"And you kept his? Well."

"Well," he echoed, then turned and went down the front steps.

Rachel followed him, catching a glimpse of Wesley's anxious face as he sat in the front seat of her car. She couldn't imagine the horror of losing a child. What Dylan's mother must have gone through. What Dylan must have gone through. Maybe it was this loss that had darkened his soul. She'd always sensed in him an inexplicable sadness.

Dylan opened his car door and pulled out a palm-sized electronic calendar. He punched in something, then looked at her. "I can clear my schedule for the next few weeks."

"Will that be enough to finish the house?"

"Probably not, but I can hire subcontractors, some local carpenters, maybe bring up one of my crews on the weekends. It's definitely doable."

"And who will pay all those people?"

"I will."

She immediately shook her head. "I can't let you do that. You're talking about a lot of money."

"You'll pay me back."

"I'm not sure I can. Not without the insurance."

"We'll get the insurance money."

"You're a real man of action, aren't you?"

He raised an eyebrow. "That sounds like an insult."

Maybe it was. She wasn't sure she liked the idea of Dylan swooping in to rescue her, making her feel like she couldn't rescue herself. She'd been in charge for a long time. She'd been the one to solve any problem in her family for more years than she could count. She didn't need a man, or Dylan, to fix things for her. She could fix them herself.

"I'm not some helpless woman," she said.

"I never said you were. But I build things, that's what I do."

"I wanted your help in finding out the truth about Gary, not this. I never asked for this."

"So I'm offering. Come on, Rachel, what's the big deal?"

She hated the casualness in his voice, hated the way he pretended they were friends, that they hadn't spent the past ten years avoiding each other, that it wouldn't feel strange to suddenly be together.

"Mommy?" Wesley said, opening the car door. "He's going to finish our house, isn't he?"

Rachel was caught, pure and simple. She couldn't give

Wesley back his father, but she could give him the house the three of them had planned. Maybe it was wrong to encourage Wesley's obsession, but he was only eight years old. Time would convince him of a reality that no amount of words could cover.

"Let me do this for you," Dylan said. "I think I need to build this house as much as Wesley needs it to be built."

She saw in his eyes a desperation similar to that of her son. Maybe that's the way it was with men and boys. They needed the action to take away the hurt. She could have used a pair of really strong, comfortable arms and a good, long cry. But she wasn't going to ask Dylan for that. "All right," she said finally. "You can build the house, but I will pay you back someday because that's something *I* need to do."

"Tell me what you need," Travis Barker said to Carly as she tried to enter the private house next door to the Rogelio Winery.

"I need you to get out of my way," Carly replied, holding her pie carefully in her hands. She'd tried to see Antonio the night before, but he'd gone to San Francisco. She'd waited until now to come back, hoping to catch him just in time for a late-afternoon snack. Or maybe she could convince him to go on an evening picnic with her. There was a beautiful spot by a nearby creek with a soft bed of grass. She could picture it in her mind, a tiny slice of heaven that could be hers if only she could get this clod, Travis, out of her way. But Travis wasn't moving. His solid linebacker body was firmly planted in front of her and his nose was twitching at the sweet smell of her apple pie.

"What you got there, Carly?" Travis asked with his usual slow drawl. The Barker family had moved to Sebastopol from Texas when Travis was thirteen, but there was still a lot of the Lone Star State in his voice and his manners. She supposed some girls would find that attractive, maybe even a little sexy, but it did absolutely nothing for her, she told herself firmly.

"It's a pie, you idiot," she said, trying to peer around him.

"I'm kind of hungry," he said hopefully.

"Forget about it. It's for Antonio. Is he here?"

"I don't think he's back from the city."

"You don't think or you don't know?"

"He's not here. Clear enough for you, babe?" he asked with a grin that told her he knew he got to her and enjoyed it.

"Don't call me babe. I'm not your babe."

"You could be."

She rolled her eyes at that. Travis had taken notice of her when she'd turned fifteen and grown breasts. Before that, he'd just been the older, obnoxious big brother of her best friend, Sandra Barker. Sandra was now devoting herself to her husband of six months and her pregnancy. Just another one of her friends to opt for marriage and children and life in Sebastopol. Carly had other plans, which included getting Travis out of her way.

She didn't know why he didn't give it up already. He'd been asking her out for years. She'd never said yes, and she was never planning to say yes. She knew what she wanted in a man and it was not this man. Not that he hadn't grown into a reasonably good-looking guy, she had to admit. Gone were the braces and the too thin, lanky body that had always been more clumsy than graceful. Now his freckles had faded, giving him a nice, even tan to go with his sandy-brown hair and golden-brown eyes. He'd buffed up over the years, his muscles defined, his stance powerful, his shoulders broad enough for a woman to rest her head on. But—and it was a big "but"—he had no ambition.

Travis was a simple carpenter. He loved living in the small town. His idea of a hot Friday night was bowling or a miniature-golf date. She wanted much more than that. She yearned for big-city noises, busy shopping malls, fancy restaurants, museums and art galleries. Oh, how she loved standing in an art gallery surrounded by masterpieces. She sneaked into the city every chance she got to do just that, but she couldn't tell anyone, especially not her family. They'd see it as a betrayal.

Rachel, in particular, was forever speaking of duty and loyalty and keeping the orchards alive for their father, for their family, for the goddamn legacy that had been passed down from generation to generation. She didn't understand that Carly's dreams were not the same as her dreams, and so far, Carly hadn't found the courage to tell her.

That's why she needed to find another reason to leave, and love was the best reason. Especially love with a sophisticated world traveler like Antonio. She liked him, so why not fall in love with him? Why not have him fall in love with her? They could both do a lot worse. It could all happen the way she wanted it to, if she could get this big oaf out of her way.

"Just move, Travis," she said with determination in her voice.

"I don't think so, not until I know what's in that pie."

"It's an apple pie. You can see that."

"Yes, but what kind of apples?"

"What are you doing here anyway?" she asked in frustration. "I thought you were working on the wine-tasting room next door."

"I'm redoing some of the hardwood floors. That pie has one of those magic apples in it, doesn't it?"

She shook her head at the knowing gleam in his eye. "Don't be silly. That tree never blooms."

"And you never bake. So tell me another one."

"I'm coming in. I'll see for myself if Antonio is here."

"Fine, but take your shoes off. I just did the floors, and those spike heels aren't going anywhere near that finish."

Carly debated whether she should just forget the whole thing. What was she going to do, stalk around Antonio's private home in her bare feet with an apple pie in her hands? Somehow, she had a feeling that would make her look desperate. It was one thing to be desperate. It was another to show it. "Never mind. I'll come back later."

"I'm sure you will," Travis said, leaning against the doorjamb.

"What is your problem anyway?" she asked, wishing the words back almost as soon as they had left her mouth.

"I don't have a problem. It's none of my business if you want to chase after some guy who will never settle down with a small-town girl like you."

"I'm not always going to be a small-town girl. In fact, I intend to get out of this town as soon as possible."

"And go where?"

"I don't know yet." She hated the smug look in his eyes. "But I know that someday I will be someone."

"You already are someone. You're Carly Wood, beautiful, crazy, impulsive—did I say crazy?"

"Did you say beautiful?" she asked, somewhat shocked to hear that word cross his lips. She might have a good body, but her face was nothing special.

"You heard me. If I say it again, your head will get even

bigger. I just don't understand what you think you can do somewhere else that you can't do here."

"A million things—go to the theater, go shopping at Neiman Marcus, have dinner in a four-star restaurant that doesn't serve chili."

"The city is an hour away. What's stopping you from going in on the weekends?"

"I have responsibilities here, not to mention very little cash."

"How about I take you to dinner tomorrow night in San Francisco? We can drive down early in the afternoon and go to the wharf. I hear they have a bunch of sea lions there."

She stared at him in amazement. "You want to take me to the city for dinner?"

"Is that a yes?"

"No. I mean, well . . ." She didn't know. She'd set her sights on Antonio. She couldn't go to San Francisco with Travis. That would be only a short-term solution, not a long-term one. What was it Rachel always said? Stay focused? Yes, that was it. She had to stay focused. "I can't. I have other plans."

"No, you don't."

"Yes, I do. And why would I want to go anywhere with you? We don't even like each other."

"Sure we do." He gave her a slow, wicked smile that for some reason made her heart jump in her chest. This was Travis, geeky, clumsy, irritating, practical-joker Travis. She could not possibly be attracted to him.

"I don't think so," she said sharply. "If you see Antonio, ask him to give me a call."

"I'll do that."

She didn't believe him for a second, but at the moment

it seemed more prudent to let it go and leave. Her body was having a strange reaction to a man who had seen her go through just about every awkward, embarrassing moment in her life.

"Carly," Travis said as she turned to leave.

"What?"

"Someday."

"It's not going to happen, Travis. I'm not interested in you. I'm sorry. But that's the way it is."

"That might have been the way it was, but not the way it's going to be," he said as he shut the door in her face.

"We'll see about that," she muttered. She looked down at her apple pie. After all, she still had her secret weapon. As soon as Antonio ate one of her magic apples, she wouldn't have to worry about Travis Barker anymore. Not even he could fight a legend.

"When do you want to get started?" Rachel asked Dylan as she let him in the front door of her house.

That was a good question. When did he want to start? He'd thrown an overnight bag into the car, thinking he might check into a local hotel for a night or two. But if he was going to finish her house, he'd definitely be staying longer than a night.

"Maybe you've had second thoughts," Rachel said. "It's okay if you have. I understand. The house doesn't need to be finished right now anyway. We have a roof over our heads, a very nice roof."

Dylan had to admit the large two-story house was warm and inviting. It was a family home, the living room filled with big, comfortable couches and chairs perfect for a man to kick his feet up on. But there were also colorful throw pillows, fresh flowers and dozens of family photographs adding a feminine touch to the room.

"Dylan," Rachel prodded.

He realized he hadn't answered her, but the answer was clear in his head. "I haven't had second thoughts. I'll finish the house that Gary started. It's what he would have wanted."

"Maybe," she conceded, not sounding so sure.

Before he could press her, an older woman came into the living room, accompanied by a very excited and chattering Wesley. It was Marge Wood, Rachel's grandmother. Dylan remembered meeting her a few times before.

Marge didn't look anything like Rachel. Her hair was a frosty gray, her eyes a bright and clear light blue. She was a tiny woman, barely five feet. Gary had once called her a pocket-sized dynamo, said she had more energy than ten people and a bigger heart he had yet to find.

"Hello," Marge said, giving Dylan a warm smile. "How are you? It's nice to see you again."

"I'm just fine, Mrs. Wood."

"Wesley has been talking so fast, I can't make heads or tails of what he's saying," Marge continued. "Something about finishing the house?"

Dylan looked over at Rachel, who slowly nodded and said, "Yes. Dylan is going to finish the house."

"That's a lovely idea. It tears my heart apart every time I see it standing there looking so lonely. A house should be finished. Then it becomes a home."

A home that Gary would never see or live in with his wife and child. Dylan noticed the tension in Rachel's face. Maybe he'd been wrong to offer. Maybe it would be too difficult for her to live there. But then again, they couldn't just leave it as it was, a skeletal reminder of a future that would never be. That would be painful, too.

"Dylan, would you like to stay for dinner?" Marge asked. "Please say yes. John will enjoy having another man to speak to. With Gary gone, John has been feeling a bit like a rooster in a henhouse."

"If you're sure it's no trouble," Dylan replied.

"No trouble at all. And there's always plenty of food, especially since Rachel eats like a bird these days. Wesley, do you want to help me set the table?"

"Sure, Grandma."

Marge took Wesley's hand and led him out of the room, leaving Dylan and Rachel alone.

As the silence enveloped them like an intimate blanket, Dylan became more and more uncomfortable. He shouldn't be here, not in this house. This was Gary's house. Gary and Rachel's. He was the outsider, the one who didn't belong, so why was he here? This wasn't right. This was Gary's life, not *his* life, never his life.

"Are you all right?" Rachel asked, a curious but wary look in her eyes.

"Me? I'm fine," he lied. "If you'd rather I didn't stay to dinner, I can make up an excuse and leave."

"I don't care. Dinner is the least of my worries. Do you want to sit down?"

"Sure, why not?" He forced himself to breathe as he sat down on the couch. He'd been here before. It wasn't like he'd never stepped foot in the house. Of course, the last time he'd been in this room was right after Gary's funeral. The breath left his chest again as he remembered the crowd of people dressed in black, their voices hushed as they whispered about what a tragedy it had been, their eyes filled with pity whenever Rachel or Wesley had come into the room.

"Dylan?"

"What?"

"You're a million miles away."

"No, I was actually right here—about six months ago."

"Oh." She sat down in the armchair across from him and laced her fingers together. "It must be difficult for you to be here."

"It feels strange."

"Well, you were pretty much a stranger the last nine years." She put her hand up to stop him from interrupting. "I don't want to talk about the past." She drew in a long breath and slowly let it out. "I want to know why you really drove all the way up here. I assume it wasn't just about the house. Was there another reason?"

"I packed up some of Gary's things. The boxes are in my car. My assistant is having a mover pick up the furniture. They'll ship it to you early next week."

"Did you find anything?"

He knew what she was asking, and he could see the worry in her eyes. He wasn't sure whom he was protecting— Gary or Rachel—but some instinct made him shake his head and say, "No, I didn't find anything important."

"That's a relief. However, it doesn't get us any closer to figuring out what Gary was doing in Lake Tahoe."

"What did he tell you?"

"He said it was a last-hurrah bachelor party weekend for one of the guys he worked with."

"Another architect?" Dylan mentally ran down the guys in Gary's office. He couldn't recall any of them being engaged or having a bachelor party. And what had Gary told him? He racked his brain, trying to remember that last conversation.

"I don't know who it was," Rachel continued. "I don't think Gary told me the name, or if he did, I've forgotten it. Didn't Gary tell you who was getting married? In fact, I'm surprised you weren't going along."

"I have no idea who was getting married or if that was why Gary went to Tahoe."

"But you knew about the weekend?"

"Gary said something about going away. To be honest, I don't remember if he told me why. I was busy that day, and he was chattering away about something. Damn!" He got to his feet, too annoyed with himself to sit. He should have paid more attention, but Gary was always talking. And Dylan had been working up a bid for a new project. He'd figured they'd catch up later.

"Stop kicking yourself," Rachel said. "It doesn't help. I should know. I've got the bruises to prove it."

He knew she was trying to make him feel better, and he appreciated the effort, but it didn't do anything to lessen his guilt. It had been bad enough when he'd thought Gary had died in an accident; now it was worse, doubts flooding his mind along with an odd certainty that something had gone terribly wrong in Gary's life.

"I'm going to check on dinner, see if my grandmother needs any help," Rachel said as she stood up. "Can I get you a drink?"

"No, thanks." Dylan was relieved when she left the room. It was easier to breathe, easier to think, easier to just be. He didn't understand why this one woman had such a strong effect on him. Maybe it was because he couldn't have her. *You always want what you can't have.* That was probably it.

And he still couldn't have her. Maybe that's why he still wanted her.

The realization shook him to the core. He'd known it; he'd just never admitted it to himself. He had a sudden desire to get the hell out of Dodge, but as he turned toward the door a small voice stopped him.

"You're not leaving, are you?" Wesley asked. "You promised to build my house."

"And I will."

"Are you sure you won't have to go on a trip like Daddy always does?"

Dylan shook his head. "I'm sure."

"He's coming back," Wesley added, a defiant note in his young voice that dared Dylan to tell him otherwise.

"I miss him, too," Dylan said quietly.

Wesley's bottom lip trembled. He fought the good fight, then a sob tore through his throat. He ran toward the stairs, the slamming of his bedroom door punctuating the shocked look on Rachel's face as she came into the living room. "What did you say to Wesley?"

"Nothing," he replied in confusion.

"You must have said something."

"I just said I missed his dad."

"Oh, Dylan." Rachel looked at him, then toward the stairs. "I better talk to him."

"Let me," Dylan said impulsively.

"He doesn't even know you."

Rachel was right. She was Wesley's mother; she should do the comforting. But he hated to have anyone else clean up his mess. "Maybe it's about time he did," he said, taking to the stairs before she could offer another protest.

He paused on the landing, figuring that the one closed door had to lead to Wesley's room. He tapped lightly, then turned the knob. Wesley had flung himself on his bed, his head buried under his pillow.

"Hey, Wesley," Dylan said, feeling somewhat awkward. He wasn't used to children. He hadn't spent much time with any since he'd been one himself.

Wesley didn't reply, but he also didn't seem to be crying anymore. Dylan sat down on the edge of the bed, trying to think of what to say. While he was thinking, he glanced around the room. It was a perfect boy's room, dark wood furniture, toys littering the floor, clothes hanging out of drawers. It reminded him of another room, one from a long time ago, one he had shared with his little brother, Jesse, only their room had been filled with airplanes.

Jesse had loved planes, probably because he'd spent so much time in a wheelchair. The thought of flying free had been his fantasy. When he was too ill to make model airplanes, Dylan had become an expert at making paper airplanes to amuse Jesse during the hard times. And there had been a lot of hard times.

Leaning over now, Dylan picked up a blank piece of paper from the top of Wesley's desk and began to fold it. He couldn't remember the last time he'd made a plane, but his fingers remembered, quickly turning the notebook paper into a sophisticated flier. The crinkling of the paper finally aroused Wesley's attention. He moved his head out from under the pillow and sent Dylan a curious look.

"What's that?"

"This?" Dylan held up the plane. "This is a high-speed jet plane. Your dad used to call this one Rudy the Rocket."

"No, he didn't," Wesley said with a doubtful look in his eyes.

"Yes, he did. I made one every day in sixth-grade science class. Your dad and I had the same teacher, Rudy Rodgers. He was the most boring teacher we ever had. Sometimes he talked so long about rocks that he put himself to sleep. He'd tell us all to put our heads down for a five-minute rest. That's when I'd make Rudy the Rocket. And one time your dad launched Rudy the Rocket right at the other Rudy, and the plane made a crash landing on Rudy's long nose. You know what your dad said?"

"What?"

"Bull's-eye."

Wesley's reluctant smile broadened. "Did my dad get in trouble?"

"Nope. Your dad was pretty good at getting himself out of trouble." As Dylan recalled, *he'd* been the one to stay after school for a week. "So do you want to launch this Rudy for me?"

"Okay." Wesley sat up on the bed and took the paper airplane from Dylan's hand. "What do I do?"

"You don't know?"

Wesley shook his head, his eyes serious. "I've never flown an airplane before. Does it have to be thrown at a certain angle to allow the wings to catch the air and lift? Or is the speed more important?"

Dylan's jaw dropped, not only because Wesley had apparently never flown a paper airplane before, but also because he seemed to have a sense of aerodynamics that was way beyond his years. He wondered why Gary had never made a paper airplane with his son. It seemed odd. But like most of his questions, that one would have to wait for another day. "Just give it a good toss. We'll see what happens."

Wesley knelt on his bed, his lips pursed in seriousness. He pulled his arm back and let the plane fly straight toward the open door and right into his mother's startled face. For a moment there was nothing but shocked silence in the boy's room. Then Wesley looked at Dylan with a big grin and said, "Bull's-eye."

Chapter 5

Rachel had come upstairs expecting to find her son in tears and Dylan trying to comfort him. She certainly hadn't expected to see matching mischievous grins or a high five between them. Nor had she expected to get bonked in the nose by a . . . what was that anyway? She looked down at her feet and saw a paper airplane. "What is that?"

"Rudy the Rocket," Wesley replied, scrambling off the bed to retrieve his airplane. He looked at Dylan. "Can I fly it again?"

"All you want," Dylan said as he stood up. "But you better make sure the landing strip is clear next time." He smiled at Rachel and she felt something turn over inside her. It had been a long, long time since Dylan had smiled at her; and she suddenly realized how much she'd missed it. "If it's okay with your mom," Dylan added.

"What?" She realized she'd lost track of the conversation.

"Fly the airplane," Wesley said impatiently.

"Oh, sure. But wash your hands now. Grandma has dinner on the table."

"Okay." Wesley set the plane on his desk, then ran down the hall toward the bathroom.

"I take it that's your handiwork," she said, looking at the plane because it was easier than looking at Dylan.

"Yes."

"Well, you made him feel better, that's for sure." She picked up the plane. "This looks like an advanced model. Are you some sort of an expert?"

"You could say that."

She heard the note of humor in his voice and it drew her gaze back to his. This time his smile was wry.

"I pretty much majored in paper-airplane design. I did my prep work in middle school and high school and got my advanced degree in college. I must admit it's been a while. I wasn't sure I remembered how until my fingers took over." He shook his head as if confused by something. "I can't believe Gary never showed Wesley how to make an airplane. When we were kids, Gary used to name them like they were real jets."

"Really?" Funny, the things you learned about your husband when you thought you knew everything. Of course, a secret penchant for paper airplanes was probably the least of her worries. "What were some of the names?"

"Rudy the Rocket, Supersonic Sam and a series of Greek names when we spent a semester studying Greek mythology—like Zeus, Odysseus and Apollo."

"He never mentioned it."

"We must have made a thousand our senior year in high

school," Dylan said. "And even after. Don't you remember that party? The luau we went to with Gary's fraternity brothers before you got married. Where was that at?"

"A Polynesian restaurant in Sausalito," she murmured.

"Yes. Trader Something."

"And Gary put on the grass skirt and did the hula," she said, floating back to that day. She could still see Gary trying to dance like a hula girl, the skirt falling off his hips as he mimicked the other dancers' movements. The entire room had been in hysterics. And Dylan . . . She looked at him with a grin. "You made a paper airplane out of the menu and tried to nail Gary in the stomach."

"I got him, too, on the third try. Remember?"

"I remember." And as she gazed into his eyes, she also remembered other times. The weeks the three of them had spent together before her wedding had been some of the happiest of her life, until she and Dylan had ruined their friendship forever. She'd attempted to push those memories aside, to concentrate on her present and her future, and she'd been successful—until now.

"Those were good times," Dylan said, daring her to disagree, but she couldn't. "We were young. We had our lives in front of us."

"They were good times. I remember how serious and intense you were. And ambitious, too. Your dreams weren't big; they were huge."

"I guess it's a good thing I got into building skyscrapers."

"I think I always knew you would."

"Gary was successful, too, despite his happy-go-lucky attitude."

"He loved his work, loved the dreaming part. That's what he used to call it." She laughed at the memory. "I used to call it the lying-on-the-backyard-hammock-and-taking-an-afternoon-nap part. But Gary always insisted that dreaming time was essential to his job."

"He could always talk his way into the right answer."

"Yes, he was very good at talking."

"And so were you," Dylan reminded her. "We had some great conversations, even though you were just a kid."

"I was nineteen."

"Just a kid," he repeated.

She shrugged. "You're right. I wasn't even old enough to have champagne at my own wedding."

"But you knew what you wanted."

"I did," she agreed. "Thanks, Dylan."

"For what?"

"For making Wesley a paper airplane, for taking his mind off things for a few minutes, for reminding me of the good times." She started as Wesley's loud voice called up the stairs that dinner was ready and they better come soon or Grandma was feeding it to the dogs.

"That sounds serious," Dylan said.

"Definitely. Around here, nobody messes with dinner, especially when my grandmother is cooking." She walked toward the door. "By the way, a word to the wise. If my grandfather offers you a taste of his homemade apple wine, say no."

"Why?"

"Because it has a lot more than apples in it."

"Thanks for the warning." He caught her arm as she moved past him. "Rachel?"

"What?" she asked, feeling his touch heat up her body.

He looked like he wanted to say something, but Wesley's voice rang up the stairs once again, and the connection between them was broken. "Never mind. It can wait."

Rachel wondered what *it* was, all the way down the

stairs and into the dining room. She suspected Dylan had wanted to say something about the past. She didn't know whether to be relieved or upset that they'd been interrupted. In some way, she felt she needed to clear the air. But then again, clearing the air meant bringing everything back, and what was the point of that? It was better to move forward, keep putting one foot in front of the other. It was how she'd gotten through the past six months and how she'd get through the next.

"There you are," Marge scolded as they entered the dining room. "It's about time."

"Sorry, Grandma." Rachel motioned Dylan to a seat next to Wesley.

"John Wood," her grandfather said, getting to his feet to reintroduce himself to Dylan. "Nice to see you again. Do you remember my daughter, Dee?" he added, putting an arm around Dee.

"Yes, I think we met a while back," Dylan said, giving her a brief handshake. "Nice to see both of you again."

"Nice to see you," Dee replied calmly, but her gaze when it swung back to Rachel's was more than a little curious.

Aunt Dee was Rachel's father's baby sister. She'd always looked out for Rachel, often acting as a second mother. Since Dee's husband had run off a few years earlier, she had become even more involved in their lives and was as dedicated as Rachel was to preserving the family farm.

"Where's Carly?" Rachel asked, ignoring her aunt's quizzical look. She couldn't explain Dylan's presence to herself, much less to anyone else.

"Said she wasn't hungry, and she went out again. I have no idea where," Marge answered with a disturbed shake of her head. "That girl. I don't know what's going on in her head."

"Maybe I should try to find her," Rachel suggested.

"You sit and eat. You have enough on your mind." Marge held out her hands, reaching one to Dylan and one to Rachel. "Let's say grace."

Rachel gave her other hand to Wesley, who connected with Aunt Dee and John, forming a circle around the table. But this time it wasn't Gary in the circle, it was Dylan. Never in a million years would she have foreseen the circle ending up this way.

Dylan didn't know what he ate for dinner. He barely tasted the food, barely heard the conversation flowing around him. He was still reeling from being included in the family circle, from hearing his name mentioned in Marge's prayer of thanks. He wasn't supposed to be here, sitting at this table, talking to these people. They were part of Gary's life, not his. He was once again flooded with the impulse to flee. And he would have gotten up if they hadn't kept including him.

Between Wesley's questions about the house building, John's questions about his business and Marge's questions about his personal life, Dylan was kept too busy talking to think up an excuse to leave. When he finally had a chance to breathe, Marge was clearing the table and offering coffee and dessert. Rachel, Wesley and Dee got up to help, leaving Dylan alone with John Wood.

John was a tall, thin man with a narrow face and sharp, light green eyes that were alert and watchful. Those eyes had been watching Dylan all through dinner, and he suspected that the questions about his business were John's way of measuring a man. Gary had mentioned more than once that he wasn't sure he was living up to John's expectations, but he'd never said why. Dylan couldn't help wondering what kind of expectations John had of *him*. It didn't take long to find out.

"You sure you're up to finishing that house?" John asked.

"I'm more than qualified to build a house."

"But that house? You want to build that house? Gary said you didn't." His eyes bored into Dylan's as if he would rip out the truth with one drilling look.

"I was busier then. My schedule has changed," Dylan answered smoothly, hoping John would leave it at that. He didn't want to get into his personal reasons for saying no.

"Rachel and Wesley don't need any more disappointments."

"I don't plan on disappointing them."

John stared at him for a moment longer, then nodded. "Make sure that you don't."

Dylan supposed he could have taken offense at the tone, but it was obvious that the man adored his granddaughter and his great-grandson. "I won't," he promised. "The last thing I want to do is hurt them in any way."

"Good. Do you play poker?"

"Once in a while."

A small, knowing smile played around the corner of John's mouth. "Figured you would. A better poker face I have yet to see. Now, Gary, he couldn't hide a damn straight to save his life."

"No, he couldn't," Dylan agreed. They'd played many a card game over the years, starting back in high school in Jimmy Baker's garage. Gary had always lost, completely unable to hide his joy in a good hand or his frustration in a bad one.

John rested his arms on the table. "Since this insurance thing came up, Rachel has some doubts about Gary. Oh, she doesn't say so, but I can see it in her eyes. What about you?"

"I think Gary died in an accident," Dylan replied firmly. "I'm going to do whatever I can to prove it."

"Good. It's hard enough to lose someone you love. Losing the good memories makes it even harder. And Rachel, she couldn't take another . . ." John's voice drifted off.

"Another what?" Dylan asked.

"Doesn't matter. I got a poker game Saturday night, seven-thirty, in the barn. We could use another player. You in?"

Dylan hesitated. He was here to finish the house, to look into Gary's death, not to play poker.

"Don't say no. The other boys will want to meet you. And they knew Gary. You might learn something."

"All right."

"Now, let me tell you about the other players," John began.

Dylan only half listened as John discussed the strengths and weaknesses of his poker buddies. His thoughts were with Rachel. He wondered what John had been alluding to—another what? Had there been another man in her life? One before Gary? But she'd been nineteen. And he couldn't remember her talking about any other relationships. So another what? Another betrayal? Another affair? Was there something Rachel and John knew about Gary that Dylan didn't? But he'd been Gary's best friend. Gary had told him everything, usually more than he'd wanted to know.

There weren't any secrets, he told himself. So why couldn't he believe that?

* * *

"Eavesdropping?" Marge asked lightly as she handed Rachel a pan to dry.

Rachel moved away from the kitchen door and took the pan from her grandmother. "No, of course not."

"I don't think Dylan scares easily."

"What does that mean?"

"That your grandfather couldn't scare him away."

"Why would he try?"

"I didn't say he would."

"Well, what *are* you saying, then?" Rachel asked in exasperation.

Marge gave a little laugh. "That I don't think Dylan needs your protection. You don't have to rush back into the dining room and save him from some third degree." Marge turned to Wesley. "Oh, dear. I forgot to feed Mr. Bones before I came over. Wesley, honey, would you run over to my house and give Mr. Bones some doggie dinner?"

"Okay, Grandma," Wesley said, bolting out the back door.

"You never forget to feed Mr. Bones," Dee observed. "So why exactly did you want to get rid of Wesley? Never mind, I know why."

Rachel frowned as her grandmother and aunt turned to her. "What now?"

"You, Rachel. You're like a cat on a hot tin roof. What's going on?" Marge asked.

"Nothing."

"Dylan makes her uncomfortable," Dee said as she put the remains of dinner in the refrigerator.

"Maybe a little," Rachel admitted. "He might have been Gary's best friend, but he's not mine. And it's not right that he's here."

"Because Gary is not," Marge said with sympathy in her eyes. "Oh, honey, I bet Dylan wishes Gary was here, too."

"Well, if Gary was here, Dylan wouldn't be," Rachel snapped, feeling a surge of anger and frustration well up within her. "The man avoided us for nine years. Now he's taking up residence in the dining room. I don't like it." And she didn't. Her stomach churned. Her head ached, and she couldn't think straight.

Dylan had been around for only a few hours, and she was feeling crazy. What would it be like to have him around for days, weeks, maybe months? She couldn't deal with it. She just couldn't. The pan slipped from her hands with a clatter, echoed by a startled silence. She shook her head in apology. "I'm sorry." She picked up the pan and set it on the counter. "I don't know what's wrong with me."

"Nothing is wrong with you," Marge said. "You're dealing with a lot of stress right now, that's all. But you're strong. You'll come through this."

Rachel supposed it was a compliment that everyone thought her to be so strong. But she didn't feel strong on the inside. Right now she felt as quivery as a bowl of Jell-O.

"If you don't want Dylan here, tell him so," Dee advised in her no-nonsense voice. But then, Dee would see it like that. She was a woman who lived by numbers that always added up. And when they didn't, she started over until she found numbers that made sense together, just the way she'd started over after her husband had left her. Or maybe she'd sent him away. Rachel didn't know the whole story. Dee had never explained. One day Uncle Jeff was there; the next, he was gone.

It suddenly occurred to Rachel that the comings and goings in marriages had become a trend in her father's generation and now in hers. What had happened to the

Wood family tradition of long marriages, long lives, long everything?

"There are other contractors in town," Dee added.

"None that I can afford," Rachel replied.

Dee appeared troubled as she nibbled nervously on her bottom lip. "I know the house is important to you and Wesley."

"And Dylan, apparently," Rachel murmured, glancing once again toward the dining room. "He seems to want to finish it. I don't really understand why."

"Then let him finish it," Marge said.

"He makes her uncomfortable, Mom," Dee said, still worried. "I'm not sure I trust him or his motives."

"But she does need the house to be completed, whatever his motives are. She can't just leave it the way it is."

"Why not? How is she going to live there without Gary?"

"I'm going to let Dylan do it," Rachel interjected, feeling that this argument would continue until she made her intentions clear, because the optimistic Marge and the cynical Dee rarely saw eye to eye on anything.

"Good. Then it's time for dessert," Marge declared with a bright smile. She was a true believer in the glass being half full, and most of the time Rachel tried to live her life in the same fashion, but the past few months had made optimism a rare commodity.

"Why don't you take these two plates out to the table? And give Dylan the bigger piece. Your grandfather doesn't need the sugar."

Rachel took the plates from her grandmother and returned to the dining room, grateful to have something constructive to do. She placed one in front of Dylan, the other in front of her grandfather, and resumed her seat across the table. Marge, Wesley and Dee joined them a moment later.

As Marge handed her a dessert plate, Rachel suddenly realized what was on it. Pie. Apple pie.

An uneasy feeling came over her. But it couldn't be the same pie. She glanced at Dylan and saw him raise a fork to his lips. She had to fight an impulse to grab it out of his hand.

The back door slammed, and Carly called out a hello. Then she came bursting into the room and stopped dead in her tracks. A look of horror crossed her face. "Oh, my God! Are you eating my pie?"

"Your pie?" Dee asked.

"I saw it on the counter," Marge said uneasily. "I'm sorry. Were you saving it for someone?"

"That's not your pie," Rachel told her sister firmly. "You gave your pie to Antonio yesterday."

"But I didn't. He wasn't home. You're eating my pie. My special—"

Rachel jumped to her feet, reached across the table and grabbed Dylan's plate. She ran into the kitchen and dumped the rest of the pie in the trash. Then she leaned over the counter and burst into tears. Dylan wasn't supposed to eat the special apples. He wasn't the one. Gary was the one, the only one.

"Anyone want to tell me what's going on?" Dylan asked, breaking the supercharged silence with his words.

Wesley was the only one who answered. "You ate a piece of Aunt Carly's magic pie."

Great; now he had an explanation, and it still made no sense.

"You used the special apples?" Marge asked Carly. "What were you thinking?"

"I was thinking Antonio needed a kick in the butt," she replied.

"But the apples . . ." Marge dropped her voice down a notch, as if she didn't want Dylan to hear. "They're very powerful."

"I know. That's why I used them. Now I'll have to wait a week until the others ripen. Or maybe I can just take Antonio a piece of this pie. There's a piece left, isn't there?"

"Yes, of course, but, Carly—"

"Don't say it. I know what I'm doing."

"You never know what you're doing," John said gruffly, an irritated expression in his eyes. "He's not the man for you."

"I think he is," Carly returned defiantly, exchanging a long, challenging look with her grandfather.

"Can I still eat the pie?" Wesley asked.

"Yes, you can," Marge said. "We all can. Except Dylan, I guess." Her eyes filled with worry once again. "Oh, dear," she murmured.

"It's fine. I was full anyway," he replied, although he had to admit the one bite of pie he'd managed to get into his mouth had been pretty damn tasty. But then he'd always loved a good, sweet apple. He glanced toward the kitchen door, wondering why Rachel had swiped his pie and rushed out of the room. And what the heck was magical about it anyway? Even reading between the lines, he couldn't figure this one out, especially not with everyone staring at him with mixed emotions in their eyes. He pushed back his chair and stood up.

"Where are you going?" Carly asked.

"I think I'll say good-bye to Rachel and drive into town, find a place to stay the night."

"There's a small hotel on Fifth Street, right off the main drag," John said. "BayBerry Inn is the name."

"Thanks."

He left the dining room, feeling their gazes follow him into the kitchen, where Rachel was wiping her eyes with a paper towel.

"I'm sorry," she said quickly. "You must think I'm crazy."

"I'm not too sure about the rest of your family either," he replied lightly. "Just tell me one thing. Am I going to need to find a poison control center before the night is out?"

She shook her head. "No."

"That's good news. So—do you want to give me an explanation?"

"I don't think so."

He waited a moment, then nodded. "Maybe later."

"Maybe," she agreed. "Are you driving back to the city?"

"I thought I'd find a place to stay in town. Then tomorrow I can pull together a plan of attack for the house." He paused, his gaze concerned. "Are you sure you're all right?"

She offered him a brief nod, as if she were afraid to open her mouth.

"I'll go, then," he said. "I'll talk to you tomorrow."

"You're really going to be here tomorrow? Really?"

Dylan could see there was more behind the simple question, perhaps a need for reassurance, to believe in someone's promise to return. When Rachel had lost Gary, she'd lost her faith in the little things, too. Maybe he could give her some of that back. It wouldn't be enough, but it might be something.

"Yes," he said. "I'll be here tomorrow."

"Gary said that to me, too. He said, 'I'll talk to you tomorrow.' That was it. Those were his last words." She shook her head in confusion. "What kind of last words are those?"

Dylan didn't know what to say. What could he say? Nothing would take the pain out of her eyes, the grief out of her heart. And he was reminded of another time, when he'd faced another woman whose eyes had bored down on him with unbearable agony. She'd looked at him and said, "Why him?" And as he'd gazed at her, no good answer on his lips, he'd wondered if she was really saying, "Why not you?" Just like now.

He was standing in Rachel's kitchen. But it should have been Gary. She wanted it to be Gary. Hell, *he* wanted it to be Gary, too.

"I'm sorry," she said again. "I didn't mean to put you on the spot."

"I'm sorry, too. Sorry I'm the one here to ask."

She met his eyes. "That's not what I was thinking."

"Sure it was."

"Dylan," she asked as he reached for the door, "what did he say to you? What did Gary say to you the last time?"

He glanced back at her, wondering if he would hurt her even more.

"You can tell me. Please," she said. "I need to know."

"He said, 'I'll talk to you tomorrow.' "

Chapter 6

Dylan's words were still ringing in Rachel's ears when she got out of bed Friday morning. In fact, they'd gone around in her head all night long, "talk to you tomorrow, talk to you tomorrow," sometimes in Dylan's voice, sometimes in Gary's voice, until they'd gotten so mixed up she didn't know who was talking.

She'd woken up in a cold sweat, confronted by her greatest fear—that she'd forget the sound of Gary's voice, the lines on his face, the way his hair curled around his ears, the certain way he smiled when he wanted to make love to her.

She didn't want to forget, not ever. But lately she couldn't quite bring his voice into her head. It had been just six months. How could she be forgetting already? What kind of a wife did that make her? How could she smile and laugh and find joy in life when Gary was gone?

It didn't seem right. And she'd always been the kind of person who prided herself on doing the right thing. Or at least trying to do the right thing.

But was bringing Dylan back into her life right? Was letting him finish her house right? Or was she making a horrible mistake?

Rachel faced herself in the mirror. She ran her fingers through the tangled waves of her hair, the hair that Gary had made her promise she would never cut. He'd loved her hair, called it honey blond. He'd always put his hands through her hair when he kissed her.

Now it wasn't honey blond, it was just hair, messy, in need of a wash, bed-head hair. It matched the rest of her, the tired lines in her forehead, the dark shadows under her eyes, the paleness in her cheeks. She looked like hell.

Was this the widow's look she would wear forever? She wasn't even thirty yet, but she'd already lived a lifetime with one man. His lifetime anyway. Hers would go on. If she lived to be eighty, she'd have another fifty years without Gary. How could that be? How could she get so much more life?

It wasn't fair. They should have grown old together, should have watched Wesley grow up, get married, have children. But she would have to do it alone. And somewhere along the way, she would have to learn how to smile again. She had a child to raise, a little boy with his whole life ahead of him. She couldn't drag him down. She had to be strong enough to go on, to live life and to let Wesley know that it was okay for him to live, too.

A knock came at her bedroom door, followed by a sleepy Wesley. "Can I have breakfast, Mommy?"

"Sure. I was just coming to get you up, but you beat me to it." She smiled at him, then impulsively swept him into her arms and gave him a long, tight squeeze. "I love you, you know."

"I love you, too. Can I have a Pop-Tart?"

She laughed and ruffled his hair. "Brown sugar cinnamon?"

He nodded, then padded back into the hall, his navy blue airplane pajamas riding low on his hips. The airplanes reminded her of Dylan and the paper plane he'd made for Wesley. Maybe bringing Dylan back into their lives wasn't a mistake. Maybe he was the bridge they needed to get from the past to the future.

Rachel ran a brush through her hair, gave her cheeks a quick blush and made her way downstairs and into the kitchen. Carly sat at the kitchen table in a pair of skimpy pajama shorts and a tank top. She was eating her usual bowl of Cheerios and reading one of the many fashion magazines she subscribed to.

Carly didn't even look up when Rachel murmured, "Good morning." Rachel decided to ignore her. She had enough on her plate without having to deal with one of Carly's moods.

She put a Pop-Tart in the toaster for Wesley, poured a glass of milk and cut up some oranges. Checking the clock, she saw it was only seven-thirty. She still had a half hour before she had to take Wesley down to the end of the drive to catch the school bus.

"Wesley," she called, just as her son walked into the kitchen. He'd put on a pair of jeans and a wrinkled T-shirt. She had a feeling the teachers and other parents who saw him at school probably thought she was a terrible mother, but forcing him into pressed clothes just didn't seem like a battle she could fight right now. "Don't forget to take your vitamin," she said when he sat down at the table. "I put it by your plate."

"Hey, buddy," Carly said. "What's up?"

"Nothing. Can I turn on the TV?" Before Rachel or Carly could answer, the *Rugrats* program was playing on the small television screen in the nook opposite the table.

Carly picked up her bowl and went over to the sink.

Rachel leaned against the counter, watching her younger sister rinse her dish and put it in the dishwasher. She thought about all the times they'd fought over the very same dishes, the same chores. They'd grown up together in this house, but Rachel had always been the responsible one, the one who had to make sure Carly grew up with some manners.

"What are you looking at?" Carly turned an annoyed glance in Rachel's direction.

"Just thinking about how many times we've had breakfast together in this kitchen."

"Too many times," Carly grumbled.

"What are you mad about this morning?"

"You don't know? How could you not know?"

"I didn't know it was your pie, Carly. I never would have served it if I'd known, but I was distracted. Grandma kept handing me plates to take to the table. I am sorry, if that makes a difference." And she *was* sorry, because she certainly hadn't wanted to put Dylan anywhere near the special family apples.

"Fine," Carly said with a sigh. "I'll have to wait a few days, though, for more of the apples to ripen."

"Maybe a few days will clear your head."

"I know what I want, and I'm going after it. You should be proud, not critical."

"Why don't you go after something besides a man? Like an education or a career or a hobby?"

"Because a man like Antonio could be an education, a career and a hobby," Carly said with a smile.

Rachel shook her head. "It's a mistake to wrap your whole life up in some man's arms."

"Why?"

"Because he could leave or he could die. You could end up alone, and then what will you have?"

Carly's smile faded. "You still have a lot, Rachel. You have Wesley. You have the family. You have the land that you love. You have the business to run."

"I wasn't talking about me," Rachel said, but they both knew it was a lie.

"I can't expect the worst. I can't live my life that way," Carly said. "And you shouldn't either."

"Kind of hard when the worst keeps kicking me in the face. Look, I don't want to see you get hurt. You're young. You're naive. You don't know what kind of a man Antonio is."

"I know him well enough. And I'm not that young or that naive. On that you'll have to trust me."

Rachel gave up. Maybe it would be better to speak to Antonio. Carly would have a fit, but Rachel wasn't about to let some playboy break her sister's heart. Although, Rachel had to admit that Carly wasn't nearly as small-town as she was. Carly was more like their mother, destined to want adventure, to roam the world. Rachel didn't understand that kind of thinking. Home was where the heart was. If you moved around all the time, what kind of a heart could you have? What sort of roots could you set down?

"I better get dressed," Carly said.

"Are you planning to do any work today?"

"I'll be down to the office later. I have some things to do."

Rachel frowned. "What kind of things? Where do you go? What do you do every day?"

"What do you mean?" Carly asked evasively.

"I mean that I seem to be seeing less and less of you. And despite the fact that you dropped two classes this semester, you appear to be busier than you were before you did that."

Carly shrugged. "I still have to study and go to the library. You're the one who hasn't been around much, Rachel. You're always working. If you weren't, you'd see more of me."

Rachel didn't quite buy that explanation, but it was obviously the best one she would get this morning. "Well, stop in at the office later on. We still need to discuss the schedule for the Harvest Festival and the second picking."

"I don't know why we're bothering to pick. There won't be anywhere to ship the apples with all the plants closing down. We need to change, Rachel. We need to plant grapes, start a vineyard."

"This is an apple farm. It's been an apple farm for over a hundred years."

"The prices for wine grapes are going up, while the prices for apples are going down. It doesn't take a rocket scientist to figure out we're in the wrong business."

Rachel shook her head. She'd been hearing the same arguments at the local growers' meetings. Even her grandmother had dared to bring up the subject. But Rachel and her grandfather were firm on the fact that theirs was an apple farm, not a vineyard. Unfortunately, the rest of the family was not so convinced. Even some of her younger cousins were starting to mutter. She'd had to find other ways to make the farm profitable.

The gift shop was beginning to make money with the offering of homemade apple butter, jellies and crisps. And recently, they'd begun offering tours of the farm and picnic lunches down by the creek on the weekends. Rachel had thoughts of using the Internet to build the business, but she hadn't really had the time to explore the opportunities.

"I'm done, Mommy," Wesley said, bringing his plate to the sink.

"Thanks, honey. Brush your teeth and get your backpack. The school bus won't wait for you."

"What are you and Dylan doing today?" Carly asked after Wesley had left the room.

"There is no me and Dylan," Rachel snapped.

Carly raised an eyebrow. "Sorry. Jeez, you're touchy."

"No, *I'm* sorry. Dylan wants to look at the plans for the house. He's coming by sometime today to get them."

"Your dream house," Carly said with a compassionate tilt of her head. "Not much left of the dream, is there?"

Rachel shook her head.

"Maybe you should tear it down."

"I've thought about it, but I can't. Wesley wants it so badly. It seems to be all he has left to hold on to."

"Won't it feel wrong to live there without Gary?"

"Yes. But it feels wrong to live *here* without him."

"Is it? I mean, you grew up here. You lived a lot of years here without him. In fact, you lived a lot of days here without him in the last couple of years."

"He was home plenty of times," Rachel said defensively.

"He was on the road every other week."

"It wasn't that much."

"Of course it was that much. I was here, too. I saw you

sitting on the porch all by your lonesome, looking out into the sunset."

"Gary had business. He provided for us with that business. He had to leave. He had to travel."

"I'm not criticizing him, Rachel, but he wasn't a saint. And you weren't always happy."

"I was happy," Rachel said fiercely. "I was madly in love with Gary, and he with me. Don't you ever say otherwise."

"I didn't mean to upset you."

"I have to believe in him," Rachel said with a quiet desperation. "I have to. It's all I have left."

"Maybe you should forget about the insurance money, go on with your life, stop asking questions that you really don't want the answers to."

"I want the answers. I just want them to be the right answers."

The phone on the kitchen wall rang and Rachel was grateful for the interruption. She picked up the receiver and said, "Hello."

"Rachel?"

Dylan's voice was not the one she wanted to hear. "Yes."

"Can I come by and look at the plans?"

"I'll bring them down to the house," she told him. "Then you can compare the plans to what's been done already."

"All right. When?"

"A half hour? I have to get Wesley off to school."

"I'll meet you there."

"Okay." Rachel hung up and saw Carly watching her. "Do you need something?"

"No. I just can't figure out why you seem so nervous."

"I am not nervous. I'm a lot of other things, but nervous isn't one of them." But she was lying, Rachel realized. She was nervous about seeing Dylan, building her house, going on without Gary, finding out things she didn't want to find out.

"You're shaking in your shoes," Carly observed quietly, a thoughtful expression on her face. "Is Dylan bothering you in some way? Is he trying to take advantage—"

"No! Of course not," Rachel said quickly, aware that her sister was veering off in a direction she definitely did not want her to take. "He just makes me uncomfortable because of his relationship with Gary."

"Gary told me once that Dylan was the brother he never had."

Rachel nodded. "I think that's the way Dylan felt about Gary."

"They probably shared a lot of things, a lot of secrets."

"Don't say that word. And don't give me that look."

"You asked Dylan to help you find out what happened. Instead he's here building a house. How is that helping you get to the truth?"

"I'll get to it eventually. I still have boxes to go through and other people to talk to."

"What other people?"

"I don't know—other people. Just let it alone, Carly." Rachel wished the words back as soon as she saw the hurt look in her sister's eyes. She hadn't meant to be abrupt; she just didn't have time to deal with Carly right now.

"Fine, I'll let it alone. What do I know? I'm just your baby sister. I couldn't help you in any way. It's not like I'm smart or anything."

Rachel sighed. "Don't do this to me, please. This isn't about you."

"No, it's not about me. It's probably about someone named Laura, someone who called Gary here a bunch of times in the weeks before he died, someone he didn't want you to know about."

Rachel's jaw dropped open. "What on earth are you talking about?"

"I thought you didn't need my help."

"Are you making this up?" A chill skimmed up Rachel's arms, raising goose bumps.

"No, I'm not. I heard Gary talking on the phone to someone named Laura. She'd called a couple of times when he was in the city. I finally gave her his apartment number because she said it was important. When I asked Gary who she was, he said she was a business associate."

"Then that's who she was."

"A business associate who didn't know his office number? Or the firm he worked for? Because she asked me those questions."

Rachel swallowed hard. "Why didn't you say something to me?"

"Because Gary told me she didn't have anything to do with you, and I believed him. After he died, I forgot all about it, until I overheard you talking to Grandma about the insurance problems."

Rachel's stomach turned over. Who was Laura? A client, as Gary had claimed—or someone else, someone who had had a more personal relationship with him? Maybe the person who'd left a perfume bottle in his apartment? Rachel moved toward the table and sat down in a chair, needing something sturdy beneath her. "You should have told me before."

Carly shook her head, looking guilty. "I shouldn't have told you now. But it drives me nuts that you won't even consider the fact that I could help you find out what happened."

"I know what happened. Gary ran his car off the road in an accident. So stop bringing up phone calls and women's names, okay?" Rachel bit down on her bottom lip as her emotions threatened to overwhelm her.

"I'm ready," Wesley announced from the doorway, wearing his backpack. "Mommy, are you okay?"

"She's just tired," Carly answered for her. "How about I take you down to the bus stop?"

"Okay. Bye, Mommy."

"Bye, Wes. Give me a kiss first." Wesley ran over and gave her a kiss on the cheek. It almost undid her, but she managed to hold herself together until he'd left the room.

Carly paused in the doorway. "I'm sorry, Rachel. Sorry if I made things worse."

She didn't wait for an apology, which was good, because Rachel didn't feel in the mood to give one. Not that it was right to take out her anger on Carly. It wasn't her sister's fault that some woman had called Gary. Not that the phone calls meant anything. Gary had women clients. He had women friends. So what?

She heard the front door close and got to her feet. She had to get dressed and meet Dylan. She didn't have time to worry about a few mysterious phone calls. But as she walked out of the kitchen and down the hall, she found herself stopping, then going into the study, past the desk and straight to the filing cabinet. Inside the top drawer was a folder marked "Phone Bills." She removed it, then paused.

She had a feeling she was about to open Pandora's box. And once it was open, would she ever be able to get it closed? But it wasn't like she had to do anything. Just looking wouldn't hurt, would it?

* * *

It hurt just to look at the damn house, to think about the man who had dreamed it up, about the family who would never live here together. Dylan leaned against his car. He'd seen a lot of buildings in his time, but none that affected him as deeply as this one did.

Dylan had had a house in the suburbs with his first family, as he thought of them. With his mother's second marriage, he'd moved into an apartment building in San Francisco. His stepfather had three girls of his own, one only two years old. The apartment had three bedrooms. His mother and stepfather were in one room, the two older girls had another and the baby had the third. Dylan had slept on a cot in the baby's room for a couple of years. Then he'd moved onto a pullout couch in the living room. They'd never made a room for him. Boys could sleep anywhere, his mother always said. They didn't need nearly as many things as girls.

Gary had lived a few streets over in another apartment building. His had been more run-down, with peeling paint on the walls, cockroaches in the hall and a cigarette smell that never went away. They'd spent most of their time together outside on their skateboards. They'd gone all over the city. Sometimes when they'd cruised through the richer neighborhoods and looked at the tall, stately houses, they'd peek in the windows and wonder what it would be like to live in such places.

Dylan shook his head at the memories. He'd been so good at forgetting. Now it was all coming back. He straightened up and looked around, wondering where the hell Rachel was. It was almost an hour since he'd spoken to her. He didn't want to stand here thinking about the past;

he wanted to get going, study the plans, figure out what he wanted to do himself and what he wanted to hire out.

His cell phone rang and he opened it, relieved by the distraction. "Hello?"

"Dylan? Mike Connolly. How are you?"

"Good. Thanks for calling me back."

"No problem. My secretary said something about Gary?"

"Right." Dylan paused, not sure exactly how to broach the subject. Mike was an architect at Gary's firm. If Gary had gone to a bachelor party in Lake Tahoe for an associate, Mike would have been invited. But Dylan didn't want to share any suspicions with Mike. He had to be careful or rumors would be flying. "I'm going to help Rachel finish the house that Gary started to build for them," he said.

Mike let out a low whistle. "The house. I'd forgotten about that. It wasn't completed, huh?"

"No, just the framing. I wondered if Gary had left anything at the office on the project."

"I think his secretary boxed everything up and shipped it to Rachel right after the funeral."

"All right. I'll check with Rachel, then. By the way, she mentioned that Gary had gone to Tahoe for a bachelor party. So who got married? Jacob?"

Mike laughed. "No way. Jacob likes to play the field."

"Following in your footsteps, huh?"

"He's a smart man. What can I say?" Mike paused. "But Gary had told me he was going to Tahoe to meet an old friend."

An old friend? These were the same words Connie had used. Why hadn't Gary told him about an old friend? And who was this person? It would have to be someone Dylan knew. An old girlfriend, maybe? There had been dozens in high school and college. Where would he even start?

"Did Gary happen to mention a name? I'm just curious."

"I don't remember if he did, but I got the feeling it was a woman. Don't tell Rachel I said that."

"Why? Was something going on?"

"No. No. I'm sure not," Mike quickly denied. "Look, I gotta run. Anything else?"

"No, thanks."

"Give me a call when you're done house building. We'll have a drink."

"Sure." Dylan disconnected the call with an uneasy feeling in his gut. Who the hell had Gary gone to see in Tahoe? If he could figure that out, the rest of the story would follow.

His chest tightened when he saw Rachel's minivan turn into the driveway and come up the hill. He wondered if he should tell her about the supposed "old friend" in Gary's life. His instinct said no. He didn't know anything specific, and until he did, he thought he should keep it to himself.

"Hi," Rachel said as she got out of the van. Dressed in a pair of tan capri pants and a light blue, short-sleeved sweater, she looked both cool and casual. She handed him a cardboard cylinder. "The plans are in here."

"Thanks. Let's take a look."

"In a second," she replied.

He saw the worry in her eyes. "What's wrong?"

"Nothing." She crossed her arms in front of her chest.

"Nothing?"

"Well, probably nothing. Oh, damn Carly anyway!"

"Carly? What did she do?"

"She told me Gary had some strange phone calls from some woman named Laura. Do you know who she is?"

"Laura? I don't think so," he said slowly. "I can't think of anyone off the top of my head."

"Neither can I. But after I spoke to Carly, I looked through the phone bills and saw some numbers I didn't recognize."

Dylan tensed. "Did you call any of them?"

"Not yet. I couldn't quite bring myself to do it."

"Any cities stand out?"

"There were a bunch—Las Vegas, New York, Los Angeles, Reno, maybe others. I scanned the numbers quickly."

"Reno?" He jumped on that one. Reno was only thirty minutes from Lake Tahoe. Maybe there was a connection there. "What about Tahoe?" he asked.

She shook her head. "No, but I don't have the bills for Gary's cell phone. Those were paid by his firm. I'm sure the calls are all perfectly reasonable and innocent."

"Probably," he agreed.

"I didn't realize Gary knew so many people in so many different places. Actually, I did realize it. I just didn't want to think about it. Just like I don't want to think about that perfume bottle in Gary's apartment, but it keeps popping into my mind. There was a woman in Gary's apartment, and a woman on the phone whom Gary didn't want me to know about. If he had nothing to hide, why was he hiding phone calls?"

"I don't know. Maybe he wasn't."

"I can't do this, Dylan. I can't question every little thing. I'll go crazy. I *am* going crazy."

Rachel struggled to hang on to her composure.

Dylan struggled against his instinct to offer comfort.

They both lost the battle.

Rachel burst into tears and Dylan drew her against his chest. "It's okay," he murmured. "It's okay."

She cried a river of tears that streamed down her cheeks and soaked through his shirt. She hung on to him like he was the only buoy in a raging sea, and he couldn't have let her go even if he wanted to.

"God, I'm sorry," she sniffed as the sobs finally began to lessen. She pulled away, wiping her eyes with the back of her hand. "I don't know why I keep crying. I'm usually pretty controlled."

"I think you're entitled. It's been a long six months, hasn't it?"

"Yes. Sometimes it feels like just yesterday that I saw him, and other times it feels like a million years ago. But crying won't bring him back or help me get to the truth. I shouldn't be wasting my time with tears."

"It's not always a waste. If you keep everything inside, it will eat you alive."

She sent him a startled look. "What did you say?"

"It's not a waste of time."

"Not that, the other part. Gary used to say that. *If you keep everything inside, it will eat you alive.*"

No wonder the words had come so easily to him. "You're right. He said that to me," Dylan admitted. "More than a few times."

"Because you keep it all in. That's what Gary said. You swallow your problems whole and have indigestion for a week."

"He said that about me?" Dylan asked. For the first time, he wondered what else Gary had shared about him. He'd never really considered himself to be a part of their conversations, their lives.

She nodded. "Was he right?"

"Partly. But I don't get indigestion, I get insomnia. I don't think I've had a good night's sleep in ten years. As soon as I lie down, my brain goes into overdrive. Everything I pushed to the back of my mind during the day comes rushing out, demanding attention."

"Gary could fall asleep in about three point two seconds," she said. "It didn't matter what time of day. If he wanted a nap, he'd lie down and take a nap, just like that. He never lost sleep over anything. He didn't worry. He didn't get riled up about small things. Anyway." She picked up the cylinder that had slipped to the ground. "The plans. You better take a look at them."

She didn't sound too keen, and in truth he wasn't ready yet either. "I have a better idea."

"You do?"

"Show me around the farm. I don't think I've ever had the full tour."

"I didn't think you ever wanted one."

"Well, I do now."

She hesitated. "All right. If you're sure, but I can pretty much guarantee you'll learn far more than you ever wanted to know about apples."

"I think I can handle it."

She smiled. "You say that now, but we'll see how you feel after one hundred and fifteen acres of apples."

"That many, huh?"

"Oh, yeah. Then there's the barn, the packing shed, the kitchen, the gift shop, the picnic area. Oh, and the pumpkin patch, which will be in full swing by next week."

"No pony rides?" he asked with a grin, pleased that his distraction had worked. Just thinking about her farm had brought pleasure to Rachel's eyes. And he was willing to look at every single tree on the property if that would keep the joy on her face for a while longer.

"Not yet. But I won't say never. The apple business isn't what it used to be. We've had to supplement our income any way we can."

He was surprised at the complexity of their operation. For some reason, he'd thought it was just trees and apples. Gary hadn't talked much about the farm. Had he? Or had Dylan just tuned out everything that concerned Gary's life with Rachel?

"Still game?" she asked.

"I think so."

"You can follow me this time." She turned toward her minivan. "You know, that fancy car of yours isn't going to stay too clean with all the dirt around here. Gary was forever washing and waxing his car."

"Gary loved that car."

"Yes, he did." She shook her head. "There it is again, that little ping in my heart. I wonder when that will stop happening. Sometimes I'm afraid it won't ever stop. And then again, sometimes I'm afraid it *will* stop. That I'll forget something I shouldn't forget."

"You won't." He held her gaze for a long second, then let it go. There were other things he wanted to say. But the words wouldn't come. It was probably better that way.

Chapter 7

Rachel had been right. Dylan now knew more about apples than he'd ever wanted to know, including the six different varieties grown at AppleWood Farms. He'd seen pickers harvesting one section of the orchard, a group of workers in the packing shed sorting apples, still more employees working the pumpkin patch, the fruit stand by the road and the gift shop in the barn that sold everything from apples to apple butter, apple pie, apple napkins and apple jewelry.

Rachel had explained the various tourist operations and pointed out the U-Pick section of the orchard, where visitors could pick their own apples and picnic by a trickling stream. She'd also introduced him to a large number of people she called cousins, including one named Wally, who was hoping to win the Biggest Pumpkin Award at the Annual Harvest Festival in two weeks' time.

Throughout the tour, Rachel had given Dylan every last

detail about planting, pruning, harvesting and shipping. It was clear that she loved the farm, loved the sights and the smells. There was pride in her voice as she talked about the land that had belonged to her family for over a hundred years. Dylan wondered what it would feel like to be a part of something so old, so treasured, so loved. He couldn't begin to imagine.

"So what do you think?" Rachel asked as she led him up the side of a small hill. She flung out her hands at the vista that unfolded before them.

It was a pretty sight, lines of trees broken up by fields of flowers and rolling hills in the distance. But it wasn't the view that stirred him, it was Rachel. Her face was pink from the sun, her hair blowing loose in the breeze, her eyes alight with a pleasure he hadn't seen since she'd shown up on his job site two days earlier.

Something inside him turned over as he looked into her eyes. He wanted to make this moment last, to keep the light in her eyes and the smile on her face. He wanted it for her, he told himself. He wanted her to be happy for a while, to be free of the sadness that she wore like a second skin. But, selfishly, he also wanted this moment for himself, when it was just the two of them, when they weren't haunted by guilt or betrayal or doubts. Unfortunately, just thinking about those emotions brought them all back.

"Well," Rachel prodded, "have I left you speechless?"

"You could say that."

"Come on. I've been working my fingers to the bone for years to keep this place going. Now I want compliments, praise. Let's hear it."

He couldn't help responding to the teasing note in her voice. "You have a very impressive farm. Is that better?"

"Yes." She let out a sigh as she gazed at the valley. "I love this place. I always have." She flopped down on the ground and picked at a piece of grass.

"I can tell," he said, sitting down next to her. "Pride of ownership in every note of your voice."

"I'm not the only owner. Everyone in the family has a share, even if it's a small one. My grandfather believes that you care more about the things that belong to you."

"He's probably right about that."

"There's no 'probably' about it, not when you're talking about my grandfather," she said with a smile. "His way or the highway, that's what my dad used to say. They argued all the time. They were as different as two men could be. My father was much more impulsive and fun-loving. Whereas my grandfather is intense, driven, dedicated. I think it comes from his being in the military when he was younger. He likes to give orders and he expects people to take them."

"So who do you follow?" Dylan asked. "Your father or your grandfather?"

She grinned back at him. "I'd like to say I have the best of both of them in me, but sometimes I think I have all their faults."

"Like what?"

"Procrastination—my father. Stubbornness—my grandfather. I'm not sure I should admit to any more."

"What happened to your mother?" he asked. "I know you told me once that she and your dad divorced. Is she still alive?"

"I have no idea. I haven't seen or heard from her in years. We weren't very important to her. She had other things in her life that she cared more about."

He heard the bitterness and had a feeling it ran deep. "What other things?"

"My mother was an artist, a painter. A really good one, too, my dad used to say. When I think of her, I see her standing in front of an easel in a corner of her studio, wearing a bright pink smock. She'd stand and stare at that canvas for hours on end."

"And what would you do?"

"Watch her, mostly. Once I tried to paint. I wanted to be like her, but I used her expensive oils and made a huge mess. She was furious. That's the last time I picked up a brush."

"You were a kid. Only natural to mimic your mother."

"She didn't appreciate it at all." Rachel's expression was distant, as if she were back in that place, that memory. "Anyway, my parents broke up shortly after that. I tried to apologize for what I'd done, but my mother went on with her life, and we came back here. She wrote and called a few times the first couple of years, but then it ended. I guess out of sight, out of mind."

"You don't think you were responsible, do you?"

"No. Well, maybe a little."

"Rachel. You weren't responsible."

"The grown-up in me knows that. The little kid inside still feels guilty."

"Tell her to get over it. It sounds to me like your mother did exactly what she wanted to do."

"I guess." Rachel picked up a pebble and tossed it down the hill. "I can't believe I'm telling you this. I've never told anyone about my mother."

Not even Gary? The question came to his mind, but he left it unspoken.

"I don't even like to think about her, much less talk about her. My dad was the same way. Once we moved back here, I never heard him say her first name. If he spoke of her at all, it was to call her 'your mother,' as if she had no other identity or meaning to him. I used to wonder how you could love someone so much and then hate them with the same intensity."

"Love and hate are two sides of the same coin," Dylan murmured.

"Is that the way your parents ended up—hating each other?"

He considered the question. He hadn't thought about them in a long time. "I don't think they had enough energy or passion left to hate each other. My brother's illness wore them down, like a constant stream of water pounding against a rock until it finally eroded and vanished completely."

"What happened to your dad?"

Dylan shrugged. "I don't know. He kept in touch for a while after my mom remarried. He drank too much. Worked too little. Drifted. Looking back, I guess he was lost. I have more sympathy for him now than I did then. I thought he'd turned his back on me. But I think everything just slipped away from him and he had no idea how to get it back. I haven't heard from him in years. I don't know where he is."

"Maybe he doesn't know where you are."

"I suspect he could find me if he wanted to."

"Or vice versa."

"True. It all happened a long time ago, Rachel."

"For me, too, but it still hurts."

"Not if you keep busy enough."

"Is that your strategy?"

"Always has been. Until now." He stretched out his legs, realizing that his strategy had changed with his trip north. He wasn't keeping busy at all. And look where he'd ended up—in a personal conversation with Rachel. "I should be working on your house." Even as he said the words, he found himself reluctant to move. "I just need to get up."

She smiled at him with complete understanding. "This place does that to you. It calms you down. Makes you feel like just sitting a while. Or else it's my conversation. I must be boring you to death with all this family talk."

"Not at all. Now, the earlier discussion on pesticides— that was boring." She laughed, and he was pleased when she flung him another smile. He was fast becoming addicted to them. "I can see why you like this place," he said. "It's peaceful here."

"This is my favorite spot. When I look out over the hills and the trees, I believe anything is possible."

"My favorite spot is the top floor of an unfinished building. You're on top of the world. It's a great feeling."

"Is that why you build skyscrapers?"

"It's a living."

"More than a living. And you have a lot to show for all your efforts. You've left your mark on the world. Not everyone can say that."

"You can." He waved a hand toward the orchards before them. "You've got all these trees that you care for like children and which will probably still be here a hundred years from now."

"They're just trees," she said modestly. "Nothing special."

"Of course they're special. Their roots go deep into the ground. So do yours. You belong here."

She turned her head to look at him, curiosity in her eyes. "Did Gary tell you that I refused to leave?"

"What do you mean?"

"Did Gary tell you that he wanted to leave and I didn't?"

"I don't think so. I don't know. Why?"

"I just wondered."

She didn't say anything for a moment, the quiet surrounding them accentuated by the sound of her breathing, which seemed somewhat agitated now.

"Is something wrong, Rachel?"

She didn't answer right away, then said, "I think I may have held Gary back."

"In what way?"

"He needed to be in the city to work. I needed to be here. This is my safe haven. As you said, I belong here." There was a plea for understanding in her eyes. "I'm not sure Gary ever did. If he was unhappy here, if that had something to do with the accident . . . I don't think I could forgive myself."

"I'm sure Gary would have told you if he wanted to live somewhere else. He never asked you to leave, did he?"

"Once," she replied, surprising him. "Once he asked me."

She didn't elaborate, and he decided not to press. He didn't really want to talk about Gary right now. Nor did he want to talk about their life together. He glanced up at the sky as a small plane came into view, the wings dipping from side to side.

"That's a first-timer," Dylan said.

Rachel followed his gaze. "The pilot, you mean?"

"When you first start to fly, you feel like you want to flap your arms. You have to sit back and relax and let the plane be an extension of your hands."

"That sounds like a comment from someone who has actually flown an airplane."

"I have a pilot's license. And a small airplane."

"No way!"

"It's true."

She stared at him as if she'd never seen him before. "Gary never told me that."

"It's no big deal."

"Did you ever take him up in the plane?"

They couldn't seem to get away from Gary. "Only once. He preferred big jets with first-class seating, movies and cocktails. He said sitting in my plane was like flying in a sardine can."

"Hmm," she murmured, turning her face away from him to gaze over the valley again. "Gary never mentioned it. Funny, how many little things he never mentioned to me."

"I'm sure that's the way it is with all marriages. You get busy. You think to say something, then you don't."

"Maybe," she replied, but she didn't sound convinced. "Did you ever fly over this area?"

"A few times when I was training."

"What's it like to fly?" she asked, wrapping her arms around her knees.

"Surely you've been up in a plane?"

She shook her head. "No. Doesn't that sound ridiculous? But we never went anywhere as kids that we couldn't drive to. And Gary flew all the time for work, so the last thing he wanted to do when he was home was go on a trip. So what's it like?"

He thought about her question for a moment, wondering if he could put into words how he felt when he was flying. "It's amazing," he said finally. "The earth falls away like a sweater that's too tight and suddenly you're free. You can do anything. Talk about the possibilities, they're limitless."

"It sounds wonderful."

"You could do it."

"Me?" She uttered a short, disbelieving laugh. "No, I don't think so."

"Why not?"

"Because."

"Because why?"

"Because of a million reasons. I'm a mom."

"And moms can't fly?"

"I drive a minivan—I've never gone faster than seventy-five on the freeway."

He laughed at that. "I bet you have. As I recall, you have a lead foot."

"Well, I grew out of it. I grew out of a lot of things." Her smile faded as she got to her feet. "I have responsibilities here. I wouldn't fly away from them even if I could."

"Not even for a little while?" He stood up. "Let me take you up one day. Don't say no. Just think about it. You could take the controls in your own hands. You'd love it."

"I can't," she said with a definitive shake of her head.

"Why not?"

"Because I'm a small-town girl who grows apples for a living. I couldn't be a pilot. I'm not that brave or that daring."

"You won't know until you try."

"Some things you just know. We should go. I still have a lot of work to do today." She turned away from the view and headed toward the path that would lead them home.

"We could take Wesley, too," Dylan said, following close behind her. He probably should have left the subject alone, but he couldn't. "Wesley would love it."

She stopped so quickly, he almost tripped over her feet. She put a hand on his arm to steady them both, but when her fingers gripped the sleeve of his shirt, he knew that her touch was in no way about comfort. "No, Dylan," she said firmly. "We can't take Wesley up in an airplane."

"Why not?"

"Because we can't," she snapped. "Just let it go."

"Not until you tell me why."

"Stop pressuring me."

He jerked his arm away from her hand, rubbing the spot where her nails had dug into his skin. "That hurt."

"I'm sorry."

But she didn't look sorry, she looked mad. "What is with you, Rachel? You don't trust me. Is that it?"

"It's not about trust."

"Then what is it about?"

She blew out an irritated breath. "Gary promised to take Wesley to Disneyland for his eighth birthday. It would have been his first plane trip. Mine, too. But Gary died two weeks beforehand, and we never took that trip. That's what it's about."

"Rachel, flying with me doesn't make you disloyal. But I'm sorry. I didn't know there was a sad connection between flying and Gary's death."

"Of course you didn't know. How could you know? You weren't a part of our lives. You stayed away, Dylan. Far away."

"So did you," he said, capturing her gaze and refusing to let go. "You stayed away, too, Rachel. And we both know why."

"I loved Gary. And I always will. I don't want there to be any misunderstandings. I came to you because you're Gary's friend. That's all you're ever going to be to me. Gary's best friend."

"I offered you a ride in an airplane, that's all," he said sharply. "There aren't and won't ever be any other strings attached." He paused. "And just for the record, I loved

Gary, too. And to me, you . . . you will always be Gary's wife."

"Yes, I will."

He nodded. In a way, he was glad she'd redrawn the line between them, because it had started to blur without Gary's strong presence. They both needed the line. There was no longer a safe distance between them, not miles and miles or years and years, just a few steps, a few breaths. "Okay, then."

"Okay, then," she echoed.

Rachel realized she was far from okay as she began walking back to the house, Dylan silent on her heels. They'd said enough, too much really, and yet there were words still left unspoken. It had been that way between them since the night before her wedding. No matter how many times they drew the line in the sand, they seemed to keep stepping over it.

For a few hours, she'd enjoyed his company. Getting caught up in the farm and the history of the family had made it easy to talk to him. He'd been a good listener, too. And it had been a while since she'd had an appreciative audience. But the tour was over. They had to refocus, regroup, get on with what they both needed to do.

I'm sorry, she silently whispered to Gary. *Sorry I got distracted. But it won't happen again. I miss you. I love you. I wish you were here and not Dylan. I swear it. I'm not going to be happy without you. I'm not.*

"I wrote the contractor's name on a note attached to the blueprints," Rachel said when they were approaching the house. "He was a nice man, but he had other jobs to do, and I realized that finishing the house was a luxury I couldn't afford. I also wrote down Travis Barker's name. He's a friend of the family, a wonderful carpenter. He might be interested in working out a deal with you."

"All right," Dylan said evenly. "I guess it's back to work."

"I still don't feel right about putting myself in debt to you with the house construction."

"It's only temporary. You can pay me back."

"I don't know if that's possible."

"I can afford it, Rachel. Whether or not you ever pay me back. And frankly, I'm doing it for Gary, not for you. He would want me to look out for you and Wesley."

"We're fine."

"Are you? I know you mentioned a small life insurance settlement, but you'll need that for Wesley's college. What about other investments? Gary must have had a retirement plan or stocks, mutual funds. Do you have a financial planner?"

She uttered a disbelieving laugh at that question. "I don't have enough finances to plan."

"Why not? Gary made a good salary. You live in a house that I would suspect is paid for. Was he investing in the farm?"

"No." She shook her head, not sure she wanted to share every last detail of her finances with Dylan, especially when she already knew that the accounts did not add up. "But I'll find a way to provide for Wesley and myself. It's none of your business, Dylan, so leave it alone."

"Why didn't Gary take out a construction loan?" he asked, ignoring her command.

She sighed. "He got a big bonus at work. He put some cash down to get started."

"Where was he going to get the rest?"

"I don't know. He didn't tell me. He just said he'd take care of it."

"And you didn't ask him how he would do that?"

"No, I didn't," she announced in frustration. "I trusted him. Maybe that was a mistake."

"We need to find out, Rachel." Dylan's eyes were alight with renewed energy. She could almost see the wheels spinning in his mind.

"Were there any recent cash withdrawals, recent being in the week before Gary died?" Dylan continued.

"Yes. Which obviously leads us to your next question— why on earth did Gary take out large sums of money before he went to Lake Tahoe? If I knew that, I never would have come to you in the first place."

"How much?"

"There were two cash withdrawals of five thousand dollars each."

"That's a fair amount of cash."

"He could have used the money for the house."

"Wouldn't he have kept some records, cash receipts?"

"I haven't gone through everything." Rachel was fast regretting her decision to involve Dylan. If she'd kept him out of it, she could have decided how quickly to move, how far to push. She could have put the brakes on when things got to be too much, but she could see there was no stopping Dylan. He'd caught the scent of something and he was on the hunt.

"Time to go through those filing cabinets, Rachel."

"You said you didn't have any doubts, Dylan. But you do, and I don't like it. You're supposed to convince me that Gary died in an accident. That there are no secrets. That's why you're here. You're not supposed to be making me feel like Gary was living a double life."

"I thought you wanted the truth."

"I want the *right* truth."

"There's only one truth." He paused. "I do believe it was

an accident. But the only way we can prove that is to answer the questions we both have. I'm not the enemy, Rachel."

"Sometimes it feels like you are," she whispered.

"I'm not," he said quietly, his gaze steady.

"I'm afraid. You're going too fast for me."

"You're not the kind of woman who can look the other way."

"Are you sure I'm not?" she asked. "Because haven't I done just that? Isn't that why I'm standing here wondering about a man I thought I knew as well as I knew myself? Isn't that why I never went through the checkbook or asked where the cash came from or found out why Gary was taking money out of his savings account?"

"So what do you want to do?" Dylan asked. "Do you want to protect Gary? Protect yourself? Hide from the truth? Or do you want to start looking in all the dark corners? It's your call, Rachel. Tell me what you want to do. But tell me now. Because once we start, really start, we're not going to stop, not until the end."

Chapter 8

It was dark in this corner of the basement, the only natural light coming from a small window just above the ground. It wasn't the best place to work, but it was the most private. Carly rolled her head onto her shoulders, hearing the tired click in her neck as she did so.

It was no wonder she was stiff; she'd been standing in front of her easel for almost two hours. The time had passed in a flash. That's the way it was when she painted. It could be one minute or one hour; she lost all concept of time until she checked her watch. But reality had finally intruded on her consciousness in the form of a big thud from above. Rachel was probably home.

She wondered if Dylan was with her. The two of them certainly had an odd, tense relationship. Sometimes Carly wondered if Dylan thought Gary had made a mistake in marrying Rachel. Other times she wondered if Dylan had wanted Rachel for himself. He had a way of looking at her that seemed far more intimate than their relationship indicated.

Rachel would be shocked and horrified to hear her say that out loud, Carly thought. In many ways Rachel was very naive. There was nothing wrong with a man wanting a woman he wasn't married to or vice versa. It was the actions that followed that mattered. As far as Carly knew, there had never been any such action between Rachel and Dylan.

She stared at the portrait in front of her. Antonio. She hadn't done his face justice. His eyes weren't right. They seemed too distant, as if he were looking away from her toward someone else. And his mouth was too tight, too sophisticated, too cold.

But he wasn't the problem. It was Carly herself. She wasn't that good an artist. Not like her mother, who actually had paintings hanging in a gallery. Carly had seen them once. She'd gone to Southern California for the weekend with some friends, and on a Sunday they'd driven over to Laguna Beach for a sidewalk art show. She'd stopped in front of a gallery, and there it was — a picture of a little girl sitting on a wicker chair next to a pot of purple violets. The little girl had been only five or six, but Carly had recognized her immediately. The little girl was Rachel, and the signature in the corner belonged to their mother.

Carly had had to borrow money from all of her friends to come up with enough cash to buy the painting, but she'd done it. She simply couldn't walk away from it. It was a link to a family she'd never known.

For Rachel, it was different. She'd had years with their mother, spent time with her, sat for a painting.

Carly couldn't help wondering why her mother hadn't painted *her*. Had she been too young? Too ugly? Too boring? Too average?

Setting down her own brush now, Carly walked over to the closet and removed the painting she'd stashed in there almost three years ago. She'd covered it with brown paper just in case anyone ventured down to the basement, not that anyone ever did. Once, about fifteen years earlier, they'd gotten water in this part of the house and as a result had moved all their storage up to the more spacious attic. The basement was just a dark stone area with a low ceiling and lots of pipes. Oh, there were still a few old suitcases and apple crates holding tools and such toward the front, but Carly liked them there because they blocked the back view of the basement, which she'd turned into her own private studio.

Lord knew she couldn't paint upstairs. She'd never hear the end of it. After they'd moved back to the apple farm, her father had refused to buy them crayons, much less paints. He'd discouraged them from any artistic endeavors, terrified that one of them might turn out like their mother.

Sometimes she wondered what her mother was like. Not that she'd tried to find her. Why should she? Her mother knew where she was, and she'd never come back, not even once.

Rachel never wanted to talk about their mother. She seemed to hate her. But she wasn't hating her mother in this painting. No, the little girl in this picture was looking longingly at something off stage—her mother, maybe? The artist who wanted her forever on paper but didn't care enough to actually stay with her?

Carly took one last glance at her mother's painting,

tracing the signature with the tip of her finger. It was a beautiful painting. Her mother was truly gifted. But along with the admiration came an almost unbearable sadness. You weren't supposed to miss what you'd never had. But she did miss it. She missed having a mother. And even though she was grown up now, she still wanted one. But all she had was this one painting. She covered it once again with the brown paper and shut the closet door. As she did so, the door from the upstairs into the basement opened.

Someone was coming. Damn! She looked at her paints strewn about, the half-finished portrait, the dozens of other sketches she'd tossed onto the old card table. If Rachel came down here, if she saw . . .

Carly dashed around the wall of suitcases and apple crates, hoping to ward off the intruder, and crashed straight into a very hard body.

"What the hell?" a low male voice ground out.

Strong hands grasped her arms, which was probably a good thing, since she seemed to have stopped breathing.

"Carly?"

"Travis?" she got out. "What are you doing down here?"

"Your grandmother said she saw a mouse in the kitchen. She asked me to set some traps down here and in the attic."

"A mouse?" she squeaked. That was right. Her grandmother had mentioned something about seeing a mouse.

"What are *you* doing down here?" he asked.

"Just looking for something," she lied.

"Looking for what?"

"Something," she said, blocking his way.

"Okay," he said easily. "I'm going to check through the rest of the basement and see if I can find any signs of a mouse."

"I've already checked," she said quickly. "And it's all clear. Tell Grandmother that you couldn't find anything."

"Are you asking me to lie to your grandmother?" he drawled. "I don't think I could do that."

She let out a sigh of exasperation. "Of course you could. And it's not a lie. There are no mice down here. You can go up to the attic and look there."

"I will as soon as I finish up down here," he said firmly, moving her to one side with his strong hands.

"Travis, wait," she said hastily.

"What don't you want me to see? Do you have a secret love nest down here or something? I know. This is where you mix the secret love potions for Antonio. I'm right, aren't I?" He gave her a big, mischievous grin.

"No, you're not right."

"Then I'll just take a look—"

She grabbed his arm and held on for dear life. "*No*."

He glanced down at her hand on his arm. "That's a mighty strong grip you got there. Never thought you'd be holding on to me so tightly. You must want something. Hmm." He rubbed his jaw with his free hand. "What could you want?"

"I want you to leave."

"If you wanted me to go, you wouldn't be holding on to me like I was the last tree in the orchard."

"Travis, would you just go?"

"I might. What's it worth to you?"

"What do you want?" she asked with annoyance, trying to curb her temper, because she couldn't give him the complete satisfaction of seeing her totally lose her cool. He loved to push her buttons and she had to stop reacting.

"I think I want a kiss."

"I don't think so. What else do you want?"

"An open-mouth kiss. Want to keep negotiating?"

"I'm not giving you a kiss."

"Then I'm going to turn right around and see what it is you're so hell-bent on hiding from me." He started to move, and she grabbed his other arm, holding him in place. In fact, she was now holding him so close, his chest grazed against her breasts and an odd tingle ran down her spine.

He looked down at her. "You've got me where you want me, babe. What are you going to do about it?"

"You cannot tell a soul," she warned.

"About what? Your secret love nest or—"

"This," she interrupted, releasing his arms to grab his face. She planted a quick kiss on his lips. At least it was supposed to be a quick kiss, but his arms went around her waist and hauled her up even tighter against his chest. When she tried to move away, his mouth came back down on hers. His lips were firm and warm and moved in a way that was far more appealing than she would have imagined. Of course she was planning to pull away. She just needed another second.

And in that second it was Travis who broke off the kiss. Travis, who smiled down on her in that frustratingly annoying manner of his. Travis, who'd just made her lose her good sense, not to mention her equilibrium.

"Fine, you got your kiss, now go," she said abruptly.

"Okay."

When he moved, she didn't try to stop him. Her mistake. He turned toward the back of the basement instead of the front, and before she could grab him, he was standing in front of her easel, the smile completely wiped from his face.

"Did you draw this?" He glanced around the small alcove containing her artist's supplies.

"You can't tell anyone. You know about my mother. You know how much this would upset Rachel, and she's had enough upset in her life."

"You're good," he murmured, staring at her painting.

"Not good enough. It doesn't look anything like Antonio."

"Because you're drawing the wrong man."

"Don't start."

"Oh, I haven't begun to start, Carly. You have talent, but your subject is all wrong. You need to paint someone you know. Someone like me."

"I don't want to paint you," she said sharply, feeling slightly bad at the wounded expression on his face. "Look, I told you before."

"I know, you don't want me. That's why you almost ripped off my clothes a second ago."

"I did no such thing."

"Then why is my shirt unbuttoned?"

She dropped her gaze from his face to his shirt, realizing with horror that the top two buttons were indeed undone, and she distinctly remembered spreading her palms across his hairy chest. Oh, God! She would never live this down.

Before she could reply, Rachel's voice rang out from far above. "Carly? Carly, where are you?"

"She can't see this," Carly said in a rush, grabbing Travis's hand and pulling him away from the alcove and up the stairs. "Please," she begged just before she opened the basement door. "Please don't tell her."

Travis didn't reply, and she didn't have enough time to wait for an answer, only to open the door and push him into the hall.

Rachel was a few feet away, followed by Dylan. "Oh,

there you are," she said. "You have a phone call. Hi, Travis."

"Thanks," Carly said.

"What were you two doing in the basement?" Rachel asked with a gleam in her eyes.

"Uh," Carly faltered, wondering how to match whatever she said with whatever Travis would say.

"Just checking for a mouse. Your grandmother thought she saw one," Travis replied. "But it's all clear."

"You better get the phone, Carly. It's Antonio," Rachel said.

"You don't want to keep him waiting, that's for sure," Travis added.

Carly shot him a grateful look. "Thanks for helping me look for the mouse."

"No problem."

"Actually, I'm really glad we ran into you, Travis," Rachel said. "I want you to meet Dylan Prescott. He's a longtime friend of Gary's and he's going to help me finish the house."

"Nice to meet you," Travis said as the two men shook hands. "Gary was a good man. Any friend of his is a friend of mine."

"Likewise," Dylan said.

Rachel watched as the two men took their measure of the other. Travis was broader, with lighter hair and not as many edges. Dylan was leaner, sharper, and seemed to dominate the hallway, even though he was the slighter of the two men. But he had a presence that couldn't be denied, a presence that continued to set her back on her heels.

She still hadn't answered his question about whether or not she had the guts to look into the dark corners of her life, because the truth was she didn't know the answer.

What she did know was that as soon as she said, "Let's go," they'd be going a hundred miles an hour, and she wouldn't be able to stop even if she wanted to, even if the truth became too much to handle.

"I need to check the attic," Travis said. "I'll see you both around."

"What's in the attic?" Dylan asked when Travis had disappeared down the hall.

"Lots of stuff. We've accumulated many things over the years. Used to drive Gary crazy. He loved to spring-clean. And I loved to pack things away, save them for a rainy day. Which are you? A spring cleaner or a pack rat?"

"I've always liked to travel light."

"Figures. Okay, Dylan, I give up."

"Give up what?"

"My misgivings. I'll open up the boxes and the files and the drawers and the rest of Gary's life. But, and I do need you to agree to this." She paused. "I might need a break every now and then, depending on what we find."

"I'm not a steamroller, Rachel."

She smiled at that. "Oh, yeah? I think you're exactly that. There's one other thing."

"Shoot."

"I don't want to start today."

"Hey, never put off till tomorrow—"

"I know, but I want to meet Wesley at the bus stop. I want to feed him milk and cookies and listen to his day and be there for him. I'm thinking that he can't let go of Gary if he doesn't have someone else to hold on to. And I need to be that someone. I need to be strong, and I need to smile, so Wesley can feel safe and so he can smile."

"I understand. I'll go back to the house, check out the blueprints, and we can talk tomorrow."

"Good," she said with relief. "Tomorrow is good."

He started to turn away, then stopped. "By the way, I hope you don't mind, but I think I accepted a spot in your grandfather's poker game tomorrow night."

"I hope you have enough money. The old boys around here like city slickers."

"I know my way around a poker table."

"Yeah, Gary said the same thing."

"Gary couldn't bluff. I can."

She thought about that. A few weeks ago, she would have agreed that Dylan was far better at keeping secrets than Gary. Now she wasn't so sure. "Maybe he *could* bluff, Dylan. Maybe he could bluff better than anyone."

Dylan stopped at the house long enough to pick up the blueprints; then he headed back to town. He wasn't quite ready to put hammer to nail where Rachel's house was concerned. He needed to go over the plans and locate some subcontractors in town willing to work for him. That part of his life here he could handle. That part of his life he could do in his sleep. Or at least on autopilot. Which was a good thing, since his mind was having trouble focusing on construction.

It wasn't just Rachel who was getting to him now, it was Gary; it was the new information he'd learned about their finances. He was disturbed to know there was missing cash, few investments, nothing substantial to provide for Rachel and Wesley in the future. Wesley was only eight years old. There would be the expense just getting him through college. Gary should have seen that, planned for it.

Okay, so Gary wasn't big on planning. He still should have had more life insurance. Granted, he'd apparently tried to rectify the problem last year. But he should have done it sooner. And if he hadn't done it earlier, what had made him suddenly decide to do it a year ago? And why the hell had he gone to Lake Tahoe?

That was the question that really bothered Dylan. Rachel didn't know whom Gary had gone with, and she had apparently bought without question Gary's tale of a bachelor party weekend. But Dylan didn't believe it for a second. Gary had gone to Tahoe for reasons other than a bachelor party. He just had to figure out what those reasons were.

Dylan pulled into the parking lot of his hotel and shut off the engine. He walked into the lobby and nodded hello to the manager, Mrs. Janet Laningham.

"How's Rachel?" Janet asked, already aware of his connection to the family and his plans to finish the house. Sebastopol wasn't the biggest city in the world.

"She's fine. I got a tour of the farm."

"Oh, it's something, isn't it? I take the grandkids out there every October during the Harvest Festival. We pick apples and pumpkins and have a grand time."

Picking apples and pumpkins had never been part of Dylan's "grand time" vocabulary, but his life was changing. Just as Gary's life had changed when he'd met Rachel on a warm September day ten years earlier.

"Did you get a chance to see Lady Elaine?" Janet asked.

"Lady Elaine? I don't remember any relatives with that name."

Janet laughed. "Lady Elaine is an apple tree named after Rachel's great-great-grandmother, I think it was. The seeds came all the way from Virginia. She's a very special apple tree, and her bounty is magical."

"Is that a fact?" Dylan asked, amused by the tale. He was

surprised Rachel hadn't told him about it. She'd told him every other little thing about the farm. But he had definitely not been introduced to any Lady Elaine.

"Well, I don't know if it's a fact, but it's quite a legend. You see, if a woman, a descendant of the first Elaine Wood, gives the man of her heart an apple from that special tree, he's hers forever. It's worked a dozen or so times in history."

"Really?"

"Yes, but some years the tree doesn't bloom, and no one knows why. And once in a while the locals have stolen into the orchard at night and tried to swipe one of the Lady Elaines and give it to their own true love, but they always break up after that. The tree only blesses the direct descendants. To others it's a curse."

"Interesting," Dylan said, unable to repress the doubtful grin that spread across his face.

Mrs. Laningham waved her finger at him. "You're not a believer, I can see that. But I've lived in this town a long time, and I've seen that apple tree work its magic. Why, it worked on Rachel's husband, Gary, just like a charm."

"Rachel gave Gary one of the special apples?" An uneasy sensation ran down his spine.

"Of course she did," Janet said with a laugh. "That's how she got that city boy so fast. She said she gave it to him on an impulse when he stopped by the fruit stand, and—"

"Oh, my God!" Dylan said, thinking back to the first day they'd met. He'd wanted to leave, but Gary had wanted to buy an apple. And Rachel, she'd turned around and pulled one out of a bin and handed it to him, saying something about a legend.

"What's wrong?" Janet asked in alarm. "Did I say something wrong about your friend? I didn't mean any harm."

"No. I just never realized." He shook his head in bemusement. "I never knew."

"Well, it's probably just a silly tale, but sometimes you need a little magic in your life, you know?"

Dylan could barely follow her words. His mind raced. His heart reeled. Because Gary hadn't eaten that apple. He had.

Chapter 9

Rachel spent the rest of Friday and most of Saturday doing exactly what she'd told Dylan she'd be doing, taking a breather from her search for the truth. When she wasn't playing with Wesley, she was burying herself in the farm office, keeping her mind busy with plans for the upcoming Harvest Festival. She filled her mind with inconsequential stuff so that she wouldn't have to think about anything serious. It worked, too, until Saturday night, when she ran out of work and excuses.

Wesley was hunkered down in the family room with his best buddy, Joey, a videotape and a bowl of popcorn. Her grandmother was in town visiting with her girlfriends while Rachel's grandfather held his weekly poker game in the barn. Carly was out with Antonio, who had apparently invited her to dinner. That left Rachel with a problem she'd been trying to avoid.

With a heavy heart, she entered the study and took a

seat behind the big oak desk. It was a man's desk, she thought with a small pang. She could remember her dad sitting here paying the bills, reading the newspaper or helping her with her homework. So many times they'd poured over a math assignment or a history book together. And he'd been so patient, never rushing her, always ready to listen. He'd been a wonderful father, and she'd loved him. He'd died of cancer a year after her marriage, and she still missed him. Just as she missed Gary.

The people she'd loved the most were also the ones she'd lost. She picked up a photograph on the desk. It was a picture of Gary, her father and herself at her wedding. Two fabulous men. She'd been lucky to have them. But they were gone and no amount of feeling sorry for herself would bring them back. She had to go on. She had to open the drawers of the desk and the filing cabinet. She had to start throwing things away.

Rachel began by reopening the file folder marked "Phone Bills," which she'd glanced through yesterday. She'd circled the strange phone numbers in red ink. Tapping one with her fingernail, she debated her options. There seemed to be only one solution: call the numbers and see where they led.

She picked up the phone on the desk and dialed the first number in Reno, Nevada. The city was the closest location to Lake Tahoe and maybe had something to do with Gary's last trip.

"Silver Legacy Hotel and Casino," the receptionist answered.

"Oh, thanks, uh, never mind," Rachel said, setting down the receiver. The Silver Legacy Hotel? Why had Gary been calling the hotel? As far as she knew, he'd spent his last weekend in Lake Tahoe at Harrah's on the South Shore.

Unless they'd taken a side trip to Reno? There was gambling there, too. But why leave Lake Tahoe, which had its own casinos, not to mention a beautiful lake and incredible mountains? Why hadn't she asked Gary more questions about his trip? Why hadn't he offered more information?

Because it had been just another trip in a lifetime of weekend trips. Gary had traveled at least once a month for almost all of their marriage. She'd gotten used to him popping in and out, and he'd always handled all the travel arrangements through his firm. His firm! A light bulb went off in her head. Gary's secretary, Beth, would probably still have all the particulars about his final trip.

Rachel let out a sigh, realizing today was Saturday. Why couldn't she have had this epiphany during the work week? Because that would have been too easy. She glanced back down at the phone bill. On impulse she dialed the next unexplained number which was in Las Vegas. She was about to hang up when a woman answered the phone in a heavy Hispanic accent.

"Hello," she said. "Tanner residence."

Rachel's heart jumped into her throat. Tanner residence? How could that be?

"Hello," the woman said again. "Is anyone there?"

Rachel's chest was so tight, she didn't think she could get any words out. *Tanner residence?* As far as she knew, Gary didn't have any relatives. His mother had died a couple of years earlier; his father, sometime before that. Cousins, maybe? An aunt or an uncle? That had to be it.

"I hang up now," the woman on the other end said.

"Wait, I'm sorry. Is—uh—Mrs. Tanner there?" Rachel asked hesitantly.

"No. Can I take a message?"

"What about Mr. Tanner?"

"He's not here either."

"Do you know when they'll be back?"

"No, sorry. You want me to take a message?"

"No. I'll call back. Oh, wait, I forgot Mr. Tanner's first name. I'd hate to call back and ask for the wrong man," Rachel improvised.

"Gary."

Rachel's heart stopped. No! It couldn't be! She wanted to demand answers, but the click in her ear told her the woman had already hung up. She set down the receiver, her hand shaky. She felt dizzy, confused. She had to think. She had to make sense of things.

Gary Tanner? It had to be another man. *It had to be.*

"Rachel?"

Dylan's voice brought her head up. She stared at him in shock. Did he know? Was he in on it?

"What's wrong?" he asked, coming toward the desk. "You're white as a sheet. What's happened?"

"Gary's alive, isn't he?"

"What?" he bit out. "What the hell are you talking about?"

She heard his anger, but she didn't care. She picked up the phone bill and waved it in the air. "I called the number. They answered, 'Tanner residence.' The Gary Tanner residence." She spit out the words. "What was it? Some elaborate scheme? Gary had another family somewhere? Oh, my God, it's just like that movie I saw where the man was married to three women and traveled all the time and none of them knew about the others."

"Rachel, stop," Dylan said firmly. He grabbed the phone bill out of her hand and ran his gaze down the page.

"Which one?" he demanded. "Which number did you call?"

"The one in Las Vegas."

"Las Vegas?"

"Yes. Go ahead, call it yourself. You'll see," she said, white-hot anger coursing through her body. How could he? How could Gary have lied to her?

"Rachel, what exactly did you say?"

"What does it matter?"

"It matters. What did you say?"

"I asked for Mrs. Tanner first. She wasn't home. Then I asked for Mr. Tanner. He wasn't home either. But the woman who answered the phone told me his first name was Gary. Gary Tanner. Ring a bell?" She knew she was taking her anger out on Dylan, but she didn't care. He'd been Gary's best friend. He must have known. And the anger was the only thing keeping her from screaming in pain.

"It does ring a bell," Dylan replied. "Did you know that Gary was named after his father?"

"What?"

"His father's name was Gary, too."

"His father is dead."

"Who told you that?"

"Gary told me that," she said flatly, her mind refusing to register this latest piece of information.

"Gary's father is alive. I spoke to him myself just after the funeral."

She couldn't believe what she was hearing. Nor could she seem to stop shaking her head in denial. "No, he's dead. He's dead."

"Your Gary is dead. His father is very much alive. And

he lives in Las Vegas with his third or fourth wife—I can't remember what number he's on now."

Gary's father was alive. Wesley had a grandfather somewhere? She had a father-in-law? No. It didn't make sense. Rachel sat back in the chair and crossed her arms in front of her chest. "You're lying. You don't want to tell me the truth. You said so from the beginning. Your loyalty is to Gary. It always has been. It always will be."

"I'm not lying about this, Rachel. Why would I?"

"Because Gary had another family." Her voice broke on the last word. She swung the chair around so she was looking out the window at her apple trees. She had to find some point to concentrate on, some peaceful focal point. But the trees blurred with the tears in her eyes. She couldn't see them. She couldn't find the peace, the harmony, the safe place.

Dylan came up behind her and swung the chair back around. He put his hands on the arms of the chair and forced her to look at him. "Gary didn't have another family. The number you called is his father's house."

"But his father is dead. Gary told me so."

"Then he lied."

She stared at him, searching his face for the truth. His gaze was unwavering. He looked like a man who had nothing to hide. But then, she'd always thought her husband had nothing to hide. Where were her instincts? Why couldn't she tell who was telling the truth and who wasn't?

"If he lied about that," she said finally, "then I don't know what to believe."

Dylan's face softened, his eyes filling with a kindness that only made her want to cry. "Gary and his father were estranged. To Gary, his father was figuratively dead. Just not literally dead."

The anger slowly seeped out of her, replaced with complete and utter disillusionment and an overwhelming feeling of hopelessness. "I can't do this. I can't."

"Yes, you can." Dylan grabbed her hands and pulled her to her feet. "But you have to stop jumping to wild conclusions."

"I can't help it. I don't know *what* to think!"

"Don't think anything. Put your conclusions away until we lay out all the facts." He squeezed her hands tightly in his.

And she found herself squeezing back. In fact, she found herself swaying forward, leaning into him. Before she knew it, her head was pressed against his chest, tucked right under his chin. His arms came around her, and she returned the favor. She needed his strength, and she selfishly took it.

He rubbed her back. "Let it all go, Rachel. Clear your mind. Stop thinking for a few minutes."

She tried to do that. She forced all the unwanted pictures out of her head and erased the confusing thoughts of the past half hour. Unfortunately, as the thoughts and the pictures exited her mind, she was left with only her senses . . . the musky scent of Dylan's aftershave, the feel of his chest against her face, the powerful muscles in his back where her hands clung to him. He was warm and solid and male, and she sensed an undeniable stirring of desire.

Guilt followed immediately, but she ruthlessly shoved it back. She was entitled to a few minutes of comfort, wasn't she? Did she have to do it all alone? Was it so wrong to want to rest in a man's arms for a brief time?

It was probably wrong to rest in this man's arms, especially with their history. But he was the only one here. He was the only one who understood. And, if the truth be told, he was the only one she would have allowed to hold her like this, to see her completely fall apart. She trusted him, she realized suddenly. Maybe that was a mistake, but it was the truth.

As the minutes passed and the comfort began to turn into something else, something that grew hotter and harder, Rachel forced herself to pull away. She tucked her hair behind her ears, feeling awkward and embarrassed now that they were face-to-face again. She couldn't tell what Dylan was thinking or feeling. His face was completely unreadable. A poker face. It suddenly dawned on her why he was here. He'd come for her grandfather's poker game, and she'd blasted him with wild accusations of bigamy.

"You must think I'm crazy," she murmured.

"I think you have a good imagination. I also think you're strung so tight these days that it doesn't take much to make you snap."

"I can't believe I thought Gary was alive and that he had another family. He wouldn't have done that. That's a movie of the week. That's not my life."

"Of course it's not."

"But I don't understand why Gary lied about his father being alive. Estranged or not, it would have made no difference to me."

"Maybe he thought you would have encouraged him to mend the relationship. You do put a lot of store in family."

"My family, not his. And what about you? Why is it you get to know everything and I don't?"

"So what? You're mad at me now?"

She sighed. "No, I'm mad at Gary."

"Good."

"Why is that good?"

"It means you're thinking about Gary like a real person and not a saint. He wasn't perfect. He had faults. He should have told you his father was alive. He probably should have told you a lot of things, but Gary didn't like to get personal. He was uncomfortable with emotions; he couldn't even stand to see a woman or a child cry."

"That's true. Gary couldn't stand it when Wesley cried. Said it made him feel helpless."

"There you go."

"But all these secrets, Dylan—they don't make sense. Maybe Gary didn't like emotion, but why hide basic facts? I knew his father ran out on him. So why couldn't I know he was still alive? I knew Gary went to Lake Tahoe, so why couldn't I know why he went there? I feel like I have only half of each puzzle piece. It's as if Gary gave me just enough information to keep me from being suspicious. But he's the last person in the world I would have thought would be secretive. He always seemed open, with not a care in the world. He could say 'I love you' without hesitation. He could kiss me in front of a roomful of people and not care what they thought. He could dance on the table with a lampshade on his head and not give a damn about the reaction. That's why nothing makes sense." She paused. "I think I'd like to talk to his father."

"I don't know if that's a good idea," Dylan said with a shake of his head.

"Well, you don't have to know. I don't need your permission to talk to my father-in-law."

Dylan held up a hand. "Take ten seconds and think about this."

"You just told me a moment ago not to think at all. Just go with my feelings. My feelings tell me that I should talk to Gary's father. He may not know Gary is dead."

"Actually, he does. He called me shortly after the accident looking for Gary, and I told him. He was shocked, but he hadn't seen Gary in a long time. And he said he wished he'd had a chance to tell his son how much he'd loved him, but he'd never been able to say the words."

"They must have spoken if Gary called him," Rachel said.

"His dad had asked him for a loan. Gary told him he never wanted to speak to him again. That was the last time they spoke apparently," Dylan replied. "He doesn't know anything, Rachel, at least not about why Gary went to Tahoe."

"Maybe you didn't ask him the right questions. You didn't know then what we know now." Rachel knew he didn't agree with her, but she also knew that she wouldn't be able to ignore the fact that Gary's father was alive. Nor could she ignore the fact that her husband had lied to her. She distinctly remembered Gary telling her his father was dead. If he'd lied about that, what else had he lied about?

"You're going down the wrong road," Dylan, said, interrupting her thoughts.

"I seem to be doing a lot of that lately."

"That's why I'm here—to keep you on track."

"Or to steer me in the direction you want me to go." Maybe she was wrong to think she could trust Dylan. She'd certainly been wrong about other things. It was disconcerting to realize that she'd always prided herself on being a good judge of character, but it was fast becoming apparent that she didn't have a clue about character.

"I think you should concentrate on the Tahoe trip for now," Dylan said.

"I will concentrate on the Tahoe trip. But I'm also going to talk to Gary's father."

"You're a very stubborn woman."

"I'll take that as a compliment. Are we still partners?"

"Yeah. Partners." He stuck out his hand, and she took it. His fingers tightened around hers.

"This is harder than I thought it would be," she said. "When I went to see you, I thought you'd be able to clear everything up in an instant. Then I'd go on the way I'd been going on. Nothing would change. It was naive of me to think like that. But I'm not very good with change."

"I like change. It means life is happening. There are choices, new directions. There are unexplored territories, uncharted possibilities."

There was an energy in his voice that told her he absolutely believed in what he was saying. And while she didn't doubt his sincerity, it surprised her, too.

"And here I thought you were a pessimist, a jaded cynic."

"A realist," he corrected her. "There's a difference."

"Is there? I always thought of Gary as an optimist and you as a pessimist."

"Why?"

"Because when we first met, Gary laughed all the time and you almost never did."

"That was a long time ago. I was getting my career off the ground. I had things to prove."

"To whom?" she queried.

He shook his head. "I don't know. To everyone, I guess. No one was particularly interested in paying for my college education. No one ever thought I'd amount to much. I wanted to prove them all wrong."

"Well, you did that."

"Yeah, I guess. It doesn't matter anymore." He let go of her hand, and it was only then that she realized how long he'd been holding it. "If you do call Gary's father back, I hope you'll keep something in mind."

"What?"

"Gary didn't want you to know him."

"I don't understand why."

"I don't think he wanted anything dirty to touch you."

"I'm not some princess living in a tower. I work in dirt every day."

"Not the kind of dirt Gary's father lived in." Dylan waved his hand toward the window. "This place of yours is like a Norman Rockwell painting. Gary told me that the first day he met you. He said he wouldn't have believed a place like this existed if he hadn't seen it with his own eyes. You have a history and roots that go back over a hundred years."

"You could live in a place like this. You could start your own farm if you wanted to. Anyone can plant seeds, put down roots."

"I don't belong in a place like this."

"Why not?"

"I like the city. I like to live where it's fast and busy and crazy and you don't have time to think. Out here, you can practically hear the grass growing."

"But there's a peace in that, a harmony to the seasons. You know to expect apple blossoms in the spring and hot nights in August, a bounty of fruit in the fall and cold, frosty mornings in winter. Predictability can feel wonderful, safe."

He stared at her as if she were speaking another language. Maybe she was. They were very different people with very different goals.

"That's what you want, Rachel? Safety? Predictability?"

"What's wrong with that?"

"It can be boring."

"Not if you're with the right people. What's so great about traffic and noise and being busy all the time?"

"You know you're alive."

"I know *I'm* alive. I have a little corner of the world. A piece of land that I cultivate and harvest. There's a beauty in that, don't you think?"

"Yeah," he said huskily. "There's a beauty in that. There's a beauty in you."

"I wasn't talking about me."

"You make me want . . ."

He didn't finish the sentence, and her mind shot ahead to complete it, but every finish seemed too dangerous to say out loud.

"Never mind," he said. "By the way, I looked over the plans. I'll start work on Monday. Travis will help me, and he gave me some other names as well. I think you'll be able to see some real progress in a couple of weeks."

"Okay," she said, not sure why she felt disappointed that their conversation had taken a right turn. It wasn't as if she wanted to have personal conversations with Dylan. It made far more sense to keep their relationship businesslike.

"I must say the plans were familiar," Dylan added.

"What do you mean?"

"Gary probably already told you this, but we used to ride our skateboards through this neighborhood in San Francisco and pretend that we lived in the houses there. It's where we first thought about what we wanted to do with our lives. There was one house in particular that intrigued us. I took a picture of it once and hung it on my wall. I told myself that one day I would build a house like that."

Rachel's smile slipped away as she thought about a Polaroid picture tucked away in one of the drawers.

"Hold on one second." She walked over to the filing cabinet and pulled out the file labeled "House." Her fingers flipped through the loose papers until she found what she wanted. She held it up for Dylan to see. "Is this it?"

"No way. It can't be. I lost that picture years ago."

"So this isn't the house? Because I found this photograph, and Gary told me that he'd always thought it was the perfect house for a family."

Dylan stared at the photograph in bemusement. "But it was *my* house. It wasn't his house," he murmured. "Gary liked another one. It was all windows, glass from floor to ceiling, and overlooked the ocean. It was spectacular. He said that was the kind of house he wanted."

Dylan seemed lost in memories, his voice hushed, as if he were talking to himself and not to her. Rachel didn't say a word, not sure she wanted to jar him out of the past. As soon as he remembered her presence, he'd probably stop talking, probably try to turn it all around. But it couldn't be turned around. Why had Gary chosen this house if it wasn't the house of his dreams?

Well, she knew why. Because she'd stumbled upon the photograph and exclaimed with pleasure over how perfect and beautiful the house was. She'd shown the picture to Wesley and he'd loved it. They'd gotten so excited, so caught up in the picture, that Gary had begun to draw before they'd even finished talking.

For her. He'd done it for her and for Wesley. But for himself? She wasn't so sure. Maybe the house of his dreams couldn't exist on the edge of an apple orchard in a small town. Maybe that's why he'd been willing to give in, because hadn't he given in already? Hadn't he joined her family in the Norman Rockwell painting? Or had he?

He'd told her he had kept the apartment in the city for purely logistical reasons, but had there been more to it than that? Had he needed to escape? If so, why hadn't he said that?

Dylan handed her the picture. "I guess there was a reason for the house feeling familiar. Although I'm sure Gary added some special touches just for you, Rachel."

She nodded, her throat thick with emotion. She slipped the photograph back into the folder. "I won't make any more calls tonight, but I think I will dive into the filing cabinet before I lose my nerve."

"Good luck."

"Thanks. You, too."

With Dylan gone, the study seemed colder than before. Rachel gave a little shiver as she turned toward the filing cabinet. She wondered if there were any other secrets to be found. Her instincts told her they weren't even close to the end. She yanked open the top drawer and ran her gaze along the file folders, looking for something, she just wasn't sure what.

Chapter 10

"I want to know all your secrets," Carly said, leaning across the dining room table. She gave Antonio her best sultry look, which apparently wasn't all that sultry, because it drew a smile instead of a kiss.

"What is this face you're making?" he asked. "Is the lemon tart too sour?"

Carly sat back in her seat and stared down at her dessert. "No, it's fine. I'm full from dinner. It was delicious."

"I'm glad you enjoyed it." His perfectly even white teeth sparkled in the candlelight. He was truly a stunningly handsome man, olive skin, black eyes, an adorable cleft in his chin. And his clothes were exquisite. No one ever dressed up around Sebastopol, but Antonio was wearing a charcoal-gray Armani suit with a starched white shirt and a grossly expensive silk tie. Carly felt a bit underdressed in her simple black cocktail dress, but it was the only thing she had that was halfway sophisticated.

"Now, why do you speak of secrets?" he inquired. "You sound so mysterious."

"You're the mysterious one. But I have to admit I like a man of mystery." Good heavens! Had that schmaltzy line just come out of her mouth? Well, she'd have to go with it. "You've lived all over the world. I bet you've known lots of women."

"A few." He smiled at her again, as if she were a mischievous child, and she frowned. This was not going at all the way she'd planned.

"How are your classes at college?" he asked, changing the subject. "Will you be graduating soon?"

"I have a few more courses to take, since I changed my major from history to business administration."

"An excellent major." He took a sip of his coffee. "No doubt it will be of much value in the operation of your orchards."

"I'm not planning to stay in the family business. I have other ideas."

"Really?" He lifted an eyebrow. "And your family approves of these ideas?"

"Of course; they're very supportive," she lied.

"I could never leave my family business. It is in my blood."

"But your business is so much more extensive than ours. You don't just operate wineries and vineyards—you have other interests as well, isn't that right?"

"Yes." He snapped his fingers. "Ah, now I think I see where this is leading. You wish me to offer you employment after you graduate, no?"

"No!"

He looked taken aback by her emphatic denial.

"I mean, no," she said more softly. "I wouldn't ask that

of you." She fell silent as Antonio's housekeeper entered to refill their coffee cups. Carly couldn't imagine having a servant. What an incredibly luxury. The only thing she'd had to do was open her napkin and place it in her lap—her white linen napkin, not even paper. She felt like Cinderella meeting the prince. It was all a bit unreal.

"Then what would you ask?" Antonio said when his housekeeper had left. "I know you've been eager to speak to me. I'm sorry I wasn't able to return your messages this week. I had to go to San Francisco to attend some meetings."

"Oh, that's all right. I know you're very busy."

"Is something wrong, Carly? Is it your sister, Rachel? I fear she works much too hard. And without a husband, she has no one to rely on. It is such a sad story."

Rachel was the last person Carly wanted to talk about, but then again, she had to come up with some reason for her persistent calls. She couldn't quite find the words to tell Antonio that she wanted him, and not just that she wanted him, but she wanted his life. "Actually, Rachel was one of the reasons I was calling you." She hesitated, searching her brain for a semi-plausible explanation. "I'm concerned about her reluctance to plant grapes. The apple market is struggling right now. I thought perhaps you could give her some advice." Rachel would probably kill her if he did, but Carly would worry about that later.

"Ah, it is a dilemma," he replied. "But I wouldn't presume to interfere in your sister's business decisions."

"Well, it's not just that," she said quickly. "I have another question for you."

"Of course. I am at your disposal."

God, he was so gallant. And the way he talked, so proper, yet masculine and powerful. When she was with him, she felt taken care of, protected, spoiled. Maybe he wasn't madly in love with her, but he could be. She just needed more time to persuade him to look at her like a woman and not like a kid sister.

"Excuse me, sir," the housekeeper said as she reentered the room. "You have a telephone call in your study. It's your father. He said it was urgent."

"I'm sorry," Antonio told Carly. "I'll have to take that. Papa can be very impatient."

"That's fine."

After he left, Carly got to her feet and wandered around the formal dining room. The house, originally built by the Rogelio family in the early 1900s, had been refurbished since Antonio's arrival. The room had lofty ceilings and arched windows. It was exquisitely decorated with a long mahogany table in the center, an antique sideboard against one wall and a slew of paintings that she was convinced cost more than a pretty penny.

For a moment she felt a twinge of uneasiness, but she pushed it away. So what if the room was a little dark, the furniture a little heavy, the smell of money a little too strong? She could get used to this life. She was sure of it.

The door opened behind her, and she turned with a smile. Her smile faded when she saw Travis enter the room instead of Antonio. He was dressed in his usual blue jeans and plaid shirt, his hair windblown, his cheeks ruddy from his having been in the sun. He was nothing like the urbane man she'd had dinner with, that was for sure.

Travis let out a low whistle when he saw her.

"Well, well, well," he said. "What do we have here?"

"What are you doing here?"

"Just picking up a check from Antonio. Where is he?"

"He had to take a phone call. He'll be right back."

"Then I'll wait."

She frowned as he settled down in her chair and had the nerve to actually pick up her fork and take a bite of her lemon tart. "What *are* you doing?"

"I thought you were done."

"Are you following me?"

He snorted a laugh. "As if I had time. I'm working three jobs as it is. Some of us actually work for money instead of trying to marry into it."

"Then why aren't you actually working? Why are you always turning up where I am?"

He swallowed before he answered. "Maybe you're the one following me. Yeah, that's it."

"As if."

"You look good in that dress. Sexy as hell. Antonio must have drooled all over the tablecloth."

She blushed, telling herself she didn't care what he thought.

"So how's the seduction going?" Travis continued.

"Fine."

"He doesn't have a clue. Come on, tell the truth. He doesn't have a clue that you're after him."

"Yes, he does. And I'm not the one doing the seducing. Antonio is. He's very suave."

"Suave, huh? There's a five-dollar word."

"Why don't you come back tomorrow, Travis? The banks aren't open tonight anyway."

"Tomorrow Antonio is leaving for New York."

Her jaw dropped. "He is not."

Travis grinned. "Yes, he is. Guess that doesn't sit too well with your plans, does it?"

"You're lying. You're trying to ruin my night."

He shrugged. "Whatever. This lemon thing is pretty good. Whatever happened to the apple pie?"

"My family ate it," she snapped, her mind still wrestling with this bombshell. Antonio couldn't be leaving tomorrow. She needed more time. Well, if she didn't have it, she didn't have it, she thought with renewed determination. She'd have to give him a night to remember, a night to think about changing his plans.

"Your family ate the pie?" Travis asked with amusement. "Boy, you're having a bad week."

"And you're making it worse."

"Does Antonio know about your portrait of him?"

"No, and you're not going to tell him. You're not going to tell anyone."

"I might forget. I might let it slip out. It wouldn't be on purpose, of course."

She sighed. "You're never going to let this go, are you?"

"Are you kidding? Blackmail, baby."

"I don't have any money."

"I don't want money."

She felt herself blush again. Damn. It was a very bad habit, and one she would definitely have to lose once she married Antonio. Sophisticated women did not blush.

"I'm never going to give you what you want," she said pointedly. "That can't be bought."

"Can't it? Aren't you trying to sell it to Antonio?"

"No. You just don't understand," she said in frustration, hating that he made her feel cheap and easy. It wasn't like that—at least she didn't think it was.

"Then explain it to me. Explain to me what Antonio has to offer you besides money."

"A different life, that's what. I told you before—I want to travel, to be someone, to fit in somewhere."

"You fit in here."

"No, I don't. I don't think I ever have. I've just been pretending. But I think deep down I'm just like . . ." She stopped herself from saying the word.

Travis's gaze turned more serious. "Just like who?"

She hesitated, then said, "My mother, if you must know. I think I'm like her. She had to follow her passion. And I have to follow mine."

He stared at her for a long moment. "You never knew your mother. How do you know you're like her?"

"I just do."

"Because you like to paint?"

"That, and other things."

"It sounds like you want to be like her. That doesn't make sense. She left you when you were a baby. You should be mad as hell at her."

"I am—sometimes. But that's just it, Travis. Everyone is mad as hell at my mother. No one will talk about her. Rachel knew her, but she won't share a memory. My father wouldn't even say her name. My grandparents pretend that she's dead. I'm the only one who wonders about her."

"I still don't get what this has to do with Antonio. Why don't you simply go look for your mother?"

"I couldn't do that. It would be a—a betrayal," she said flatly. "Everyone would hate me."

"I don't think they would."

"Well, I do, and I know them better than you do."

"So what? Are you hoping you'll marry Antonio and

somehow wind up in the same social circle as your mother? You don't even know if she's still alive, do you?"

Carly shook her head. "No, I don't."

"I think you need a better plan."

"My plan is not to find my mother. My plan is to marry Antonio and live a cosmopolitan life. Why shouldn't I want that? What's wrong with it?"

"Nothing is wrong with wanting that kind of life. But marrying a man you don't love isn't the way to get it."

"*He* will love *me*. I still have the apples."

"Oh, right, the magic apples. You don't really believe that story, do you?"

"Yes, I do. The magic has worked before. Why shouldn't it work for me?"

"Well, good luck getting Antonio to eat one. I think you'd have a better chance trying to push some caviar down his throat." Travis shoved back his chair. "Tell Antonio to leave my check with his housekeeper, would you? I don't think I have the stomach to watch you sell yourself tonight."

"That's mean. You make what I'm doing sound cheap and degrading."

"It *is* cheap. You're worth more, Carly."

"No, I'm not." Because if she'd been worth more all those years ago, her mother never would have left.

"Sure you are."

"I'm a flake. I'm a terrible student. I'm even worse at business. The only thing I can do, I can't do."

He looked confused. "What are you talking about?" He snapped his fingers. "The painting? Is that what this is about?"

"No," she immediately said.

"It is. My God, Carly, if you want to paint, paint. Why go after Antonio? Or is this still about his money? He can set you up, get your career going, is that it? Is that what he promises you?"

"He doesn't know anything about my painting, no one does except you, and I wish you didn't. I'm going to marry Antonio because he's my ticket out of here. If I get married, I can leave without feeling like I've betrayed my family. This is my chance, so don't blow it for me."

"Carly, I'm— Oh, Travis, you're here, too," Antonio said as he returned to the dining room. "My apologies for leaving you alone so long," he told Carly.

"No problem."

"I have your check, Travis. In my study." Antonio sent Carly another apologetic smile. "I will be right back, I promise. Then we can discuss what's on your mind."

"Take your time," she said, because suddenly she wasn't so sure exactly what was on her mind.

Antonio left the room first, but Travis paused at the door, giving her one last look.

"Don't sell yourself short, Carly. Just like that painting in your basement, you're still a work in progress. I think you could turn out to be spectacular. And Antonio is in no way your only chance."

His words left her reeling. Before she could respond, he was gone, and she was alone. She turned away from the door and caught sight of her reflection in the ornate mirror. She looked out of sync with everything else in the room, a cheap imitation, not the real thing. And she wanted to be the real thing, to have the real thing. She wanted to belong somewhere, but the real question was, did she belong here?

*   *   *

He did not belong in this big old barn with these good old boys, Dylan thought as he perused the cards in his hand. The conversation, as well as the beer, had been flowing for the better part of two hours. While he'd won more hands than he'd lost, he had the feeling that he was losing something else—maybe a little bit of himself. His city life seemed far away. He wondered if Gary had felt the same, if he'd hung on to his life in the city for reasons other than mere convenience.

The men at the table ranged in age from thirty something to seventy something, but there was a camaraderie among them, a sense of connection. They were either related or friends or business partners. Most important, they all seemed to be happy. Dylan couldn't remember the last time he'd sat with a group of people who weren't complaining about one thing or the other.

Here, there seemed to be an acceptance of life, whether they were talking about the disappearing apple-processing plants, the latest pest to attack their crops, the sudden heart attack of a good friend or even Gary's tragic accident. Maybe their acceptance came with farming, with relying on the seasons and the generosity of Mother Nature. Maybe that's where the sense of fate and destiny came from.

Another reason Dylan didn't belong here. He wasn't a man to leave his life to fate. He wanted to control every aspect of it, live every moment the way he wanted to live it. Just being here tonight made a mockery of that thought. He wasn't controlling anything right now, except perhaps this poker hand.

"You need any cards?" John Wood asked in his gruff, no-nonsense voice.

"No, I'm good," Dylan said as the deal continued

around the table. He bet when appropriate, his mind only half on the game. His thoughts kept drifting back to Rachel. He wondered if she was still going through her filing cabinet or had given up and gone to bed. He wondered if she'd found anything. His instincts told him something was wrong with the way Gary had died, with how his best friend had acted in the days before his death. But what was that something?

Dylan tossed in his cards when it became apparent he did not have a winning hand. "That's it for me," he said, getting to his feet with a stretch of his hands over his head. "I'm done. Thanks for allowing me to play. I enjoyed it."

There was a murmur of good-byes and see-you-arounds as he headed toward the door. It wasn't until he stepped outside that he realized John had followed him.

"A word with you," John said.

"Sure."

"Walk with me, would you?"

Dylan followed him across the yard and into the garage, wondering what on earth John had up his sleeve. He waited in front of a storage locker while the older man inserted a key into a padlock. Once the door was open, John hesitated. He scratched his chin as if he didn't know where to start.

"I've been thinking about something for a while now, especially since Rachel didn't get that insurance money. I've always respected a man's privacy. The women don't need to know everything, you know?"

Dylan didn't know, but he had a feeling that agreeing was his best option, so he simply nodded his head.

"I think Gary went to Lake Tahoe to see a woman," John said, surprising Dylan with his words.

"Why do you say that?"

John reached into the locker and pulled out a small jewelry box. He opened the lid to reveal a short gold necklace with a pearl in the center of a heart, lying on top of a small, folded piece of white paper.

"This was in the car," John said. "The police sent over a box after the accident with whatever was salvageable. I went through it myself. I didn't want to make Rachel do it. I found this in the box."

Dylan stared hard at the necklace, his gaze then straining to see the words inked on the other side of the paper.

"Go on, take it out. Read it," John urged.

Dylan slid the piece of paper out from under the necklace and opened it slowly. The writing was small and feminine.

"Gary—remember this? You said you'd always love me. Now I need you. Please call me back as soon as you can. Laura."

Dylan let out a breath as he finished reading the last word. "I don't know what to say."

"How about telling me who Laura is?"

"I don't know. Rachel asked me earlier about a Laura."

"Rachel knows about this?" John was shocked.

"Not this, no. Carly overheard a phone call between Gary and someone named Laura. She mentioned it to Rachel."

"Carly shouldn't have done that. She should be minding her own business. Rachel doesn't need to know about any of this." Her grandfather took the paper from Dylan's hand and folded it. "I want you to make sure she doesn't find out."

"Then why did you bring me out here?"

John looked at him through narrowed eyes. "So you can discover what happened before Rachel does. Then you can tell her what she needs to know and keep the rest from her."

"I'm not going to lie to Rachel."

John shrugged. "I didn't ask you to lie. Rachel needs to know Gary didn't kill himself. After that, I don't think she needs to know anything. She loved Gary. He loved her. That's all there was to it. Seems to me, being Gary's best friend and all, you'd like to see it turn out that way, too." He held up a hand as Dylan started to reply. "Don't say anything now; just think about Rachel and Wesley. That little boy thinks of his daddy as a hero. You don't want him to lose that, do you?"

"No," Dylan said slowly, his mind wrestling with this new wrinkle. "But Rachel is determined to figure out what happened, and this is a big clue. I don't know that I can keep it from her. I don't know that I should."

"Because you want her for yourself?" John barked. "I knew I was taking a chance showing you this, but—"

"I don't want her for myself," Dylan broke in. "What the hell gave you that idea?"

"I've got eyes."

Dylan ran a hand through his hair. Damn. John was a lot more perceptive than he'd given him credit for, a lot sneakier, too, keeping this necklace hidden away all this time. "You got anything else to show me?"

"Nope. You think about what I said, Dylan. I have an instinct about you says I can trust you not to hurt my granddaughter."

"That's the last thing I want to do."

"Well, telling her about this necklace will hurt like hell."

"And knowing you've been keeping it a secret all these months would probably hurt her even more."

John shook his head, his face a picture of stubbornness. "I did what was right. You didn't see her after the funeral. She was devastated. The last thing she needed to see was some love letter from another woman to her husband." He paused. "Don't tell her, Dylan. Just find out who this Laura is and make sure she stays in the past where she belongs."

"Rachel is already going through the phone records."

"Then stop her. If you love her like I think you do, you'll stop her."

"I don't love Rachel," Dylan said firmly, defiantly.

"Only one thing keeps a man away from his best friend, and that's his best friend's wife," John declared.

Dylan wanted to deny that fact, but John had already walked away from him. He took in a long, deep breath and let it out, trying to calm his raging pulse. Laura? Who the hell was Laura? He closed his hand over the jewelry box. Something else to hide.

A moment later, he walked out of the garage and into the moonlit yard. He glanced over at the house. Most of the lights were out except a couple upstairs. Rachel's room? Carly's? He saw a figure silhouetted against one of the curtains, a female figure, but he couldn't tell who. The light went out. He told himself to go, but he couldn't seem to move his feet.

Rachel was too close and the night was too still. It was so quiet he could hear the hum of a distant creek, the breeze blowing through the trees, the low bark of a neighbor's dog. None of the noises were familiar to him. He wondered if Gary had stood in this yard and felt the same sense of wonder that he had ended up here—in this place far from the city where they had grown up.

Had Gary looked up at the moon and the stars and wondered why they were so bright? Had he been happy in this idyllic setting or had he felt the pull back to the city, the pull back to the past? Had this Laura been a part of that past?

Who was she? Why didn't he know the name? Why hadn't Gary told him about her? Gary must have told him. He just wasn't remembering. And he had to remember.

Then what? Keep it a secret—or tell Rachel? Was his loyalty to her or to Gary? Damn. How had everything gotten so complicated?

"You were supposed to be the simple one," he whispered into the night, wondering if somewhere Gary was listening. "You weren't supposed to be able to keep a secret. That's why I never told you any. I knew you wouldn't be able to hold it in. But I was wrong about that. What else was I wrong about, Gary? What else?"

The sound of hammering grew louder as Rachel walked through the woods to her new house on Sunday afternoon. She paused at the edge of the trees, the back end of the structure just barely visible from her vantage point, but she could see the valley beyond and was reminded again of what a glorious view she'd have from her front porch and her upstairs bedroom balcony. Unfortunately, Gary wouldn't be there to share it with her, to sit on the balcony and sip a glass of fine wine and talk about their day, their son, their lives.

Although . . . it occurred to her now how rarely they'd ever done just that. There was a porch on the family house with a big, comfortable swing, but she could remember only a couple of occasions when they'd sat out there and talked. Maybe in the beginning, when they were "courting," as her grandmother had called it. But then marriage had come, and a child, and Gary's business had grown. The alone time had dwindled down to nothing. She hadn't really fought for it, hadn't insisted on it, and now it was too late.

Thinking of Gary brought Gary's father back into her mind. She'd called his number again this morning, but there was no answer, only an answering machine requesting that she leave a message. Her heart had stopped for a brief second when the machine picked up. She'd been afraid that the voice on the recorder would sound like Gary's, for surely a father and a son would sound alike. She could hear echoes of Gary in her own son's voice. The legacy of family. But the woman's voice on Gary Senior's recorder had been completely unfamiliar. And Rachel had hung up without leaving a message.

Rachel moved closer to the house. It was a warm Sunday afternoon, well past eighty degrees. The farm had been busy all day with tourists stopping by to pick their own apples, picnic, take a tour of the farm or browse in the gift shop. With a bountiful harvest, the trees were offering up many a juicy, plump apple, and fortunately for the family's financial coffers, the tourists had been coming in droves.

Normally Wesley enjoyed helping her with the visitors, but when Dylan had stopped by earlier to pick up some tools, Wesley had convinced Dylan that he needed his help. Rachel had tried to argue, but one look at Wesley's eager face had told her she was fighting an uphill battle. Her son was determined to get his house built, and Dylan hadn't seemed to mind the idea of Wesley's company.

Maybe it was good for the two of them to be together. Maybe Wesley felt closer to Dylan because of Dylan's long friendship with Gary. Or maybe it was bad for them to be together. Maybe Wesley would get attached to Dylan, only to be disappointed again when Dylan returned to his own life.

Rachel let out a deep sigh. There were suddenly far too many "maybes" in her life. And she was tired of worrying about all of them. In fact, she was just plain tired. It was time to relax, and she had just the idea, an early picnic supper with Wesley down by the creek. They could go wading, throw a Frisbee and be happy for a while.

She entered the house through the back door and called out a hello. The hammering didn't stop. When she walked into the kitchen area she saw Wesley and Dylan, and her heart skipped a beat. They looked like a father and a son. They were both wearing blue jeans and no shirt, both down on their knees, hammering a board.

It was the most incredible, poignant, touching picture she'd seen in a long while. She didn't know whether to laugh or to cry. And when they stopped hammering to look at her, she felt like laughing and crying at the same time. Because this picture in front of her, this beautiful family portrait, had the wrong people in it, and yet they were the right people, too. It was all so confusing.

"Hi, Mommy," Wesley said, bounding to his feet, his face alight with enthusiasm despite the sweaty dirt streaks along his cheeks. "We're getting a lot done today."

"I can see that," she murmured as Dylan stood up as well. She heard Wesley say something else, but she wasn't sure what. A bare-chested Dylan consumed all of her attention. His skin was twice as dark as Wesley's, his chest broad and muscular, with just the right smattering of dark hair that drifted down in a vee over incredibly flat abs. She halted her gaze right there and forced it back up.

"What are you doing down here?" Dylan asked somewhat sharply, as if he'd caught her wandering eye and didn't appreciate it.

"Lemonade," she said hastily, holding out the pitcher in her hand. "I thought you might be thirsty."

"I am," Wesley said, taking one of the paper cups from her other hand and filling it with lemonade.

"Why don't you give that one to Dylan?" she suggested.

"It's fine. I can get my own." Dylan took the pitcher from Wesley and poured himself a cup. He drank it all in one long swallow, then wiped the edge of his mouth when he was done. "Very good. Not store-bought, I'll bet."

"Squeezed from our very own lemon tree."

"You could sell this, you know."

She laughed. "We do sell it, along with everything else we can think of."

He smiled back at her. "Right, I forgot. You live on a farm. You grow your own vegetables, too, don't you?"

"My grandmother has the touch with the vegetable garden. She's far more patient than I am."

"I can grow tomatoes," Wesley said proudly. "And pumpkins and watermelon and squash. Can you grow anything?" he asked Dylan.

"Buildings. I grow buildings."

Wesley nodded. "I guess it's the same thing."

"In a way," Dylan agreed.

"How's it going?" Rachel asked as Wesley wandered away with his lemonade.

"Good. Just going over some of the basics today, making sure everything is where it should be." He grabbed his T-shirt off a nail and pulled it over his head. Rachel was both relieved and disappointed, then annoyed with herself for having any kind of reaction whatsoever.

"I hope Wesley isn't too much trouble."

"Not at all. He asks a lot of questions, but I like it. He's got an incredible mind. I bet he gets good grades."

"He used to. I'm not so sure what's going on now. In fact, I have a meeting with his teacher tomorrow. She said she had something important to discuss with me. I'm sure it's about Wesley's reluctance to admit Gary is dead." She glanced down the hall to make sure Wesley had moved far enough away not to hear her. "He keeps telling the other kids that Gary is coming back as soon as the house is finished."

"He'll figure it out," Dylan said quietly. "That's the way of things, you know."

"You're probably right. So how did the poker game go last night?"

"They cleaned me out. Your grandfather is hard to read."

"I'm glad you went. He liked having you there."

"I enjoyed it."

"Even though you didn't think you would."

He looked a little uncomfortable and she knew she'd hit the mark. "I must admit it was more fun than I thought," he said.

"So the country boys showed you a good time after all?"

"Poker is poker, no matter where it's played."

"But some things are better in the country, aren't they?" she teased.

He smiled. "Now, that sounds like a loaded question."

"Not at all."

"Yeah, right. Some things are definitely better in the

country, but I'm not sure poker is one of them. I found needles of hay in my shorts last night. Your grandfather doesn't seem to believe in chairs."

Rachel cleared her throat, not wanting to think about Dylan's shorts. "Hay can be softer than a chair."

"Really? Tell me, have you spent a lot of time rolling around in the hay?"

"Dylan!"

"Rachel!" he returned with a laugh. "It's a simple question."

"It's a personal question."

"Like you haven't asked some personal questions?"

"Okay, truce. We'll talk about something else."

"Fine. Tell me what you've been doing with yourself all day. Did you call Gary's father back?"

"He wasn't home. I didn't find anything in the files I went through last night. I still have to go through the boxes you brought me from the apartment. I didn't have time to do any more searching today. Sundays are busy. Not that I'm complaining. We can use all the business we can get. At any rate, things have quieted down, and it's such a beautiful day, I thought . . ." She hesitated. What on earth was she thinking? She was about to invite Dylan on her picnic supper. She couldn't do that. Could she? He looked hot and sweaty, and he'd been working hard all day, not to mention entertaining her son.

"And?" he prodded. "You have something on your mind?"

"A picnic," she said, throwing caution to the wind. "With Wesley and me, if you want. We go to the creek, take off our shoes and wade up to our knees. Not that you have to do that. But if you want to come, please do." She tried to make it sound like she didn't care one way or the other.

"A picnic, huh?" He looked as indecisive as she felt. "Are you sure that's a good idea, Rachel?"

"Probably not. Do you want to come anyway?"

Chapter 11

She'd asked him on a picnic. Dylan couldn't quite believe it. Nor could he believe that he'd accepted the invitation. But a half hour later, he found himself a passenger in a rickety old farm truck with Rachel in the driver's seat and Wesley in between them. In the back of the truck was a golden retriever named Rusty and an enormous picnic basket. Dylan had questioned the wisdom of allowing Rusty to guard the food, but Rachel had only laughed and told him there'd be plenty for all of them.

It wasn't really the food part he worried about, it was the all-of-them part that had his stomach rolling. This little picnic wasn't about the house or about Gary or about anything that had brought him north of the Golden Gate. He was losing his focus, and when he lost his focus, bad things happened. Just like the time nine years earlier, when he'd let himself think for a mere moment that Rachel was having second thoughts about marrying his best friend and that maybe he could slide in and change her mind. . . .

Rachel cast him a sideways look. "All you all right? I know the truck is kind of bumpy, but it handles the dirt road better than my minivan."

"It's fine."

"We're almost there anyway."

"Are you going swimming with us?" Wesley asked.

Dylan glanced down at his jeans. "I don't have my suit."

"You don't need a suit. Mommy and I go swimming even if we don't have suits."

The thought of Rachel romping nude in a stream did little to ease Dylan's discomfort.

"Wading—we go wading," Rachel corrected her son, a flush creeping up her cheeks. "Not skinny-dipping."

"Too bad. That sounds kind of fun." Dylan was pleased to see he wasn't the only one whose thoughts had taken a wayward turn.

"Mommy went skinny-dipping once," Wesley said.

"Wesley, Dylan doesn't want to hear that story."

"Oh, I think I do."

"It was after midnight," Wesley began impressively. "Mommy and her friends were supposed to come home right after the dance, but they stopped at Sullivan's Lake and took off all their clothes and went swimming. Mommy got grounded for a year. Aunt Carly said Sam Waterstone saw her—"

"Wesley!" Rachel interrupted. "Sam Waterstone did not see anything; I don't care what Aunt Carly told you. And I didn't get grounded for a year. It was for a month."

Dylan laughed at her chagrin. "You were a wild thing, weren't you?"

"I wasn't, and no one saw anything," she said defensively.

"Or so they told you. Who is Sam Waterstone? An old boyfriend?"

"Just a local kid who took me to a dance. That's all."

"So you were a skinny-dipper—interesting."

"It is not at all interesting, and it was one time. I didn't make a habit of it."

"You never did it again, not even with Gary?" Skinny-dipping certainly seemed like an activity that would have appealed to Gary.

"No. Gary didn't like to swim."

Gary didn't like to swim? Since when? Dylan caught Rachel's gaze, but she gave a firm shake of her head, and he let the subject drop. A few minutes later, she pulled the truck over to a large tree and shut off the engine. As soon as they were out of the vehicle, Wesley and Rusty went running down the path toward the creek, leaving Dylan to carry the picnic basket and Rachel to carry the blanket.

"Gary loved to swim," Dylan said.

"He didn't have time on the weekends. There always seemed to be too much to squeeze into Saturday and Sunday."

"Then why not say he was too busy?"

"Because Wesley heard those words too many times. They started to mean something else, like 'I'm too busy to be with you.' It was easier to say Gary didn't like to swim."

Dylan frowned, not liking what he was hearing. "Gary was too busy for his son? I don't understand."

Rachel's expression indicated she was sorry she'd brought it up. "The last few years Gary was only home on the weekends, and even then he was often catching up on work," she explained. "Like a lot of fathers, he didn't have extra time to play with Wesley. And they never really seemed to be on the same wavelength. Wesley's constant questions used to drive Gary crazy."

"He's a curious kid, but that's great."

"You've only been around him for a few days," she said with a shrug. "I'm sure the constant questioning would get on your nerves, too."

"I don't think so," he said flatly. "I don't think Wesley gets on your nerves either. You have a great relationship."

"Well, it's been the two of us for a while now."

"And you're not just talking about since the funeral, are you?" He could see the discomfort in her eyes, the guilt, as if she didn't want to say one bad thing about Gary. He supposed he could understand the loyalty, even though he thought that in this instance, it was misplaced. Then again, Gary's distance from his son didn't make sense.

Gary had always longed for a father's love. It seemed strange to Dylan that he wouldn't have doted on Wesley, his only son. And what about that "only"? Why hadn't they had more children?

"I'm not criticizing Gary," Rachel said.

"No, you wouldn't, would you?"

She cleared her throat. "At any rate, I appreciate your letting Wesley work with you today. It meant a lot to him. I think he feels closer to his dad when he's with you."

"Is that the way *you* feel?" Dylan asked, not sure he liked being a stand-in, or whatever she wanted to call it.

She hesitated, then shook her head. "No, I don't feel closer to Gary when you're with me. If you want to know the truth, I feel even farther away."

He met her gaze head-on. "Do you want me to leave?"

"Do you want to go?" she countered.

"No."

"Then you should stay." She turned away and spread out the blanket. Dylan set the picnic basket down and began unpacking it. Rachel talked about the weather and the creek. Dylan nodded and asked questions when needed. Through it all, underneath it all, he felt like they'd just crossed over the line they'd been so desperately trying to stay behind.

Two hours later, Dylan lay back on the blanket and rubbed his stomach. The sun was going down, turning the sky into a dusky blue. There were only a few wispy clouds overhead, but even those seemed to be disappearing into the night. He felt full, sated and more relaxed than he'd been in weeks. It probably had something to do with going barefoot in a creek, with the blades of grass pushing up between his toes, and throwing a Frisbee to an eight-year-old and a dog.

It was the most unsophisticated outing he'd been on in years, but maybe—just maybe—it was one of the most enjoyable. And they'd laughed—a lot. More than he would have expected. Rachel had a whole slew of jokes that Wesley had prodded her into telling, obviously a favorite ritual between them, since Wesley often jumped in with the punch line before Rachel could get the words out.

They'd begged Dylan for new jokes, but in searching his mind for something appropriate, he realized that he didn't know any jokes he could tell to an eight-year-old. He realized, too, that he hadn't spent much time laughing in the past few years. Nor had he spent much time arm wrestling, trying to catch butterflies with a net or watching the way a woman smiled with genuine pleasure.

This was family, he thought. The kind of family he'd always wanted. The kind of family Gary had gotten. But had he cherished this family? Dylan had always believed that—until now.

Would it get old, this low-pressure, low-tech life? Had Gary grown tired of it? Had he wanted out when he'd always thought he'd wanted in?

"You're doing it again," Rachel accused, interrupting his thoughts. She stretched out on her side, her head propped up on one elbow, facing him.

"Doing what?"

"Thinking. Your brows get pointed and your lips get tight."

"They do not," he said, but he could feel his eyebrows drawing in.

Rachel laughed. "It's okay. You're entitled to think, although we might have burned out all your brain cells with silliness. Wesley hasn't been this playful in a long time." Her gaze drifted over to her son, who was back to throwing the Frisbee to Rusty. "I hope he'll have more of these happy moments in life than sad ones, you know?"

"He will. You'll make sure of it. Even if you have to dig up some more dirty jokes."

"They were not dirty. They were all rated PG."

"I bet you know some dirty ones," he said.

"I'm not that kind of girl. You, however . . ."

"Me, however, what?"

"You'd probably never tell a dirty joke in mixed company. You're too gentlemanly."

"That sounds dull," he said, feeling vaguely irritated by her comment.

She laughed again. "You try to compliment a man, and he turns it into an insult. Gentlemanly is a good thing."

"Exciting is better," he said with a wink in her direction.

She blushed, and he smiled, propping his own head up on one elbow as he turned onto his side. They were face-to-face now, closer than was wise, but neither one of them pulled back.

"I like how you do that."

"What?" she asked, a nervous, edgy note in her voice.

"Blush like an innocent girl."

"It's a family trait. Even Carly turns red at the least provocation. And my grandfather can still make my grandmother blush with just a smile."

"A knowing smile, I'll bet. They seem very much in love."

"They are. They've been together fifty years."

"That's amazing."

"Yes," she said quietly. "What are we doing, Dylan?"

"Talking?" He reached out and tucked a piece of hair behind her ear. He saw a leap of something in her eyes. His heart wanted to call it desire. His head knew better than to call it that. But there was something between them, something unspoken, untried; something better left alone, no doubt.

"Mommy!" Wesley squealed. "Rusty got all wet."

Rachel sat up and Dylan followed. They looked at Rusty, who sat in the middle of the stream, the Frisbee in his mouth.

"I guess he needed a bath," she called. "Come on back now, Wes. We need to pack up and get home. You have school tomorrow."

"I haven't heard those words in a long time," Dylan muttered.

"We lead different lives," Rachel said as she began to put away their things. "But you already knew that."

"Yeah, I knew that." He grabbed her wrist. "The line is back, isn't it?"

"It never went away."

"I think it did—for a few hours anyway."

"I can't be on my guard all the time."

"I don't want you to be on your guard with me."

"I can't help it. I don't know what to do about you, Dylan," she whispered. "You make me feel things I don't want to feel. You always have." She pulled her arm away and got to her feet. "Rusty, come here, boy," she called.

And as Rachel surrounded herself with a bouncing dog and an equally bouncing boy, Dylan understood that she'd just put on an armor he couldn't possibly penetrate. Nor did he know if he even wanted to. She might not know what to do about him, but he had even fewer ideas on what to do about her.

Carly stared at the open drawers in the filing cabinet, the pile of papers on the desk and the boxes on the floor. An uneasy feeling made her stomach turn over. Rachel was looking for something. But had she found it?

Probably not, Carly decided. If she had, surely she would have said something to someone. Despite the evidence of a search, Carly suspected that Rachel still didn't know what had happened to Gary.

Maybe she should tell her more of what she knew. But if she did that, she'd have to tell Rachel how she'd gotten the information. She couldn't do that. Rachel wouldn't understand.

Only Gary had understood. And Gary had understood because he was more like her than he was like Rachel, yet Rachel couldn't see that.

Carly didn't want to be the one to tell her that either. In

fact, she regretted her earlier outburst. She never should have mentioned the phone calls from the mysterious Laura. But she'd wanted Rachel to stop shutting her out. Judging by the chaos in the study, she was afraid she'd opened a door that couldn't be closed again.

Speaking of doors, the front door of the house slammed, and Carly heard Rachel tell Wesley to go upstairs and wash up. Then her footsteps came down the hallway, pausing in front of the door to the study. Carly turned around, feeling somewhat nervous as Rachel entered the room.

"Oh, you're here," Rachel said. "I can explain all this."

"Did you find something?"

Rachel hesitated. "Some phone numbers I didn't recognize."

Carly wondered if one of those numbers belonged to Laura. It still bothered her that Gary hadn't told her who Laura was. She'd thought they were close friends, confidants. But on the subject of Laura he had been silent, unusual for him, which had made his behavior even more disturbing.

Rachel sat down behind the desk. "What a mess. I have to get a better filing system."

Carly perched on the edge of the desk. She picked up a phone bill upon which Rachel had circled several numbers in red. "Did you call any of these?"

"One," Rachel admitted.

"And?" Carly prodded when Rachel didn't continue.

"The number belongs to Gary's father. He apparently lives in Las Vegas."

"What? Gary said his father was dead. Why would he lie about it?"

"Who knows?"

"Did you speak to his father?"

"No, but Dylan confirmed the fact he is alive."

Carly stood up and began to pace. She felt strangely betrayed by the information. She'd trusted Gary with her darkest secret, but he obviously hadn't trusted her. Of course, she didn't have nearly as much right as Rachel did to feel betrayed. She wasn't Gary's wife, only his sister-in-law, but still, the lie stung. Actually, it didn't so much hurt as make her mad. "What the hell was he thinking?" she said out loud.

"I don't know. Families aren't supposed to lie to each other. Husbands and wives, especially, are not supposed to lie to each other. Trust is the foundation of a relationship. And I thought we had trust. I thought we had truth."

Carly looked away from the pain in Rachel's eyes, knowing that she hadn't been completely honest either. "Maybe he thought he was protecting you," she muttered. Because wasn't that *her* reason?

"Protecting me from what?" Rachel lifted up the file folder. "I wonder if the answer is somewhere in here, or maybe it's in Gary's apartment, or maybe it's in one of the boxes sent home from his office. Maybe it's in my own bedroom, and I've been walking right past it."

"You do have a tendency to put blinders on. I'm not saying that to hurt you. But sometimes you don't see what's right in front of you."

"Meaning what?"

"I'm not sure Gary was as happy living here as you were."

"Did he tell you that?"

"He didn't have to. I saw the smile on his face every Monday morning. He was eager to get back to the city."

"To get away from me," Rachel said, a dismal note in her voice. "That's just what I needed to hear, Carly."

"I'm sorry. Maybe you're not as ready for the truth as you think you are."

"Maybe I'm not," Rachel said with a sigh. "So what happened with Antonio? Did you feed him an apple yet?"

"No. He went to New York. He'll be back on Tuesday."

"Ah, a reprieve, time for you to come to your senses."

"I have all my senses in fine working order," Carly retorted. "I want that man, and I'm going to get him."

"Such single-minded determination. If you could only turn it in a more productive direction."

"My plan will be very productive. You'll see. Just like you, I'll get the man I want."

Rachel frowned. "About that, Carly. I was younger than you, and possibly even more foolish, which I'll admit now. You should learn from my mistakes. Don't rush into this. Get to know Antonio. If it's meant to be, it will be."

"I don't have that kind of time. He's leaving for good in a couple of weeks."

"And you're going to leave with him? How can you do that? Won't you miss us?"

"Of course I'll miss you. I love you." Carly stumbled over words that she always meant to say but never quite got around to saying.

"I love you, too. I would miss you terribly if you left."

"But I can't stay just because you'll miss me," Carly said.

Rachel suddenly looked stricken. "God, you sound just like Mom. 'I can't stay just because you'll miss me.' " Rachel shook her head in bewilderment. "I think that's what she said to me. 'I'll miss you, darling, but I have to go, and you have to let me go.' As if I had a choice in the matter. She was going no matter what. And you are, too, aren't you?"

"Well, not yet," Carly said, panicking. "Not yet."

Rachel's gaze bored into hers. "You really hate it here so

much? Do you think that's how Gary felt? Am I some kind of a monster, holding people back from their dreams?"

"You're not a monster, Rach. You just love really deeply when you love. Sometimes your grasp gets too tight."

"Because if I don't hold on, people leave. I never did believe in that old saying—'If you love something, let it go free, and if it was meant to be yours, it will come back to you.' Because nothing, no one, ever seems to come back. And apparently it doesn't matter how tightly I try to hold on. I just can't keep the people I love in my life." Rachel paused. "The blinders are finally off, Carly, and this time they're off for good."

Chapter 12

Rachel wanted to put the blinders back on late Monday afternoon, along with a good, strong pair of earplugs, because she couldn't believe what she was hearing. This had to be wrong. Mrs. Harrington, Wesley's teacher, had to be wrong.

"The test scores are very accurate, Mrs. Tanner." Mrs. Harrington tapped her number two pencil against the score sheet in front of her.

"But no one has ever said anything before. I don't understand." Rachel gazed at the test scores that had just turned her world upside down. She'd always known Wesley was bright, but not this bright.

"He is very gifted, Mrs. Tanner. Wesley is a third grader reading at a tenth-grade level. He answered every single one of his math problems correctly, ten percent of which involved calculations not taught in our school until the sixth grade. He didn't miss one, not one."

"Maybe he just got lucky or the test was too easy or something. I mean, he's a smart kid, but—"

"He's more than smart. He's truly remarkable."

"I don't know what to say."

"You'll need to think and do some research, but I'd be happy to help you in any way I can."

"Research? What would I be researching?" Rachel asked awkwardly. Mrs. Harrington frowned. She was probably wondering where Wesley had gotten his brains, definitely not from Rachel's side of the family, judging by how many times Mrs. Harrington had to repeat herself.

"Schools, of course. This is a wonderful elementary school, but we don't have the technology, the science labs, the art classes, the math projects that will stimulate and challenge Wesley. There are some very good small, private schools in San Francisco. I can give you a list if you like."

"Wesley isn't going to change schools," Rachel replied, dumbfounded by the suggestion. "We live here."

"I understand it's a lot to digest all at once. But I hope you'll think very seriously about making a move. Your child deserves a chance to challenge his incredible mind."

"Couldn't you move him up a grade?"

"I'd have to move him up to middle school at the very least, and that would be difficult socially and emotionally."

"Middle school? He's eight years old."

"Exactly. That's why he needs a special school where he can be with children his own age who are also very bright. If he stays at his grade level in our school, he'll simply be bored and probably lose all interest in learning, and who can blame him? I have twenty-seven other children to consider. I don't have the time to give Wesley extra projects, not without it coming at the expense of the other children."

"I don't know. I can't think right now. I bet that sounds funny. I'm the mother of a genius, and I can't even think."

"It's understandable. It's a lot to take in all at once." Mrs. Harrington pushed a file folder across the desk. "I've collected some information that will get you started."

Rachel took the folder but didn't bother to open it. She doubted she could read a word with her mind spinning the way it was. She'd come to the conference thinking it was about Wesley's reluctance to admit his father was dead, not about his IQ or some tests that he'd taken. He'd always done well in school. He'd read at an early age, but she hadn't noticed anything abnormal. Had she been wearing blinders with Wesley, too?

"Mrs. Tanner?"

"What?" Rachel started, realizing that the teacher was regarding her with some concern.

"Are you all right? You look pale."

"I'm fine. Thank you."

"There is something else," Mrs. Harrington began. "While Wesley's test scores are exceptional, in the past week I've noticed a deterioration in his actual schoolwork. In fact, today he deliberately misspelled several words on a spelling quiz. Words that he had spelled correctly three times before."

"Okay, now I'm totally confused."

"I believe Wesley's determination to stick to his fantasy of his father's eventual return is due in part to his extreme intelligence. For the first time in his young life, Wesley doesn't want to believe the facts in his head. So he's rejecting them. Perhaps he believes that if he's right about the spelling, his brain might be telling him the truth about his father, which is unacceptable. So he purposely makes errors."

"Wesley doesn't want to believe himself? Is that what you're saying?"

"Yes. Although I'd highly recommend that you speak to a counselor who has greater training in this area than I do. Of course, that's up to you. Wesley is a wonderful child, a bit more complicated than most, but perhaps that's the other side of genius."

"Genius," Rachel echoed, still not believing that word could possibly relate to her son. She got to her feet, desperate to leave before Mrs. Harrington told her something else she didn't want to hear.

"I'm available if you wish to speak further about this," Mrs. Harrington added as Rachel opened the door.

"Thank you." Rachel walked out into the hall and shut the door behind her. Wesley sat at a table in the hall. He didn't even look up at her, so engrossed was he in coloring something on a piece of paper.

The sight reminded her of her mother. In her mind she could see her mother with a paintbrush in her hand, completely absorbed in her work. Now it was Wesley with a crayon in his hand, completely absorbed in his work. Neither one of them looked over at her, and she felt them both slipping away. Oh, God!

But this wasn't the same situation. It wasn't even close. She pulled out a small chair at Wesley's table and sat down.

"Hi, there," she said, forcing any hint of anxiety or panic out of her voice. "What are you doing?"

"Do you like my picture, Mommy?" Wesley moved his hand so she could see his drawing. It was a house, a house very much like the one they were building. His drawing was excellent, too, the lines straight, the curves in the right places. There was a purpose to the sketch, a sense of planning and organization. It could have been drawn by a much older child or maybe even an adult. Maybe even his father.

"It's very good," she murmured.

"Does it look like the ones Daddy draws?"

"Yes, it does. Maybe you'll want to be an architect when you grow up."

"And work with Daddy." He sent her a defiant look. "I can't wait till our house is done and Daddy comes back to live with us. Then we'll be together all the time, not just on the weekends."

He dared her to deny that claim. She could see it in every taut little muscle in his body. "I can't wait until the house is done either," she said. Maybe she did need to take Wesley to a counselor. She didn't know whether to keep correcting him or just let him accept things in his own time.

"Am I in trouble?" Wesley asked, changing the subject when he failed to get the reaction he'd been expecting. "Is that why Mrs. Harrington asked you to come in?"

Rachel shook her head. "You're not in trouble. But I would like to know why you spelled some words wrong on your test when you knew the right spelling."

"I forgot," he mumbled, avoiding her gaze.

"Really? Or did you stop trying?"

"It's just a stupid quiz. And the words are stupid, too. They're too easy."

"So you did know how to spell them?"

"I guess. Are you mad at me?"

How could she be mad at his sweet angel face, his expression so clearly worried as he was caught between defiance and confusion? So she did what she'd wanted to do all along: she pulled him into her arms and gave him a hug. She still couldn't believe her little boy was a genius. Where would he have gotten those genes? She'd never been more than an average student in school. And her father hadn't put much store in test grades. Which left only Gary or . . .

Not her mother! Definitely not her mother.

Her mother had been an artist, not a math whiz. Although Rachel remembered her father using the same word, "gifted." He'd once said her mother was a gifted artist. And her mother had left because of that gift.

Now they wanted her to take Wesley to some place where he could use his gift. But their home was here. This was where they lived, where they would always live. She couldn't uproot her child. Especially not now. They were building their dream house, for heaven's sake. They were going to live there together. Wesley wouldn't want to go to a private school. Even if she wanted him to, he wouldn't. There had to be some other solution.

"Can we help Dylan work on the house now?" Wesley pulled away from her arms with another show of independence. "I promised to help him after school."

"What about your homework?"

"I already did it."

"You did?"

He nodded and reached into his backpack to remove several sheets of math problems. "See?"

Rachel ran her eye down the problems, noting the neatness and accuracy of his answers. "Did you do this in class?"

"No, I did it while you were talking to Mrs. Harrington. It was easy."

"So it didn't take you very long?"

Wesley shrugged. "Nope."

"Do you have anything else?"

"I already read the story and answered the questions, too. I'm done, so can I go see Dylan?"

Rachel glanced at the clock on the wall. It was three-fifty-five, and she'd begun her appointment with Mrs. Harrington at three-twenty. In thirty-five minutes Wesley had finished three pages of math problems, read a short story and answered questions about it, not to mention drawing an incredibly detailed picture of a house. Had he always been this fast, this creative, this confident about his homework?

She certainly hadn't thought about it before. But then, she hadn't thought about much in the past six months beyond getting on with her life and making sure Wesley was reasonably happy. Now she felt guilty for not noticing. Even Dylan had remarked on Wesley's intelligence and he'd barely spent any time at all with him. She had to start opening her eyes and ears. She had to start listening, and seeing what was happening right in front of her.

"Mommy?" Wesley asked uncertainly. "Are you okay?"

"I'm okay," she answered with a smile as she ruffled his hair with her fingers. "Let's go home."

"To our new house?" he asked with a persistence that couldn't be denied.

"I have a better idea. Ice cream." Wesley looked disappointed, so she added, "Chocolate in a waffle cone dripping with hot fudge sauce, and we'll sit at the counter and spin on the stools."

His eyes lit up. "Okay."

Ice cream wasn't exactly a stiff drink, which was more along the lines of what Rachel needed, but then again, chocolate had always been her drug of choice.

"Can we have two scoops?" Wesley asked.

"We can have three." It was the easiest decision she'd made all day.

"Can I buy you a drink?" Dylan asked the young woman sitting across from him.

Beth Delaney patted her stomach, where he noticed a small bulge. "I'm afraid nonalcoholic only."

"Congratulations."

Her face lit up with a bright, joyful smile. "Thank you. Mike and I are so happy. We've been trying for three years."

"When are you due?"

"In the spring."

He looked up as the waitress came to take their order. "A beer for me and a—"

"Seltzer," Beth answered. "Thanks." She folded her hands on the table. "Now, do you want to tell me just why you're buying me a drink?"

"It's about Gary," he said. "As his secretary for the last few years, you might be able to help me with something."

"Does this have something to do with Gary's cell-phone bills?" Beth asked, the previous pleasure in her face completely gone. "I spoke to Rachel this morning. She asked me to send her copies of the bills. She wouldn't say why, and I hesitated to ask."

Dylan waited as the waitress set down their drinks. The bar was getting crowded; the large iron clock in the corner struck five-thirty. Soon, happy-hour would be in full swing and J&B's Bar was one of the hottest happy hour spots in downtown San Francisco. He and Gary had shared many a cocktail here over the years; the bar was just down the street from Gary's office.

He didn't remember the place being this loud, this

chaotic. Probably because he'd spent the past few days in the country. Last week he would have told anyone who asked that this was the kind of noise he preferred, this energized bar filled with intense and ambitious people, passionate about their careers, living life in the fast lane. Now he wasn't so sure.

"Dylan," Beth continued after the waitress left, "can you tell me what's going on?"

"I can't," he said. "But I need to know if Gary told you who he was going to see in Lake Tahoe the weekend he died."

Beth didn't answer right away. He saw a battle going on behind her green eyes. She'd always been devoted to Gary.

"He didn't say exactly," she said. "But he was worried about something, Dylan. The two weeks before he died, he was taking off at strange hours, usually after he got a phone call from a woman named Laura."

Dylan's heart sank to the floor. Laura again? Who the hell was she? "Laura who?" he asked. "Do you know a last name?"

"No, and I was irritated that she wouldn't give me one. At first Gary seemed reluctant to take her calls, but then he made it clear she was to be put through to him wherever he was."

Dylan took a sip of his beer. "Do you think he went to Lake Tahoe with this woman?"

"I don't know, Dylan. He mentioned something about a party. I didn't ask. It was the weekend."

"What was his mood, Beth? Was he happy, worried, depressed?" He still couldn't get the idea of suicide out of his mind. It certainly didn't seem plausible, but neither did this thing with another woman.

Beth ran her finger around the edge of her glass. She

seemed to be choosing her words carefully. Why? Was she trying to protect Gary? A loyal secretary to the end?

"He was nervous," she said. "And Gary was never nervous. He was the most confident, happy, daredevilish kind of guy I'd ever met. He didn't take things to heart. He didn't get stressed when problems arose. I marveled once that his blood pressure was probably zero. He just laughed and said he'd live longer that way." She bit down on her lip. "God, I can't believe I just said that."

"It's okay. He'd probably laugh if he heard you."

"I miss him so much, Dylan. They reassigned me to Harry Trent, if you can believe it."

"Old Harry? Ouch."

"I'm thinking about quitting after I have the baby." She paused. "How is Wesley doing? I used to love hearing Wesley stories. Gary was really proud of his boy."

"He's a great kid," Dylan replied. "I wish Gary could see him grow up."

"Me, too. Have I told you what you wanted to know?"

He smiled but shook his head. "No, but thanks anyway."

"I told Rachel I'd fax her copies of Gary's cell phone records. Would you like me to send them to you, too?"

"That would be great."

Beth gave him another long, thoughtful look. "Do you think Gary was having an affair?"

"Do you?" he countered.

"I never called him at a motel, if that's what you mean."

"You never called him on anything but his cell phone; he could have been anywhere."

"I think he really loved Rachel. Although . . ."

"Yes?"

"I'm not sure I could have put up with my husband staying in the city during the week and only coming home on the weekends. I used to tell Gary to take off early some days and go home. He always acted like he wanted to, but then something would come up. He said Rachel was the most understanding wife in the world and the best thing that ever happened to him. It always sounded like true love to me."

"Yeah, true love." Dylan raised the beer bottle to his lips and took another swig. It didn't taste right. This bar didn't feel right. He had the sudden urge to go home, but it wasn't his apartment he was thinking about, it was the house in the country that called to him.

"Thanks for the drink," Beth said, getting to her feet. "I should go home. If you need something else, let me know. And if you see Rachel, tell her again how sorry I am, would you? I didn't really know her, but I felt like I did after hearing Gary talk about her. She sounded pretty special."

"She is special," Dylan agreed. Pretty damn special.

She couldn't possibly be missing Dylan, Rachel told herself as she loaded the dishes after dinner Tuesday evening. The man had avoided her for nine years. There was certainly no reason that she couldn't go two days without seeing him.

But the two days had seemed endlessly long. She'd stopped by the house three times, hoping to find him there. Instead she'd found Travis and a plumber. Travis had said that Dylan had run into San Francisco to tie up some loose ends. What loose ends? Had he changed his mind about finishing the house himself? Travis seemed to think he'd be back soon, but maybe Dylan wasn't coming back at all.

He would have told her if that were the case. He wouldn't have left her hanging. Would he?

Rachel wiped her hands on a dishtowel and walked out of the kitchen. Wesley and Carly were watching television in the family room, and her grandparents had retired to their house after dinner. Pushing open the front door, she stepped onto the porch and took a seat on the swing. It was a beautiful night, filled with bright stars, a big old moon and a cool breeze. Rachel shivered, wrapping her arms around herself. She needed a coat or a blanket or a man's arms, she thought with a yearning that stretched down deep into her soul.

But there was no reassuring voice coming out of the darkness, no strong male upon whose shoulder she could rest her head. She was alone, a truth she had to face. She wasn't a wife anymore. She was a widow. But she was still a woman. A woman alone.

Some would say she wasn't really alone, not with her grandparents nearby, her sister and child living in the house with her, an assortment of cousins and aunts and uncles in the surrounding few miles, but still she felt lonely. In recent years she'd been too busy for girlfriends. Heck, maybe she'd been too busy for her husband. And why had she been so busy? Had her priorities been wrong? Had she spent all of her time trying to save the farm, save the family, when she should have been more concerned with saving herself and her marriage?

But she hadn't thought she was in trouble.

Now she knew she was in trouble. There was no doubt about it.

"Rachel?"

She stiffened when a male voice did come out of the darkness, but it wasn't Dylan's voice, she quickly realized. It was her grandfather's.

"Yes," she said as John came into view. He walked up the steps and sat down next to her on the swing.

"You should have turned the porch light on. I could hardly see you," he said.

"I like the dark."

"Easier to hide in, that's for sure."

"You think I've been hiding? Carly said the same thing earlier. Why didn't you tell me before? Why didn't you grab me by the shoulders and give me a good shake?"

John put his arm around her. "I think you've spent a lot of time and effort trying to make everyone in this family happy. Now it's time to concentrate on yourself."

"But I should have concentrated more on Gary. Maybe if I'd made him happy . . ." She couldn't finish the sentence or the thought.

"You did just fine by Gary. Don't be thinking you short-changed him in any way."

"It's hard not to think that. I'm beginning to realize that my husband was not as happy as I was."

"That wasn't for your lack of trying."

"I guess not."

"Is something else bothering you, Rachel?"

She supposed she should tell him about her conversation with Wesley's teacher, but she couldn't quite make herself bring up the subject. Once it was out in the open, she'd have to make a decision, and it was too soon for that. "I'm just restless," she said instead. "I feel keyed up, and I don't know why. It's as if I'm waiting for something to happen, but I don't know what."

"Dylan came by earlier this afternoon," John said abruptly.

"What did he want?"

"He didn't say. Just asked you to give him a call. I meant to tell you at dinner, but I forgot. Thought I better come back in case you want to call him tonight."

"Thanks." She tried to ignore the little jump in her pulse. Dylan was back. Well, that answered one of her questions. Unless he'd come back to tell her he was leaving, or to tell her something else—something about Gary? She shook her head as the thoughts chased each other around in a circle, making her dizzy.

"Are you all right, Rachel?" John asked.

"I'm hanging in there. Can I ask you something, Grandpa?"

"Sure."

"Do you think you know Grandma? I mean, really know her."

"Nope."

"You don't? Not even after fifty years of marriage?"

"Everyone has secrets, including your grandmother, including me."

"You? What secrets do you have?"

He laughed. "If I told you that, they wouldn't be secrets."

"Doesn't it bother you to think that Grandma might be keeping something from you?"

"Well, I'll tell you something. About ten years ago I came across a picture of a young man in your grandmother's Bible. I flipped it over, thinking it was some family member of hers, but on the back it said, 'Margie, I'll always love you, Andy.' " He shook his head. "Andy? I had never heard of an Andy. We'd been married forty years and Marge never once mentioned an Andy, but she'd kept his high school picture in her Bible all those years."

"Did you ask her about it?"

"Damn right I did. Shoved that picture right in front of her face and told her to come clean."

That sounded like Rachel's no-nonsense, serious-minded grandfather. When he had a goal, he went after it one hundred and fifty percent.

"Who was he?"

"An old flame, she said. They were sixteen when they met, but after graduation he went into the military and was killed in a training exercise."

"That's so sad."

"Marge said she didn't love him, just liked him a lot and still felt a sadness that he'd never gotten to grow up and fall in love, the way she'd fallen in love with me."

"Did you believe her?" Rachel asked, sensing something in her grandfather's voice.

"Not for a second. I think she still has a place in her heart for that Andy. That's why she kept his picture and why she never said. She didn't want to share him with me, because she didn't think it had anything to do with me."

"Did you feel the same way?"

"Hell, no. I was jealous. Still am, if the truth be told. But he's long gone, and I'm still here. I've got the woman I love, so I figure in the long run I'm doing a whole lot better than that poor guy."

"Why are you telling me this?"

"Because you're worrying about Gary. And you shouldn't be."

"I didn't find an old picture, Grandpa. I found a perfume bottle in his apartment." She couldn't see John's expression, but he didn't seem all that surprised. "It probably means nothing," she said tentatively.

"Probably doesn't," he quickly agreed. "Maybe he bought it for you."

"It was already half empty. And the worst thing is that I can't ask him. I can't go to Gary and ask him like you asked Grandma. What if you'd found that picture after she'd died? What would you have thought?"

"I don't know. I'd probably try to remember the good times. When you get to be my age, Rachel, you realize that life is about going on. People die, they leave sometimes, they screw up your life. But you just keep putting one foot in front of the other, breathe in and out and try to be happy."

"That sounds easier than it is."

He patted her on the shoulder. "It will sort itself out. Just don't put Gary under too harsh a light. Not many of us could stand the glare."

"Not even me," she muttered. For didn't she have her own secret? Wasn't there a moment in her life that she hadn't shared with Gary?

Her grandfather got to his feet with a stretch and a groan. "Lord, I'm getting old."

"No, you're not. You'll always be young."

He smiled. "Don't forget to call Dylan."

"I won't. Thanks. For everything." After he left she stood up and went into the house. Picking up the phone on the hall table, she dialed the number of Dylan's hotel. It was busy. Making an impulsive, probably foolish decision, she grabbed her sweater out of the hall closet and paused in the family room doorway. "I need to go out for a while," she told Carly. "Can you get Wesley into bed for me?"

"Where are you going?" her sister asked.

"I have to talk to Dylan about a few things."

"Why don't you call him?"

"The line is busy, and frankly, I could use a little air."

"Can I go, too?" Wesley asked as he looked up from his television program.

"No, honey. It's a school night and it's almost bedtime."

"But I want to ask him about the house."

"I'll find out how it's going."

Wesley turned his attention back to the television. Carly, however, still had her gaze fixed on Rachel.

"Is something going on?" she asked.

Rachel shook her head. "It's probably nothing."

"Be careful, Rach. I'm not certain you and Dylan want the same things."

Chapter 13

Dylan stared at the monitor on his laptop computer, disturbed by the information Beth had sent him earlier that day. Gary had received many incoming calls from Lake Tahoe, Nevada, on his cell phone, beginning almost six weeks before his death. Dylan had already called the number several times, but either it was busy or there was no answer and no answering machine. The number had to belong to a residence, which only made him that much more suspicious.

He didn't want to believe that Gary had been unfaithful, but the numbers were adding up to that inescapable conclusion. Still, it was circumstantial evidence, he reminded himself. A perfume bottle, a lace teddy, a necklace, a phone call from a woman . . .

He hated the doubts running through his head. He wanted to believe what he'd always believed: Gary loved Rachel.

It was a fact Dylan would have bet his life on. Actually,

he *had* bet his life on it. He'd walked away from Rachel, kept their kiss a secret, stayed out of their marriage, because he'd wanted them to be happy together. He'd wanted Gary to have the storybook ending. Now he wondered if it had all been for nothing.

Had Gary and Rachel been happy? There seemed to be too many discrepancies in the story of their marriage.

The knock at his door startled him. The voice that followed surprised him even more. He strode over to the door and flung it open. Rachel stood in the hallway wearing faded blue jeans and a peach-colored tank top, her blond hair flowing loose about her shoulders. For a second he wondered if he was dreaming; she was the last person he'd expected to see.

"What's wrong?" he asked immediately. Surely she wouldn't have come here unless there was an emergency of some sort. "Is it Wesley?"

"Nothing's wrong," Rachel stuttered. "Why?"

"What are you doing here?"

"My grandfather said you called."

Right. He had called, but he'd expected her to call him back not appear at his door.

"Can I come in?" she asked.

Could she come in? He flung a quick glance over his shoulder at the modest hotel bedroom, made even smaller by the king-size bed he'd requested. There was no reason that she couldn't come in. They were friends, partners. But he still wanted to say no. Self-preservation, he realized. No matter how many times Rachel told him she didn't want him, that didn't lessen his attraction to her.

"Dylan?" she questioned.

"Come in," he said gruffly, waving her into the room. "You could have just called."

"The line was busy."

It was obviously an excuse, but he let it go.

Rachel hesitated uncertainly in the middle of the room. "I heard you went to San Francisco."

"I needed some more clothes." He tipped his head toward the two suitcases he had yet to unpack. "It looks like I'll be staying a while."

"Was that the only reason you went to the city?"

"I had to stop in at my office, make sure my jobs are proceeding smoothly and on schedule."

"They must wonder what the heck you're doing up here."

"They're not paid to wonder."

She smiled. "Now, *that* sounds like a boss talking. You have a large company, don't you?"

"Over thirty full-time employees and a couple hundred independent contractors."

"Wow. I'm impressed."

"You should be," he said with what was probably a ridiculously proud grin. But he was proud of what he'd accomplished. And it was nice to finally share it with Rachel. In many ways she'd been the impetus for much of his success.

Rachel walked over to the desk and sat down in the chair he'd just vacated. "Looks like you brought your work with you." She glanced at his computer. "I'm sorry if I'm disturbing you . . ." Her voice drifted away as she read what was on the screen. "What's this?"

"I asked Gary's secretary for his cell-phone records."

"I already did that."

"I know. I spoke to Beth yesterday."

"And she sent the records to you instead of to me? I don't understand."

"I thought she was going to fax them to you, too."

Rachel shook her head in amazement. "I can't believe she went to you before me."

"We've been friends a long time."

"And she worked for my husband a long time. Her loyalty should be to me, not to you."

"Look, Rachel, we're in this together. What does it matter who she sent them to? I called you earlier so we could go over what they contain. I'm not holding out on you. We're partners."

She wanted to believe him, but there were so many lies in her life right now. So many shadows that hid what she wanted to see. "All right," she said at last. "What did you find?"

"Numerous calls to a number in Lake Tahoe, a personal residence. I haven't managed to connect with anyone yet. It could be nothing."

"Or it could be something. It could be the clue we've been looking for. Let's call the number again now."

"It's late."

"It's not that late." She moved toward the bed and picked up the phone receiver. Then she hesitated.

Dylan wondered if she could go through with it. Despite her brave words, he often sensed an ambivalence in her, as if she wasn't sure she wanted to learn the truth. "Want me to do it?" he asked.

"No. I have to do it. I just don't know what to say. *How do you know my husband? Why were you calling him eight months ago? Were you sleeping with him?*" She sat down on the edge of the bed. "What do I say, Dylan? Tell me what to say."

He shook his head. "I don't know. Maybe you shouldn't call tonight. Another day won't make a difference."

"It will to me. I won't be able to sleep. Not that I ever sleep anymore."

"Then you better make the call."

She stared at him. "That's the difference between you and Gary. He would have persuaded me to put down the phone. He would have laughed off the coincidence. He would have told me he'd take care of it. And I probably would have let him."

"I think you can handle it, Rachel."

"Why on earth would you think that? What could have possibly given you the impression that I can handle anything?"

"Because you can," he said steadily. "You're a strong woman. Strong from the inside out."

"I think I have you fooled."

"I think you have yourself fooled."

"I don't know who I am anymore, what I want, what I need. It's all mixed up in my head. Part of me wants to know. Part of me doesn't."

"Which part is winning?"

She glanced at the phone. "Give me the number," she said, squaring her shoulders.

Dylan read it off the screen as she dialed. He dug his hands into his pockets, feeling anxious, as if they were about to take the wrapper off something that could explode in their faces.

"It's ringing," she told him. "Maybe no one is home. Oh, hello."

Dylan started as he realized she'd made a connection. Was it Laura? Was it someone else?

"Um, I was wondering," Rachel began, tripping over her words. "Who is this?" She paused. "Who am I?" She looked over at Dylan, pleading for an answer. He pointed to his ring finger and saw her glance down at the wedding ring Gary had placed on her finger nine years ago. "I'm— I'm Gary Tanner's wife," she said, her voice gathering strength. "I saw your number on Gary's phone bill, and I wondered who you were. What?" She paused again. Her face paled as she listened, and Dylan had to stop himself from ripping the receiver out of her hands. "Wait," Rachel said. "Don't go. Hello? Hello?" She slowly set down the receiver. "She hung up."

"What did she say?"

"She gasped when I said Gary's name. Like I'd just brought someone back from the dead."

"What else did she say?"

"She said, 'My relationship with Gary is over. Don't call here again.' They had a relationship, Dylan, some kind of relationship."

"You don't know what kind," he told her, forcing himself to go to Gary's defense when what he really wanted to do was put his arms around Rachel and hold her until the end of time.

"I think I do. I think you do, too," she said with a note of defeat in her voice. She got to her feet and came over to him. "I think we just found the owner of that perfume bottle."

"Rachel, you don't know."

"Don't I?"

"We need to find out her name and who she is and all the rest." He stopped as she put her hands on his waist. A reckless gleam had entered her eyes. "What are you thinking?"

"I'm not thinking," she said, her gaze fixed on his face. "I don't want to think anymore. I don't want to pretend or tell lies or draw lines between us."

She pressed her body against his, her breasts flirting with

his chest. He had to fight to keep his hands in his pockets.

"This isn't a good idea," he managed to get out, even though his body was telling him otherwise.

"It's the best idea I've had all day. Kiss me, Dylan."

"No."

"Kiss me, Dylan," she repeated yearningly, her gaze drifting to his mouth.

"No." But he wavered inside. Why shouldn't he take what she was offering? Why shouldn't he indulge? Because she was scared and confused and hurting, that's why, he told himself with ruthless determination.

"Don't you want to?" she asked.

"I won't take advantage of you."

"Then I guess I'll have to take advantage of you." She stood on tiptoe and put her mouth to his.

His eyes closed at the contact, the delicious, unbearably sensuous contact. He wanted to pull away. This wasn't the right time, the right moment, but damn if her mouth wasn't working his in the most incredible way, her sweet kiss turning to pure sin as she opened her mouth and invited him inside.

And he went. God help him, but he went, sweeping her mouth with his tongue, tasting her from the inside out.

She wrapped her arms around his neck and pulled him as close as she could get, her soft hips cradling him, her legs intertwining with his. It was better than any dream he'd ever had about her. If he'd been a better man, a stronger man, he would have pushed her away, but in truth he was just an ordinary man who'd wanted her for a long, long time.

He put his hands on her waist, his fingers bunching the material of her shirt, a shirt that covered her curves, curves that he wanted to travel, and travel slowly, caressing every last inch of her. But they had too many clothes on. He wanted nothing but skin, nothing but her.

Rachel moaned restlessly as if she also wanted more but wasn't sure how to get it. They moved toward the bed, stumbling slightly as they hit it with their legs. A second later, he was lying on top of her and she was looking up at him with desire in her beautiful blue eyes.

Desire for him? Or revenge against Gary?

He suddenly wasn't sure. Did she want him? Or did she just want to prove something?

"Don't stop," she whispered, cupping his face with her hands. "For God's sake, Dylan."

He didn't want to stop, but the voice in his head grew louder. It was too fast, too soon.

"We have to." The words came out before he could stop them, his mind winning out over his heart and his body. He got up before the other parts of him could argue that she wanted him and he wanted her, so what the hell was he acting so noble about?

"Dylan?" She propped herself up on her elbows, her face a picture of hurt. "Don't you want me?"

"Not like this," he said sharply. "Get up. For God's sake, get up." He walked away from her and stared out the window, trying not to think about the look on her face, the expression of shame and embarrassment. Embarrassment for what they'd done or what they hadn't done?

"I'm up," she murmured from behind him. "And I guess I'm leaving, if that's what you want."

He whirled around. "Did you even know who you were kissing just now?"

"I'm pretty clear on who you are, but I guess I was wrong about what you wanted. No surprise there. I seem to be consistently wrong these days."

"You weren't wrong. I do want you. I always have. That's why I stayed away from you—so I wouldn't have to see you, wouldn't have to think about you. It's hell wanting someone you can't have, knowing they're with someone else, loving someone else, loving your best friend." He ran a hand through his hair, annoyed with himself for the words that had just come from his mouth.

"I'm sorry." She reached for him, but he sidestepped her touch. He couldn't handle that now. Not if he wanted to keep his wits about him. Her hand dropped to her side. "I didn't know. I thought you'd moved on."

"I didn't want you to know. You married Gary, end of story."

"If it was the end, we wouldn't be here right now."

"We're here because of Gary. We've always been to-gether because of Gary."

She didn't say anything, just stared at him with an ex-pression that he couldn't read. Well, what did it matter? He knew what he had to say and he would say it. "Even though Gary is dead, he's still between us. I won't be his stand-in. I won't be the way you pay him back for the affair you think he had."

"It wasn't like that," she protested. "I wasn't making you a stand-in."

"Yes, you were. You were angry with Gary. You wanted to punish him. That kiss had nothing to do with me. I know you didn't come here tonight to make love to me."

She didn't reply right away, then said quietly, "Are you sure about that?"

"Yes," he said forcefully. He couldn't let himself believe she'd wanted him for himself.

Rachel picked her purse up off the bed, "You're wrong, Dylan. I'm afraid that's exactly why I came here tonight.

And I'm also afraid that kiss didn't have anything to do with Gary."

Rachel's mouth still burned two hours later when she lay in her bed, the moonlight pouring in through the curtains of her open window. If Dylan hadn't stopped, she would have made love with him. And she probably would have hated herself for it.

He'd been right to call a halt. She was too confused to be making love to any man, especially Dylan. She hadn't even consciously considered the idea until she'd been in the middle of kissing him. Then it had seemed like the absolutely right thing to do. But how could it be right?

She turned over, reaching her hand across the queen-size bed, resting her palm on the space where her husband had once slept. He hadn't been beside her in months, six months. And they hadn't made love in more months than that. In fact, there were two creases in her mattress, one for her body, one for his, the middle of the bed rising slightly between the indentations made by two people who had slept beside each other, but not together.

When had that happened? When had they stopped meeting in the middle? When had sleep become more important than making love?

She couldn't remember a specific day, a big argument, a frustrating fight. She couldn't remember any of those things. There should have been something significant to recall. Otherwise it would mean that they had just drifted apart. What kind of wife let her husband just drift away? What kind of man let go of his wife?

They had loved each other. She knew that deep in her heart. But the passion between them, so fiery in the beginning, then tender after Wesley was born, had turned into something more comfortable than lustful. She'd enjoyed making love, but a distance had grown between them, and they couldn't seem to breach it. Just having weekends together wasn't enough for her to feel emotionally connected.

Making love had become unimportant. And that wasn't right. She realized that now. Why hadn't she realized it then?

And why did it seem to matter now—with Dylan?

How could she want another man so soon?

Maybe because she'd always wanted him?

Rachel felt her cheeks grow warm with guilt, embarrassment and shame. How could she have jumped on Dylan that way? She'd asked him for a kiss, and he'd said no. Instead of accepting that, she'd kissed him. Why? Out of lust? Out of revenge? Out of loneliness?

Maybe it had been a little of each.

Her feelings for Dylan had always been complicated.

At first he'd just been Gary's best friend, a friend who didn't appear to like her all that much. That had changed as the three of them began to spend time together. Their weekends had been filled with parties and adventures, canoe trips down the Russian River, dancing at the local club in town, sometimes driving up to the University of California at Davis, where Gary had even more friends.

It had been three months of pure, unadulterated fun. But in retrospect, Rachel realized that while Gary was busy being the life of the party, she had been with Dylan. She couldn't remember what they'd talked about, but she could remember feeling smart and challenged and provoked by their conversations.

Yes, her feelings for Dylan had always been complicated, from their first meeting to that painful conversation the night before her wedding. Even now she could remember feeling anxious and light-headed. The lights were too bright, the music too loud. She'd escaped to the restaurant veranda for a breath of fresh air . . .

Rachel leaned against the concrete wall and looked out over the moonlit valley. It was difficult to find the peace she craved. The rehearsal dinner was in full swing in the private room behind her.

She tried to calm down, but inside, the butterflies in her stomach did somersaults. What was she doing, marrying a man she barely knew? Gary was handsome and sexy and fun, but would he be happy living on the farm?

She had to believe he would, because she didn't want to leave. She couldn't leave. The farm was where she belonged, the only place she belonged.

She turned, hearing someone step out onto the veranda. It was Dylan. Her heart sped up as he came toward her. She didn't want him here now. He saw too much.

But she couldn't stop him from moving closer, couldn't say the words that would send him back inside, couldn't do anything but meet his dark, questioning gaze.

"It's not too late, Rachel," he said, his face in the shadows. "You can have second thoughts."

The words terrified her. "Of course it is. I'm getting married in the morning."

"Does Gary know how scared you are?"

"I'm not scared."

"Your mouth is trembling."

"It's not."

He touched a finger to her lips and they quivered even more. "There's no crime in waiting, making sure."

"Gary is a good man," she said desperately.

"The best," Dylan agreed. He cupped her face with his

warm, strong hands. "But you have to be sure, Rachel. This is too big a step not to be sure."

"I know," she whispered. She looked into his eyes and saw the glitter of desire, the gleam of recklessness as his head drifted down toward her.

She had plenty of time to move, but she didn't. She had plenty of time to say no, but she couldn't. It seemed to take forever for his mouth to touch hers, each second strung out like a long, taut wire, until finally, finally, he kissed her.

His mouth was hot and firm, stubbornly determined. He didn't taste like the bubbles and champagne she associated with Gary; he tasted like a dark red wine, mysterious, potent. His mouth moved against hers, pushing her lips apart until his tongue could slide inside. She melted into him, her tongue dancing with his, her hands holding his head as he was holding hers, their hips stirring restlessly against each other. It was the most carnal, passionate kiss of her young life, and it scared her to death.

What was she doing? This was Dylan. This was her fiancé's best friend.

He must have come to the same conclusion at the same time, for he pulled away with a rough and furious "No."

They stared at each other for a long moment. Then she went back inside, telling herself that she loved Gary. And she wouldn't look back at the man in the moonlight. She wouldn't.

Chapter 14

Dylan filled Wednesday, Thursday and Friday to the brim. He hired electricians, plumbers, Sheetrock workers and carpenters. He bought supplies and tools, set up accounts in town and met with the appropriate building department inspectors. When he wasn't working on the house, he was working on his other projects, in constant contact with his office and his crews in the field.

But every day, come three-thirty, he found himself looking around for a short, blond, freckle-faced kid who had become his afternoon shadow. Today was no exception, he thought, wiping the sweat off his forehead as he checked his watch. It was three-forty-five. Wesley was late. He hoped nothing was wrong.

He supposed he could call Rachel. He hadn't spoken to her at all since she'd left his hotel room late Tuesday night. He was a coward, that's why. He hadn't known what to say, how to act, so he'd avoided her. But he couldn't avoid her forever. They still had the issue of Gary's death to deal with, and yet another complication that he needed to share with her.

Might as well be now, he decided.

After asking Travis to make sure the tools were secured in the locked shed he'd put on the site the day before, he hopped into his car and drove over the hill to the apple farm. He stopped at the house first and found Wesley waiting on the step with a small suitcase and a sleeping bag.

"Hey, buddy," he said. "I was wondering where you were. Are you going somewhere?"

"The Cub Scouts are having a camp-out by Sullivan's Lake," Wesley said with a heavy sigh at the end of his sentence.

Dylan sat down next to him. "You don't sound too excited."

Wesley shrugged. "It's a father-and-son camp-out."

"Oh, I see."

"Grandpa is going with me."

"That's good."

"I guess. He can't go hiking because of his arthritis. And he won't be able to do the three-legged race or the swimming relay with me. He says the lake water is too cold for him. I don't even want to go on the stupid camp-out, but Mom says I have to." He added another sigh just in case Dylan couldn't tell how unhappy he was.

He needn't have bothered, because Dylan had a pretty good idea of how he was feeling. Dylan hadn't had a dad around to do the father-son things either. Once or twice his stepfather had filled in, but he'd made it clear he didn't want to be there.

"So how long do you go for?" Dylan asked.

"Just one night. We come back tomorrow at five." Wesley paused. "Hey, Dylan?"

"Yeah?"

"Do you think you could go on the camp-out with me?"

"Uh . . ." Dylan didn't know what to say. He wasn't Wesley's father. He didn't belong on a father-son camp-out, that was for sure. But there was a pleading look in Wesley's eyes that told him how much the boy did not want to go with his elderly grandfather. "I don't know, Wes."

"Please. Grandpa doesn't want to go anyway. He'd be happy if you took his place. And you could do all the cool stuff with me, the hikes and the swimming and everything."

"But you'd have fun with your grandfather."

"Right." Wesley rested his head on the sleeping bag in his arms.

He looked completely dejected, and even if half of it was an act, Dylan couldn't help but respond. "Where's your mom?"

"She's making us some food to take."

"I'll be right back."

Dylan went into the house without bothering to knock, a habit he'd only recently begun to acquire, but it appeared that locked doors and knocking irritated people out here in the country; they preferred you just let yourself in and help yourself to whatever you needed. He'd never lived in a house like that, and it still didn't feel right to him to be walking down Rachel's hallway without her knowing it, but he pushed the feeling aside and ventured into the kitchen. He found her half hidden behind the freezer door.

"I'm almost ready, Wesley. I just have to fill the ice

chest," she said, shutting the door. She stopped when she saw him. "Dylan."

"Hi."

"Hi," she said with a breathless catch in her voice.

He'd thought a couple of days would be enough to banish the memory of their last kiss, but seeing her now, her lips softly parted, her gorgeous blue eyes focused on him, he was taken right back to where they had been. And he wanted her—again. He shouldn't have sent her home. He should have taken what she'd offered. He still remembered her parting words. Had she actually told him that she'd come to his hotel room to make love to him? Or was he remembering it the way he wanted to remember it?

He'd told himself he'd been right to stop. If he hadn't, they would have made love. And they both would have been sorry.

"What are you doing here?" Rachel asked.

"Oh." He had to think for a moment. Why was he here? Wesley, that's why. "I came to see if something was wrong. Wesley didn't show up at the house, and I was worried about him."

"He's fine. He's going on a camp-out."

"Yeah, I saw him on the porch."

"Oh." She paused, licking her lips. "Then was there something else?"

He hesitated. "Is your grandfather excited about this camp-out?"

"Hardly, but he doesn't want Wesley to miss out. Why do you ask?"

"I was thinking that maybe I could go in his place."

Rachel looked shocked by the suggestion. "I don't think so. You're not Wesley's father."

"I'm not trying to be," he said slowly. "Wesley is concerned that your grandfather won't be able to keep up. He asked me if I could go instead."

"He doesn't want to go with his grandfather?"

"His great-grandfather," Dylan reminded her. "He's eight years old, Rachel. John seems like a million years old to him."

"I didn't realize. Why didn't Wesley say something to me?"

"He probably doesn't want to hurt anyone's feelings."

"But he can talk to you." She shook her head in confusion. "I guess that's good."

"We've become friends, bonded over hammer and nails," he said. "It's a guy thing." He wanted to take the pressure off her. She tried to be all things to Wesley, but she couldn't. It was too much to ask anyone to be a perfect mother and a perfect father at the same time.

His words drew a smile from her. "A guy thing, huh? And this camp-out is a guy thing, too?"

"Oh, yeah, we'll pound our chests, howl at the moon, make a fire. We'll be in hog heaven."

"Sounds like a fabulous time," she said with a short laugh. "I guess you can go if you're sure you want to. I better call Wesley. Wes—"

Dylan laughed as Wesley came bursting through the kitchen door, He'd obviously been eavesdropping.

"Can Dylan go?" Wesley asked eagerly.

"Yes, he can go."

"Yea!" Wesley cried, launching himself into Dylan's arms.

Dylan laughed and swung the boy up off the floor. "I think I need some stuff, though."

"What kind of stuff?" Wesley asked.

"A sleeping bag and a pillow."

"We have a couple extra," Rachel said as Dylan lowered Wesley to his feet. "Why don't you go get them, Wesley? And tell your great-grandfather he's off the hook."

Rachel stared at Dylan after Wesley left the room, an expression on her face he couldn't quite interpret.

"What?" he finally asked.

"Wesley really likes you."

"I'm a likable guy. Don't sound so amazed."

"Sorry. You know, last year's Cub Scout camp-out was the last thing Gary and Wesley did together. Gary tried to get out of it, but he just couldn't come up with the right excuse."

"Gary hated to camp. He was like a girl when it came to sleeping on the ground with bugs crawling around him."

"Hey, I think I resent that girl comment," she said with a grin. "I am a very good camper."

"Well, your husband wasn't."

"No, he wasn't." The smile slipped off her face. "I don't feel like we're getting very far very fast, Dylan. I should call that number again or do something. I've been putting it off, but I can't keep doing that."

"Speaking of that number, I called it again yesterday. I should have done it the day before. It was stupid not to."

"Did you talk to the woman again?"

"I didn't talk to anybody." He paused, hating to deliver more bad news, but he had no other choice. "The phone number was changed, Rachel."

She took a step back, her hand going to her heart. "I don't understand."

"She had her phone number changed to a private number after she spoke to you. My guess is she didn't want to take a chance that you'd call her back."

"I still don't get it."

"She could be married. She could have children. She could be protecting someone."

"Protecting them from me?" Rachel shook her head in bewilderment. "Why do I feel like I'm in the wrong?"

"You're not in the wrong, but you might be in the way."

"What do we do now?"

"Well, I'm going camping. I think you should look through every drawer and box in this house that belonged to Gary. It's time, Rachel. What do you say? Deal?" He stuck out his hand.

"You don't know what you're asking."

"I think I do."

She stared at his hand for a long minute, then finally slipped her hand into his. "Deal."

Her fingers were warm and curled around his. He wanted to pull her closer. It took everything he had to let go. He moved to the door. "Do I have time to run into town and change my clothes?"

"Sure. In fact, they're meeting in town at the steps to City Hall. The mayor is one of the dads. You can take Wesley with you and stop at your hotel on the way, if you want. Unless you think I should come along."

"No, I can take him."

"You know, people are going to wonder about you . . . and about me."

"We're friends, Rachel. That's all they need to know."

"But not all we are," she murmured. "You can lie to them, Dylan, but don't lie to me, okay? I can't take any more lies."

Rachel spent the evening as she'd promised Dylan, going through the drawers and closets of her life. She'd done a halfhearted job a few weeks after the funeral, but nothing since. Then, she hadn't wanted to throw anything away or to make changes. Now she didn't know why she'd resisted the chore. Gary was gone. Keeping his clothes in her closet wouldn't bring him back. But as she'd told Dylan once before, she was a pack rat by nature. And throwing things away did not come easily.

More than once she found her eyes tearing as she picked up something of Gary's, a pair of cuff links she'd given him on an anniversary, his favorite bottle of cologne, the gold watch he'd inherited from his grandfather that would one day go to Wesley. They were just things, she told herself. Without them she would still remember the way Gary smiled, the way he hugged, the way he snored, the way he laughed, the way he loved.

The tears in her eyes finally spilled over, and she sat down on the bed and cried for everything she'd lost and everything she would miss. For the first time in six months, she let herself think and feel and remember. Each memory hurt more than the last, each thought made her heart break and the tears stream down her face, but she stopped fighting and let them come. When she was finally spent, she felt like a wrung-out sponge. There were no more tears left. She was empty. Completely empty. It felt good.

The weight was lifted from her shoulders. The queasiness was gone from her stomach; the sense of having to stay in control had disappeared. She went into her bathroom, blew her nose, washed her face and decided to get on with the task at hand.

When Carly came home around ten, Rachel had filled two large plastic bags with Gary's clothes, as well as a couple of boxes. She was just about to go through Gary's jewelry box when Carly paused in the doorway.

Rachel smiled at the wary expression on her sister's face. "Hi."

"What's going on?"

"Just doing some cleaning."

"Looks like more than a little cleaning."

"Once I got started, I just kept going. It needed to be done."

Carly walked farther into the room. "What are you going to do with all this stuff?"

"Give it away to charity. A lot of Gary's suits are in excellent condition. I think they'll come in handy for someone looking for a job or trying to hold one down." She opened the small wooden box that Gary had kept on top of the dresser. Inside was the silver chain she'd bought him as a birthday gift a few years earlier. "Maybe Wesley would like this," she murmured.

"I'm sure he would." Carly sent Rachel a thoughtful look. "Did something happen tonight to trigger all this?"

"It just felt like the right time."

"Can I help?"

"You can help me take these bags downstairs."

"Oh, sure, now you let me help when there is manual labor involved. I should have figured."

Rachel gave a little laugh at the disgruntled expression on Carly's face. "You did ask. Thanks, by the way."

"No problem."

"Not for taking the bags out, but for not judging me, for not saying it's about time or the alternative—how can you just throw Gary's life away in two plastic bags and a couple of boxes?"

"You're not throwing his life away, just his things, things that don't mean anything to anyone."

"Right. You know, I just realized that I'm starving. Want to share a banana split like we used to?"

"With whipped cream and nuts on top?"

"As big as we can make it."

"Absolutely." Carly picked up a bag. "By the way, I saw Grandpa in the yard. He said Dylan went on the camp-out with Wesley. How did that happen?"

"Wesley talked him into it. He thought Grandpa would be a little too old for some of the activities."

"And Dylan agreed? Did you by any chance warn him about what actually goes on during the annual father-son camp-out?"

Rachel laughed. "Are you kidding? He was acting like the original bear hunter."

"He's going to kill you when he gets back."

"Hey, he wanted to go."

"Quite the volunteer, isn't he? First your house, now your son's camp-out. He's certainly going beyond the call of duty." Carly paused, her eyes narrowing on Rachel's face. "But this isn't about duty anymore, is it?"

"I don't know what you mean," Rachel said, looking away.

"He cares about you."

"What do you think about some new curtains in here? Maybe even a new carpet. I feel like a change."

"What you're changing is the subject."

"I know. Let me, okay?"

Carly hesitated, then shrugged. "All right. But I hope you know what you're doing, Rachel. I don't want to see you get hurt."

"Dylan won't hurt me. He's a good friend." As Carly left the room, Rachel realized that she'd done just what she'd asked Dylan not to do—she'd lied about their relationship.

Their relationship—whatever the hell that was. Maybe they *were* friends. She didn't really know anymore.

"Got more than you bargained for, didn't you?" Lance Daniels said to Dylan, giving him a friendly punch on the arm.

Dylan wiped the face paint off his cheeks with a paper towel and a big scowl. "Wesley did not tell me we were going to act like warriors."

"An old tradition," Lance said with a laugh. "Started back a gazillion years ago when they used to play cowboys and Indians. With the politically correct movement, the game transformed into warriors and adventurers. You did great capturing the flag, by the way. I haven't seen Wesley smile so big in a long time."

"I'm glad I could help," Dylan mumbled, tossing the paper towel into the trash can. The boys were supposed to be getting ready for bed, but the flashlight beams were bouncing off the walls of the tent, followed by laughter, giggling and squealing. Dylan smiled to himself at the sound of such unrestrained joy.

"Want a beer?" Lance asked as they sat down in side by-side camp chairs by the dwindling campfire.

"Beer? You've got beer?"

"Private stash. What do you say?"

"I say yes." Dylan replied with a grin. He watched Lance pour the beer into two plastic cups and hide away the offending bottle. Some of the other fathers had gone to bed, a couple had taken a walk down by the lake and another two were playing cards on the other side of the fire.

"Hell of a thing that happened to Gary," Lance said. "He was a good guy." He raised his cup in a silent toast and Dylan did the same. "Heard you were friends from way back.

Gary used to tell me some of the things you did when you were kids. He was a real cutup."

"And good at exaggeration. I hope you didn't believe everything you heard."

"Nah. I figured his tales got taller with the amount of liquor he drank. How's Rachel doing? I don't see her much. My wife, Kristie, says Rachel is usually too busy to talk."

"She's all right." Dylan realized the third degree he'd been avoiding had finally arrived. Most of the dads had just accepted him without question, but Lance obviously wanted information.

"Tough being a widow at her age, not even thirty yet. Damn shame." Lance took a long drink. "You know, Gary and I shared a beer at last year's camp-out. I think that might have been the last time I spoke to him. Hard to believe he's dead now. Makes you think about your own mortality, you know?"

"Yeah, I know," Dylan said heavily.

Silence fell between them for a few moments, broken only by the crackling of the fire.

"Wesley likes you," Lance observed. "He's a good kid."

"So is your boy, Palmer. Is that a family name?"

"My wife's father. Had to get the old man off my back somehow."

Dylan smiled at that. "Good decision."

"You ever been married?"

"Nope."

"Smart man. You get married and have kids and this is how you'll spend a lot of Friday nights."

"Ah, this isn't so bad," Dylan said, leaning back in his chair. Actually, it wasn't bad at all. He'd enjoyed himself more than he cared to admit. He was changing bit by bit,

piece by piece. He wondered if he'd recognize himself
when it was time to go home.

"It's not bad, but it's not exactly exciting. Gary brought
his cell phone on the last trip. Spent half the night making
phone calls to people on the other side of the world. I
don't know anybody who doesn't live within a fifty-mile
radius of my house. He was talking to Japan, I think.
Amazed the hell out of me."

"Gary's firm designed buildings all over the world."

"And you built them, right?"

"Some of them."

"Impressive stuff."

"Thanks."

"Me, I'm a small-town guy. I run the pharmacy in
Miller's Drugstore. If you need any aspirin, I'm your man."

"I'll keep that in mind."

"I wonder if Gary ever got that ticker of his checked
out. I told him he better slow down if he was having chest
pains."

"Gary was having chest pains?"

Lance shrugged. "I think it was just stress. He told me
he was going through some heavy-duty stuff and wanted
to know if I could recommend a tranquilizer or an energy
booster. I told him to get himself to a doctor. He said he
would. I don't know if he ever did."

"He was awfully young to have chest pains," Dylan said.
Another new wrinkle unfolded itself in front of his eyes. If
Gary had been having chest pains, why hadn't he mentioned it to him, his supposed best friend? Had they talked
at all that last year? Until a couple of weeks ago, Dylan was
sure their friendship had never wavered. Now he realized
that there had been plenty left unsaid. He wondered why.
Had he withdrawn from Gary in some subtle way? Had it

been the other way around? Or just the business of their lives that had intruded?

"Life in the fast lane," Lance murmured. "Not my style." He crumpled the empty cup in his hand. "I'm going to turn in. What about you?"

"In a few minutes. Thanks for the beer."

"No problem. Don't stay up too late. There's a lot more fun to be had tomorrow."

When Lance had left, Dylan stared into the last lingering flames of the fire and let his mind roll around what Lance had just told him. Chest pains? Stress? He had thought Gary looked tired. Had he been sick?

Maybe the accident hadn't been suicide. It was possible that the eyewitness who saw Gary driving erratically had, in fact, seen something else. Maybe Gary hadn't killed himself. Maybe he'd had a heart attack.

Chapter 15

"You scared me," Rachel said as her pulse leapt with Dylan's appearance in her gift shop Saturday evening. She'd seen him drop Wesley off earlier that afternoon but had been too busy with a group of tourists to ask how the camping trip went.

"Sorry." Dylan flashed her an apologetic smile. "I saw the Closed sign, but the door was open, so I let myself in. You were engrossed in something."

"My sales receipts." She shut the cash register. "Wesley said he had a good time. I understand the two of you won three blue ribbons."

"We were certainly the best at Trivial Pursuit. Not because of me, because of your son. He knew answers that blew the rest of us away."

There was that genius thing again. She would have to deal with that soon. She couldn't believe five days had gone by since she'd spoken to Mrs. Harrington, and she hadn't even opened the private-school folders. She had to be the queen of procrastination. After the Harvest Festival, she promised herself; she'd deal with it then.

"But I did hold my own with the arm wrestling," Dylan added, drawing her attention back to the conversation at hand.

She smiled at the male pride on his face. "Congratulations. What did you think of the warrior games?"

"I particularly enjoyed painting my face," he said dryly. "No one bothered to mention that little tradition to me."

Rachel laughed out loud. "I figured it was something you had to live through. But you seem to be in one piece."

"One tired and hungry piece. What do you say to treating me to dinner?"

"Treating you?"

"Hey, you owe me. I just spent a night on the very hard rocky ground by Sullivan's Lake with your kid."

"Okay. You're right, I owe you. But—I hate to admit this. I'm not a very good cook. Grandma usually does the honors, and she went to visit a friend. When I called up to the house a minute ago, Carly said she and Wesley were eating SpaghettiOs out of a can."

"Good. You can take me out, then. The kids are already fed."

"Don't let Carly hear you call her a kid. She'll have your head."

Dylan grinned. "Now you definitely have to take me to dinner."

She hesitated, knowing there were a lot of reasons why they should not have dinner together. The only problem was, she couldn't think of what they were at this very second.

"I don't think it's a good idea," she got out.

"Since when has anything we've come up with been a good idea?"

She felt herself weaken at his mischievous wink. He looked so damn good. His hair was damp from a recent shower, his skin glowing from a fresh scrubbing. He looked delicious, he smelled even better. She was hungry, she realized. Unfortunately, it wasn't for food. But food was what Dylan had in mind. At least, she thought it was. There was a little gleam in his eye that she didn't quite trust, but what the heck. "All right. I'll take you to dinner. What kind of food are you in the mood for?"

"Hot and hearty and plenty of it."

"Then we'll go to Shenanigans. Uncle Harry serves up a mean Irish stew."

"Uncle Harry? Is everyone in this town related to you?"

"Just about."

"How did Uncle Harry escape the apple-farm tour of duty?"

"He married my aunt Shannon, whose father used to run Shenanigans before she married my uncle Harry. They contributed most of my cousins, by the way. They had nine children and now have a bunch of grandchildren, too."

"Sounds like a lot of shenanigans were going on in their house."

"Very funny. By the way, I did what you asked. I went through all the boxes and closets in the house."

"And?"

"The Goodwill people are going to love me and the garbageman is going to kill me. But I didn't find anything, Dylan, not even in the boxes from Gary's apartment. What do you think we should do next?"

"I think we should have dinner."

"That's not what I meant."

"I know, but for the moment, it's all I can handle. Your kid wore me out."

"Poor baby. I thought you said real men loved to camp."

"Real men don't have to take seven different eight-year-olds to the outhouse seven different times during the middle of the night."

"What about the other dads?"

"They seemed to be dead asleep. Nothing could rouse them."

"The old possum trick," she said with a nod. "Gary said they did it to him the first time he went on the camp-out, too. Some of those dads have older boys."

Dylan laughed. "The old possum trick? I should have figured that one out. I'm an idiot."

"No, you're not an idiot." She reached out and touched his shoulder. "You're a nice guy. A really nice guy."

Nice guy—the kiss of death, Dylan thought as he dipped his overly large spoon into a huge bowl of Irish stew. No self-respecting guy ever aspired to be nice. Successful, charming, good-looking, maybe even a little bit bad—those were positive goals. But nice; ah, hell. She might as well have told him she thought of him as a brother.

"How's the stew?" Rachel asked.

"Huh?"

"The stew. You were scowling at it like something tasted really awful."

"It's fine. I was thinking about something else."

"Want to share?"

"Not really. How about some more bread?"

She pushed the basket of warm rolls across the table

and watched while he slathered a piece with some particularly fine-tasting garlic butter.

"This is great," he mumbled, his mouth still full.

"I'm glad you like it. So was the camping trip really a pain?"

"No, it was fun. I had a good time."

"Really? Or are you just being nice again?"

"I am not nice," he grumbled. "Stop saying that."

"It's a compliment."

"Not to a guy it's not."

She rolled her eyes. "I will never understand men if I live to be a hundred."

"We're not the mysterious ones. That's you and your female cohorts."

"Is that something you men came up with at the campfire after the boys were in bed? Gary used to say that the dads gossiped like a bunch of hens at the campfire."

"Men don't gossip. We share information."

"Good. Then how about sharing some of that information with me?" She leaned forward, and he felt a catch in his chest as her blond hair caught the light and her blue eyes sparkled. She really was a beautiful woman, not the pretty young girl he remembered but a woman with life and love sharpening her features, adding wisdom to her eyes and tenderness to her smile.

"Dylan, I asked you a question," she said.

"Sorry. I got distracted."

"By what?"

"You."

"Oh."

He smiled at the familiar flush that crept up her cheeks. "There it goes again, like a red flag saying stay back."

She put her glass of water to her cheeks. "It's warm in here, don't you think?"

"It's always warm when we're together."

"I think you're trying to distract me from my question. What happened at the campfire? Did the other dads wonder who you were and why you were there?"

"Let's see . . . there were the usual questions, nothing too intense. I did have a private chat with Lance, the pharmacist."

"He's a good guy. Gary liked him a lot."

"Lance liked Gary, too." Dylan paused. "He did say something, Rachel. It's probably completely irrelevant, but it made me wonder."

"What?"

"He said Gary told him he'd been under a lot of stress and had had some chest pain."

"Chest pain? You mean like a heart attack?"

"Just some pain, tightness. I think it was probably stress. Lance told Gary to see a doctor. Do you know if he did?"

Rachel thought about that for a moment. "Yes, I think so. He had a doctor in the city, a woman. Her last name was Flanders. I could check the bills again, see when he last went in. He didn't have regular checkups, but I know he mentioned seeing her a couple of times."

"It's something to look into."

"Why? I don't see the connection. *Oh.*"

He saw the light come on in her eyes. "If he wasn't feeling well as he came down the mountain . . ." he began.

"He could have swerved across the divider or lost control of the car," she finished. "Maybe that's it, Dylan. Maybe we've been going down the wrong road."

"It's possible. It doesn't explain the rest, but . . ."

"You mean Laura."

"Yes. We still have to figure out her place in all this. Hey, you better eat; you still have a full bowl."

"I'm not that hungry."

"Sorry. We should have saved this conversation for later."

"It's fine. I'm saving too many things for later as it is."

"Like what?"

"Wesley."

"What's wrong with Wesley?"

"Nothing's wrong. Everything is right, too right." She folded her hands on the table. "Okay, here's the deal. I met with Wesley's teacher on Monday and she told me that Wesley is a genius."

He relaxed at her words. "I told you he was a smart kid."

"He's not just a smart kid. He's reading at a high school level and doing math problems that no one has taught him how to do. And his writing is way up there, too."

"Wow, that's amazing. Great, though."

"It would be great, but Mrs. Harrington says Wesley needs a special school for gifted children so he can be truly challenged and still be in an environment appropriate for his age and emotional development. Needless to say, there aren't any such schools around here."

"Where are they? San Francisco?"

"And other big cities. But I can't move Wesley. I can't uproot him. This is where he feels safe and loved."

Now Dylan saw her problem, and saw it more clearly than she had probably intended. "This is where *you* feel safe and loved," he said quietly. "Isn't that the real problem?"

"I'm a horrible person," she whispered, "always putting myself before everyone else. I've got to stop doing that."

"You're not a horrible person. You've made a good life for yourself here, and you don't want to leave."

"But by staying I might be denying Wesley the education he deserves."

"You know what?"

"What?"

"You need some time to think about what you want to do. It's been a rough year. Give yourself a break. You don't have to do anything about Wesley's schooling right this second, do you?"

"Not this second, but probably sooner than I want, which would be when Wesley is eighteen years old. I'm not even sure I'll be able to let him go then. Carly seems to think my hold on people is the same as a death grip."

He gave her a grin. "What do younger sisters know?"

"More than you wish they knew."

"True."

"Are you close to any of your stepsisters?"

"Grace and I keep in touch. She's the baby of the family. She never knew a life without me in it, so she accepted me as her brother. The other two always felt like I was an interloper."

"Where is Grace now?"

"San Diego. She's a mom, has a two-year-old of her own. Married a great guy. And they'll live happily ever after."

"You could have the same."

He laughed. "Not tonight I couldn't."

"I wasn't talking about tonight."

"Well, that's all I want to think about right now. In fact, I have another idea."

"Another one," she groaned. "I don't think I can handle any more of your ideas."

"This one is easy. Darts."

"Darts?"

"Gary said you were pretty good, but I have my doubts." He tipped his head toward the dartboard in the corner of the bar area. "What do you say?"

"I'd say I'd have to know if the stakes were worth playing for."

"Stakes, huh? Five dollars?"

"I don't think so."

"A hundred bucks."

"Jeez, how about something in between?"

"What do you want, then?"

She leaned forward slightly. He could see the swell of her breasts as her low-cut blouse shifted slightly. His body immediately tightened. He didn't know what the hell she wanted, but he knew what he wanted.

"A dance," she said.

"I don't dance."

"To my choice on the jukebox."

"And if I win?"

"Well, if you really want to waste time thinking about that possibility . . ."

"You go flying with me," he said with a snap of his fingers. "One hour over your apple farm and your precious valley."

She tensed. "I don't think so."

"Hey, I thought you were confident."

"I am, but I don't want to fly."

"Why not? Are you afraid of crashing? Because I promise I won't let anything happen to you."

"It's just not me. I like my feet on the ground."

"You won't know it's you until you try it. Hey, you're not going to lose anyway, right?"

"That's right. Fine. You're on." She got up from the table

and pointed to the opposite wall. "By the way, see that board over there?"

Dylan turned his head to see a list of names on a plaque, one name repeated over and over again, Rachel's name.

"Five years running, Annual Darts Champion," she said with a confident smile of her own. "I'll get the darts from Uncle Harry. You better warm up. Make sure you have a steady hand."

He wanted to tell her that he was already warm. He took another drink, finishing the beer in his glass. So much for a steady hand. Hell, who was he kidding? His hands hadn't been steady since Rachel had come back into his life.

Rachel handed Dylan the darts a few minutes later. "What do you want to play? Three-zero-one, Cricket?"

He raised an eyebrow. "I assume those are games."

"Yes, they're games. Three-zero-one begins by hitting a double. Then the score is determined by subtracting from three-zero-one the score of each dart thrown. You have to reduce your score to exactly zero to win."

"That sounds complicated."

"You can go first. I'll explain as we go."

"Maybe I don't want to go first," he said warily. "I sense you have a strategy."

"And I sense you're chicken," she said with a little laugh.

"Okay, now you've made me mad."

"So get even. Beat me."

"Maybe I will."

"I doubt it."

"Awfully cocky, aren't you? How about we do just three darts, high score wins?"

"Fine. Throw your first dart. Show me up."

He rotated his arm a few times in an exaggerated warm-up. "The center dot is what I want, right?" he asked.

"It's called a bull's-eye, remember?"

"It's coming back to me." He drew his arm back and threw. He hit the bull's-eye dead center and heard Rachel gasp at the same time the dart stuck in the board. He turned his head to see her jaw drop.

"What was that?" she demanded.

"I think it was a bull's-eye. Actually, I think it was a double bull's-eye."

"And I think you've been hustling me."

"Me?" he asked innocently. "Hustling the five-time world champion?"

"Hardly world," she said, annoyed with herself for having believed his innocent routine. The man had already demonstrated his prowess with a paper airplane. She should have figured he'd be just as good at darts. "Go on, let's see what else you've got. Maybe you were just lucky."

He quirked an eyebrow at that. "Luck had nothing to do with it. It's all skill."

"We'll see." But as Rachel watched him pull back his arm and take aim, she began to worry. If he did somehow beat her, she'd have to go up in an airplane with him. She didn't want to do that. She couldn't. So she cleared her throat just as he threw. It startled him enough to hit the outer ring, worth only eighteen points.

"You did that on purpose," he accused.

"I had something stuck in my throat."

"Yeah, I think it was your pride. But I've still got one dart left." He twirled it in his fingers. "Want me to try it with my eyes closed this time?"

What she wanted was to find his arrogant smile irritating, but in truth she was enjoying this relaxed side of Dylan. He was clearly having a good time. Of course, it was at her expense, she reminded herself. And if he didn't mess up this last shot, she had a terrible feeling she'd be soaring over the valley as early as tomorrow. She simply could not let him win. Drastic measures were called for. But what?

He was looking at her, waiting for her to make some remark about his dare. "Actually, I don't want you to close your eyes at all," she said, her fingers rolling around the top button of her shirt. In one quick movement, she undid it, impulsively revealing the top of her lacy white bra. It was the most audacious, foolish thing she could do. But it had the desired effect. Dylan's eyes fixed on her fingers as they played with the next button on her shirt. "Go ahead, take your last shot."

He started, as if he'd suddenly remembered where they were. When he drew his arm back, it was nowhere near as steady as it had been. The last dart went wide of the board altogether.

"Oh, too bad," she said. "But still a good score." She walked over to the board and removed the darts.

"That wasn't fair. You distracted me. And I must say I'm shocked."

She laughed at his outrage. "All's fair."

"In love and war. Which is this?"

She ignored that question. "My turn." She threw her first dart before he could do anything to distract her. "Bull's-eye."

"Not bad," he said grudgingly. "But you've got to hit at least two more to beat me."

"How about this one?" she said, landing her second shot with unerring accuracy. Of course, Dylan didn't know how many hours she'd spent playing darts while growing up.

"You know I can't dance," he told her. "I'll probably step all over your feet. Unless, of course, you hold me real close."

"I don't think so."

"What do you think about this, then?" His hand dropped to his belt buckle. "Tit for tat?"

She swallowed hard as her gaze traveled to the very male bulge just below his fingers. "You wouldn't dare." She looked around, ready to point out all the people watching them. Unfortunately, no one was. The nearby pool table was empty, same with the dance floor, and the other dinner customers were seated across the room. Still, she felt compelled to utter another protest. "You could be arrested for indecent exposure."

"And you could be arrested for looking," he said, reminding her that she was now indeed fixating on a very personal part of his anatomy.

She immediately turned away. She took a deep breath. Focus, concentrate. Hit your mark. The commands ran through her brain, and she drew her hand back and threw, a perfect shot to the center.

"Well," Dylan drawled. "I guess your concentration is better than mine."

"Well," she echoed. "I guess it is. I believe this is my dance." She walked over to the jukebox and studied the songs listed. Something fast and upbeat. That's what she wanted, nothing slow, nothing where they'd have to hold each other.

Dylan joined her a moment later. "You know, flying is really incredible."

"A bet's a bet. Are you a sore loser?"

"I wouldn't know. I don't usually lose," he grumbled.

"I believe that," she said. "But you lost this time."

"And you cheated by giving me a peep show."

She laughed at the disgruntled look on his face. "Men are so easy. One little glance at a bra strap and you completely lose your concentration."

"I didn't lose it. It just went somewhere else," he replied, dropping his gaze to her breasts, which unexpectedly began to tingle. "I could show you some real concentration if you'd give me a chance."

"Are you flirting with me?"

"Hey, I'm not the one showing my underwear."

For a split second, she wondered whether he wore boxers or briefs.

"Boxers," he said.

"I was not thinking that," she lied.

"Red polka dots."

"No way."

"What about you? Sexy thong or practical cotton?"

"I am not discussing my underwear with you."

"Then you shouldn't have brought it up."

"I need a quarter," she said.

"What?" he asked mockingly. "You need a quarter to show me your underwear?"

"Don't be ridiculous. That would cost a lot more. I need a quarter to play a song so we can dance. Don't think by distracting me that I've forgotten our bet."

"The bet was for a dance, not a quarter. If you don't have a coin, that's not my problem."

"Fine, I'll get one myself." She walked over to their table and dug into the bottom of her purse. Sure enough, a loose quarter. She held it up triumphantly. "I found one."

"Great," he said with a dismal sigh.

Rachel popped the quarter into the machine and selected the funniest, most amusing song she could find. " 'Saturday Night Fever' okay?" she asked. "Do you have your best John Travolta moves ready to go?"

He groaned. "You did not pick that."

"Oh, but I did." She stopped abruptly as a song began to play, but not the one she'd requested. This one was slow and romantic and sensuous.

"A love song?" Dylan asked with a raised eyebrow.

"This isn't the right one."

"Well, it's the one that's playing, and this is our dance. Come here," he said softly, holding out his hands.

"I picked a fast one."

"Too bad. You get one dance. Take it or leave it."

She considered leaving it.

"However, if you default on the bet, I win," he added. "You and me and the wild blue yonder—here we come."

"Okay, I'll dance with you. But if you step on my foot, I'll kick you on the shin."

And with that little bit of romance, she went into his arms.

Chapter 16

In a moment Rachel felt like she'd always belonged in Dylan's arms. She knew in her head that it was not supposed to feel this easy, this comfortable. It should have been awkward. Their legs should have bumped, their feet should have gotten tangled up. They should have kept a proper distance between their bodies.

Instead her hand crept up from his shoulder to the back of his neck, where her fingers played with the waves of his dark hair. In response, he drew her close against his heart, his chin brushing the top of her head as she breathed in the scent of him. He smelled like soap, like strong, manly soap with a touch of lavender. But it wasn't just his smell that undid her; it was his hand, the rough, callused palm that brushed her own fingers, making her very much aware of how hard he was and how soft she wanted to be.

She thought she heard him sigh. Maybe the sound had come from her own throat. She felt like purring like a contented cat that had just found the perfect spot to nestle into.

The music swept through her, the lush words of romance a perfect accompaniment to the way their bodies were talking to each other. It was a good thing there were no words required. She couldn't have spoken even if she'd wanted to, and she didn't want to. She wanted to have this dance, this one dance, this one moment when everything felt good and right.

Dylan's lips pressed against the top of her head. If she moved slightly, if she raised her head, she could kiss him the way she wanted to. She tried to resist the call, but a moment later hopelessly surrendered as want overrode reason. He was waiting for her.

His mouth claimed hers, his dark lashes sweeping against his cheeks as he closed his eyes. It was the last thing she saw before she gave herself up to his kiss, a kiss that lasted to the end of the song, until the soft romantic harmony was replaced by the pounding beat of "Saturday Night Fever."

Dylan drew away. His eyes glittered with desire, or was it something else? Rachel was afraid to read more. Afraid for him. Afraid for herself. She took a step back. He did the same.

"I'm not dancing to this one," he told her.

"Neither am I."

"Why don't we leave?" he suggested.

"All right." Leaving was good. Cool, fresh air would be good, too.

As Rachel turned, she caught sight of her aunt Shannon

and her uncle Harry standing behind the bar, watching her. Their expressions were solemn, worry lines creasing their faces as they stood together, a solid, protective unit.

Rachel picked up her purse from the table. Dylan put a hand on her back as they walked toward the bar.

She paused in front of her aunt and uncle, feeling very much like a child whose hand had been caught in the cookie jar. "Thanks for dinner," she said lightly. "It was great."

"How much do we owe you?" Dylan asked.

"Nothing," Uncle Harry replied, his tone sharp. "Rachel doesn't pay for food. She's family."

And Dylan was not. Rachel could hear the words as clearly as if Uncle Harry had spoken them out loud. Unfortunately, Dylan could hear them, too. She didn't want him to feel that he was the odd man out, that he was unacceptable. He'd already had too much of that kind of rejection in the past.

"Well, I'd be happy to pay for mine," Dylan said.

"No, no," Aunt Shannon said, putting a soothing hand on her husband's arm. "Why, you were Gary's best friend. You're practically family."

"Didn't appear to be his best friend a minute ago," Harry remarked, obviously referring to their kiss.

"That wasn't what it looked like," Rachel said quickly.

"Yes, it was," Dylan said, contradicting her. "It was exactly what it looked like." He dared her to counter him, but the last thing she wanted to do was get into an argument over a kiss, especially here.

"Dylan, would you mind bringing the car around front?"

"So you can explain. Sure, why not?" He departed without a backward glance. In fact, Rachel wondered if he'd actually bring the car around or leave her to find her own way home.

"You don't have to explain, honey," Aunt Shannon said. "You're entitled to do whatever you like with whomever you like. You're not cheating on Gary."

Uncle Harry snorted his disapproval. "Not right for a man's best friend to step in before his body is even cold."

"It's not like that," Rachel said. "And Dylan isn't stepping into anything. We're friends. He's helping me."

"We just worry about you, honey," Aunt Shannon murmured. "We don't want to see you get hurt."

"It's too late for that. I've been hurt more than I could have ever imagined. But not by Dylan. He won't hurt me."

"I hope not," Aunt Shannon replied. "But then, there's different kinds of hurt, some that come from hate and some that come from love."

"I don't hate him or love him," Rachel said firmly. "We're just . . ." She threw up her hands in defeat. "Oh, I don't know what we are. And I don't care. I like him. I just like him."

He had to stop kissing Rachel, had to stop wanting her, had to stop liking her. Dylan pulled the car up in front of Shenanigans and waited for Rachel to appear. He knew her aunt and uncle had been less than thrilled to see their niece in the arms of another man.

Another man? Hell, when had he become the other man?

It wasn't his style to get involved with married women. He'd always steered clear of that kind of entanglement. Until now.

He wondered if it had something to do with that damn apple he'd eaten all those years ago. Not that he believed in legends or magic, but he certainly felt a pull to Rachel that never lessened, not with distance or marriage or death or even anger. It was always there behind everything he did, everything he said. Rachel got into the car and shut the door, sliding her seat belt on with a rapid, nervous movement. "We can go now. Sorry about that."

"They're worried about you."

"Well, they don't have to worry about you."

"Are you sure about that?" He glanced over at her and saw the telltale blush spread across her cheeks.

"No," she said. "Don't look at me like that."

"Like what?"

"Like I'm your favorite ice cream on a cone."

"I think you might be. I'd need another taste to be sure."

"What are we doing, Dylan?" She turned slightly in her seat so she could face him. "Do you know?"

"No. I keep telling myself to keep it casual, keep it business, or at the very least friendly, but there's more between us; there always has been."

"A connection," she agreed. "You're the only one who knows that I had any doubts about marrying Gary. I never told anyone else."

"I never did either."

She stared at him, her blue eyes darkening with her somber mood. "When I'm with you and I find myself smiling or having a good time, I feel guilty because you're here and Gary's not. And I remember those doubts I had. I wonder if I hadn't had the doubts or wished for something more in my marriage, if Gary would still be here. I can't have fun with you without feeling like I've done something terrible to Gary. Like I wished him away."

"You didn't do that. You couldn't."

"My head believes you, but my heart has trouble letting go. I loved Gary, and I say that with all honesty, Dylan. The doubts that I had in the beginning were put to rest by our years together. We had a child. We lived through sickness and health and all the rest. We had good times. I know we did. No matter what anyone else thinks."

"I know you did, too. Gary was happy with you, Rachel. Whatever happened in the last year doesn't change that fact. You and Wesley gave him the family he wanted. It was a tremendous gift. Don't ever doubt that."

"I'm trying not to."

"You didn't do anything to cause Gary's death. Even if you'd hated him, he wouldn't have died. I don't like a lot of people and they're still alive and kicking."

His comment drew a reluctant smile. "That's not very nice."

"People aren't always nice. We're not perfect, we're human. Give yourself a break. You did the best you could in your marriage. That's all that matters."

"Why didn't you ever marry?" she asked, turning the conversation to him.

He stiffened. "What brought that on?"

"You wanted a family as much as Gary did, but you didn't go after one."

He shrugged. "Someday I will."

"There hasn't been anyone?"

"There have been a lot of someones, just no one I wanted to marry. Actually, I was engaged a few years back. It didn't last."

"Why not?"

"A lot of reasons. She wasn't the right one."

"I'm sorry."

"Don't be sorry. A woman would have slowed me down. I've gotten to the top of my game by working night and day."

"Building a career, but not a family. It sounds lonely."

She didn't know the half of it, but then, she never would. For Rachel, family was everything. "It's been profitable," he said lightly. "I've been very successful."

"What was her name, the woman you almost married?"

"You don't want to know that."

"Yes, I do."

"Sheila."

"Sheila." She rolled the name around on her tongue. "She sounds sophisticated, a good dresser, very stylish, a career woman. Am I right?"

He didn't appreciate her accuracy. "She's an attorney."

"And very beautiful, I'll bet."

He nodded. "Stunning."

"So what happened?"

"She didn't want children, a little fact she neglected to mention until after we were engaged. She assumed that I felt the same way, that with our lifestyles of work and travel, a child would be impractical."

"Children are always impractical, but they're wonderful. They change your life in ways you could never imagine. You should have children. You'd be a wonderful father."

"I would like to have kids," he admitted. He hadn't known how much until Sheila had told him she didn't want any. It was then he realized how wrong their relationship was. He'd felt that it was time to marry, to have children, to make a family, and he'd figured she'd probably want all that, too. And why not marry a beautiful woman with whom the sex was all right? It wasn't like he was ever going to have that head-over-heels, stomach-churning kind of love anyway. That woman was gone, out of reach. Until now.

The thought came unbidden into his mind and refused to leave. Maybe he could have Rachel now. God! The same guilt that Rachel had spoken of earlier swept through him. How could he be happy at Gary's expense?

"Dylan?" Rachel interrupted his train of thought. "Do you want to take me home now?"

He wanted to take her back to his hotel room and make love to her. That's what he wanted to do. But he'd shock the hell out of her if he said that.

"Sure," he said instead, putting the car into drive. "I'll take you home."

Rachel didn't say anything on the way home. It wasn't until he pulled into her driveway that she turned to him. "I had a good time tonight. It was fun to play darts with you. You're a serious competitor."

"So are you. I had a good time, too."

"I'm glad."

"Rachel." He hesitated. She'd say no. He knew it. So why was he bothering to ask?

"What?"

"Tomorrow is Sunday. The weather is supposed to be clear and warm, a perfect day for flying."

"I can't. Besides, you didn't win the bet, so I don't have to."

"Will you at least think about it?"

"Why? Why do you keep asking me? Why does it matter to you?"

Why *did* he keep asking her? He wasn't sure. He just felt a compelling need to show her a world she'd never seen before. He hated the way she limited herself. She didn't know what she was missing. "I want to share it with you," he said. "I want you to see the world, *your* world, from another perspective. We can take Wesley with us."

"I'm busy."

"It will take an hour, tops."

"Oh, Dylan, you do tempt me, and not just to fly with you."

He smiled. "Then say yes."

"No."

"Yes."

"Maybe."

"Yes," he persisted.

"Okay, all right, yes. But I'm probably going to hang on for dear life the whole time or, worse yet, throw up all over you."

"I'll take my chances. What time?"

"I don't know—early? I have some tour groups to deal with in the afternoon. Don't we need a reservation or something?"

"I think I can find a plane for us to use."

"Any plane? I mean, I want it to be safe, especially if we're taking Wesley. Oh, dear, I don't know if I should do this. Flying is dangerous."

"*Life* is dangerous, Rachel. But I promise I'll do everything I can to keep you safe. Now, don't think about it anymore. I'll pick you up at eight o'clock tomorrow morning."

"Am I going to regret it?" she asked.

"You won't regret going up in a plane with me, but you

might regret this." He leaned over and covered her mouth in a long, deep kiss.

"How fast are we going to go? How high? Are we going to flip over and fly upside down?" Wesley asked excitedly, the questions streaming out of his mouth one after the other.

"Whoa," Dylan said with a laugh as he swung Wesley up into his arms. "We'll go fast and high—"

"But we are definitely not flying upside down," Rachel finished.

He smiled at her as she nervously fidgeted with the necklace around her neck. She looked pretty as a picture this morning in a short floral skirt and sleeveless blouse. He just wished the expression on her face was relaxed instead of tense. Maybe he was wrong to push her into this. But he knew she would love it. And he wanted to give her this flight, this moment, this experience that Gary had never given her.

Was that what this was all about? He refused to go there. He didn't want this day to be about Gary. Maybe that was selfish or wrong, but that's the way it was.

"What do we do now?" Rachel asked.

"We get in."

"Are you sure we're ready? Did you check everything?"

"Three times. And I went over every inch of the plane, including the maintenance done over the past year."

"Maintenance? What kind of maintenance?"

"The kind that keeps the plane in the air."

"Mommy is scared," Wesley told him.

"I'm not scared; I'm just concerned. It's good to be concerned," she replied.

"Flying is very safe, Mom," Wesley said as Dylan put

him back on the ground. "Did you know that you have a greater chance of being hit by lightning than crashing in an airplane?"

She shook her head in amazement. "Where do you learn this stuff?"

Dylan helped Wesley into the plane, then turned to Rachel. "If you don't want to do this, it's okay. I want it to be your decision."

"It would be easier if you picked me up and threw me in."

"Not my style."

"I know. You want me to make courageous decisions all by myself. All right, then. I'll do it. I'll go."

"This isn't a root canal. It will be fun."

She forced a smile onto her face. "Fun. I can't wait."

He laughed and helped her into the plane. When they were ready to go, he glanced over and saw her gripping the armrest so tightly her knuckles had turned white. "I never really thought the expression white-knuckled flier was true."

"Just do what you have to do to get this thing in the air," she said. "Before I lose my nerve."

"Go really fast, Dylan," Wesley encouraged from the backseat.

"Don't go too fast," Rachel said.

Dylan shook his head and turned his attention to the flight plan. He hoped by the end of the trip they'd both be satisfied.

They were going up. They were really doing it. Rachel felt every muscle in her body tense as the plane gathered more and more speed. She felt every bump on the runaway, winced at every jolt, heard every tiny ping in the plane.

Her nerves screamed that this was wrong, humans were not meant to go this fast. But before she could tell Dylan to put on the brakes, they were up, off the ground, airborne.

The land below fell away in a dizzying fashion. Rachel couldn't believe the sight unfolding before her. The airport below vanished, giving way to hills and fields, long, winding roads and cars that looked like ants.

"Wow," Wesley said, and it seemed to be the only word appropriate for the experience they were having.

She felt Dylan's gaze on her and turned her head. "Wow," she echoed with a smile.

He smiled back at her. "You haven't seen nothing yet. I'm going to make your head spin."

"It already is. This is incredible."

"Want to see your apple farm?"

"Can we?"

"Oh, yeah." He turned the plane slightly toward the left. "In about five minutes."

The hour passed far too quickly as Dylan pointed out familiar sights below, far below. And while Rachel eagerly strained to catch a glimpse of her apple farm, her cozy green hills and her beautiful valley, she found her gaze drifting to the horizon, wondering what was over the next hill and the next.

What if they kept flying? What else would they discover? What beauty would they see? She'd never thought she needed to cross the next bridge or go over the far hill. She had what she wanted, all she wanted. Now she wasn't as sure.

Dylan landed the plane much too soon. Neither Rachel nor Wesley had had nearly enough, which Wesley told Dylan in no uncertain terms as they got off the plane.

Dylan laughed. "I think Wesley liked it," he reported to

Rachel, who was still trying to get her land legs back under her. Wesley had no such trouble, running over to the nearby hangar to check out some of the photos they had on the wall. "What about you?"

"It was fabulous. That's the biggest word I can think of, but it's not big enough." The pure pleasure in his eyes made her heart turn over. He'd wanted her to like it more than she'd realized.

"I'm glad," he said softly. "I'm glad you had enough faith in me to go up."

"I'm glad you had enough faith in me to push me into it. Sometimes I need a good, swift kick . . ."

"That isn't what I want to give you."

"Let me," she murmured. "You've already given me enough today." She put her palms on his chest and kissed him on the mouth, wanting to thank him in a way that words couldn't express. "Mommy?" Wesley's questioning voice ended the kiss.

She turned and saw the confusion on his face and silently berated herself for forgetting that he was close by, that he wouldn't understand.

"How come you kissed Dylan?" Wesley asked.

She cleared her throat as she tried to think of something that would make sense. "I wanted to thank him for taking us on a great ride."

"Oh." Wesley hesitated. "Can I thank him, too?"

She glanced over at Dylan. "If it's all right with you?"

Dylan didn't have time to answer, because Wesley had jumped into his arms and planted a big, wet kiss on his cheek. Rachel felt a knot rise in her throat when Dylan kissed Wesley's cheek in return. It was a tender, sweet moment, and one she knew she would cherish.

"Ready to go home?" Dylan said.

"I won't be able to look at my home in the same way. I always thought the farm was big, but it's really very small. Maybe I made it more important than it is. You were right, Dylan. Flying over it gave me a whole new perspective."

Chapter 17

Rachel's head was still in the clouds Sunday evening as she closed up the gift shop and walked across the yard to her house. It had been a busy, full, satisfying day, though she wasn't thinking about the tourists or the sales they'd made, but about that incredible, uplifting flight over the valley.

She paused on the steps leading to her porch and glanced up at the sky. It was a dusky evening, a bluish-purple tint the last remnant of a beautiful sunset. She would never look at the sky the same way again, she realized. Because she'd been up there. She'd flown through the clouds. She'd been as free as a bird.

A smile crossed her lips at her silliness. People flew every day; millions and millions of people had been where she'd been, seen what she'd seen. Were they changed by it? She didn't think so. They just accepted it as a way of life, a means to an end. Gary certainly hadn't raved about the experience; he'd spent far more time complaining about the delays, the bad food and the watered-down drinks. It hadn't been an incredible mind-blowing experience, just one he took for granted, part of his life, a life she didn't know.

The screen door opened behind her. She turned her head. She wasn't surprised to see Dylan standing there. He seemed to be everywhere these days.

"Hey," he said softly.

"Hey."

"I brought Wesley home. We worked on cabinets today."

She nodded. They'd been planning to work on the house after their plane trip. "How did it go?"

"We're making excellent progress. There are some things you'll need to think about, though."

"Anything I have to think about right now?"

"No."

"Good. I'm too tired to think. Have you eaten?"

"Actually, your grandmother just asked me to chase you down and tell you dinner will be ready in a half hour. She's got a roast baking in the oven that smells incredible."

"I suppose you're invited to share it with us."

"She did mention something about it. You look tired. Long day entertaining the city folk?"

"You could say that." She tipped her head toward the porch swing. "Want to sit a spell?"

"I'm not really a porch-swing kind of guy."

She sat down and patted the seat next to her. "Live a little dangerously."

"Fine." He took the seat next to her.

"You know, I don't think you *were* a porch-swing guy,

but I have a feeling that might be changing." She gazed into his eyes. "Am I right?"

"Maybe."

"I'm changing, too. This morning made me very aware of that fact. My life used to be predictable. Now it's not. Getting married was the boldest thing I ever did, but you know what? I realize now I did it on my terms. I made Gary fit into my life. I made no effort to fit into his. It's no wonder he started to look elsewhere."

"You don't know he did that."

"I think I do. That woman wouldn't have disconnected her phone if she didn't have something to hide."

"I've been thinking. I believe it's time to call in a private investigator."

Rachel didn't like the sound of that. There was only one thing worse than having dirty linen and that was showing it in public. "Why?"

"Because I'm a builder. You're a farmer. We need help, Rachel, professional help."

"I agree, but I'm not sure it's a private investigator we need," she said wryly.

Dylan answered her with a grin. "Good point. Maybe a shrink, huh?"

"Definitely. Do you think an investigator can find something we haven't?"

"Laura's address, for one. What about the doctor Gary was seeing in San Francisco? It might be interesting to talk to her as well."

"I want to say no, but when you're around, I find myself saying yes."

"You shouldn't tell me that, Rachel. Makes me want to ask you something else."

She laughed and held up her hand. "Don't. I've had

enough earth-shattering experiences for one day. I need to get my feet under me again. The week ahead will be nuts."

"Why is that?" He put his arm along the back of the seat, his fingers brushing against her neck.

She probably should have moved away, but when he began kneading the tight muscle in her shoulder, she simply sighed and let him do it.

"The Harvest Festival starts next Friday and runs through the weekend," she said, trying to remember what she'd been saying.

"Right. I've been seeing signs for it all week."

"All the local growers take part as well as the town. There are events at every farm and also a dance at the Recreation Center on Friday night, a parade down Main Street on Saturday and a free concert in the park on Sunday afternoon."

"Sounds like an old-fashioned blast."

"It is—if you like that kind of thing. Gary missed last year's festival. I think he planned it that way. He was a city boy at heart." She paused. "What was I thinking, giving one of our special apples to Gary?"

"Did you happen to notice that Gary didn't like apples?"

She sent him a puzzled look. "What do you mean?"

"He never liked apples."

"I'm sure he did. We made tons of pies and tarts and breads and . . ." She frowned. "Actually, he said he didn't care much for dessert. Hmm. Maybe you're right. Another little thing that slipped by me. I guess I was lucky he ate that first one."

"He didn't."

"Excuse me?"

Dylan looked like he wished he could take the words back. "Never mind."

"No, not 'never mind.' What did you just say?"

"Gary didn't eat that apple. When we got in the car, he tossed it to me. I ate it."

She stared at him in amazement. "I don't believe you." But she did. Suddenly it made sense. She jumped to her feet and walked over to the railing, grabbing it with both hands.

"It's true." Dylan got up to stand beside her. "I didn't know until recently that that apple had any particular meaning."

"But Gary did. He knew all about the legend. He never once mentioned that he hadn't eaten it. Why didn't he tell me?"

"Maybe he thought it would have changed things. Would it? What if he'd told you before the wedding? Would you have married him?"

"Oh, God! Don't ask me that." She looked away from him. She could see the special tree in the distance, rising like a beacon in the night on the hills behind her grandparents' cottage. It had always stood there like a sentinel, guarding their property, nurturing their family, protecting their love.

Dylan laid a hand on her shoulder. "It's done, Rachel. It was done a long time ago."

"But you don't know. You don't know what it all means."

"Tell me, then. Tell me the whole story. Mrs. Lanigan told me a little bit, but I want to hear it from you."

She hesitated. She didn't want to tell him, didn't want him to know how powerful the magic was, how strong it could bind two souls together, because they weren't talking about her and Gary anymore. They were talking about her and Dylan. Was that why they had this strong connection? This inability to break apart and stay apart? Although they'd managed to do just that for nine years. Kept apart by Gary, by the man who was supposed to eat the apple, by the man who'd never told her that he hadn't.

"Come with me," Rachel said, holding out her hand. She led him across the yard and up the small incline. The branches of the tree were lit by the early moonlight, as if Mother Nature wanted nothing to upstage her special tree.

"This is it," she said in a hushed voice. "This is Lady Elaine."

"Should I shake hands or—"

"You should be respectful," she admonished.

"Oh, believe me, I am, because if she's responsible for what I've been feeling all these years, she has a lot of power."

"She does. The story begins with my great-great-grandmother Elaine," Rachel said. "She grew up in Virginia, the daughter of a poor farmer and in love with a rich boy named William. He was beyond her station, as they used to say. But one day he happened by her farm and saw her in the garden. It was a hot day, and she offered him something to drink and something to eat, a fresh apple from her tree. It was said that he took one bite and fell madly in love with her."

"I don't suppose she happened to be beautiful."

"Shh," she said, putting a finger to her lips, for she wanted him to hear the whole story. "She kept the seeds of that special apple and planted them outside her bedroom window, her heart full of hope for their future together. But William's parents were furious when they found out he had feelings for Elaine. In an attempt to break them up, they sent William to California to live with his uncle.

"Elaine was devastated. But she refused to accept the

idea of a life apart. So she joined an expedition, a wagon train to California. And she took with her the seedling, nurturing it and protecting it all the way across the country. It was a dangerous and hard trip for a young, innocent girl, but she was determined to make it, and she did."

Rachel saw Dylan smile. She walked away from him and touched one of the apples hanging from the tree. As she did so, the story came alive in her head. She could almost see Elaine and William, their joyous reunion, their overwhelming love.

"When Elaine got to California, she found William with his bags packed. She'd almost missed him; he was on his way back to find her. They were overwhelmed with love and married immediately. William's family disowned him, told him he would get nothing unless he dissolved the marriage. But William didn't need anything but Elaine. They planted the seedling behind their house right here," she said, glancing back at Dylan. "The tree grew and blossomed, the beginning of their family, my family."

"That still doesn't explain the magic," Dylan interjected.

"I think it explains a lot, but if you want more, there's more. Six years after their marriage, a fire swept through the orchard, burning all of the trees to the ground except this one. There was no reason the fire should have skipped this particular tree, but it did. Oh, you can say the wind turned at the right moment, but what made it turn?"

"Magic?"

"Exactly. My great-great-grandparents started over again with this one tree. They came to think of it as their salvation. The apples were especially tasty but only grew sparingly, and only during certain years was the bounty worth picking. No one knew why. They just knew that each apple was special, each apple was love.

"Elaine told her children, all five of them, that if they fed an apple to their true love, that love would last forever. They had to be careful, because if it was given to the wrong person, the results could be disastrous. For the most part, they made the right choices, with a few exceptions."

"It's a nice story," Dylan said.

She was disappointed by his pragmatic response. "You don't believe me?"

"I've never had much cause to believe in magic or long marriages. And I wouldn't think you would either. What about your own parents? What happened to the magic then?"

"My mother hated apples. I'm not sure why she married my father. I think it was to escape her parents. They were very controlling. Getting married was her way out. Having children was what she gave back to my father. Once they both had what they wanted, there was no reason to stay together. But I've seen it work lots of other times."

"What made you choose Gary? You didn't even know him."

Rachel rolled the apple in the palm of her hand. It was smooth and cool. She could still feel the texture of the one she'd handed to Gary, still feel the butterflies in her stomach when she'd made the decision to give it to him, still feel the excitement.

"He was so . . . happy," she said, settling for a word that wasn't really right but was the only one she could think of. "He made me feel like I could be happy, like I could catch whatever he had." She paused. "I knew my dad was sick. I was losing him, losing my life, and I wanted to hold on. It was a rash thing to do. My grandmother was really worried when she found out what I'd done. But everyone came to love Gary. They figured the apple tree had worked its magic once again. Of course, they didn't know Gary never ate the apple."

"What do you think—now that you know?"

"I don't know."

"Don't you?" He put his hand under her chin and looked into her eyes. "There's been a connection between us since that first day, and it's never gone away. You can call it magic. You can call it whatever you want, but I call it truth."

She swallowed hard at the expression in his eyes, for there was a question there, a question she couldn't answer. *What do we do now?* The branches from the tree cast shadows on his face. Maybe the shadows had always been there, always hiding what they felt for each other.

"I can't wipe away the past nine years," she said. "I can't pretend they didn't exist, that I didn't live with and love someone else, because I did."

"I'm not asking you to do that."

"What are you asking me?"

"I don't know, Rachel. You tell me. You're the one who believes in the legend. If the magic is real, if an apple from that tree binds two people together for all time, then what are you going to do about me?"

"What do you want me to do?"

"How about you stop answering questions with questions, to start with?"

"You're confusing me. I don't know what you want me to say."

"Sure you do. You're just afraid to say it."

She saw the challenge in his eyes and wanted to rise to the occasion, but she couldn't seem to get there. "I need to go. I'll tell my grandmother you have other plans for dinner."

"That scared, huh?"

"I think we need some time apart."

"I think we've had too much time apart. But go, Rachel. Just remember this—you can run, but you can't hide," he said as she turned away.

"Oh, yeah?" she muttered, "Watch me."

Chapter 18

"You are impossible," Carly told Travis, fighting back the urge to stomp her foot. That would be childish, and she didn't want to be childish. She wanted to be mature and sophisticated and way out of this oaf's league. But he was being nice, and she hated him for it, hated him for making her feel anything but irritation.

"What is your problem? I just did something incredible, if I don't say so myself. I thought you'd be happy." He waved the tickets in front of her face, and she immediately grabbed them and tucked them out of sight.

"Someone could see you," she snapped, casting a quick glance into the hallway behind them. Her grandmother and Wesley were in the kitchen, but Rachel would be back any second. "How would I explain tickets to the opening of an art gallery in San Francisco? Where did you get these anyway?"

"A friend of mine works for a radio station in the city. I asked him to let me know if he got free tickets for anything arty."

"I can't go," she said flatly, even though she couldn't believe she was turning this opportunity down.

"Why not?"

"Because it's for Friday night, the night of the Harvest Dance, and Rachel would ask where I'm going. I can't tell her that I have an interest in art."

"You'll have to tell her someday. In fact, you should show her. I went into your basement earlier, and—"

"You did what?" she asked, her jaw dropping.

"I looked at some of those other paintings you got tucked away."

"You had no right."

"They were incredible. You have a talent, Carly, a talent you shouldn't be hiding."

"A talent my family would hang me for."

"I'll take you to the gallery opening," Travis said. "Tell Rachel we're going out on a date. She'll be happy it's me and not Antonio."

That reminded her. "I was going to take Antonio to the dance, another reason I can't go anywhere with you."

"He's still in New York, isn't he?"

"He should be back soon."

"I assume he hasn't called you?"

"I'm sure he's busy."

Travis sent her a thoughtful look. "You didn't sleep with him, did you?"

"As if that's any of your business!"

"You didn't. I'm glad."

"It has nothing to do with you." She didn't like the

gleam in his eyes. It was more than just a knowing look, it was a look filled with something else, a something else she wasn't going to give him. "Why did you do this?"

"Because I want you to have what you want," he said.

She couldn't have what she wanted, not at the expense of her family. She couldn't bear to lose them, and she would lose them if they thought she was like her mother. They'd feel betrayed by her painting. She knew that as surely as she knew her name was Carly Wood.

"You want to go, don't you?" Travis asked.

"Of course I want to go," she grumbled. "I would love to go."

He smiled. "Then let's do it."

"What about the dance? Rachel won't believe I'd go on a date with you instead of to the Harvest Dance."

"We'll figure something out."

"But why would you want to go to an art show? You don't even like art."

"How do you know what I like?" he challenged. "You think you know exactly who I am and what I want, but, baby, you don't have a clue. I'll pick you up five o'clock on Friday. Be ready to go." He grabbed the tickets out of her hand. "If you aren't ready, I'll go without you."

"Like you'd go by yourself."

"You want to take that chance?"

"Maybe I do," she said uncertainly, because this wasn't a step she was sure she wanted to take. She'd started down this road once before but had chickened out. Maybe she really wasn't that good. And if she wasn't that good, why risk losing everything else for a dream that would never materialize? It would be easier to just get married. Then whatever she and Antonio did would be part of their new life together. Rachel wouldn't see it as a betrayal. A woman was supposed to support her husband, and if Antonio's interest was art, then Carly's would have to be, too.

"Boy, I can see the wheels turning in your head," Travis observed. "You take the longest route of anyone I know to get from point A to point B. You want to be an artist, start by going to a showing. Don't start by marrying some guy you don't love."

How could he know what she was thinking? Had she spoken out loud? Before she could ask him, the front door opened and closed. Rachel was home. "Fine, I'll go with you," she said quickly. "But don't tell Rachel."

"Don't tell me what?" Rachel asked as she came into the living room. "Nothing," Carly replied abruptly. "I guess Dylan found you, huh?"

"Yeah, he found me."

Rachel didn't sound too happy, and Carly wondered why. "You look flushed."

Rachel put both hands to her face, looking guilty. "It's warm in here. I think we need to get a ceiling fan."

"Or maybe just send someone back to the city," Carly said pointedly.

"What are you doing here, Travis?" Rachel asked, changing the subject. "Looking for another mouse?"

He smiled. "We can't seem to find the little bugger. Carly thought she saw one run in here, but I couldn't find anything."

"It was probably just my imagination," Carly interjected. "Thanks for coming by." She walked over to the doorway, hinting that he should leave. For a moment she thought he was going to say something else, he so enjoyed yanking her chain, but all he did was murmur a good-night in Rachel's direction. Then he stopped in front of Carly and said, "Don't forget our date. Wear something pretty."

She silently counted to ten before turning back to face Rachel's inquiring gaze.

"You're going out with Travis?" Rachel asked.

"Just for dinner next weekend. He wants to plan a surprise party for his mother's birthday next month, and I said I'd help him." It was amazing how easily the lies came where her art was concerned. Sometimes Carly was amazed by herself. Or maybe she was amazed by how easily Rachel seemed to buy into her lies. Then again, Rachel didn't even seem to be listening. "What's up with you?" she asked.

"I told Dylan the Lady Elaine story."

"Was he impressed?"

Rachel shrugged, then sat down on the couch. "I don't know what he thought. But when I was telling him the story, I started thinking about more than the apple tree. I was thinking about Elaine's journey west. How brave she was. How much she was willing to sacrifice for the man she loved. She must have been an amazing woman. I'm beginning to wish we'd inherited more than the tree. I wish I could be that bold, that daring, that willing to throw away everything I know for everything I don't know."

Carly wished she could, too. Just as she wished she could share with Rachel the most important part of herself. But she'd rather have her sister believe she was in love with an Italian playboy than that she had the same passion for painting as their mother. Where was her bravery?

Their mother had had courage, maybe more courage than compassion. She'd chased her dream and to hell with the consequences, leaving behind a family shattered by her actions. "She stole it from us," Carly said, not realizing she'd said the words aloud until she saw the quizzical look on Rachel's face. "Mom. She stole our courage. She took it with her when she left. Because she ran away, we've been afraid to lose what we had left."

Rachel stared at her as if she'd never seen her before.

"You don't agree?" Carly asked sharply, feeling somewhat foolish.

"No. I mean, yes. Actually, I do agree. I've just never thought of it that way."

"We couldn't hold on to her, so we have to hold on to other things."

"Like the farm."

Carly nodded, even though for her it wasn't the farm at all, it was Rachel's love. It wasn't until this very moment that she realized what it was all about. She'd lost her mother and her father, too, for that matter. She couldn't afford to lose her sister.

"But you don't care about the orchards like I do," Rachel said slowly. "What is it you care about, Carly? What are you afraid to lose?"

It was the best opening she'd ever had to reveal her secret; she just needed to find the right words. Unfortunately, while she was thinking, Wesley came running into the room.

"You're back," he said, jumping onto Rachel's lap. "Dylan and I made a cabinet today. I want to show it to you."

"We'll go see it tomorrow, honey."

"Okay. Grandma says it's time to eat. Where's Dylan?"

"He had to go home."

Wesley's face fell. "But he said he was going to stay."

"Something came up," Rachel said. "You'll see him tomorrow, don't worry. Tell Grandma we'll be right there.

"Okay."

"Guess we better go eat," Rachel said to Carly, getting to her feet. "You were going to say something, though. What was it?"

Carly shook her head, for the moment had passed. "Nothing."

"Was it about Travis?"

"No! Goodness, why would you think that?"

"Because I don't believe for a second that Travis was here seeking a phantom mouse," Rachel said with a smile. "I think he's mad about you. He has been for a while."

"He's mad, but not about me."

"Oh, come on, surely you've noticed."

"I'm not interested in him that way."

Rachel frowned. "That's right. You want Antonio. Be careful, Carly. Be careful what you wish for. Sometimes it comes true and then you find out it's not at all what you wanted."

"You know what I wish?" Wesley asked Dylan when he stopped by the house on Monday after school.

"What do you wish?" Dylan asked as he sat back on his heels and gazed into the little boy's face.

"I wish that Daddy would come back now and help us with the house instead of waiting for us to finish it." Wesley's blue eyes challenged Dylan to refute the fact that Gary was coming home.

Dylan wasn't sure how to respond. This was the one conversation they hadn't had, the one they'd both avoided. Now that it had arrived, he didn't know what to say. He didn't want to make things worse, but he also didn't want to lie. They'd established a trust between them, a trust he wanted to protect.

"Do you really think your dad would just wait for us to finish the house?" he asked, the words coming out slowly. "Don't you think he'd want to help if he could?"

Wesley wet his lips with his tongue. "He's very busy. He has a lot of work to do. He can only come home on the weekends. And sometimes not even then. He wants to be with us, but he can't."

Wesley sounded like he was reciting a familiar refrain. Were these the words Gary had used to explain his frequent absences? And why had Gary been such an absent father? Hadn't he realized how much Wesley missed him when he was gone? Maybe Dylan was to blame, too. Maybe he shouldn't have offered Gary the convenient city apartment. Maybe he should have urged his friend to spend more time at home with his family. Well, it was too late to do anything about the past. But he could do the right thing now.

"That's true," he said easily. "Your dad wants to be with you more than anything. But he can't, can he, Wes?"

Wesley shook his head as the tears began to fall down his cheeks. Dylan put down his hammer and gathered the boy in his arms, feeling his small body shake with the sudden release of sobs. Rachel said Wesley hadn't cried much since the funeral. But he was crying now, weeping like his heart was breaking. It was the worst sound of pain Dylan had ever heard. He wished he could make it go away, but all he could do was hold on.

Finally, the sobs began to break. Dylan loosened his grip so he could wipe away the traces of Wesley's tears with the sleeve of his shirt.

"It's okay to cry," he told him. "I cried enough to fill a big bucket when I found out your dad had died."

"Why did he have to die? Why did he have to go away

and not come back? It's not fair. Everyone else has a dad but me."

Wesley's simple questions broke Dylan's heart. They reminded him not only of Gary but of Jesse. He could remember clinging to his mother, asking her why Jesse had to die. *Why did God have to take him to heaven? Why couldn't he have more time?*

"It's not fair," Dylan agreed, giving Wesley another hug. "But I know this. Your dad loved you a lot."

"He did?" Wesley stepped back, digging his hands into the pockets of his blue jeans.

"Yes. Did you know he called me the night you were born? He was so excited to have a son. He told me he was the luckiest man on earth, and no one in the world could ever mean more to him than you did."

Wesley sniffed, taking in every word like a long, cold drink that he was thirsty for.

"I'd never heard your dad sound so happy. And over the years, he'd tell me how proud of you he was, every little thing you did—when you first learned to talk and walk and read and ride a bicycle. He loved being with you, Wes. And the only reason he's not here with us today is because he can't be."

"Sometimes I think he's still coming back," Wesley confessed. "Like his car will come up the driveway and he'll honk three times, the way he did when he came home after a trip. Sometimes I stay up all night listening for the horn. Don't tell Mommy. She doesn't want me to stay up at night."

"I won't tell her."

"She misses my dad, too."

"I know she does."

"Do you think she's going to like the house if Daddy isn't here?"

Dylan looked at the house taking shape around them. He had followed Gary's plans carefully, not wanting to veer off in the wrong direction, but sometimes he wondered if this was truly the house Rachel wanted. Could she be happy here on her own? Or would it always feel empty? Would it always be just a house and not a home?

Gary would want Rachel to be happy. Whatever he had or hadn't done with other women, Dylan knew with a deep and unyielding certainty that Gary had loved Rachel on some level and her happiness had always been important to him.

"Mommy wanted a big bathtub in her bedroom," Wesley said. "But Daddy said he'd never get her out of it, so he drew in a shower."

Dylan smiled, seeing a new light in Wesley's eyes. "You think your mom would rather have a bathtub?"

He nodded. "A really big one, the kind you can swim in."

"With jets and bubbles?"

"That would be cool. And I could use it, too."

"Then maybe we should put one in. What do you think?"

Wesley's smile went from ear to ear. "I think we should."

"Then we will."

"I can't help you very long today. I have a soccer game at five. It was supposed to be this coming Saturday, but it got rescheduled because everyone is going to the festival."

"That's okay."

Wesley hesitated. "Do you think you could come to the game? Do you have time?"

Once again Dylan had the sense that Wesley had asked this question more than a few times.

"We'll make time," he said firmly. "How about we go out to the field a little early and warm up?"

"Really?"

Dylan tousled Wesley's hair. "Yeah, really. Now, hand me those nails. We've got some work to finish before we go."

"What are you doing here?" Rachel asked Dylan as he parked in the spot next to hers at the soccer field.

"Wesley and I are going to take some warm-up shots. Didn't he tell you? Hey, Wes," he said as her son got out of the minivan.

"Hey, Dylan." Wesley squatted down to retie his shoe.

"No, he didn't tell me," Rachel said. "What's going on?"

"I told you, a warm-up." Dylan gave her a little wink with his smile, and she had a feeling there was more going on than soccer.

Wesley had been acting differently since he'd come home an hour ago. Something had gone on between these two males, but she didn't have a clue to what it was.

"Toss me the ball, Wes," Dylan said.

Wesley tossed him the soccer ball. Dylan rolled it around in his hands. "It's been a while since I've kicked one of these."

"Are you planning on kicking one now?" Rachel asked.

"Maybe."

"What's going on with you two?"

"We just had a little man-to-man chat," Dylan replied. "I'll tell you later. Let's go, Wes."

They were off before Rachel could protest, not that she wanted to. Wesley had been struggling with his soccer skills since the season had begun a few weeks earlier. Since she'd never played soccer, she couldn't do much to help him. And Gary had never had the time. Or made the time, she thought with a sigh. But then, neither one of them had realized just how little time they would have.

Rachel wandered over to the bleachers and sat down. One of the other moms, Ellen Connor, sat down next to her.

"Who's that?" Ellen asked.

"Dylan Prescott. He's working on my new house."

"Ah, that's the sexy contractor. I should have guessed," Ellen said with a laugh. "My sister, Melissa, says all the single girls in town have their eyes on him. Is he available?"

Rachel felt a little discomfort with the question. Was Dylan available? Well, of course he was. He was an attractive man with a successful business. And he was good with kids, that was for sure. Athletic, judging by the way he was juggling the soccer ball. Sexy? He certainly did fill out a pair of tight blue jeans. Oh, heavens! She felt the warmth rush to her face and hoped to God that Ellen was still looking at Dylan and not at her.

"Sure, he's available," she said, deliberately infusing a breezy note into her voice.

"He was friends with Gary, wasn't he?"

"Since they were kids."

"It's nice of him to help out now." Ellen shot Rachel a sideways glance. "I heard you and Dylan heated up the dance floor at Shenanigans the other night."

"We danced. I don't think there was any smoke."

"Too bad. I mean, I know you're still grieving, but he seems like a great guy." Ellen sighed as her son called out for a Gatorade. "Can I get you anything at the snack bar?"

"No, thanks."

Rachel should have known that dance would stir up

gossip. She should have thought about that before she'd insisted on the silly bet. Of course, she hadn't been thinking at all, just floating along on the tide of desire that always arrived with Dylan. But she had to start thinking, start acting better or at least differently. She wasn't being fair to Dylan.

As Ellen had reminded her, Dylan was free, single, available. He'd make a great husband, a wonderful father. Someday he'd marry and wear both of those titles. Someday he'd find a woman who'd make him feel like he was first in her heart. He was right; he deserved that. She could never give him first. She could only give him second. And that wouldn't be enough for him.

She had to step back, keep her distance, give him a chance to get on with his life. She'd already had her turn on the merry-go-round to grab the brass ring and spin crazily around. It was Dylan's turn. And there were women who wanted him, probably dozens, she thought, feeling even more depressed.

"Why the long face?" Dylan asked.

She was startled to find him standing next to her. Wesley had joined the rest of his team on the field for the official warm-up. He already looked like a different kid, like someone who felt more comfortable in the huddle. Dylan had given him that confidence. She owed him a lot. More than she could ever repay.

"Rachel, you're a million miles away."

"Thanks for helping Wesley. He looks better already."

"He just needs to believe in himself, that's all. Move over," he added, climbing onto the bench next to her.

"So what was the subject of your man-to-man talk?" she asked, subtly scooting a little farther down the bench so their thighs weren't touching, but Dylan closed in on her again. Aside from running into the family of four sitting next to her, she had no choice but to stay where she was.

"We talked about Gary. Wesley brought it up, Rachel. I just listened and held on when he started crying."

"He cried?" Her gaze immediately darted back to her son. Wesley wasn't crying now. He was laughing and kicking a ball and having a great time.

"Cried up a storm. He needed to get it out."

"He admitted that Gary is dead?"

"Pretty much. It's a start."

She put a hand on Dylan's knee. "Thank you."

He covered her hand with his own, a warm, tender touch that almost undid her previous resolve to let him go. How could she let him go when he was holding on to her?

"I didn't do anything but listen."

"That was enough. By the way, I found the number for Gary's doctor. He had a checkup a month before he died. The doctor told me that Gary was given a clean bill of health."

"One less question," Dylan said.

"Yeah, one less question. I also spoke to his father this morning. He was surprised to hear from me."

"I'll bet."

"He doesn't know why Gary went to Tahoe. He also didn't seem to remember anyone named Laura. In fact, he said the only thing he and Gary had talked about was a small loan. Apparently, Gary had sent him money over the years." She paused. "He sounded very sad, a man with a lot of regrets. I told him I'd send him some pictures of Wesley. After all, he is family."

"You're a good person."

"I try." As the stands began to fill, Rachel tried to pull her hand away, but he wouldn't let go.

"Dylan, people will talk."

"Who cares?"

"I do. And you should, too. See that blond woman talking to the coach?" Rachel said, pointing out Ellen Connor. "She asked me if you were available. Her sister is gorgeous. Her name is Melissa. She works at the coffee shop on Main Street."

"I think I've met her."

"Ellen says half the single women in town are after you."

"Only half?" he asked dryly. "I must be slipping."

"You could have anyone you want."

He squeezed her hand. "If that were true, I'd have you."

"But you don't want me. You said so yourself. You don't want to be second best. You don't want to be someone's second husband—someone's stepfather," she added. This time when she pulled her hand away, he released it. "The game is starting," she said unnecessarily as the referee blew his whistle and the boys lined up on the field.

Dylan didn't reply, nor did he offer a counter argument. So that was that. He agreed that he didn't want to be second best. They'd finally drawn a line between them that would stick. It wasn't about Gary anymore. It was about what could never be.

Chapter 19

"Careful," Dee said as Rachel took the sign out of her hand Thursday afternoon. "The paint isn't quite dry."

Rachel looked at the carefully scripted letters announcing the pumpkin prices for the upcoming festival. "It's great, but did we really need something so artistic? It's just a sign."

"Your cousin Tracy spent a long time making those pumpkin faces. Be sure you say thank you," Dee said reprovingly.

"I will." Rachel set the sign behind the counter and checked her watch. "Wesley is probably driving Dylan up the wall about now."

"He's over at the house again?"

"Every day after school." No matter what other enticing adventures Rachel had offered up, Wesley always chose to go to their house. Sometimes she wasn't quite sure if the "their" referred to her and Wesley or to Wesley and Dylan.

And she wasn't brave enough to ask. It was bad enough that every sentence coming from Wesley's mouth was punctuated with what Dylan said or Dylan did. So much for trying to put the man out of her mind.

She'd spent the past few days avoiding him. After their conversation at the soccer field, she'd told herself to stay away, and for the most part, she'd done just that, having only minimal contact with Dylan, a brief conversation now and then when she dropped off Wesley or picked him up. It hadn't helped. He was still in her head, under her skin, driving her slowly mad.

"I understand the house is coming around very quickly," Dee said, interrupting her thoughts. "Dylan has half the town working on it. At least the half that isn't working on the festival. Speaking of which, don't forget to tell Dylan to vote for your cousin Christie tomorrow night. She really wants to be the Harvest Queen. He can vote at the dance."

"I'm not sure if Dylan will go to the dance."

"Of course he will—everyone goes."

"He doesn't like to dance."

"That's not what your aunt Shannon told me."

Rachel made a face at her aunt. "I was wondering when you would bring that up."

"I heard there was a long kiss at the end of that dance."

"It was nice, but the world didn't end. I wish everyone would stop talking about it."

"It's not a crime to care about someone else."

"It's not like that with Dylan."

"Are you sure?"

"I'm trying to be sure," Rachel admitted. "He confuses me. He always has."

"A little confusion can be good."

"Frankly, I'd prefer more clarity. I don't know who I am anymore. I was a wife. Now I'm a widow. I was part of a couple; now I'm alone. People look at me differently. They treat me differently. I want to be normal again."

"You will be. It takes time."

"How long did it take you to feel normal after uncle Jeff left?"

Dee frowned at that question. "Longer than it should have. But Jeff left me. He didn't die. There's a difference."

"It was just as final. And we're both alone. I'm sure you didn't expect to be alone. I know I didn't. I thought that damn apple would take care of forever."

"Ah, the magic of Lady Elaine. You were depending on that."

Rachel smiled. "You gave uncle Jeff one of the Lady Elaines, didn't you?"

"No, I never did," Dee said, surprising Rachel.

"Why not? Didn't you believe in the legend?"

"You can only give the apple to one man, and I'd given the apple to someone else a few years before I met Jeff."

"Really? I had no idea. Who was it?"

"It doesn't matter. It didn't work. He married someone else."

"Was he a local boy?" Rachel persisted, certain she was onto something when Dee avoided her gaze. "Was he?"

"You're certainly nosy."

"And you're evasive."

"It was a hundred years ago."

"Not that long. Tell me."

"All right. It was Malcolm Jennings," Dee said, waving her hand in the air.

"The butcher?" Rachel stared at her aunt. "Malcolm's wife died three years ago."

"I know that. So?"

"So do you still have feelings for him?"

"Don't be silly."

"I don't think I am. Why did you give him the apple in the first place? You must have felt something."

Dee didn't reply right away, her eyes taking on a dreamy expression, as if she were traveling back to that time in her life. "I fell in love with him in the second grade, I think. He sat behind me and pulled my braids."

"How romantic."

"In the third grade, he pushed down a bigger kid who teased me about something, and I loved him even more. By high school I thought he was the man I would marry. The day he asked me to the prom was the day I gave him the apple. We ate it together. I was so happy. A few days later, Malcolm told me that a few weeks earlier, he'd gotten drunk and slept with Lucille. She was pregnant and he was going to marry her. That was that."

"What about now?"

"I'm too old to start over, Rachel. I invested so much time in Jeff that it is unthinkable to consider doing it all again, going through those nervous first dates and pretending to be prettier and thinner and more interested in sex than I really am." She smiled at Rachel. "I'm set in my ways. It would be difficult to bring a new man into my life."

"What about an old friend? What about Malcolm? He's alone. You're alone."

"Too much water under that bridge. It's different for you, Rachel. You're young. You have a child to raise."

"It doesn't seem fair to Gary. That I can go on, that I can be happy again. Where is the justice in that?"

"There isn't any. Life is about accepting what is and letting go of the rest. It's about being happy. If that means falling in love again, then fall in love. The marriage vows don't say forever; they say 'until death do you part.' "

"I never thought of that."

"Maybe you should."

"It sounds like you're giving me permission."

"You don't need my permission. Listen to your heart."

"I was faithful to Gary. From the minute I said I do until the last time I kissed him good-bye." Rachel felt as if she had to make that clear.

Dee stepped up and gave Rachel a hug. "I know you were."

"People are going to think that Dylan and I—"

"No one who knows you would ever think anything."

"But there was something," Rachel heard herself confess. "A long time ago, before the wedding. It was just a kiss. Actually, it felt like a lot more than just a kiss, but we put it aside, and we went on with our lives. And I loved Gary. I tried to make him happy."

"He's gone now. It's time to make yourself happy. You should start worrying about your future instead of your past."

"I *am* worrying about my future," Rachel said with a sigh. "Dylan doesn't belong here any more than Gary did."

"I wouldn't be so sure about that."

"Mommy, Mommy!" Wesley's excited voice cut through their conversation, and Rachel turned around as the door banged open and Wesley literally flew into the shop. "Look what Dylan gave me. I'm a carpenter!" He pointed proudly to the smallest tool belt Rachel had ever seen.

"That's wonderful." Rachel squatted down so she could see the belt better. "You look great in it."

"What do you think, Aunt Dee?" Wesley asked, seeking more compliments.

"I think you're official now."

"I'm going to show Grandpa. If he needs a screwdriver again, he doesn't have to swear about not finding one. I'll have one right in my tool belt."

Rachel laughed as Wesley ran out of the shop to share his good news. Her laughter quickly faded when she saw Dylan standing in the doorway. Their gazes met and caught, a myriad of emotions flowing back and forth between them without a word being said. They must have looked at each other for far too long, because Dee cleared her throat and said, "I've got to go back to the office. I'll catch up with you later, Rachel. Dylan," she murmured as she passed by him.

"You made Wesley really happy," Rachel said. "Thank you."

"It was nothing." He paused. "You've been avoiding me."

"You've been avoiding me."

He tipped his head. "Old habit, hard to break."

"I know what you mean."

"I did something I thought you should know about."

"Okay." She braced herself for the sound of yet another shoe dropping.

"I hired an investigator. I gave him Laura's phone number and asked him if he could figure out who she was and where she lived. He said he'd check in with me by tomorrow at the latest. I didn't tell him anything else."

Rachel didn't know how she felt about this latest development. Obviously her own search had stalled for several reasons: the Harvest Festival, procrastination and a real ambivalence deep down about learning anything more.

Nothing they'd turned up so far had been good, that was for sure.

"Okay," she agreed.

"That's it, just okay?"

"For the moment. I wanted to talk to you about the house. I've been thinking about some things." Things that had more to do with her future than her past.

"Like what?" Dylan asked.

"Like that room at the back. Instead of making it an office, I wondered if it could be a sunroom with lots of glass and double doors opening onto a deck. Gary thought we only needed a deck off the kitchen for barbecuing, but I was thinking that a deck off that side of the house would offer a nice view of the trees. You know how much I like my trees."

His expression didn't waver the whole time she was talking. She nervously plunged ahead. "If you don't like it, we can leave it as is. I mean, maybe we should build the house exactly the way Gary planned it. It's the way he wanted it."

"He's not going to live in it," Dylan said flatly.

"What do you think about a sunroom and a deck?"

"I think you should have a Jacuzzi tub built into the deck with drink holders so you can sip a glass of wine and look out at your trees and your valley."

"That sounds fabulous. Thank—"

"I don't want any more words of thanks," Dylan told her as he moved slowly and deliberately toward her. "If you really want to thank me, you'll have to be more creative."

He didn't put out a hand to her. He didn't even lean in her direction, but she knew what he wanted. More important, she knew what she wanted. She pressed her mouth to his and once again they went up in spontaneous combustion.

It was a delicious, warm, late-afternoon kiss that went on far too long for a simple thank-you. Rachel didn't want to pull away. Neither, apparently, did Dylan, giving her back kiss for kiss until somewhere in her consciousness she heard voices and footsteps, and it occurred to her she had once again lost her mind.

She pulled away just in time, smoothing her hair down as Wesley and her grandfather approached the shop.

"Someday we won't be interrupted," Dylan said huskily. "Someday we'll find out what lies down that road. Neither one of us will be able to go on until we do."

"You need to go on with someone else," she said. "We need to let go of each other. So you can get on with your future, and I can get on with mine."

"What was that kiss about, then?"

"That was good-bye."

"It didn't feel like good-bye."

"It was supposed to."

"You might have to try again."

Rachel shook her head. "Not now."

"Because you're not ready to say good-bye. I'm not either." And with that, he turned and left.

Dylan was still thinking about that kiss Friday night when he walked down Main Street toward the Recreation Center, where the Annual Harvest Festival Dance was about to kick off. He'd spent most of the day telling himself he wouldn't go, but by the time the tenth person he'd run into had said he'd see him there, Dylan realized he would be going because Rachel would be there. And, damn his soul, he couldn't seem to stop showing up where she was.

She'd told him she was setting him free. He deserved to have a wife and children who put him first, who called him Dad and not Stepdad. He should have been happy that she understood he couldn't take Gary's place. But he didn't feel happy. He felt restless, as if she'd changed the rules of the game in midstream.

Who was she to set him free? Who was she to tell him when to let go? He'd let go when he damn well pleased.

"Hey, Dylan."

He nodded to Conrad, the plumbing contractor, waved hello to some of the Sheetrock guys and smiled at his innkeeper, Mrs. Laningham. The brunette waitress from the coffee shop asked him to save her a dance, as did the cute cashier from the market who always made a point of asking him if he'd found everything he needed. It amazed him how many people he knew. He'd been in town a couple of weeks, and already he felt like an old-timer.

"Dylan, you made it." Rachel's aunt Dee came forward to greet him. "Did you bring Rachel with you?"

"No. But she called earlier and said I should come and vote for someone named Christie to be Harvest Queen, or something. I assumed she'd be here."

"Oh, she will," Dee said with a wave of her hand. "The voting table is against that wall, and Christie sure would appreciate your vote. We haven't had a Harvest Queen in our family since Rachel won the title."

"Rachel was Harvest Queen?" Why didn't that surprise him?

"She sure was, the year she turned eighteen. She was as pretty as she could be with that apple tiara on her head."

"I'll bet she was. I can't think of a more appropriate queen. She does love her apples."

Dee grinned back at him. "That she does. I'm glad you came. She'll need you later on."

"Why?" he asked.

But Dee wasn't looking at him anymore; she was saying hello to an elderly couple and offering to show them to the voting table. He decided he might as well follow behind and cast his vote, which was, after all, the main reason he was here.

Actually, it wasn't the reason at all. The reason was Rachel. And there she was, standing by the table, filling out a ballot. She wore a short, clingy dress the color of raspberries. Her legs were bare, her feet encased in the highest pair of heels he'd ever seen her wear. For beauty, he wondered, or for courage?

She turned and saw him watching her. In that second when their eyes met, he saw nothing but pleasure, attraction, desire. Then she blinked, and caution appeared as an afterthought, a reminder of who they were, what they were and where they were. How he wished they were meeting for the first time; no past, no friend, between them.

"Dylan." Rachel took a step forward. "Have you voted yet?"

"I was just about to."

She handed him a ballot. "You know what to do, right?"

"I think I can handle it." He took the pencil from her hand and put an X next to the name Christie Wood. When he was through he deposited his piece of paper in the voting box. "So where is this Christie, and whose kid is she?"

Rachel took his arm and pulled him over to the side. "She's right by the stage, the blonde in the blue dress with the spaghetti straps. She is one of my uncle Harry's daughters."

"Not bad," he murmured.

Rachel rapped him on the shoulder. "Down, boy, she's engaged."

"Engaged? She looks about fifteen."

"She's twenty, and this is her last year of eligibility. She'll be married by next October, and only single girls can be the Harvest Queen."

"I hear tell you once wore the crown," he said with a grin. "What was your talent? Apple bobbing?"

She made a face at him. "Very funny. There is no talent competition."

"Bathing suit?" he asked hopefully.

"It's pretty much a popularity contest."

"The person with the most friends, or should I say the most family present, wins. Is that it?"

"That's it."

"And what do you do once you're queen?"

"You reign over the rest of the dance. You ride in the mayor's convertible in the parade. You get to pick the winners of the various contests tomorrow afternoon. You know, the biggest pumpkin, the best face painting, et cetera." She shook a finger at him. "Don't even say whatever it is you're thinking."

"Why? What am I thinking?"

"Probably that this is all very foolish and schlocky."

"Is that a word, schlocky?"

"I have no idea. How about schmaltzy, is that a word?"

"I'm not making fun of you, Rachel, or any of your friends."

"I know we're not very sophisticated. But most of the people here work really hard on their farms or in their businesses during the year. This is the one weekend when we get to show off our goods, so to speak."

"So defensive," he murmured. "Why? Do I seem like I'm judging you?"

"Gary used to say it was hokey."

"As long as you enjoy it, what does it matter?"

"Are you enjoying it?" she asked. "I'm sure it's not the kind of party you're used to."

"I'm having a great time. In fact, I'm feeling so popular, I think . . ." He dropped his voice down a notch and whispered in her ear, "I think I could be the Harvest King."

Rachel burst out laughing. "You?"

"Yes, me," he said with mock pain. "Why not me?"

"Because you're a city boy."

"I'm not a boy, I'm a man," he corrected her.

"Oh, I know that. Believe me, I know that."

The laughter and teasing between them suddenly stilled. The rest of the room faded away, the noise, the music, the chatter. It was just the two of them.

"It always comes back to this," she murmured. "No matter what we say, how far we step back, it always comes back to this."

Before he could reply, the microphone on the stage gave a shrill scream, and a woman called for attention.

"Let's get out of here," he told Rachel.

"I can't. They're about to announce the queen."

"I'm sure someone will tell you later who won."

"I can't," she repeated. "Not yet."

"Fine, but we're going to discuss this one-step-forward, two-steps-back thing before the night is through."

"Actually, you're going to have the chance to do some stepping sooner than that," she muttered.

"What?"

"Listen."

"As is tradition," the large woman on the stage boomed

out with an enthusiastic smile, "while we're counting the votes, our previous Harvest Queens will dance with their personal kings. Ladies, don't be shy. Come on out to the dance floor, please."

"That's us," Rachel said.

"That's you," he countered.

"You just said you were a king. I happen to be in need of a king." She slipped her hand into his. "It won't hurt a bit."

The pain was exquisite. Rachel felt as if her nerve endings were on fire. And the pain was made worse by the fact that she couldn't do what she really wanted to do—couldn't run her fingers into Dylan's thick, wavy brown hair, couldn't pull his head down and kiss him, couldn't slip his coat off his shoulders and undo the buttons on his shirt.

It was true what she'd said earlier. No matter how many times she told herself she didn't want him, couldn't have him, would never cross that last line between them, they kept coming back to this place where desire battled with reason.

Reason told her to back off, to keep her distance. It was too soon. It was too late. Either way, she was vulnerable. But desire told her to move closer, to let herself go, to lose herself in him.

Dylan's hand tightened on her waist; his chin brushed the top of her head. She wouldn't look at him, wouldn't let those lips get close to hers. They weren't in Shenanigans in front of her aunt and uncle; they were in the recreation center in front of the whole damn town. The friends watching her now were the friends who had come to her wedding and to Gary's funeral. They wouldn't understand this relationship she had with Dylan.

"Relax," he murmured. "It's just a dance."

She wanted to believe him. But he was wrong. There was a lot more going on between them than just a dance.

The music finally stopped to a smattering of applause. With relief, Rachel turned her attention back to the podium. Mrs. Bailey, the Mistress of Ceremonies, motioned for a drumroll.

"The winner of this year's festival, our new Harvest Queen, is Miss Christie Wood," she said.

Rachel clapped her hands with genuine pleasure as she watched her younger cousin rush up to the stage amidst a flurry of congratulations. After she was given a bouquet of flowers and a tiara, a speech was called for.

"Thank you so much," Christie said, her eyes welling with tears. "This means so much to me. I'm an apple girl all the way down to the tips of my toes. Nothing gives me greater pride than to be this year's queen."

"I'm so happy for Christie," Rachel said to Dylan.

He smiled back. "An apple girl down to the tips of her toes. Must run in the family, huh?"

"I used to be that apple girl."

"Not anymore?" he quizzed.

"Not anymore." It was the truth, she realized. Somewhere along the way she'd grown up, she'd changed. She wasn't a girl anymore. She was a woman. And she didn't want just apples in her life. "Let's go."

He raised an eyebrow. "Where?"

She hesitated as he gave her the opening she needed to break away for home, for safety, for everything she knew and held dear. But was home really where she wanted to go?

Chapter 20

Dylan didn't say anything as he unlocked the door to his hotel room. But then, he hadn't said anything after she'd told him she didn't want to go home. He'd simply walked her out of the building and down the three short blocks to his hotel. Since everyone was at the dance, there was only a teenager manning the front desk, a teenager who didn't even glance at them. That hurdle aside, Rachel had a bigger one to face, the one inside herself.

She went into Dylan's room and waited while Dylan flipped on a light by the bed. The room was neat and tidy, but Dylan was the kind of guy who had a place for everything and everything in its place. Where was her place? Where did she belong? She held her purse in front of her like a shield of armor, afraid to put it down, afraid to take a step forward.

"You can have second thoughts," Dylan said, watching her closely.

His words triggered a memory of another time they'd stood like this, stiff and uncertain. The night before her wedding, he'd said the same thing. *You can have second thoughts.*

She'd pushed those second thoughts aside. She'd run back into the restaurant, looking for Gary, her dad, herself. There was nowhere to run this time, no one whose arms would envelop her in a big bear hug, no one except Dylan. If he opened his arms, she would run into them. But his arms remained at his sides, his hands in his pockets.

"Is it supposed to be this hard?" she asked.

"Maybe it's hard because it matters."

"I don't want it to matter. It could just be sex. Casual sex."

"It will matter. And it won't be casual," he said in a husky voice. "You and I both know that."

"I wish it had just happened, that we'd been swept away, no rational thinking involved."

"As soon as we touch each other, that will probably be the end of all rational thought," he said with a small smile.

She felt better with his smile, felt like she could handle this Dylan, the one who was amused and lighthearted. But what of the other Dylan, the one with fire and passion and complexity? The one who'd stayed in her head all these years. The one she'd instinctively known would over-whelm and consume her if given the chance. What about him? Could she handle him? She felt anxious, excited and scared all at the same time. Like a woman in love.

No. She wasn't in love with him. This wasn't love. It couldn't be. She'd promised to love one man for all time. But here was another. She cared about him deeply. He'd al-ways had a piece of her heart. Was this love, too? Could she love two men in her lifetime? Was that fair to either one of them?

"Are you nervous at all?" she asked him.

"Yes."

"Really? Because I'm feeling very unsure of myself." She wet her lips as she thought about what she wanted to tell him. "I've only been with one man. Doesn't that sound ridiculous in this day and age? Most people have had a dozen lovers at least. But I was nineteen when we got married. Before that, I just didn't like anyone enough to—you know."

"I wasn't asking, Rachel."

"I feel like I need to tell you. Not that you have to tell me. You don't. Your past is your past. I just don't want you to expect someone really experienced and . . . Oh, God, I don't even know what I'm trying to say."

"Maybe you're trying to talk yourself out of this. Like I said before, it's up to you. I'm not holding you." He opened his arms wide to emphasize his point.

"I want you to hold me," she whispered.

"Are you sure? I want you to be sure of what you want and who you want."

She hated the hardness that came into his eyes. "I'm not here because I'm lonely and I'm missing Gary. Even though I am lonely and I do miss Gary." She let the words sink in, then went on. "That's a different issue. I'm here because of you. Because everything has changed in the last few weeks. I'm tired of looking over my shoulder. I'm tired of looking back, trying to grab onto something that is gone. I have no idea what's ahead, tomorrow or next week or next month."

"None of us do."

"I used to feel like I was walking on solid ground. I knew the path. I knew the sights. But I don't feel that way anymore. And it isn't just Gary's secrets that have made that ground shaky, it's you, too. You're in my heart. You're under my skin. You're in the air I breathe. I can't stop thinking about you. I can't stop wanting to touch you, wanting to be with you."

"I know what you mean." His eyes darkened with the desire he'd been holding in check.

"I want to live in the present, in this moment, at least for tonight. Is that wrong?"

"Not wrong, but tomorrow will come and probably regrets right along with it. You've always felt guilty about me. I've always been your deep, dark secret, haven't I, Rachel?"

She saw the challenge in his eyes and said, "Yes. But haven't I been yours? Haven't you felt guilty?"

"So where does that leave us? Do you want something to really feel guilty about?"

"No. I'm not going to feel guilty about this." She lowered her purse, then tossed it onto the bed. "I want to be with you tonight. There's no one else in this room, no one but you and me. There's no past and no future; there's only now."

"You're not going to change your mind, are you? I don't think I could take that, Rachel."

"I'm not going to change my mind." She walked over to him and cupped his face with her hands, speaking straight from her heart, from her soul. "I want you, Dylan."

"God, I want you, too," he groaned, grabbing her by the waist and hauling her body up against his. His mouth came down on hers in a fiery burst of passion. They no longer needed words. What had to be said could be said with their lips and their hands and their bodies.

Their conversation had been slow and deliberate, yet

their lovemaking was anything but. Rachel had wanted to be swept away and she was. She was barely aware of Dylan stripping the clothes from her body. She sensed that somewhere along the way she became impatient and helped him do it. And somewhere along the way she helped him get rid of his clothes.

When they fell onto the bed, they were completely naked. Rachel thought she'd be shy and awkward, but being with Dylan was like the most natural thing in the world. She reveled in the freedom of being able to touch him in every conceivable way. His body was rough and textured as only a strong, powerful man's body could be, a man who worked outdoors with his hands and his back. His muscles rippled under her fingers; his heart beat faster with each touch; his groans deepened with each kiss.

She wanted the luxury of time to enjoy him, but Dylan was moving impatiently, hungrily, kissing her mouth, then her neck, his lips drifting to her breasts, her sensitive nipples, her belly and lower still. Each sensation, each kiss, set off another wave of pleasure. She couldn't think. She didn't want to think. Feeling was everything.

She selfishly took what Dylan eagerly gave. And when he finally filled her body, he also filled the lonely little corners, the guilty little desires. When the pleasure seemed too much, she tried to retreat. Dylan forced her to look at him, to move with him to each new peak, until she finally cried out, "No more." Their climaxes rolled over each other like two waves hitting the beach at the same time.

For a long while, the only sound in the room was breathing: fast, short gasps, finally settling into deeper, more satisfied breaths. Rachel was aware of Dylan's weight now, but she liked it, liked the way he surrounded her, enveloped her.

"I'm too heavy," he murmured.

"Don't go." She rubbed her hands over his buttocks, feeling him stir within her as she did so. A wonderful sense of possession, of completeness, came over her. She felt whole again.

Dylan kissed the base of her neck, then pushed the sweaty strands of hair off her face. "Are you all right?"

"Oh, yeah. Better than all right."

He smiled and rolled off her. Before she could protest, he'd moved her onto her side, with her head resting on his chest. She could hear the pounding of his heart against her cheek; she didn't think she'd ever forget the beat.

"How about you?" she asked, suddenly feeling self-conscious about how generous Dylan had been with his attention and how she'd soaked it all up like a hungry sponge.

"I'm great."

She lifted her head to look into his eyes. "Really?"

"Really," he reassured her with a warm, tender smile.

"Good." She dropped her head back onto his chest and smiled. "Because you were magnificent."

"Well, I like that."

"Like a forest fire."

"That hot, huh?"

She laughed. "I shouldn't have said that. You won't ever let me forget it, will you?"

"It's indelibly printed on my brain."

She traced a circle on his chest with her fingernail. "Did I tell you that Wesley is spending the night at a friend's house?"

"No."

"Well, he is." She lifted her head one more time. "Do you want me to stay?"

"Yes," he said without any hesitation, but his eyes were somber when he added, "If you want to."

"Can I be on top next time?"

The smile came back into his eyes. "You can be wherever you want. Hell, you can tie me to the bedpost."

"That sounds interesting," she said, her words abruptly cut off by the ringing of the phone.

Dylan glanced over at it. "I'll just let it ring. You've got your cell phone, right? In case Wesley needs you?"

"Yes, but it might be important."

"On a Friday night? How important could it be?"

But she saw the shadow in his eyes and knew he was thinking the same thing she was, that it could be about Gary. The investigator had promised to call by today. "I'm going to use the bathroom. Why don't you answer it?" She slid off the bed before he could protest.

When she'd finished in the bathroom, she put on the white terry-cloth robe hanging on the back of the door and returned to the bedroom. Dylan had retrieved his boxer shorts and was jotting something down on a piece of paper. A moment later, he said good-bye and hung up.

"Work stuff," he told her. "A call from one of my foremen on a job I'm running in San Francisco."

"Everything all right?"

"Good enough. They still don't think they can handle some of these things without me."

"You're the man."

He smiled. "You want to come closer and say that?"

She laughed. "I'm coming. But do you think I could borrow a T-shirt?"

"Well, you won't be wearing it for long, but sure you

can borrow one," he said with a grin. "Top drawer of the dresser."

She moved to the dresser and was just opening the drawer when he said, "Wait." He jumped out of bed. "I'll get it for you."

"I can do it," she said, reaching into the drawer. Unfortunately, what she pulled out wasn't a T-shirt. It was white and lacy and silky. It was a teddy, a woman's teddy. "Whose is this?"

Dylan cleared his throat. "I'm not sure."

"You're not sure?" she asked incredulously. She turned the teddy over in her hand, the design suddenly very familiar. She'd seen this before. She'd admired the cut but had thought it too daring for herself. "Oh, my God!"

"What?"

"This is Carly's teddy."

"Carly?" he said, sounding shocked.

"What is Carly's teddy doing in your drawer?"

"It's not what you think," he said quickly.

"You're fooling around with my sister?"

"No! Hell, no," he said forcefully. "I brought the teddy with me. I found it in—"

"You found it in . . ." She put a hand to her heart. "No." She shook her head in disbelief. "Tell me you didn't. Please tell me."

"I don't want to tell you anything. I don't want to hurt you, Rachel."

"Where was it, Dylan? I think you have to say the words."

"I found it in Gary's apartment," he replied heavily. "But I didn't know it was Carly's."

"Why didn't you tell me?"

"I wasn't sure it meant anything."

"And that perfume, I wonder if that was hers, too." Rachel's mind raced. Her stomach churned and bile rose to her throat. She put a hand to her mouth, feeling nauseated. "My husband and my sister? Oh, God! When is it going to end? When will I finally know everything?"

"You have to talk to Carly."

"I don't think I ever want to talk to her."

"There might be a reasonable explanation. I'm sure there is."

"I don't see how there could be." She threw the teddy back in the drawer and slammed it shut.

"Do you want to go home?" he asked quietly.

She looked at him with despair. "Where is that, Dylan? Where is home? I don't think I know anymore."

He put his arms around her and drew her against his chest. "It's right here, Rachel," he whispered. "It's right here."

"I have had the best time," Carly said, twirling the empty champagne glass in her hand.

Travis smiled at her. "You're lit up like a Christmas tree."

"The bubbly did me in."

"Nah. It was the art. You're a cheap date. A few pictures and you're in heaven."

Carly waved her hand at the beautiful paintings adorning the walls of the gallery. It was after ten and the crowd was beginning to thin. She supposed they should go, too, but she was having a hard time tearing herself away. It had been an evening to remember, with conversations that at first had intimidated her but then had fascinated her.

"Isn't it all incredible?" she asked Travis.

He loosened his tie. "Not bad."

"It's not your thing, is it?" She didn't know why she felt disappointed. Travis was a country boy. He didn't belong here.

"It's your thing, and that's what matters. I'm glad you had a good time."

"I had a fabulous time, the best ever. I wish I could do this stuff all the time."

"Which one do you like the best?" He nodded toward the wall.

"The mirror," she said, walking over to the painting that had caught her attention the minute she'd come through the door. It was a shimmering abstract impression of a mirror, reflections barely there, hints of something, but no definition. "It's a trip into the imagination, into the world of the inner mind."

Travis tilted his head, considering her words. "I think the artist drank too much wine."

She made a face at him, but he just smiled back at her. "I don't pretend to get any of this. But I get you, Carly. That's all you should care about."

"Maybe I don't want you to get me."

"Don't you? Wouldn't you like to be with someone who understands you?"

She turned away and put her champagne glass on a tray of empty glasses. "It was nice of you to bring me here, but it doesn't change anything. Antonio and I are having dinner tomorrow night."

"Does he know about it yet?"

"Yes. He called me as soon as he got back from New York."

"Carly, give it up. He's not the man for you."

"He *is* the man for me, and tomorrow night we'll share

an apple tart for dessert," she told him, that desperate feeling returning to her stomach.

If she didn't get that apple into Antonio soon, she was afraid she never would. She was nowhere near as confident about him as she wanted Travis to think. But she had to succeed with Antonio. This gallery opening was the kind of thing Antonio did on a daily basis. He lived a cosmopolitan existence filled with champagne and beautiful people in beautiful clothes. That was the kind of life she wanted to lead, too.

"Travis? Miss Wood?"

Carly looked up to see a tall, thin man with glasses bearing down on them.

"Roger, I didn't think you would make it," Travis said, shaking the other man's hand.

"I got delayed at the opera. Wouldn't you know it?"

"Actually, I wouldn't. I'm not much of an opera guy."

"I forgot. Please introduce me to your friend."

"Carly Wood, this is Roger Bentley."

Carly shook his hand, a little ill at ease because of his intense scrutiny. What on earth was this man looking at? Was there something stuck in her teeth?

"Beautiful," Roger murmured. "Just as you said. Did you enjoy the opening, Miss Wood?"

"Very much, thank you."

"Roger's brother is the owner of this gallery. You met him earlier, Carly," Travis said. "Roger owns another gallery in Union Square."

"A much larger one," Roger said with a wicked glint in his eyes. "Travis tells me that you are a painter. I would like to see some of your work."

"You—you would?" Carly stuttered. She could hardly believe her ears. "But I'm just an amateur."

"I am interested in art, not in résumés. Travis tells me you're good. I would like to judge for myself. Could you bring me some of your paintings one day next week?"

"Yes, of course."

He pulled out a card and handed it to her. "I make no promises, you understand, but I will give you a fair and unbiased opinion, if you like."

"I would like that. Thank you."

"Wow," Travis said as Roger walked away.

"Wow," she echoed. "You told me your friend who works for a radio station got you the tickets."

"I didn't want to get your hopes up in case Roger couldn't make it."

"You told him about my paintings," she said in wonder. Then it occurred to her that he'd had no right to tell anyone about her paintings. "How could you do that?"

"Don't even pretend to be angry." He shook a finger at her. "This could be the opportunity of your lifetime. You're ambitious and realistic enough to recognize it. So say thank you, Travis, and then kiss me."

"I'm not going to kiss you."

"Do I have to do everything?" he asked with a dramatic sigh. He leaned over and kissed her on the lips, long and deep and filled with promise. "Now say thank you."

"For what?" she asked, completely befuddled. "For the kiss?"

"For the contact," he said with a laugh. "You don't need Antonio. You need me." And he kissed her again and again until someone laughed and said they'd better find a private room.

Carly broke away in embarrassment, still a small-town girl for all her pretense otherwise. She ran out of the gallery, not stopping until she hit the sidewalk. The cool air blew against her face in welcome relief. What had she been doing? What had she been thinking, kissing Travis like that? She didn't want him. She didn't. She wanted . . . Why couldn't she remember his name? Antonio! That was it. She wanted Antonio.

But Travis's arms came around her waist and he nuzzled her neck with his lips, driving Antonio once again to the recesses of her mind.

"Don't," she protested.

"All right, I can wait."

She pulled away from him. "You'll be waiting a long time."

"You know what I love about you? Your stubbornness."

"Yeah, that's what you love."

"And your passion."

She swallowed nervously. "I'm not getting a room with you."

"I didn't ask you to."

"You seem to be full of surprises tonight."

"I was thinking the same thing about you, but not just tonight. I wish I'd known about your painting before. It explains a lot, the way you can't settle down with a college major or a job. Because you know what you want to do, only you can't bring yourself to say it out loud. So you go about it in a very peculiar way, like trying to seduce Antonio. What is that all about anyway?"

"It's about love."

"It's about everything *but* love. And what of the other guys?"

"What other guys?" she asked with a shiver, for it was a foggy night in San Francisco, and she was getting chilly.

Before she could protest, Travis had whipped off his suit jacket and placed it around her shoulders. It was a touching gesture for a man who was at that very moment questioning her about other guys.

"There was Karl and Maxwell and what was that other guy's name—Steve?"

"Do you have a point?"

His expression turned serious. "My point is that you've been trying to grab onto every guy who passed through town, hoping he'd take you with him, only at the last second you don't go. Why is that?"

"Because those guys were wrong for me."

"They were, and so is Antonio." He rubbed his chin. "The one I can't figure out—I shouldn't even say anything."

"Don't stop now. You seem to be on quite a roll."

"Gary."

"Gary?" she echoed, rocking back on her heels. "Rachel's Gary? What are you talking about?" Even as she asked the last question, her heart sank to her stomach. He couldn't possibly know.

"You tell me, Carly. Tell me what was going on between you and Gary."

Chapter 21

"You don't have to stay with me," Rachel told Dylan as she paced back and forth in her living room. It was almost midnight, and Carly still hadn't come home from her date with Travis.

"I want to stay with you." Dylan sat on the couch, his eyes worried as he watched her move restlessly around the room. He hadn't said much since he'd driven her home almost an hour earlier.

"This probably wasn't the evening you were hoping for."

"I wasn't hoping for anything. We were living in the moment, remember?"

"It seems like a long time ago that we made . . ." Her voice faltered. How was it possible that she could go from being completely fulfilled to being completely shattered in only a matter of hours? And it always came back to Gary. The man was dead, but in the past few weeks he'd been more alive in her life than he had been during the past two years.

"Sit down, Rachel."

"I'm too restless."

"What are you going to do? Jump on Carly as soon as she walks through the door?"

"Maybe."

"You should think about this."

"I have thought about it." She ran an impatient hand through her hair. "And it makes me sick."

"I don't think anything happened between Carly and Gary."

"How can you say that?"

"I believe it."

Reluctantly she sat down next to him. "You think I'm wrong?"

"I think you're scared. It's easier to feel anger than to feel pain."

A car door slammed, and Rachel stiffened. "She's home."

She looked into Dylan's eyes. "Don't leave, okay?"

"Are you sure you want me to be here?"

"Positive. And that's the only thing I am sure of."

He squeezed her hand. "I'll stay."

She stood up as Carly came in through the front door and paused in the entry.

"What's up?" Carly asked.

Rachel stared at her younger sister, wondering how she could appear so innocent, so beautiful, so much like the little girl she'd grown up with. Since she'd discovered the teddy in Dylan's drawer, Rachel had begun to think of Carly as a stranger, an enemy. But here, in person, Carly just confused her.

And Carly did look guilty about something, her eyes darting from Dylan to Rachel, then back again. "Is someone going to tell me what's going on?"

Rachel drew in a deep, steadying breath. "I found your white lace teddy."

"So?"

"The white lace teddy you bought last year—the one I said was beautiful but too sexy for me? I found it."

"Okay," Carly said slowly, "Is there a problem?"

"Don't you want to know where I found it?"

"If you want to tell me."

"In Dylan's drawer."

Carly's jaw dropped as her gaze swung to Dylan. "I was never with Dylan. What did you tell her?" she asked him accusingly.

"Dylan brought it with him," Rachel said quickly, realizing they were going down the wrong road. "Dylan found the teddy in Gary's apartment." She squared her shoulders. "Do you want to tell me how it got there? How your teddy got in Gary's apartment?"

Carly turned white. "Oh, God, Rachel. It's not what you think!"

"Did you stay at Gary's apartment in the city?" Rachel asked, trying to hang on to her last bit of sanity. It was difficult, because Carly looked stricken, like a deer caught in the headlights. "Did you?" she repeated forcefully. "Dammit, Carly, answer me."

"Yes, I stayed there one night. But Gary wasn't there. He was on a business trip. I must have left the teddy by mistake."

"When did you go there? Why did you go there?" Rachel still wasn't sure she believed Carly's innocent explanation, not the way Carly avoided her gaze.

"It was last year sometime. I don't remember."

"You don't remember going to the city and staying in my husband's apartment?" Was that her voice shrieking? It must be, because Carly recoiled as if she'd been struck.

"Okay, it was a couple of weeks before Gary died. He offered me the apartment because I had a late date in the city and I didn't want to drive home that night. How could you think that Gary and I would . . . we *wouldn't.* That would be like incest." Carly turned to Dylan in desperation. "You believe me, don't you? Tell her it's crazy, Dylan. Gary was like my big brother. I never, ever . . . I couldn't."

"You never told me you stayed there and Gary didn't either. Why? What was the secret?" Rachel asked.

"All right," Carly said. "I should have told you before, but I've never been able to find the courage. Maybe I should just show you."

"Show me what?" Rachel asked.

Carly hesitated, then said, "Follow me."

Rachel looked at Dylan, who shrugged. "I think we better follow her."

"Carly, what's this about? I just want a simple answer."

"There isn't a simple answer, but there is a complicated one. Do you want to know it or not?" She marched out of the room, leaving them to follow.

Rachel was surprised to find Carly leading her down to the basement. She was even more surprised to see Carly push a couple of boxes aside, turn on a light and motion her forward.

"This is my studio," Carly said.

Her studio?

Rachel walked around the wall of boxes and stopped abruptly. She couldn't believe the sight before her—the painting on the easel, the sketches on the cardboard table, the boxes of art supplies, the other pictures lying against the wall. It was a strangely familiar sight, one she'd seen a long, long time ago. But that studio had belonged to her mother.

"What is all this?" Rachel's throat was so tight she could barely get the words out.

"It's my art," Carly answered. "I'm a painter, Rachel. An artist—like Mom."

Like Mom?

Rachel heard the words but couldn't process them. "I don't understand. You don't even like to draw."

"That's what I always told you, because that's what you wanted to hear, you and Dad."

"You lied?"

"Oh, yeah, I've lied, just about every day of my life for at least the last fifteen years."

Rachel put a hand to her temple. It was already throbbing from her earlier discovery. Now this! What was this? A studio hidden away in her basement? Her sister leading a secret life? Maybe her husband doing the same?

She'd always thought of herself as living a normal, uneventful life tucked away in the safety of an apple orchard where nothing ever changed but the seasons. But it was only a facade, a cover-up for lies and secrets and strangers. Who were these people in her life? She was looking at her sister, but she couldn't even see her. So she turned away.

"Don't do that, Rachel—please don't turn away," Carly pleaded. "I didn't tell you because I was afraid you'd hate me the way you hate Mom."

Rachel turned back around. "She left us. She left us for her art. She broke up our family. How could you like it? How could you want to do it?"

"I don't know. It's just in me. It's in my blood. I found

out a long time ago I was good at it. But I couldn't tell any-one. Daddy wouldn't even let us have crayons or watercol-ors in the house."

"So you did it in secret? All these years? But someone knew, didn't they?" Another piece of the puzzle fell into place. "Gary knew."

Carly nodded, her eyes begging for understanding. "He came down here one day to clean things out. He found the paintings and asked me about them. So I told him the truth."

"You told him the truth," Rachel echoed tonelessly. "Which was what?"

"That my real ambition was to go to school at the San Francisco Art Institute. That's why I've never been able to finish college. Business doesn't interest me." Carly drew in a shaky breath. "Gary encouraged me to apply to the school and he let me use the apartment for my interview. That's the only reason I was there, Rachel. You have to be-lieve me."

"I don't know what to believe!"

"Well, believe that. It's the truth."

"I have to go," Rachel said. She was having a hard time breathing in this place with no air and far too many paint-ings. "I can't do this right now." It was all she could do to climb the stairs instead of running up them. Once she'd slammed the basement door behind her, she ran as fast as she could down the hall and out of the house. When she hit the front yard she stopped, dazed, shocked, scared. Where could she go now? Her safe haven had just turned into a world she didn't recognize. Where the hell was she going to go now?

* * *

Dylan wanted to follow Rachel, but first he had a sobbing young woman to deal with. Carly had burst into tears the second the basement door had slammed shut.

"She'll come around," he said soothingly.

Carly shook her head, the tears running down her face. "I don't think she will. She hates me."

"She doesn't hate you. She loves you. You're her sister."

"She thinks I'm like Mom now," Carly said, sniffling. "And I am, you know. I'm just like her. That's why I don't fit in here. Why I should be leaving. Rachel wants me to love this place, but I don't. I mean, it's okay, it's home, but tending to the orchards is not my dream."

"It doesn't have to be. I think once Rachel thinks about it, she'll realize that you have to live your own life and go wherever that life takes you."

Carly looked at him with a small glimmer of hope in her eyes. "Are you just being nice or do you really believe that?"

"I really believe it," he said firmly. "Don't underestimate your sister."

"I wish she could understand that I have to paint. It's in my blood. My relationship with our mother was different than hers. I missed having a mom, but I didn't really miss my mother as a person. I was three years old when she left. I didn't know her. Rachel was my surrogate mom. I had my dad and my grandparents, my aunts and uncles, to fill up my life. But Rachel remembers being with Mom. She remembers the way things were before she left."

Dylan nodded. He understood completely, because he'd had a family for a while, before everything had been torn and ripped and broken beyond repair. Maybe it was harder to go on when you knew what you were missing.

Carly turned to look at the portrait on her easel. "I don't even know if I'm any good. I'm probably cursed with a desire that doesn't match my talent."

"That one looks pretty good to me. What did the Art Institute say?"

"They said I could come if I could pay for it."

"Did Gary give you the money?"

"No. He said he was going to, but something came up. I don't know what. Maybe the house construction cost more than he thought. I didn't want to beg. And he was preoccupied. Then he died, and it was too late."

Dylan wondered again about Gary's preoccupation. What on earth had been going on in his life that had distracted him to such an extent?

"I asked Gary not to say anything to Rachel," Carly said. "That was probably a mistake. Because now Rachel feels like Gary kept something from her."

He nodded. "Yes."

"He urged me to tell her. I never found the right time."

"Did Gary ever say what was bothering him?" he asked her, more interested now in Gary's preoccupation than in Carly's big secret. She stiffened slightly, and he wondered why. "You stayed at his apartment. You didn't notice anything odd? Out of place?"

"Like what?"

"Like other women, phone calls, notes, clothes that didn't belong there. Let's cut to the chase, Carly. Rachel thinks Gary was having an affair. That's why she went nuts when she found your underwear. Obviously, it wasn't you. What do you think?"

"I already told Rachel about the phone call Gary got here from some woman named Laura."

"Was that it?"

"Well, no. The same woman left a message on Gary's answering machine the night I was there. I didn't answer the phone, just let the machine pick up."

"Do you remember the message?"

"I wish I didn't," she said.

Dylan didn't like the sound of that. "Will you tell me?"

"I don't want to. Maybe I heard it wrong. Maybe I mis read the intent."

"Why don't you let me be the judge?"

"All right. She said she needed to speak to Gary immediately and that if he'd ever loved her, he'd call her back." Carly snapped her fingers. "Oh, and she said something in Italian, like *amore* something. Or 'Remember Venice.' I don't know exactly. I just remember that it sounded foreign and mysterious and kind of romantic. God, I shouldn't say that."

Dylan's mind began to whirl. Hadn't Gary spent a few weeks in Italy? Yes. The summer after their senior year in high school. His pulse accelerated as he recalled the postcards. *Wish you were here. I met an incredible girl. I think I'm in love.*

Dylan hadn't thought much of it. Gary had always been in love. But he'd acted differently when he came back, in a more somber, less joyful manner. He'd said things hadn't worked out. They'd broken up. What was her name? Was it Laura? Damn. Dylan wished he had a better memory.

"I should have told Rachel," Carly continued. "But I couldn't figure out how to tell her about the message without mentioning that I'd been in San Francisco."

"A tangled web, huh?" he asked with sympathy.

"It certainly turned out that way. One lie led to another.

Even tonight I lied about going to dinner with Travis. We went to an art gallery in the city. It was incredible. I wish I could tell Rachel about it."

"You will. Just give her some time. I better go find her."

Carly nodded, then reached for an afghan hanging over one of the boxes. "Take this; you may need it."

"Why, where am I going?"

She smiled. "Where do you think?"

The answer came to him immediately. He took the blanket out of her hand. "Thanks."

"You're welcome. And if you feel like putting in a good word for me, I'd appreciate it."

The grass was cool beneath her fingers. Rachel leaned back and stared up at the sky through the branches of Lady Elaine. She'd have a better view of the stars from somewhere else, but it was here, under this shadowy tree with its protective branches, that she felt the safest. Although she'd come to realize in the past few weeks that it wasn't always the obvious that could hurt. Sometimes pain came in subtle, unexpected, surprising ways.

Secrets. She'd never thought much about them. They were the gossipy little tales you told when you were young and swore you'd never tell another soul. They were about goofy things like who liked whom and where you stashed your chocolate and what you'd really bought at the bookstore when your dad asked.

Rachel smiled, remembering the elaborate lie she'd made up just so she could buy a sexy novel. She'd read it at night with a flashlight under her covers when she was fifteen years old. And no one had known. No one had suspected that she had questions about sex and love and desire. Her grandmother had tried to do her duty by giving her the motherly talk, but the abstract conversation had done little to help Rachel in terms of what going to second base meant when you were a sophomore in high school.

Rachel had tried to do better by Carly, to be open and honest and frank. She sighed, thinking of how she'd failed. Not about sex, maybe, but about everything else. Carly had had her own secret, her own desire, her own worries. And Carly had had no one to talk to either. She hadn't hidden in her bedroom. She'd hidden in the basement.

Secrets. So much more a part of her life than Rachel had ever known.

Gary and secrets. There was another combination that Rachel didn't want to think about but couldn't avoid. Maybe he hadn't done with Carly what she'd initially feared, but he had kept her visit to the city and her passion for painting a secret. Why? Why had his loyalty been more to Carly than to her, his wife? Had it not been that important to him? Had he thought of it as Carly's secret, rather than his own?

How she wished she could talk to him, ask him all the things that were bothering her. Ask him how they'd gotten so off the track, how they'd lost touch with each other, how they'd gone from being intimate to being distant. Had it happened overnight, in a week, in a month, in a year? Or had it happened over time? If he'd lived, would they have stayed together?

She'd never know. No matter what she and Dylan found out, she'd never know that.

The crunching of leaves and the soft sound of footsteps told her someone was coming. She didn't have to turn her head to know it was Dylan.

He'd followed her again. The way he'd followed her before. And it wasn't until just this moment that she realized how disappointed she would have been if he hadn't come after her.

He draped an afghan around her shoulders, then dropped down next to her, not saying a word, not needing to.

A second later, she put out her hand and he took it. They sat there for a long time, just listening to the night. She'd come to this spot searching for peace, for a connection to the past, to the strength of those who had lived and loved before her. But the tree hadn't given her the comfort she craved. It had come now, with Dylan.

"How is Carly?" she asked finally.

"Worried."

"I should go back and talk to her."

"It will wait. How are you?"

"I'm better now. Now that you're here."

He squeezed her fingers. "It's been a long night. Are you cold? Do you want to go inside?"

"Not yet. You don't have to stay, though." She felt compelled to say the words, even though the last thing she wanted him to do was to go.

"You're not getting rid of me that easily. So what about Carly? What are you thinking?"

"I overreacted, didn't I?"

"It's just art, Rachel. A lot of people in the world like to paint. It doesn't make them deserters."

"It made my mother one."

"Carly is not your mother. She isn't married or with children. She's free to do what she wants to do. And she wants to paint. More than that, she wants your blessing to paint."

Rachel shook her head in bewilderment. "I still don't

understand how she could like art. After everything we lost because of it."

"She was just a baby when your mother left. She doesn't remember."

"I remember. I remember that the only time I had with my mother was when I sat for a painting. Then I'd have her undivided attention. The rest of the time she didn't even see me. I wanted her to see me so badly. I loved her."

"What was she like?"

"Beautiful. Her voice was soft, her laughter like music. She didn't laugh much with us, but when her artist friends came over, she couldn't stop. I'd sneak downstairs and listen to their parties. We weren't enough for her. Now I feel like we're not enough for Carly."

"You mean *you're* not enough for Carly."

"It sounds so selfish when you say it like that. I want her to be happy, Dylan, I really do. I love her. I just don't want to let her go. But I know I have to. I have to let her be who she is." She glanced over at him. "I'll tell her in the morning."

"Good," he said approvingly, and she felt a surge of pleasure.

His opinion had become terribly important to her. *He had become terribly important to her.* She'd known it all along, but tonight the words wanted to be spoken.

"I'm glad you're here," she said. "You're fast becoming a huge part of my life, in case you hadn't noticed."

"You've always been a huge part of mine."

"Even with all those years between us?"

"They seem like nothing now, don't they?"

"Like the blink of an eye. Times passes faster than we realize."

"Which is why we shouldn't waste one second of it."

"You're right."

They fell silent for a moment. It was a beautiful night, filled with stars.

"I never realized how much I liked quiet until I came here," Dylan mused. "I've always lived with noise, radios blaring while we work, the roar and hum of power tools, the television on when I'm at home. Quiet was never one of my goals."

"Quiet gives you time to think."

"And regret and feel sorry for yourself. I preferred to keep busy."

"Outrun your thoughts?"

"It worked for a long time."

"Until you came here and found the quiet."

"And you. You were the only secret I ever kept from Gary," he said. "I thought it was a big deal to have that one."

"I know what you mean. I told myself what happened with you didn't matter, because once I took those vows, I was completely faithful. But I still kept it a secret. It was probably wrong. How can I accuse Gary of withholding information when I did the same thing? I realize now that there was a distance between us from the very beginning. I thought that love meant knowing each other inside and out, but that wasn't the case with us."

"Maybe it's unrealistic to believe that you can know someone inside and out. Maybe the mystery is part of the attraction."

A little shiver ran down her spine at his words. "Is that why we're attracted to each other? Because of the mystery? Because of our secret? Does the guilt make us want each other more?" She wished the moon were brighter; his expression was too shadowy to read.

"Maybe it's all of the above and then some."

"You're a stranger in some ways, Dylan, and yet I feel like I know you. I feel like I understand you, like you're a part of me." *I feel like I love you.* She licked her lips, wondering if she could really say those words out loud. But the moment passed, and they remained unsaid.

"I feel the same way. Frankly, Rachel, I don't care anymore what comes next. Being with you now is important. Whatever happens after this, I'll live with it."

"We can't always just live in the moment."

"Why not?"

"It's not very responsible or reasonable or smart."

"We've been all those things. Where have they gotten us?"

She heard the teasing note in his voice. "Well, you've made a lot of money, built a lot of buildings. I've picked a lot of apples, kept my family business going."

"All very boring, practical and adult. I don't know about you, but some days—make that nights—you need to act like a teenager, no responsibilities."

"And what would a teenager do right now?"

"Let's see. A pretty girl, a warm blanket, some soft grass, a lot of moonlight . . ."

"Sounds like you've got a few ideas."

"A few."

She laughed. "You are quite the smooth talker, but I'd suggest a little less talking and a lot more action."

"Action, huh?" He gave her a gentle shove, so that she was on her back and he was leaning over her. "I'll show you action." He ran his hand down the side of her face in a tender caress. "I want to make love to you."

"Uh. We're outside. Do you think we should?"

"Absolutely not. Let's do it anyway," he said with a wicked smile. "Are you feeling reckless?"

"Yes, I'm ashamed to say. But do you have anything with you? Like protection?"

"Still trying to be responsible, huh?"

"I'm trying." She swallowed hard as his hips moved against hers with just the right amount of pressure to create a great deal of pleasurable friction. Soon, she believed, she would not be remembering her name, much less protection.

"I have one in my wallet," he said.

"Thank God!" she said with heartfelt enthusiasm.

He smiled down at her, his finger tracing the curve of her lips. Then his eyes grew more serious. "I want you, Rachel, everything you're willing to give. Maybe you don't know this about me yet, but I'm greedy as hell."

"I'll give you everything I can—tonight. I can't make any promises beyond that."

"I'm not asking for any."

"Are you sure? I don't want to hurt you. I don't want to hurt me. But I'm scared, not of you, but of the way I feel when I'm with you, like I'm losing control. I don't have a road map. I don't know where we're going. And I'm not sure how we're going to get there."

"We'll find out together, Rachel." He paused. "Maybe we should take a page out of Gary's book and just go where the road takes us. To hell with maps. After all, that's how we met the first time around."

She put her hands around his neck and pulled him down to her. "Show me the way," she murmured.

He answered her with a kiss, his lips warm and hungry. She wanted Dylan inside her again, as close as they could be to each other. She wanted to hold on and never let go.

Dylan must have felt the urgency in her kiss for his mouth answered hers, and his hands moved under her dress. She helped him pull it over her head, welcomed his mouth to the corner of her neck, his fingers to the clasp of her bra and finally, with great relief, his callused palms to the swells of her breasts.

"So soft," he murmured, taking a moment to just look at her. "I want to do this slow, but I don't think I can."

"We can do slow later," she murmured, pulling his head down to hers. "Right now I need you."

"I need you, too," he murmured. Then he proceeded to show her just how much.

Chapter 22

Rachel awoke to the sun breaking through the branches of the apple tree. Her head was on Dylan's shoulder, her arm around his waist, their bodies still bare as they lay on the grass, the afghan their only protection against the bright, piercing eye of dawn. It was another day. Tomorrow had come after all.

Dylan stirred against her. "Is it morning?"

"Yes. We better get dressed before anyone wakes up and finds us here." She tried to grab her clothes, but Dylan rolled her onto her back and nestled his face into the side of her neck. "It's not that early, the sun is barely up."

"This is a farm, people get up early."

He ran his tongue around the edge of the mouth she was trying to keep closed. "You are so disciplined. I find that very sexy."

She laughed at that. "Right. I have a feeling you find everything sexy in the morning."

"Just you," he said with a boyish grin that made her heart turn over. She liked seeing him this way, relaxed and happy.

"I'm glad," she said, reaching for her bra and dress. She slipped them on while Dylan quietly collected his clothes.

When she had finished dressing, she folded the blanket and got to her feet. "Today will be crazy. The festival is only half over. I need to pick up Wesley, then get back to work."

"Back to reality," he said somewhat grimly.

"You knew it would come."

"It always does."

They walked down the hill. They didn't say another word until they reached his car. Then he turned to her. "This isn't over, Rachel."

"I didn't think it was." She drew in a breath. "But I'm not sure I can give you what you want."

"I'm not sure you know what I want." He leaned over and took a kiss. "We'll figure it out together."

"Our lives are in different worlds. And I don't have much luck holding on to people."

"Maybe you've been trying to hold on to the wrong people. Maybe you need someone who wants to hold on to you."

She looked at him in bewilderment, wanting to believe him, but afraid. "Where do I find that someone?"

"I don't think you'll have to look too far."

"Oh, Dylan." She touched his face in a gesture of love.

He caught her hand and pressed it against his lips. "Don't worry. The answers will come, all of them."

"That's what I'm afraid of."

Carly was asleep on the couch in the living room when Rachel entered the house. She paused and studied her baby sister's face. She'd been looking at Carly asleep for twenty years, she realized, watching over her like a mother hen. It would be hard to let her go, but she would do it because, more than she wanted Carly home, she wanted her happy.

Carly slowly stretched and opened her eyes, coming fully awake when she saw Rachel watching her. She sat up, her tangled hair falling about her shoulders, her eyes still red from the traumatic events of the night before.

"I'm sorry," Rachel said.

"You are?"

"Yes." She sat down at the other end of the couch. "I love you, Carly. I want you to do what makes you happy. I want you to live where you feel comfortable, where you belong."

"Even if that's not here?"

"Even if. I don't know why I expected you to stay. Look at our history. Elaine came across the country in a wagon train to follow her heart. Why shouldn't you go where love takes you?"

"I thought it would be easier if I went with a man. That you would understand love and marriage more than you would understand a passionate desire to paint."

"Ah, so that's where Antonio comes in. I wondered."

"He's not really interested in me. I guess it's a good thing I didn't actually feed him one of our special apples."

"You wouldn't want to tie yourself to the wrong man for all of eternity, that's for sure."

Carly looked tremendously relieved. "I can't believe you're being so great about this. I should have told you before."

"You should have, but I probably wasn't ready to hear it then. I've had tunnel vision and a steel grip on the people

I love. I know now that I can't hold on to someone who doesn't want to be here."

"It's not that I don't love you, Rachel. You've been the best sister ever."

"You've got that right. Now, you better get dressed so you can help me today. You can't leave until after the Harvest Festival, deal?"

"Deal."

Rachel got to her feet, then paused. "You weren't really planning Travis's mother's birthday party last night, were you?"

Carly's face lit up. "He took me to the opening of an art gallery in San Francisco. It was so cool, Rachel, and Travis knows this man who owns another gallery and he wants to see my paintings."

"That's great."

"Nothing will probably come of it, but I can't believe someone wants to see my work."

"It was nice of Travis to set that up."

Carly waved a hand as if she didn't care, but Rachel sensed that she did. "He's always butting into my business."

Rachel smiled. The path of love just got bumpier and bumpier. She wondered if it had occurred to Carly yet that leaving Rachel and her family wouldn't be half as hard as leaving that annoying, irresistible Travis. And wasn't it a complete and utter irony that Carly would fall for a country boy and Rachel would fall for a city guy? Just went to show the best-laid plans . . .

"We always do things the hard way, don't we?" Rachel said.

Carly nodded. "I'll deal with Travis. Don't worry."

"First we deal with the festival. I'll meet you at the barn in an hour. I have the perfect job for you."

"What's that?"

"Face painting. After all, you're the artist in the family."

At precisely five o'clock on Sunday, Rachel declared the Harvest Festival officially over. Unfortunately, she had no one to declare it to except herself. The family, the temporary workers they'd hired for the weekend and the tourists had all vanished. Most had headed off to enjoy the free concert in the park. The others had no doubt gone to find rest, relaxation and cooler temperatures, Rachel thought, fanning herself with the last of the gift-shop brochures.

It was time to take herself off for something or somewhere, but she'd been living from moment to moment for the past forty-eight hours and hadn't given much thought to what she'd do this evening. Wesley and Carly had gone into town with her grandparents, leaving her alone to finish putting things away. Of course, they'd begged her to come, too, but she'd refused. In truth, she'd been looking forward to some quiet time.

Too much had happened in her life these past few weeks. She wanted a chance to let it all sink in. She wanted a moment to absorb everything she'd discovered. However, now that she had that moment, she felt more restless than peaceful. She wondered what Dylan was doing—if he was sitting on the grass listening to the musicians, or holed up in his hotel room doing some paperwork, or working at her house.

He hadn't stopped by or called since he'd left her the morning before. He'd known she'd be busy. It was no wonder he hadn't been in contact, but she couldn't help feeling irritated. She'd slept with him, for God's sake, and the least he could do was call and say, "Hello, how are you? I miss you."

She smiled at her own foolishness. She was such a girl. They weren't high school kids. They weren't dating. He didn't have to call her. And she didn't have to wait by the phone.

Of course, it was easier to figure out what they weren't than what they were. Two adults having a casual relationship? No, not even close. Two people who'd always been attracted to each other, finally free to be with one another? Closer, but not quite right. Two people who had fallen in love with each other, who had a second chance to make that love work if they had the courage to take it?

Rachel shivered as the truth gave her chills. It would come down to courage. And she'd had so little of that commodity over the years. Could she find it now? Could she risk losing her safety net for the opportunity, the love of a lifetime? And could Dylan risk giving his carefully guarded heart to a woman who'd been married to someone else, who'd had that person's child, that man's love?

It would be easier to do nothing, to let Dylan finish the house and go back to the city. And for her to go on with her life. To raise Wesley the best way she knew how. It would be safer to travel that route. She knew that road. She knew how to keep things even. It was the highs and lows she wasn't so sure about.

Rachel took one last look at the shop, then stepped outside and closed the door behind her. She glanced toward the house, but she wasn't quite ready to go inside. For the first time in a long time, she had the property to herself. She wandered through the garden and up the path, knowing all along where she would end up, under the branches of Lady Elaine.

They'd lain on the grass and made love in the shadow of this tree. It had been perfect. Rachel closed her eyes and let herself remember, for just a moment, every kiss, every touch. The memories were so alive, so real. The taste of Dylan lingered on her lips, the feel of his skin on her fingers.

A small voice inside told her that it was wrong to remember Dylan in such vivid detail when Gary had become a faded photograph. She'd made love to Gary for nine years. Why couldn't she remember with such clarity the way he tasted, the way he felt? Was this how life was? Was it right to go on or was it wrong? Did what she feel now lessen what she'd felt before?

Rachel opened her eyes and looked at the tree that had stood proudly on this spot for over a hundred years. She thought about her great-great-grandmother following her heart through numerous and mountainous hardships. Elaine had had no certainty when she'd made her perilous trip. But she had done it anyway. Courage, Rachel thought again. Love took courage.

She'd never thought that before. Loving Gary had been easy. His smile, his joy in life, had washed over her like a warm summer breeze. Nothing about their love had been hard. Nothing about their love had been spectacular either. That evenness again. No ups or downs, no highs or lows. She'd been content with that. She'd thought he'd been content, too. She should have known better.

Gary had always wanted the highs and lows. He'd needed the outside stimulation. But just how far had he gone seeking what he hadn't found at home?

Who was this Laura who'd had a relationship with him? How much did she matter? What had she offered Gary that Rachel had not?

She needed the answers to those questions, and she would have them by the end of the week, if not sooner. The festival was over. The seasons were changing. It was time to move on with her life. Rachel reached up and pulled a ripe apple off the lowest branch. It was ready to be picked. Everything had a season.

She heard the soft crunch of feet on the grass and turned around. It was just like last time. She knew it was him even before she saw him.

Dylan stopped a few feet away from her. "I had a feeling I'd find you up here." He tipped his head toward the apple in her hand. "Who are you planning on feeding that to?"

She smiled, rolling the apple around in the palm of her hand. An idea took root and blossomed. "You?" She held it out to him.

Dylan looked at the apple, then at her. "I think I know how Adam felt. I should say no."

"You already ate one once."

"I didn't know there was magic to it then."

"And I didn't know you were the one who was getting the magic. Maybe that's why things went haywire. Do you want to try again?"

"I'm not sure."

She was disappointed in his answer, and her arm drifted down to her side. "I see."

"We've got some things to settle."

"Like the fact that your life is in the city and mine is in the country?" That fact had been bothering her more and more with each day. For even if she could let go of Gary, could she really let go of everything else in her life?

"Partly. I do have a business there."

"And there aren't a lot of skyscrapers to build around here."

"Thank God, right?" he said with a smile. "You wouldn't want anything to ruin this valley."

"No, I wouldn't."

"But it's not just that, Rachel. It's Gary. We have to settle this once and for all. I didn't want to say anything until after the festival, but the private investigator I hired called me yesterday and gave me the address of one Laura Gardner. She lives on the south shore of Lake Tahoe."

Rachel forced herself to breathe. "That's the Laura who was calling Gary? The one I spoke to?"

"I think so. She changed her phone number right after you called."

"Do you have the new one?"

"I do. But I don't think we should call. I think we should go there. Meet her face-to-face."

Rachel started shaking her head even before he finished speaking. She couldn't go to Lake Tahoe. She couldn't confront this woman. What would she say?

"We've come this far. We can't stop now," Dylan said. "Let's drive up there tomorrow. We can leave as soon as you drop Wesley off at school and be back before dinner."

"I'm scared. What if we find out Gary was in love with someone else? What if we find out he was having an affair? What if we find out that she broke it off, and he killed himself on the way home?"

Dylan grew more pale with each of her questions. But his resolve only seemed to strengthen. "We'll deal with the truth, whatever it is. I loved Gary, and so did you. Nothing will change that."

"I'm not sure that's true. I'm not sure my feelings won't change."

"All right. Then they'll change. But not knowing has to be worse than knowing. You don't want to spend the rest of your life wondering. Will you come with me tomorrow?"

She made a decision she hoped she wouldn't regret. "Yes."

"Good."

Rachel raised the apple in her hand to her lips and took a bite. The fruit was tart, juicy and delicious. She swallowed her bite and saw Dylan watching her. "If it can't bring me love, maybe it will bring me courage."

She raised the apple to her mouth once again, but this time Dylan's hand stopped hers. He gave her a long look, then surprised her by leaning over and taking a bite out of the apple.

"I thought you didn't want any," she said.

"You're not the only one who needs a little courage. As for the love part . . ." He covered her mouth with his and kissed her deeply. She could taste the apple on his lips, the lingering juice on his tongue. A little zing of lust, love or maybe simply magic ran through both of them.

Travis plopped himself down on a corner of the blanket Carly had spread out on the grass near the jazz-band stage. "Hi, babe. All alone?"

"My grandparents took Wesley to get an ice cream. The band is on a break."

"Weren't you hungry?"

She looked into his eyes and smiled. "I saw you coming this way. I decided to wait for you."

His eyes darkened. "You waited for me?"

"I wanted to tell you that I selected some paintings to show your friend Roger. I thought I might drive into the city one day next week."

"Sounds like a good idea."

"I was wondering if you'd like to come with me."

He stared at her. "Me? You want me to come?"

"He is your friend, and you did get this opportunity for me." She tried to sound casual, as if she didn't care, but she found herself foolishly crossing her fingers.

"You don't need me to pull it off. Your talent will speak for itself."

She uncrossed her fingers in disappointment. "I'm not sure I'm that good."

He laughed. "That's the first modest comment that's ever come out of your mouth."

She made a face at him. "Well, it's true. My art is personal. I can't always tell if it's right."

"It's right. Have a little faith."

"I'm trying. I told Rachel about my paintings. I showed them to her, actually."

"And you're still breathing?"

"She was crazed at first, but she came around. She said she'll support whatever I do."

"Does this mean you don't have to marry Antonio?"

"That would be difficult to do. I saw him yesterday, and he told me he got engaged when he was in New York."

Travis shook his head in mock disappointment. "That's too bad."

She threw her rolled-up napkin at him. "As if you care."

He caught the napkin and threw it back at her. "I care. Too much, if you want to know the truth."

And when she looked into his eyes, she saw the truth. She suddenly realized that she was falling in love as well. But how could she love this man and still have what she wanted most in life?

"Why now?" she murmured. "Why now, when everything that I ever wanted is coming true?"

"You don't have to choose."

"Don't I? You live here."

"So could you."

"I want to paint."

"You could paint from here. And when you needed to go into the city, you could go."

She shook her head. "I watched Rachel and Gary try to make that kind of relationship work, but it failed. You can't do love long distance."

"You can do whatever you need to," he said seriously. "I'm just glad you finally realize that you love me."

"I didn't say that."

He smiled. "Yes, you did."

"I don't think so."

"Then why are we talking about living together?"

"We're not. Are we?"

"Yes."

Her breath caught in her throat at the look in his eyes. "Travis, I don't know."

"That's okay. We can figure it out together. And it doesn't have to happen tomorrow. I'm not letting you go, Carly. Get used to it."

"My father couldn't hold on to my mother," she argued. "I'm like her. I have a passion that speaks to my heart in a way that a man can't."

"Your father wanted to compete with that passion. I want to embrace it. I don't want to hold you back. I want to hold you close."

She felt her eyes begin to tear. "That's the nicest thing anyone has ever said to me. I could fall in love with you."

"I think you already have." He leaned over and kissed her tenderly on the lips. "Now, you know what I want?"

She was confused for a moment. "What?"

He nodded toward the picnic basket. "You know."

She suddenly smiled and reached over to take a Tupperware container out of the picnic basket. "Is this what you want?"

"If it has one of those damn apples in it, it is."

Carly pulled off the lid to reveal a slice of apple cobbler. "Try it and see."

Travis picked up a plastic spoon and took a big bite of the apple dessert. He chewed lustily, then swallowed. "I'm yours forever," he proclaimed. "Let's get married."

Carly laughed so hard she thought her sides would split. Finally, she caught her breath enough to say, "There was not a bit of magic in that dessert."

"Oh, yeah, we'll see about that." He pushed her back onto the blanket and lowered his head, his mouth hovering over hers, just long enough to make her want him even more.

"Kiss me already," she demanded.

"You are such a bossy woman. Maybe I won't kiss you."

"Maybe I won't wait until you make up your mind," she said, but she didn't try all that hard to get away.

Travis grinned at her. "You're not going anywhere."

"You think you know me so well."

"I do. And you know me. You know I'm stubborn."

"And annoying," she added.

"Persistent."

"And arrogant."

"Generous."

"And generous," she agreed as his mouth came down on hers. Because he wasn't just giving her a kiss, he was giving her the dream she'd been dreaming since she was a little girl.

Chapter 23

There was something symbolic about shutting the car door, listening to the motor come to life, watching the farm fade in the distance as Dylan drove toward the highway. Rachel didn't travel beyond the town borders very often, but today she was going far beyond the boundaries of her life.

She and Dylan were on their way to Lake Tahoe to see a woman named Laura Gardner, who was quite possibly the last person to see Gary alive. Rachel still couldn't believe they were on their way. She'd tossed and turned most of the night, imagining every likely scenario. When those imaginings grew too frightening, she thought of excuses, reasons that she couldn't go.

But when Dylan had arrived at her door, she'd known exactly what she had to do. She had to finish what she'd started. She had to find out what had happened to her husband. She couldn't go on with her life until she did that.

Dylan's hand covered hers. She appreciated the warmth and strength of his fingers. He was a rock in her wild, chaotic sea of emotions, a rock to which she could cling, lean on, stay afloat on. She wanted to be strong for him, too. She wasn't the only one with illusions to lose. Dylan had a faith in Gary that could be sorely tested today.

She glanced over at him. "I was thinking last night about this Laura. Did the investigator tell you anything else about her? Her age? What she looks like? I wish I could be more prepared."

"He gave me her name, her address. And as for her age, she's the same age as Gary."

"How did he find that out?"

"Copy of her driver's license."

"Did you see it?"

"No. But we'll see what she looks like soon enough." He hesitated. "Actually, Rachel, there's something else I want to talk about."

"Something else." Her heart sank down to her stomach. "What now?"

"It's just a hunch, but I think Gary may have met this woman when he traveled through Europe."

"Europe?"

"He went for the summer. Right after high school. The point is, there *was* a girl on that trip, someone he met. He sent me a dozen postcards raving about her. But when he got back, the subject was closed. It was over, and he wouldn't tell me anything more about her."

"You think it was this Laura?"

"Carly said there was a message on the answering machine in Gary's apartment from a girl who talked about Italy and remembering what they'd been to each other."

Rachel shook her head, trying to keep up with the information. "Carly heard this on an answering machine?"

"She couldn't tell you, because—"

"I get it. I wasn't supposed to know she was in the city. Go on."

"Okay, one last thing. Don't kill me."

She shook her head, her lips set in a frown. "Do you promise this is the last thing?"

He smiled tenderly. "I promise." He reached into his pocket and drew out a small jewelry box. "Do you recognize this?"

Rachel opened the box and saw a gold chain with a heart and a pearl in its center. "No."

"It came with a note. Read it."

Rachel slowly unfolded the piece of paper and read the brief message. "Where did you get this? Gary's apartment?"

"Your grandfather found it in a box that came from the police department. The box was apparently in Gary's car."

"Why didn't I see this before?"

"Your grandfather didn't want to upset you."

"So he gave it to you?"

"He thought it might be a clue, but he didn't want to worry you if it wasn't."

Rachel tried to drum up some anger, but fell short. Her grandfather loved her. He only wanted to protect her. She could understand that. "You're sure this is it, Dylan? No more surprises?"

"I'm sure. Whatever we find out now, we find out together."

She looked out the window at the scenery passing by. This was her valley, her beautiful, safe valley. But she was leaving it, leaving behind everything she'd known, everything she'd loved. She'd come back. Of course she would come back. And the valley would still be the same. But she had a feeling that she would be different.

Three and a half hours later, the scenery had changed considerably. Thick forests surrounded the two-lane highway that climbed to an altitude of eight thousand feet, then descended to a clear mountain lake that was awesome in its size, its clarity, and its beauty.

These were the sights Gary had seen that last weekend of his life, Rachel realized. The view was breathtaking, and when she rolled down the window she could smell the pines and feel the cool, crisp air of autumn. Soon it would be winter. The mountains would be covered with snow. The animals would hibernate, the world would change. She'd always welcomed the seasons, but this year they felt especially symbolic.

They came to a stoplight and Dylan glanced down at the address he'd jotted on a piece of paper. He made several more turns, finally stopping in front of a modest ranch-style house in a heavily wooded area.

"This is it," he said, turning off the engine.

Rachel stared at the house. There was a swing on the porch that reminded her of home. Had Gary and Laura sat on the swing with their arms around each other? Had they watched the sun go down? Had they shared an intimacy that should have belonged only to her and Gary? Rachel's stomach churned uneasily as she thought of all the possibilities.

"Ready?" Dylan asked.

"I'm scared."

"Fear only retreats when you look it in the eye. You can

do this, Rachel. You were Gary's wife. He chose to marry you. He chose to stay married to you. You're not the other woman. You're not the one who should be afraid."

"What if he was leaving me? What if he rushed down the mountain because he wanted to get home and ask for a divorce?"

"What if he rushed down the mountain because he missed you so much he couldn't wait to get back to you?"

"I don't think that was it. He wouldn't have come here if he hadn't had a reason."

"Let's go find out what that reason was." Dylan flipped the automatic locks and opened his door.

Rachel hesitated, then did the same, joining Dylan on the sidewalk. Every step they took toward the house felt like a step toward the edge of a cliff. Dylan rang the bell. Rachel listened for some sign of life. It came far too quickly, the sound of feet, a dog barking, someone telling the dog to quiet down. Then the door opened.

Rachel saw a woman through the screen, a petite woman with light brown hair and green eyes. She was strikingly pretty. Rachel's heart skipped a beat. This was her. This was Laura.

"Can I help you?" the woman inquired, looking from one to the other, no recognition in her eyes.

"Are you Laura?" Rachel asked.

"Yes, I'm Laura Gardner."

"I'm Rachel Tanner." Dylan was right. The fear went away when you looked it right in the eye.

Laura's face turned white. "Rachel—Tanner?" She made a move to shut the door.

"Wait." Dylan opened the screen, putting his hand against the door she was trying to close. "We need to talk to you."

"I don't have anything to say. Go away." Her voice shook with emotion.

"Please," Rachel said. "You have to tell me about your relationship with my husband. I think you were possibly the last person he spoke to before he died. I need to know why he came here to see you. I need to know what you talked about." Rachel's voice grew stronger with each word. "Please let us in."

"I wish you hadn't come," Laura said, shaking her head. "You shouldn't have come."

"You shouldn't have changed your phone number," Dylan said sharply. "We're not leaving until you talk to us."

Laura looked from Dylan to Rachel. She licked her lips, checked her watch, then finally nodded. "All right. Since you're here. Come in." She stepped back, allowing them to enter.

The furnishings were as modest as the house; the cluttered living room had nothing particularly special about it. Rachel moved toward the mantel, glancing at the photographs of Laura, a man—her husband, perhaps—and a girl—their daughter? They looked like a happy family. So why had this happy family woman been seeing Rachel's husband, calling him all over town, leaving messages for him, sending him back necklaces in the mail?

"Were you having an affair with Gary?" Rachel asked. The words came out blunt and sharp. There was no more fear left in her body, only anger and a desire to know the truth.

Laura's hand went to her neck as if she were checking for a necklace, but there was none there. Rachel opened her purse and removed the jewelry box. "Is this what you're looking for?"

Laura took the box from her and flipped open the lid.

She bit down on her lip, then closed the box again. "I wondered where it had gone."

"Why did you send it to my husband?"

"I needed Gary's help. I needed to remind him of what we once were," Laura said.

"What exactly were you?"

"We were lovers." Laura met Rachel's gaze head-on. "Many, many years ago. When we were teenagers."

"In Europe?"

"Yes." She appeared surprised. "I didn't think Gary had told you about us."

"He didn't. Dylan guessed."

"Dylan? You're the Dylan Gary spoke of so fondly?" Laura shook her head in bemusement. "I always wanted to meet you. I never anticipated it would be now."

"Why did you come back into Gary's life?" Dylan asked. "I thought your relationship was over years ago."

"It was." Laura sat down on the couch and motioned for them to sit as well.

Rachel wasn't sure she wanted to sit, but it didn't appear that Laura would speak until she did so. She sat down in a hard-backed chair. She didn't want to be comfortable in this house.

"We met on a gondola in Venice. It was wildly romantic for a pair of eighteen-year-olds." Her expression grew dreamy. "We fell in love and spent every moment we could together. Then my brother told my parents about our affair. My father arrived and whisked me back to the States before I could say good-bye to Gary. I called him when I got home. I told him that I loved him but I couldn't be with him right now. He was hurt and angry. He didn't understand that my future was dependent on my parents' will-

ingness to pay for college, which they threatened to with-
hold if I ever saw him again. They were strict Catholics and
ashamed that I had had sex before marriage."

Rachel's pulse took another jump as reality set in. This
woman had been with Gary. She'd laughed with him.
She'd seen him naked. She'd made love to him. Yes, maybe
it was years before Rachel had met Gary, but damn, it still
felt wrong.

"Unfortunately," Laura continued, "my parents were
further shamed a few months later when they found out I
was pregnant."

Rachel started, a gasp coming from her throat. Laura
had been pregnant? She'd been carrying Gary's child? "Oh,
God," she muttered, putting a hand to her mouth.

"Are you all right?" Dylan asked, drawing her gaze to his.

She wanted to scream that no, she wasn't all right. This
woman had been with her husband. She'd been carrying
his child.

"Rachel?" Dylan said.

"Go on," she bit out. "Tell me the rest."

"I tried to find Gary again," Laura said. "But he had
gone off to college, and I couldn't track him down. My
parents insisted I marry someone as soon as possible, so I
married a friend of mine who was willing to give me his
name. It wasn't love, but it worked. I went on with my life
the only way I knew how. And my dear friend, Bill, stuck
with me, raising my daughter as his own."

Rachel looked over at the family pictures once again
and saw the resemblance she'd missed before. The truth
was right in front of her eyes. The veil had been lifted.
"Your daughter is Gary's daughter?"

Laura slowly nodded. "Yes. Her name is Allison."

"Allison," Rachel echoed. "Well." She shook her head. What did you say when someone told you your husband was the father of her child?

"She's sixteen years old," Laura added. "She didn't know about any of this until last winter. Before that, she had accepted Bill as her father."

"What happened last winter?" Dylan asked.

"At my wedding anniversary party, someone made a joke about how I must have gotten pregnant on my wedding night; I'd had Allison so soon. It was a silly comment. But Allison heard it and started counting. We'd always figured that we'd just say she was premature, but to tell the truth, it never came up until that night. Allison figured out I must have been pregnant when I got married. At first she just teased me about sex before marriage. Then my brother, my stupid brother, mentioned my infamous tour of Italy, and Allison wondered how I could have gotten pregnant by her father if I was in Italy at the time. To make a long story short, she put two and two together and asked me if her dad was really her dad. I couldn't lie to her. I wish I had now. Allison is very headstrong and impulsive. Once she knew she had a father out there somewhere, she wanted to find him. She insisted on it. I couldn't talk her out of it." Laura uttered a harsh laugh. "She did a far better job than I did. She found Gary over the Internet in a couple of days. Then she ran away to see him."

"That's why you started calling him," Rachel said.

"She had found his home phone number. At first I called to warn him. Then I was worried when she ran away, and I needed him to find her. I didn't want her roaming the streets of San Francisco by herself."

Rachel sat back in her chair. "How did Gary react to the fact that he had a daughter?"

"He was shocked at first that I had even called him. He didn't understand that it was about Allison. He wouldn't call me back for days. I guess he was still angry after all those years." Laura shook her head. "I didn't want to leave a message about a daughter with his secretary or at your house. So I finally sent him the necklace he'd given me in Italy, hoping to play on the memory, at least, of the love we'd had."

"And he called you back after that?" Rachel didn't like the idea that Gary's return call had been motivated by a memory of love for Laura. She told herself again that their love had nothing to do with her. It had happened years before. But why hadn't he ever told her about Laura? Or even about his trip to Europe? Why had he kept so many things a secret?

"When I told Gary about Allison, he understood that I'd had a real reason for calling." Laura looked at Rachel. "But he was worried about you, about hurting your family. He didn't want me to talk to you until he had a chance to explain."

"Explain what? That he loved you?"

Laura hesitated. "We did love each other very much. But it was before . . ." She shrugged. "It was separate from you. Gary wanted to keep it that way."

"I see," Rachel replied. Even though she really didn't see. Maybe their relationship had been separate, but the fact that he had a daughter certainly involved her.

"Gary agreed to help me find Allison. He tracked her down in San Francisco in a seedy motel. Thank God he did. She could have gotten herself into all kinds of trouble. They spent some time together. Then Gary sent her home on the bus. He promised to come up for her sixteenth birthday party."

"Oh, God," Rachel whispered as her mind raced ahead.

Laura's eyes filled with pain, but she went on. "We had a good weekend together. Gary and Allison talked incessantly. They had the same laugh, you know, the same eyes. It hurt me to see them together, but it felt good, too. My husband, Bill, was jealous of Gary and Allison's relationship. But he realized that they needed to know each other, that it was important to both of them." She put a hand to her mouth as her lips began to tremble. "I didn't know it would be the last time. I didn't know that."

Rachel's eyes blurred with tears. She had to bite down on her own lip to keep from crying. Why had Gary's last weekend been with this woman? With this family?

Laura cleared her throat. "Bill saw the accident on the news that night. We told Allison the next day that Gary had been killed. She was devastated. She completely fell apart."

Rachel tried to swallow, but the lump in her throat grew bigger as she was taken back to that awful day when she'd received a terrible telephone call. "We were all devastated," she said, choking on the words.

"I didn't mean that you weren't," Laura said haltingly. "I know you must have been. And your son, too. I'm sorry. I never contacted you, because . . ."

"Because Gary hadn't told me about you or Allison."

"He said he would tell you when he got home."

"He did?" Rachel jumped on that like it was a lifeline. "He was going to tell me? Are you sure?"

"Yes. He wanted Allison and Wesley to know each other. And he hoped that you would understand that Allison needed to be part of your lives. I wasn't sure you'd accept her. Another woman's child? But Gary said you had a generous heart. You would never turn your back on a child in need. And family was everything to you."

"I wouldn't have, you know," Rachel said, brushing away a tear from her cheek. "I wouldn't have turned my back on your daughter—on Gary's child."

Their gazes met, woman to woman, mother to mother. And the rest slowly slipped away.

Dylan broke into their conversation. "Was Gary planning to support Allison?"

Rachel sent him a quick look, noting the hard glint in his eyes. She wondered what he was thinking. He seemed angry. With whom? With Gary? With Laura? With her? Or maybe he was angry at himself. Gary hadn't told him about Allison either. Not his wife. Not his best friend. They'd both believed they'd had a close relationship with Gary. They'd both been wrong.

"Gary gave Allison some money to put toward college. He wanted to set up a trust fund, but Bill and I didn't want his financial support. We just wanted Allison to have a relationship with him."

"The missing cash," Rachel murmured. "Ten thousand dollars?"

"Yes. We'll return it, of course."

"No. He gave it to you. It's yours," Rachel said. "There should be more, too. Allison should have something." She glanced again at Dylan. "Don't you think she should have something?"

"Whatever you want, Rachel. One thing bothers me." He looked at Laura. "Why did you change your phone number after Rachel called? Why hide all this now? Gary's dead."

"I panicked. Allison has had a terrible few months. She

blames herself for Gary's death. If he hadn't come up here for her birthday, he'd still be alive." Laura paused. "I was afraid you'd blame her, too, Rachel."

"It was an accident," Rachel said. "It could have happened anywhere." It took a lot for her to say that, because there was a part of her that did blame them for having Gary drive up to the mountains.

"I've tried to tell Allison that. I've gotten her into counseling, but she's very fragile. I didn't want anything to disturb the little peace she's achieved. I hope you can understand. I wanted to protect her, and I didn't know what you would say to her. She's at school now. That's why I let you in."

"I understand," Rachel said. "I'm a mother."

"Does Wesley look like Gary?" Laura asked.

"The spitting image."

"Allison, too," she said softly. "I guess he left us both something special."

"Yes, he did. Maybe someday I could meet Allison. And she could meet Wesley. They are brother and sister, after all. They should know each other. You can never have too much family."

"Gary was right. You are generous."

"I wish he had trusted me with this," Rachel said. "I wish he had told me. I still don't really understand why he didn't."

"He was afraid of losing you. He wanted to protect you and Wesley. When he realized Allison and I weren't going to be a threat to your family, he decided to tell you."

Rachel thought about that for a moment. She saw Laura play nervously with the wedding ring on her finger and she wondered about something else . . .

"Was it all in the past—for both of you?"

Laura looked up, her expression guilty but honest. "It was for Gary. After he came up here that weekend, it was for me, too. I had toyed with the idea of a romantic reunion, but it wasn't meant to be. My summer with Gary was a long, long time ago. He'd moved on. We both had."

"Thank you for telling me the truth." Rachel got to her feet. "There's one last thing. What did Gary say to you when he left?"

"He was happy the weekend had gone so well. He kissed Allison on the cheek and said, 'I'll call you tomorrow.' That was the last thing he ever said to us. 'I'll call you tomorrow.' "

"To us, too," Rachel said. "It's time to go home, Dylan."

He nodded and stood up.

Rachel gave Laura a sad, watery smile and said, "I won't call you tomorrow, but soon. We'll get the kids together. It's what Gary would have wanted."

Back in the car, Dylan and Rachel didn't say anything for a long time. They both needed the silence to sort through their emotions.

"I guess it's over," Rachel said finally. "We know everything now—all the secrets, the cash, the perfume, the teddy, everything."

"And we know Gary didn't kill himself." Dylan shot her a sideways glance. "He was coming home to you, Rachel. Whether or not the insurance company believes that, I'm convinced."

"Yes, I believe he was coming home."

"How do you feel?"

"I don't know yet."

"Me either."

Rachel twisted the wedding ring on her finger. "I guess

my marriage had a few holes in it. That's probably an understatement. But it wasn't all my fault. Gary shouldn't have kept so many secrets from me."

"I guess my friendship with Gary had a few holes in it, too," Dylan said heavily. "I don't know who was to blame. Maybe no one. Maybe it just happened. I always thought he told me everything, but he didn't, and not just recently either. That whole thing with Laura, whatever it was, he never discussed it with me."

"Because it was private, something he couldn't share. The way we couldn't share our kiss."

"You're right. That's it, then."

"That's it," she echoed, wondering why she felt so hollow. They had all the answers, so why didn't she feel complete? Because there was a question left unasked, a question left unanswered. *What now? What happens now?* "Will you go back to the city?" she asked, hedging away from her real question.

"I'll finish your house first," Dylan replied.

Then what? Will you ask me to go with you? Will you tell me you love me? Will you just walk away and say good-bye?

Rachel couldn't quite put the questions into play. She knew Dylan's life was in the city. She knew hers was in the country. Where did that leave them? She didn't know, so she sat back in her seat and looked out the window.

A few minutes later, another thought occurred to her. "Do you know where it happened? The accident?"

Dylan hesitated. "A little ways from here. I asked."

"Will you show me?"

"Are you sure you want to see it?"

"My eyes are wide open, Dylan. I want to see everything. No more hiding. No more wishing away the bad stuff."

"All right." Five minutes later, Dylan pulled into a turnabout at the edge of a steep drop. "It's a half mile down the road, where there's no shoulder, just the rail."

Rachel nodded and opened the door. She got out and stood at the edge of the road, looking around. There were sharp curves behind and in front of her, curves that could be deadly if taken too fast, too recklessly, too impatiently.

She'd never know what had really happened—if Gary had been speeding, if he'd gotten distracted by the ringing of his cell phone, if he'd tried to dodge a deer. But what she did know was that her husband had not committed suicide. He had not driven himself off the side of a mountain. He had been coming home to her, to Wesley, to the life they shared.

She closed her eyes and drew in a long breath of the cool mountain air. There were awful places to die, but this wasn't one of them. She opened her eyes and looked at Dylan, now standing beside her. He stared at the spot down the road.

"He must have felt like he was flying," Dylan said quietly. "For a few seconds there, he was flying."

"He would have loved that," she said.

"Yeah, he would have loved that."

She heard the catch in his voice and saw the emotion in his eyes. She put her arms around him and held him close. She felt his body shake as he fought for control. "It's okay," she murmured.

"I miss him. He was my best friend."

"I know. I miss him, too. I think we always will."

"Yeah."

"I have an idea. Do you have a piece of paper in the car? And a pen?"

"I think so. Why?"

"Could you get it?"

Dylan retrieved the sheet of paper with the directions to Laura's house. "Will this do?"

"Actually, it's perfect." She took the pen out of his hand and wrote: *To Gary, with love from your family, Rachel, Wesley, Allison, Dylan and Laura. We'll always miss you.*

She saw Dylan's quirked eyebrow and smiled. "Family is not always about blood. Will you make an airplane for me?"

He took the paper out of her hands, folding it sharply as he turned it into an airplane. Then he handed it to her. "Do you want to do the honors?"

"Yes." She took the airplane out of his hand and raised her arm. Then she hesitated, her fingers tightening on the paper. Was she really ready to say good-bye?

"Can you let go, Rachel?" Dylan asked.

Was he asking her to let go of Gary? Or to let go of him?

"I can let go," she whispered. "To you, Gary, may you soar high in the heavens as only you could do." She tossed the airplane into the breeze. They watched it fly down the mountain, over the stream, into the trees and beyond. "Good-bye. Rest in peace."

Epilogue

Three months later . . .

"I can't believe it's done." Rachel looked at her brand new house with the purple ribbon draped across the front door.

"What do you think?" Dylan asked.

"My dream house is better than any dream."

"I'm glad you like it. I know it's not exactly what Gary envisioned. We made some changes along the way. Having the insurance money come through for you helped."

"It's perfect. Unfortunately, I'm not sure I'm going to live in it."

Dylan sent her a questioning look. "Why is that?"

She licked her lips, feeling a bit nervous. They'd taken a lot of steps together in the past three months, but not this last one, not the one that needed to be taken. They'd mutually decided to give themselves some time, but time was up. The house was done. Dylan had a life to go back to. And Rachel had a decision to make.

"I've fallen in love with someone who lives in the city," she said. "I need to be with him."

"And leave this incredible house?" he asked, a smile playing around the corners of his lips. "You could do that for some guy?"

"Not some guy—you. I could do it for you. And as you know, only for you."

His eyes darkened with emotion. "You don't have to do this, Rachel. I know how much you love this place, the land, the trees."

"I love you more." She took both of his hands in hers. "I know that you said you couldn't be second best, but you're not, Dylan. The love I have for you is different from what I felt for Gary. But it's strong, and it's good. I know it will last. I wasn't ready for you before, but I am now. And I think you're ready for me. I'll go wherever you want. I don't need a safe haven to hide in. I need you." She smiled at him with all the love she had to offer. "You set me free from my past, from my fears of losing the people I loved to their dreams. I can give you what I couldn't give Gary. I can move to the city for you. I can give up my life here. Maybe it's not the title of first husband, but I hope it's enough."

"It's more than enough," he answered, crushing her in his arms. "I want to be your husband, and I want to be Wesley's father, and the numbers and the steps don't count. We can live wherever we want."

"You need to be in the city and so does Wesley. I found the perfect school for him. He can start next September."

"You hate the city."

"I don't hate it anymore. It was never about the city; it was about feeling safe, and I feel that with you wherever you are."

"To tell you the truth, I'd give up my business for you and not miss it for a second. I built things to fill the emptiness in me. But you do that now. You and Wesley."

Her eyes blurred with tears of happiness, but she could still see clearly enough to kiss him.

"Goodness, do you two ever stop?" her grandmother asked, a note of amusement in her voice.

Rachel stepped back as the rest of her family joined them, urging her to officially open the new house. It was silly, really. They'd all been a part of the construction, but they acted like they'd never seen the house before.

"Wait one second," Carly said. "I almost forgot." She ran back to her car, then reappeared a few moments later holding a small pot. "This is for you, Rachel, to plant behind your house. It's a seedling from the Lady Elaine."

"But we said we'd never try to duplicate the tree."

"I think it's time. You're just as brave in love as our great-great-grandmother. I think Elaine would want you to have this. It will protect your new home and your new family."

"Thank you, Carly."

Carly dropped her voice down a notch. "By the way, Travis and I are going to Paris this summer—for our honeymoon." She let out a little squeal at the end of her sentence.

"Paris? Honeymoon? Oh, my God." Rachel put the pot on the ground, then threw her arms around Carly's neck and gave her a big hug.

"We're planning to live in the main house."

"What about your painting?"

"I don't need to live in the city to paint. In fact, I find a certain annoying man actually inspires me."

Rachel laughed. "How the world keeps spinning."

Dylan put his arm around Rachel's shoulders. "The world is spinning without me in it?"

"Oh, you're always in it."

"You better believe it. Now, cut the ribbon so we can go inside."

"Let's do it together, the three of us," she said, motioning for Wesley to join them on the steps.

They put their hands on top of one another's and cut the ribbon.

"There's only one thing left to do," Dylan told her with a tender smile.

"What's that?"

"Carry you across the threshold." He swept her up in his arms with a laugh.

"But we're not married yet," she protested.

"We will be," he promised. "We will be."

Your mother always told you to marry a doctor . . .

If we all listened to our mothers we'd have married doctors, lawyers, or perhaps nice accountants. Men with steady jobs, good salaries . . . no muss, no fuss—no danger!

But sometimes even Mom is wrong . . .

Especially for the heroines of the Avon Romance Superleaders! No regular-job guy for any of them. These women want someone special . . . and they all manage to get him . . .

Join Susan Andersen, Kathleen Gilles Seidel, Barbara Freethy, Rachel Gibson, Kathleen Eagle, and Judith Ivory on the search for the perfect man . . . one even Mom will love!

We know not all mothers are like this—this is just for fun!

In *HEAD OVER HEELS*
BY Susan Andersen
Available January 2002
Veronica Davis learns differently . . .

Veronica walks through the doors of the Tonk—the local watering hole—searching for answers about her sister's murder. What—or who—she manages to find is Cooper Blackstock. He works as a bartender, but there's much more to him than meets the eye. Could he have the answer she's been looking for?

He looked up as she stepped forward and gave her a comprehensive once-over. "You're new around here," he said in a low voice. "I'd remember that skin if I'd seen it before." His gaze seemed to track every inch of it before his eyes rose to meet hers. "What can I get you?"

Veronica blinked. *Wow.* She was surprised the men of Fossil didn't keep their women under lock and key around this guy, for even she could feel the sexuality that poured off of him in waves, and he wasn't at all her type. "Are you Mr. Blackstock?"

"Yeah, but call me Coop," he invited and flashed

her a smile that was surprisingly charming for someone with such watchful eyes. "I'm always tempted to
look around for my dad whenever I hear anyone call
me mister, and he's been gone a long, long time."
Then he became all business. "Since you know my
name," he said, "I assume you're here for the waitress
job."

"No!" She stepped back, her hands flying up as if
they could push the very idea away. *Oh, no, no, no*—
She'd sworn when she graduated from college that she
would never serve another drink as long as she lived.
It was a vow she'd kept, too, and she intended to keep
on keeping it right up until the day they planted her
body in the cold, hard ground.

Seeing those dark brows of his lift toward his blond
hairline, she forced her shoulders to lose their defensive hunch and her hands to drop back to her sides.
*Oh, smooth, Davis. You might wanna try keeping the idiot
quotient to a bare minimum here.* "I'm sorry, I should
have introduced myself." Head held high, giving her
fine wool blazer a surreptitious tug to remind herself
she'd come a long way from the Tonk, she stepped
back up to the bar. "I'm Veronica Davis. I just stopped
by to see how the place is doing."

"You want to know how it's doing?" Coop demanded coolly. "Well, I'll tell you, lady, right this
minute not so hot. But things are looking up now that
I've got you in my sights. Here." He tossed her something and reflexively she reached up to snatch it out of
the air before it hit her in the face. "Put that on," he in-
structed, "and get to work. We're shorthanded."

She looked down at the white chef's apron in her
fist, then dropped it as if it were a cockroach, her head

snapping up to stare at him in horror. "I'm not serving drinks!"

"Listen, Princess, I've got one waitress who called in sick and another who just quit. You want the Tonk to close down and lose a night's receipts, that's up to you. But don't expect me to knock myself out if you're too high-toned to sully those lily-white hands schlepping a few drinks."

Who *was* this guy, with his farmer's body and his warrior's eyes, to tell her what to do? What gave him the right to threaten her with the bar's closure? She was the owner here, and that made her his boss. If anybody should be giving orders, it was she.

But she was just too worn out and emotional to get into it, particularly with someone who looked the type to relish a good fight, the more down and dirty, the better. Not to mention he might simply quit like Rosetta—and wouldn't *that* just be the icing on her cake.

Still, it didn't keep her from resenting his attitude. He didn't have the first idea how hard she'd worked to get away from this place, so how dare he look at her as if she were too snooty to do an honest day's work?

If she was smart, she'd just walk away right now, the way she should have done earlier.

Except . . . the Tonk was her niece Lizzy's inheritance, and now that Crystal was gone, she had to protect it.

WHAT MOM SAYS:
"If you want a man who's a success, stay away from small towns! The city is where the action is."

In *PLEASE REMEMBER THIS*
BY Kathleen Gilles Seidel
Available February 2002
Tess learns all about love in a small town

Tess comes to Kansas searching for the truth about her famous mother. What she discovers is unexpected love in the arms of Ned Ravenal. Ned's a dreamer, and Tess has always seen herself as a woman with her feet firmly planted on the ground. But sometimes love is just a dream away . . .

Ned tilted his head, his dark eyebrows pulling close together. "You're not interested in your family's stuff?"

"I can't imagine that my family had much stuff. That's why they had to leave. They were broke, the Dust Bowl and all."

He waved his hand, dismissing everything that she knew of her family's history. "No, not those people. I'm talking about the ones on the riverboat. We probably won't be able to identify the owners of most of the personal belongings, but the Laniers had so much more money than anyone else. If we find rich-people stuff, it was probably theirs."

"Whose? What are you talking about? There were Laniers on the riverboat?"

He drew back. "You didn't know that?"

"No." Tess had never heard anything about this. The banks taking away the farms, she knew about that. Her grandparents each having an uncle killed in World War I, she had heard about them. But Laniers being on the riverboat? Her family ties to Kansas were even stronger than she had realized.

"Their names were Louis and Eveline," Ned was saying. "He was the younger son of a reasonably important New Orleans family. They had an adult daughter named Marie with them, and Eveline was pregnant. Six months after the wreck Herbert was born. He was the one who built the Lanier Building."

Tess wondered if Nina Lane had known this. Of course she had. Everyone said she had been obsessed by the riverboat.

So why hadn't Tess's grandparents told her?

Were they afraid that I would become obsessed too?

"Apparently they were going to spend the summer in the St. Louis area," Ned continued, "and I don't know what made them decide to continue west, and I doubt that we'll find out. No paper onboard—no books, diaries, or correspondence—is going to have survived. But the Laniers certainly were luckier than everyone else. The boat sank in less than five minutes. People only salvaged what they had on their backs, but Eveline Lanier had three hundred dollars in gold coins sewn into the hem of her petticoat."

"Three hundred dollars ... that was a lot then,

wasn't it?" Tess had never heard of any Laniers having money.

"It certainly was. It was more than enough to have gotten them back to New Orleans, but they stayed on and used the money to build a decent house and get a sawmill started. Years later she wrote an account of the wreck. I suppose you haven't read it or you'd have known about your family. But I'll make a copy of it for you."

"That would be nice." This was all so surprising. "I would like to read it."

"Don't be so sure," he said bluntly.

WHAT MOM SAYS:
"If you break up with somebody—or even if he breaks up with you—you should never date his best friend!"

In ***LOVE WILL FIND A WAY***
BY Barbara Freethy
Available March 2002
Rachel Tanner discovers that
this is one rule worth breaking!

Years ago, Rachel Tanner handed her husband an apple. But not just any apple—this one came from a tree in her family's orchard. Legend had it that if a woman handed a man a piece of that succulent fruit he would marry her. Rachel always believed her late husband had taken a bite—but she didn't know the truth . . .

There were moments in time when Rachel forgot the sadness. But then she'd feel guilty that she'd forgotten her pain, if only for a second. Some things, some people, should never be forgotten, and Gary was one of them.

Dylan was too, unfortunately.

The two men were as different as night and day: Gary with his golden blonde looks, Dylan with his midnight black eyes; Gary with his sunny disposition, Dylan with his dark moods. *Dylan*. Today her faded memories had suddenly been washed in bright, beautiful color, and the shadowy figure in her mind was now vibrant and real and distinctly unsettling.

As she got into her car she told herself it was the circumstances that bothered her, not the man. And there was too much at stake to allow a momentary indiscretion from a long time ago to get in the way of what she needed to do. Dylan had probably forgotten all about it by now. Chalked it off as no big deal. He probably didn't even realize she'd been avoiding him all these years. After all, it had been easy not to see each other. She lived more than an hour away, and when Gary was home on the weekends he was with her family, her friends. Dylan had rarely invaded that space, just three times that she could remember: Wesley's christening, Gary's thirtieth birthday, and Gary's funeral. Never had Dylan stayed more than an hour.

Gary had always told her that Dylan felt more comfortable in the city, and she'd accepted that explanation. Whether or not it was true didn't matter. And whether or not Dylan Prescott made her uncomfortable didn't matter. What did matter was that Dylan had been Gary's best friend for more than twenty years. If anyone could help her figure out what had been going on in Gary's mind the last day of his life it was Dylan . . .

WHAT MOM SAYS:
"Whatever you do, don't date a cop—or a secret agent—or anyone else who runs around getting shot at!"

In *LOLA CARLYLE REVEALS ALL*
BY Rachel Gibson
Available April 2002
Lola finds that with guys like Max Zamora dangerous is awfully appealing . . .

Max "borrows" a yacht, which happens to be the one Lola's staying on. Together they outrun drug dealers, but Lola can't outrun her past—and they can't outrun the passion they feel for each other. But what happens when Max discovers the whole truth about Lola Carlyle?

"Who are you?" she asked.

"I'm one of the good guys."

"Good guys don't steal boats and kidnap women."

She had a point, but she was just plain wrong. Sometimes the line between the good guys and the bad guys was as hazy as his sight. "I didn't steal this vessel, I'm commandeering it. And I'm not kidnapping you. I am not going to hurt you. I just need to put some distance between me and Nassau. I'm Lieutenant Commander Max Zamora," he revealed, but he didn't give her the whole truth. He left out that he was retired from the military and that he currently worked for a part of the government that didn't exist on paper.

"Let go of me," she demanded, and for the first time Max looked down at the blurred image of his hands wrapped around her wrists. "Are you going to take another swing at me?" he asked.

"No."

He released her and she flew out of his grasp as if her clothes were on fire. Through the dark shadows of the cabin, he watched her take a few steps backward before he turned to the controls once again.

"Come here, Baby."

He looked over his shoulder at her, sure he hadn't heard her right. "What?"

She scooped up her dog. "Did he hurt you, Baby Doll?"

"Jeesuz," he groaned as if he'd stepped in something foul. She'd named her dog Baby Doll. No wonder it was such a nasty little pain in the butt.

"If you're really a lieutenant, then show me your identification."

Even if every piece of identification hadn't been taken from him when he'd been captured, it wouldn't have told her anything anyway. "Take a seat, lady. This will all be over before you know it," he said, because there was nothing more he could tell her. Nothing she would believe anyway.

"Where are we going?"

"West," he answered, figuring that was all the information she needed.

"Exactly where in the West?"

He didn't need to see her to know by the tone of her voice that she was the kind of woman who expected to be in charge.

"Exactly where I decide."

"I deserve to know where I'm being taken."

Normally, he didn't enjoy intimidating women, but just because he didn't enjoy it didn't mean it bothered him either.

"Listen real close," he began, towering over her and placing his hands on his hips. "I can make things easy for you, or I can make them real hard. You can sit back and enjoy the ride, or you can fight me. If you choose to fight me, I guarantee you won't win. Now what's it gonna be?"

She didn't say a word, but her dog propelled itself from her arms and sank its teeth into his shoulder like a rabid bat.

WHAT MOM SAYS:
"If he's living alone in the woods some-where he's probably not husband material!"

In *YOU NEVER CAN TELL*
BY Kathleen Eagle
Available May 2002
Heather Reardon learns that sometimes
a man who's been alone for a while has
more than conversation on his mind!

Kole Kills Crow is the man of every woman's fan-tasies—sensual and mysterious . . . a man who walked away from the limelight at the height of his fame. Now reporter Heather Reardon has sought him out. But you never can tell when a man's right for you!

"Your cat looks pretty well fed," she said, stroking affectionately.

"She's an excellent hunter."

"So am I." Heather looked up from her ardent stroking to find Kole leaning over the back of his chair, his face closer to hers than she'd anticipated. "I found you, didn't I?" She hadn't meant to whisper, but that was how it came out.

"Let the feeding frenzy begin," he whispered

back as he braced his left elbow on the back of the chair and cupped her face in his right hand.

His eyes were hard, hungry, resolute. She saw his kiss coming, but those eyes mesmerized her. She didn't close hers until his lips covered her mouth, stealing her breath along with her senses. Good Lord, he was as demanding and as deft and as delicious as she'd imagined when she was a green girl watching him make news. His tongue tasted of beer and bread, but better, bolder, spiced with the zest of his masculinity. She sampled it with wonder, even as she stanched the urge to reach for him and take more than a sample. She kept her hands on the cat.

Kole came up smiling. "Your lyin' lips taste very sweet."

"I haven't lied to you," she said in a voice that was remarkably steady, considering she didn't know where her next breath would be coming from.

"You said you weren't hungry."

"You're misquoting me." She met his amused gaze. "Something I promise never to do to you."

"Promises don't faze me, honey. I inherited a pretty good immunity to promises."

"And I'm allergic to 'honey.' "

He drew back with a laugh. "Reporters always did bring out the smart-ass in me."

"Not always," she recalled. "But that was the role you generally played, wasn't it? You were the tough guy."

"How'd you come up with that?"

"Short of checking in men's drawers, I really *do* do my homework."

"Good girl. If I had a red pencil, I'd give you an A."

He pushed himself off the chair and turned to clean up the bread and cheese. "But you won't be taking your report card home for a while."

"I've been looking for you for a long time. Why would I want to go home now?" She reached for a slice of cheese, again politely shaking off his added offer of bread. "I wouldn't mind going back to the lodge, though. I don't see an extra bed here."

"What you see is exactly what I've got. Do you prefer one side over the other?"

"I prefer, um . . ." She shared her cheese with the cat as she glanced from the bed to the recliner to the door.

"Exactly what I've got."

She assessed him with a frank look. "If I decide to leave, you're not going to stop me."

"Who says?"

WHAT MOM SAYS:
"Never talk to a man you have not been properly introduced to . . . after all, you don't know if his intentions are honorable."

In **BLACK SILK**
BY Judith Ivory
Available June 2002
Submit Channing-Downes
breaks that rule . . .

Submit was young and proper—a woman who lived strictly within the guidelines of English society— when suddenly, because of a legacy in a will, she's thrust into the embrace of a man she has just met. Aristocratic Graham Wessit is roguish, dangerous, and tempts Submit into sensuous surrender. Soon, she's engaged in a tumultuous battle of wills with a man who is a most improper stranger.

"It's a small enough thing to ask."

Tate sighed.

Clouds rumbled distantly. The weather dwarfed the lawyer's stature. Outside his book-lined office, he was an insignificant smear of color—yellows, reds, and browns on the grey steps to a grey building. The woman in black was part of the darkening sky, her strength of purpose as palpable as the smell of rain in the air.

After a moment, he said, "All right, you're going to take the box to him, as the will asked. But remember he's a black sheep, if ever there was one. Don't be misled by a glossy exterior."

"Ah." She lifted her head and gave an ironic little smile. "He is handsome."

Tate made a gust of objection through his lips, the sound of a middle-aged, slightly paunched man trying to minimize such an attribute. "Just don't be misled by that."

"I won't be. Nor put off by it."

"Handsome men don't have to account for themselves as often as they should."

She thought about this. "You're probably right."

"And he's worse than just handsome. He's selfish. Unruly. A breaker of rules, a builder of nothing."

"You don't like him, I take it."

"I didn't say that." Tate paused, frowning. "He's rather likable," he corrected. "But he's also one of the most frustrating young men I have ever met. Not your sort at all."

"Ah, young too." She smiled and looked down. "Young and handsome. No, definitely not my sort."

Tate pulled a glum mouth, then contradicted himself. "Actually, he's not so young anymore. He must be approaching forty." After a pause, he added, "He's one of those men one doesn't expect to age very well: perpetually eight years old. He has no vocation, no avocation, no occupation—except drinking and gambling and women. He lives with a married woman, an American."

She laughed, gently shaking her head. "Arnold,

having impugned the man's character, you are now trying to slander his taste as well. Stop being so smug." She continued to smile, not meanly but with a kind of teasing forbearance. "If the man is shallow or dissolute or immature or whatever you're trying to say, I'm sure I'm not so stupid as to miss it. And in any event, I'm only delivering a harmless little box Henry wanted him to have."

The lawyer clamped his mouth shut.

They stood in what would seem to be the silence of opposition, Tate frowning with a slight mouth, she looking down, trying to minimize her faint, intransigent smile.

Five minutes later, Graham sat in the vacant chair between his solicitor and barrister. He wedged himself into it, folding and bending a body never meant for the narrow, curved design. In uncomfortable situations, Graham became particularly conscious of his own height and doubly conscious of it when he saw others fidgeting and standing up straighter.

Tate rose and pushed his chair in, as if he would stand for the whole proceeding. Then he stretched, got books out from a case behind the desk, and laid them out on the desktop, three, four, eight, more; fortification.

Tate was a balding man of perhaps fifty-five, of medium height, with a tendency to carry slightly more than medium weight. He was squarely built and bluntly shaped with small feet and short, spatulate hands. He had to strain at the high shelves, the heavy law. Graham could have spanned several volumes at once with his long fingers.

"Shall we begin?" The Q.C., in a valley of books, aligned papers on the desk.

Graham had a sense of the past repeating itself. The barrister still seemed the adversary. The sound of his voice—mellifluous, Olympian, full of sincerity—worked undoubtedly to his professional advantage, but it was not reassuring. It implied that truth could afford to be questioned.

Graham claimed one last trivial digression, a curiosity he couldn't quite dismiss. "Her complete name," he said, "I should know—" He could vaguely recall old letters, bits of remembered conversation, and these memories made him want to smile for some reason. "You didn't tell me her first name. I'm sure Henry told me once, yet I can't recall—"

Tate looked up, his cheeks puffed as if he might blow Graham away.

"It is a sound, virtuous, old name," he said. Then his cheeks sagged, as did his head. "Her first name is Submit."